the
Wizard's Ward
DEBORAH HALE

LUNA™
www.LUNA-Books.com

LUNA™

First edition April 2004

THE WIZARD'S WARD

ISBN 0-373-81113-6

Copyright © 2004 by Deborah Hale

Digital photography of the author by Jennifer Berry,
for Studio 16
For more information: 888-929-5927

www.LUNA-Books.com

Printed in U.S.A.

For my twarith,
the people who help me and believe in me,
no matter what challenge I tackle—
my family, with all my love!

ACKNOWLEDGMENTS

I would never have been able to make the jump from historical romance to high fantasy writing without the invaluable assistance of my fantasy consultants:
Ian and Patricia Galbraith, Robert Hale,
and Ivy and Mike Moore. Thanks for all your help, guys!

I also owe a special thank-you to the team at Harlequin/LUNA for their belief that I could contribute to this exciting new imprint: Mary-Theresa Hussey, Margaret Marbury and Laura Morris.

THE KINGDOM OF UMBRIA

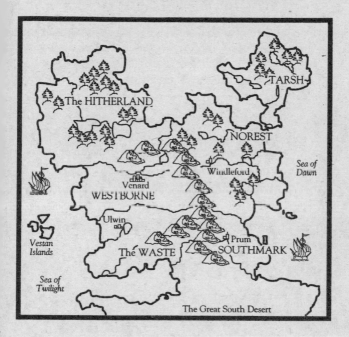

1

Her time has come.

Maura Woodbury only glimpsed those words before she'd been summoned to tend an injured child.

Whose time? Time for what? Those questions plagued her every step of the way into Windleford, a small village in northern Umbria. Unless she had misread the message or the haunted look in Langbard's eyes, she feared she would not like the answers.

Now, as she examined the little boy's hand, she struggled to keep her mind on her task.

"I have something here that should make it feel better." She pitched her voice loud enough to carry over the boy's exhausted sobs, yet soft enough to soothe and reassure him.

Lifting a small earthenware crock from her basket, she pried off the lid, scooped out a generous dollop of green salve, then smeared it on the child's blistered skin. The wholesome tang of freshly bruised merthorn and marshwort infused the air, making Maura's nose tingle.

The boy's mother hovered close watching every move, all the while wringing her hands and looking anxious. Was it on account of her son's injury, Maura wondered, or because she had the wizard's ward under her roof?

It never seemed to bother Langbard that the villagers scarcely spoke to him or Maura unless someone was ill or injured. Then again, hardly anything ruffled the old wizard's composure...until an hour ago when that messenger bird had arrived.

"What happened to you?" Maura asked the boy once his tears had subsided. "Did you see something good in your mama's stew pot and try to fish it out?"

His injuries looked worse than a simple burn, somehow.

The child sniffled. "I know better 'n that. Me and my friends was playing and I seen this queer gray twig. When I picked it up, my hand took to paining worse than a hundred bee stings at once!"

"A pain spike?" cried Maura. "Curse those soldiers! How dare they leave such vile things lying about? Windleford is hardly a hotbed of rebellion. Ordinary weapons do well enough to keep country folk like us under their thumb."

Since before her birth, Umbria had been ruled by the Han, invaders from the south, greedy for the perilous riches of the Blood Moon Mountains.

"Them younglings had no business playing so close to the garrison!" snapped the boy's mother, though she looked angrier at Maura than at her son. "The soldiers has to keep order, don't they? If it was a pain spike, they probably meant to use it on the outlaws. I hear tell there's a gang of 'em camping over in Betchwood, if you please."

"Perhaps so." Maura chided herself for failing to hold her tongue. If it got around Windleford that she'd voiced such rebellious sentiments, the villagers would shun her worse than they did already.

Besides, the woman's excuse might be true. Any unnatural weapons of the Hanish garrison might only be meant to combat outlaws, some of whom had grown insufferably bold of late. Maura despised their kind at least as much as she did the Han She'd suffered more on their account than she had from the invaders.

"How does your hand feel now?" She turned her attention back to the boy. "Better?"

He had stopped crying. That was a good sign. Already his fingers looked less swollen.

The child nodded. "Still pains some, but not like it did."

Now that she understood it was no common hurt, Maura realized it would need stronger healing. "I know just the thing to put your hand right—fresh queensbalm."

It would be blooming now. Queensbalm always bloomed on Maura's birthday. During her childhood, she and Langbard had often celebrated by packing a lunch and going gathering. Maura felt a wistful longing for those carefree days.

"I hope you learned your lesson about meddling with metal." Anxious to get home she repacked her basket in a hurry. "Some of it is not harmful, if it has been properly tempered. But most is tainted with mortcraft, which can do even worse things to you than make your hand pain. The next time you see something metal, do yourself a good turn by keeping your distance."

The boy's eyes widened at the notion of worse things than he had already suffered. Meanwhile his mother nodded in grudging agreement. Though she might not like Maura's implied censure of the Han, who used metal and mortcraft to dominate the people of Umbria, the woman clearly approved of her warning.

Rising from the low stool beside the boy's bed, Maura handed his mother the crock of salve. "Spread on more of this whenever he wants it, though mind you do not rub it in too hard. I will bring some queensbalm tomorrow."

"Don't trouble yourself." The woman shoved the crock into her apron pocket. She looked torn between gratitude and wanting to get Maura out of her house as quickly as possible. "This looks to have done the job fine."

Maura glanced at the boy whose eyelids were beginning to droop. "It will ease his pain, not cure it. That salve would have done well enough for an ordinary burn or a pest bite. Mortcraft needs something stronger to combat it."

She headed for the door. "If you would rather not have me seen coming to your house again, I can ask Sorsha Swinley to fetch the queensbalm here."

"That would be far better!" The woman immediately repented her hurtful eagerness. "I am sorry, Mistress Woodbury. I do not mean to sound ungrateful. It was good of you to come so quick. Poor little Noll hurt so bad, I was beside myself. It's just…well…I expect you know how it is."

"Aye." The word wafted out of Maura on a sigh.

Part of her did understand. Wizards and their kin could be

dangerous folk to know. Healers of any kind were frowned upon by the Han, who lived according to a harsh creed: *The strong thrive as they deserve and none should mourn the weak who perish.*

That knowledge did not make it any easier to be kept so firmly at arm's length.

"I'm glad you're not offended." The woman slid her door ajar just wide enough to peer out. Then she had a quick look up and down the road before throwing it open for Maura. "I'd be much obliged if you would send that other balm when you get it."

She spoke the words in a rush and when Maura turned to reply, she found the door already shut tight behind her.

Telling herself she must not mind it, she pulled up her wrap to cover her head and set off back to the snug thatched cottage north of town where she had lived for as many of her twenty-one years as she could remember.

Had she ever lived anywhere else? How had she come into Langbard's care? Who were her parents and what had happened to them? For years Langbard had gently but firmly discouraged such questions. Because he was the only family she had and because he was so good to her in every other way, Maura had grudgingly reconciled herself to ignorance about her past. That had not stopped her from wondering and guessing.

Now she wondered if Langbard's mysterious message had anything to do with her mysterious past.

As she neared the edge of the village, Maura spied her friend Sorsha some distance ahead. She opened her mouth to call, but before she could get the words out, a pair of Hanish soldiers turned onto the main road, talking together in their own language. To Maura's ears it had a jarring, strident sound.

The Han were taller than most Umbrians, with the hard, muscular build of their race and long, pale manes of hair they pulled through holes in the tops of their helmets to trail like plumes.

Maura lowered her head and averted her gaze, as Langbard had taught her. She did not slow her step, but neither did she walk faster. Though the soldiers passed quite close, they did not seem aware of her at all, for which she was grateful.

Once they had past, she broke into a run and soon caught up with Sorsha, who was returning home from market.

"Maura!" she cried. "If I had known you were in town, I would have waited for you."

When Maura explained about her errand in Windleford, Sorsha nodded, her generous mouth pursed in a disapproving frown.

She was shorter than Maura, and after three babies in rapid succession, a fair bit stouter. Her wild tumble of curls was ruddier than Maura's and she had a splash of freckles over the bridge of her nose. Perhaps her most attractive feature was her air of exuberant sociability.

Better one Sorsha for a friend, Maura had often thought, than four or five others…not that she'd ever had a choice.

"The gall of that Prin Howen!" huffed Sorsha. "I will give her the sharp edge of my tongue when I see her tomorrow. If young Noll hasn't sense enough to keep from picking up things he shouldn't, she ought not to let him out of her sight. Then to treat you so rude after you came to help. Fair makes me boil!"

"Do not say anything, Sorsha, please! That will only make

it worse. Langbard has never been anxious for me to make friends in the village, anyway."

Sorsha did not protest…but neither did she agree. Instead, as was her wont, she steered their talk to another subject. "Will you come up to my place for a cup of tea? The younglings are always so anxious for you to visit."

"Another day." Maura shook her head reluctantly. "I must get home now. A message came for Langbard just before I was called away to Howen's. I have never seen him look so worried."

"Langbard worried? It must be serious." Sorsha's brow furrowed. "I always thought he could walk over hot coals without turning a hair…not that he has much to turn, on top. Who did the message come from? Someone in the village?"

"I do not know who sent it, but I reckon it came from far away. A messenger bird brought it."

By this time, the two friends had reached the foot of the lane that wound up to Hoghill Farm. Maura's gaze strayed toward the low hill that shielded Langbard's cottage from view of the north road. "I hope he will confide in me. He does not seem to realize I have grown up."

"Older folk are like that and I reckon we will be too when our time comes." Sorsha reached for her friend's hand and gave it a reassuring squeeze. "You know, if there is anything Newlyn and I can do to help, you have only to ask. We owe Langbard a good deal after all he did to help us."

"I know we can count on you both."

The last time Maura had been this worried about anything was when her friend had gotten involved with a dangerous fugitive from the living death of the Blood Moon mines. It had all turned out better than she'd dared hope between Sorsha and her husband, the man now known as Newlyn.

But as she waved goodbye to Sorsha and started over the hill, Maura recalled the levelheaded ease with which Langbard had handled that whole perilous situation. Suddenly the spring sun seemed to sparkle with a false brightness and the brisk breeze sent a chill up her back. Anything that caused Langbard to fret must be ominous indeed.

Stifling that worrisome thought, Maura hurried toward the cottage. She found Langbard sitting in his favorite chair in front of the hearth, still clutching the scrap of parchment he had peeled off the bird's leg.

He was a tall man, taller than many of the Han, but lank of figure and gaunt of face. The crown of his head was bald, but the thick gray fringe around it grew long enough to braid into a plait that hung down his back.

He glanced up with a preoccupied smile of welcome when Maura entered. "The child—how is he?"

"The poor little fellow got hold of a pain spike." She set down her basket. "But he should be fine once I make a queensbalm ointment for him."

Langbard winced at the mention of the pain spike, then nodded to endorse Maura's choice of treatment.

She knelt by his chair. "Before I go off to Betchwood gathering queensbalm, you must tell me about the message you received. I have been so worried."

"Gathering queensbalm?" Langbard surged out of his chair. "Why, it is your birthday!"

"So it is, Uncle…but the message?"

"All in good time, my dear, I promise you." Langbard took

Maura's hand and helped her to her feet. "Let us pack a lunch and go gathering in Betchwood, like we used to."

The melancholy tenderness of his smile was impossible to resist.

"We do have some mutton sausages in the cold hatch," she said, "and I made oatloaf fresh this morning. Unless you have been foraging, there should be some marshberry tart left, too."

"Splendid!" Langbard cried. "A wonderful birthday feast. You pack the basket and I will make ready."

"On one condition, Uncle."

"What might that be?"

Maura lifted the trap door to the cold hatch. "On the way to Betchwood, I want you to tell me what that message meant."

"Of course, my dear." Langbard glanced down at the scrap of parchment in his hand, as if he had forgotten it for a moment and regretted being reminded.

More to himself than to her, he murmured, "I cannot put it off any longer."

He gazed around the large room that served as both kitchen and parlor. "It seems like only yesterday you were a wee thing, crawling around the cottage floor, popping everything into your mouth. No wonder you have such an apt hand for magic— you ate enough potion ingredients before you could walk!"

While Maura climbed down into the cold hatch to repack her basket with food, Langbard hunted up his walking staff, his cloak, his hat and the many-pocketed sash he wore when- ever he went any distance from the cottage. It held emer- gency supplies of vitcraft ingredients most necessary for healing and defense.

A while later, as they cut across the Swinley's north pasture, heading for Betchwood, Maura asked Langbard once more about his cryptic message. "Who sent it to you? It is bad news, isn't it?"

Though Langbard shook his head, he still looked too anxious to ease Maura's fears. "Grave, perhaps, but not bad. Indeed, it may be the best possible news for the people of Umbria. Perhaps it is selfish of me not to welcome it as such."

If he meant the words to reassure her, they did not. "Please, Uncle, you are talking in riddles."

"Your pardon, my dear. I do not mean to. Only, it is hard to know where to begin. Perhaps I should have begun preparing you long ago, but I dared not take the chance you might let a careless word slip. And you were always such a happy child, I could not bear to burden you with it until I had no choice."

"Goodness, Uncle, you make these tidings sound very dire." How could anything that concerned her be something other than quiet and commonplace?

Langbard heaved a regretful sigh. "Perhaps I was wrong not to tell you as much as I knew about your parents when you asked."

Her parents? Was she going to find out about them at last?

She had been quite an age when she'd come to realize that most children had mothers and fathers to look after them. From there it had been a short step to wonder if her parents had given her away because they'd been displeased with her. Sorsha had been quick to soothe her worries on that score, suggesting the more dramatic possibility—that Maura's parents might have been murdered by outlaws.

For years Maura had preferred to believe it over the likelihood that she'd been abandoned. Deep in her heart, though, the gnawing doubt had never quite gone away.

Langbard gazed off toward Betchwood, yet Maura sensed he was looking back into the past. "This might all make more sense if I begin at the beginning. Do you remember the stories I used to tell you about King Elzaban?"

"Of course, I do. They were always my favorites."

Long ago, perhaps a thousand years, Elzaban, the Margrave of Tarsh, had forged the provinces of Umbria into one strong, proud nation. Many heroic tales were told of his brief but glorious reign. One in particular had stirred Maura's fancy.

"Then," said Langbard, "you recall he disappeared during the Battle of the Three Castles and was never seen again?"

"Yes, Uncle." Did he truly suppose she could forget? "King Elzaban had taken a mortal wound in the fighting. But his beloved Abrielle spirited him away and wove a powerful sleeping spell around him to hold back death and time."

Maura could not keep a tender, dreamy note from her voice. Her only knowledge of such passionate attachment between a man and a woman came from such tales. Often she had fallen asleep picturing herself as Abrielle. Only in her dreams, she always found a way to heal her dying lover, so they could wed and enjoy a long lifetime of happiness.

"Do not forget the most important part of the story." Langbard's deep, resonant voice intruded on Maura's fanciful musings. "In his country's hour of greatest need, the Waiting King will be woken from his magical slumber by his Destined Queen. Together, they will reclaim and restore his kingdom."

Under her breath Maura muttered, "I wish they would hurry up about it."

She had thought that often over the years. Whenever she saw Hanish soldiers harassing villagers in the market. When she had heard of what Sorsha's husband had suffered in the mines. Just this morning, when she had seen the boy hurt by a pain spike. What was keeping the Waiting King and his Destined Queen?

If Langbard heard her, he did not acknowledge it. "Did I ever tell you what became of Abrielle?"

"No." Maura started to ask why any of this mattered, but her curiosity got the better of her. "What happened to her?"

"Few people know that part of the story," said Langbard. "She lived. She wed the man who had been her lord's champion. She bore him a daughter, and years later, her daughter begat a daughter. For centuries the princess enchantresses of the House of Abrielle served as counselors to the kings of Umbria. It was rumored that one of their line would be the Destined Queen."

He stopped and turned his gaze upon Maura. "That message came from the Vestan Islands. From scholars who have studied the ancient writings of the Elderways to determine when the Destined Queen must begin her quest. The message said..."

"'Her time has come,'" Maura murmured in a daze as she guessed what Langbard was trying to tell her.

Guessed, but could not believe.

"*My* time is come?" The words squeaked out of her, followed by a burst of thin, overwrought laughter. "Uncle, this is too important a subject for jesting!"

"I could not agree more, my dear. I assure you, I am completely in earnest." His steady gaze told Maura he believed what he was saying.

"It cannot be." She spoke gently, coaxing him to see reason. "I am nobody special."

"Nonsense!" When a wizard spoke in that tone of authority, it was impossible *not* to give him one's full attention…and respect. "You do not know enough of the world to appreciate how special you *are,* my dear."

Special, perhaps. But the Destined Queen of Umbria?

She could not just stand there and listen. The shadow of Betchwood beckoned in the distance. Maura began walking toward it. Perhaps if she kept moving, she could somehow keep one step ahead of Langbard's disturbing revelation.

But her guardian was not about to stop now that she had persuaded him to talk. Maura heard him hurrying to catch up with her. She could picture his dark cloak billowing out and his blue-gray robe swirling around his feet with each long stride.

"I have not always lived in this quiet corner of the kingdom, you know." His voice sounded a bit winded as he fell in step with her. "When I was a young man, I made quite a reputation for myself as a scholar of the Elderways. I had hoped to lead a revival of our forgotten culture."

Maura cast him a sidelong glance, trying to imagine what those familiar craggy features must have looked like in their youth. "What changed your mind—the coming of the Han?"

"No. It was the Oracle of Margyle. She told me that one day I would be father to the Destined Queen. Of course, I did not understand the truth of what she meant at the time." Langbard shrugged. "That is the trouble with oracles. They are not always as plain as they might be."

Ahead of them, the outermost trees of Betchwood stretched their budding branches skyward for the sun's warming kiss.

"Let us eat now and talk more." Langbard handed the lunch basket back to Maura, then settled himself on a fallen tree trunk, well cushioned with thick moss. "We can do our gathering later, if you still wish to."

"Yes...of course." Maura sank onto the grass and began to unpack the basket.

Somehow, it felt as if her body, her mind and her heart were no longer fully connected. The sun shone bright and warm. Nearby a narrow stream of water cascaded over some rocks. Both had lost their accustomed power to soothe her.

She could not bring herself to ask any of the scores of questions that clamored for answers. Putting them into words would be taking a dangerous step toward something from which she would rather turn and flee.

Having finally broached this momentous subject seemed to restore Langbard to his old, unruffled self. He munched away on oatloaf and cold mutton sausage with obvious relish. Between bites, he continued his story. At least, that was what it felt like to Maura—a story. A bedtime tale like all the others he had told her over the years. Except that this story had grave consequences for her... if it were true.

"I was not anxious to believe my part in these events, either." The slope of Langbard's bushy brows and the soft glow of his eyes communicated fond concern and an earnest desire to lessen the impact of what he was telling her, if only by identifying with it. "I was wedded to my work, then, and had not thought it fair to ask a wife to take second place in my life. That would have to change if I was meant to sire a daughter.

So, with some regret, I gave up my studies. When I took my nose out of my books and looked around at the world, I discovered there was a lady of my acquaintance who fancied me."

All these years later, he still looked so pleasantly shocked by the notion, that Maura could not help smiling...for a moment.

"We were very happy together." Langbard lapsed into the soft murmur of a man musing to himself. "Even with war swirling around us and dark days for the people of Umbria. We made our home here, in a quiet corner of the kingdom that might easily be overlooked. As safe and wholesome a place to raise a child as we could find...but no child came."

He turned his face away from Maura, staring at the tiny waterfall in silence for a moment before he spoke again. "The winter my wife sickened and died, I wanted to die with her. Happy as we had been together, I wondered if I had wasted my life. I questioned my belief in the Elderways. Were they no more than foolish stories people clung to for comfort and hope when they had too little of either?"

"And then?" Maura found herself hunched forward, hanging on his words.

"Then—" abruptly Langbard swung about to fix her with his most penetrating gaze "—one winter night I heard your mother calling for my help."

Questions she should have asked years ago poured out of Maura. "What was she like? Where did she go? Why did she leave me with you? Who was my father?"

She still feared the answers, but now the *unknown* seemed far more menacing.

"Your father?" Langbard seized on her final question first, perhaps because it was the most easily answered. "I do not

know. Your mother never told me, and I did not ask. I though
perhaps I would find out during her ritual of passing, but she
kept that secret to death and beyond."

"She died, then? Here?" So her mother had not abandoned
her. At least not in the way she had feared.

Langbard gave a slow nod as he chewed on a slice of oatloaf
"When?"

"Not long after you were weaned. I am sorry you have no
memory of her. She was so very beautiful, and so very sad. I
believe she died of a broken heart."

Never in twenty-one years had Langbard so much as raised
his voice to her. Now Maura felt as though he had struck her.
"Did her child bring her no joy?"

"Oh, my dear!" Springing from his seat on the fallen tree
trunk, Langbard dropped to his knees before Maura and took
her hands in his…oblivious that he was kneeling in the ruins
of her marshberry tart. "Believe me, her love for you was all
that sustained your mother!"

The part of her that clung to all that was safe and ordinary made Maura cry out, "Langbard, your robe! Nothing
stains like marshberries. I must put it to soak as soon as we
get home."

"Maura." Langbard crooked his forefinger under her chin
and tilted it so she must look him in the eye. "You have more
important matters to concern yourself with now than stained
robes and salves for the village folk."

"How can I?" The thought of it made her tremble. "I have
never been farther from home than Windleford. All my life
you have taught me to avoid trouble or drawing attention to
myself. How am I supposed to find the Waiting King when

no one else has stumbled upon him in hundreds of years? What part can I have in driving the Han out of Umbria?"

With every word her breath came faster and more shallow. Her heart raced as if it meant to fly out of her body.

"I do not want this, Langbard! I would rather stay here in Norest, washing clothes and baking tarts and making salve. It is all I know. How can you be certain I am the girl the Oracle told you about? Perhaps your wife was not meant to die. Perhaps you were supposed to wed again and sire a real daughter."

"You *are* my daughter, Maura, in every way that matters. And I believe you can do this. Umbria needs a queen who can perform humble tasks as well as high ones. A queen who can help her people find peace and simple happiness again, because she has known them herself."

While those words penetrated her buffer of denial and aversion, Langbard went on. "It was only during your mother's passing ritual that I discovered who she was and consequently who you are. After my wife's death, I had rejected the Oracle's prophesy. But when I learned that you were the last of Abrielle's line, it restored my faith in the Giver and the Elderways. You must have faith in them, too, and faith in yourself that you can fulfill your destiny."

The steadiness of his gaze and the conviction in his voice helped calm Maura's mounting panic.

"Until this morning, I did not know I *had* a destiny. This is so much to take in. I believe in the Waiting King. I want him to return. But for me to bring it about…?"

Langbard's hand fell. "I am sorry I waited so long and have broken all this to you so badly."

Was there any *good* way to tell such tidings? "If all this is true, how soon must I leave and where must I go?"

"I wish the scholars of Margyle could have given us more warning." Langbard's busy brows knit together. "The ancient writings say the Waiting King must be woken during the full moon of Solsticetide."

Maura's shield of numb disbelief slipped. The sharp edge of panic slashed through her. "But that is only…ten weeks away! How far must I go in that time?"

"I wish I could tell you, my dear. First we must obtain an ancient map that will lead us to the Secret Glade. For many years, the map has been hidden in a town called Prum at the edge of the Southmark steppes."

"We?" Maura prayed that meant what she hoped. "Us?"

"Did you think I would send you off on a quest like this all by yourself?"

"Uncle!" She caught Langbard in an embrace that was all the tighter for knowing something of what he had sacrificed for her.

His arms closed around her. "We will manage, somehow, my dear. You will see."

The woolen weave of his robe scratched softly against Maura's cheek as she nodded. She would not disappoint Langbard by questioning his reassurance.

But neither could she bring herself to believe it.

2

"I am not sure this is a good idea," said Langbard a while later, as he packed the remains of their lunch back into the basket. "Are you certain you will be all right by yourself?"

"Quite certain." Maura shook the cloth free of crumbs, then folded it. "I must get a few queensbalm flowers for that boy in the village."

What she truly wanted was a little time, peace and privacy to absorb everything Langbard had told her about her past... and her future.

She tucked the cloth over the remnants of food in the basket. "I do not plan to run away, if that's what worries you."

Not that part of her wouldn't like to. But where would she run? Norest was one of the safest, most peaceful places in the kingdom. Yet turmoil and danger had still found her.

"That does not worry me in the least. The trouble is I have

spent the past twenty-one years fretting about your safety."
Langbard picked up his staff from where it leaned against the
fallen tree trunk. He pointed it toward the little waterfall. "I
cannot stop all at once any more than that water can bring itself to a halt at the top of those rocks."

"I will be fine, truly." Maura held out the basket for him to
take. "If we are to go in search of the Waiting King, it is past
time I learned to look after myself, don't you think?"

How easily those preposterous words formed themselves
on her lips!

Langbard mulled the notion over for a moment, then gave a
resigned nod. "I suppose you are right, though it will take some
getting used to. Promise me you will be home before sundown?"

"I promise."

He made no move to take the basket from her. Instead
Langbard dropped his staff and unfastened his cloak so he
could remove his sash.

"At least oblige a worrisome old man by taking this." He
handed Maura the sash, exchanging it for the lunch basket.
"There are one or two empty pockets you can fill with queensbalm when you find it. As for the rest, you will find anything
you might need in an emergency—powdered stag hoof, spidersilk, madfern."

"I know what is there, and where to find it." Maura slipped
the sash over her head. "I have filled most of the pockets in
it, remember? Besides, it is quiet as can be around here. I will
not be in any danger."

"Do be careful, just the same." Langbard slung his cloak
over one arm then stooped to retrieve his walking stick.

"I will." After having been taught all her life to avoid danger, Maura doubted she could commit a reckless act if she tried. "When you get home, do not forget to change your robe and set that one to soak. Otherwise I will be scrubbing for a week to get the marshberry stains out."

He assured her he would, all the while walking so slowly and turning so often to glance back at her, Maura doubted he would reach home before nightfall. Perhaps once she was out of sight he might reconcile himself to her going.

Inhaling a deep breath of bracing spring air, she strode into Betchwood Forest, willing herself not to look back. She ducked behind the first large tree she came to—a tall gnarled goldenoak with a thick trunk and rough bark. Leaning against it, Maura let her legs go limp and sank to the ground under the weight of her own dread and bewilderment.

"The Destined Queen?" Her words came out in a faltering whisper.

She stared at her hands. Her fingertips were stained green from the juice of fresh herbs. Her palms had calluses from the rough rope she pulled to draw water from the well. There was a tiny blister, almost healed, where she'd burned it retrieving fish pasties from the oven. They were not the hands of a queen, regardless of what Langbard might say.

Wrapped in her warring, whirling thoughts and raw emotions, Maura staggered to her feet and wandered deeper into the forest. Dead leaves from the previous autumn rustled beneath her feet. Soft fronds of new fern whispered against her legs beneath her gown. A shoot of bramble rasped across the flesh of her ankle.

Those familiar sensations bound Maura to her familiar

world, when the fateful, foreign power of Langbard's story threatened to seize her and carry her away against her will.

Why me? The question trembled through her with every step she took.

Of course she wanted to see the Waiting King restored to his throne! No Umbrian of goodwill would wish to have his coming delayed an instant longer than need be. But surely there must be other young women more capable and more willing than she to undertake the task? Even with Langbard by her side, Maura quailed to think of the hardship and danger they might face.

Around and around it went, one moment rejecting the notion as altogether impossible, the next moment terrifying herself with a reluctant glance into the future.

"I must get back," she whispered to herself at last.

She had hoped a quiet interval to think over Langbard's words would help her make sense of it all. Instead she found herself in a worse muddle than ever.

And which way was *back?* She had never wandered quite so far into Betchwood before.

Maura looked around, trying to judge her location. Off to the west, the trees appeared to thin out. It might not be the most direct route home, but suddenly it felt more important to find her way out of the forest before the sun dipped lower.

Besides, queensbalm grew at the edge of the woods and Maura remembered her need for it. A fleeting thought crossed her mind that when the Waiting King regained his throne no one would leave Hanish pain spikes around for children to find. Would that not be worth a certain amount of hardship to gain?

Just ahead, she spotted a patch of queensbalm. Maura knelt

and picked enough of the delicate flowers to fill the empty pockets of her sash.

A soft hiss, followed by a sharp snap, made her glance up. An arrow stuck out of a nearby tree trunk, still quivering from the impact. From beyond the edge of the forest a wave of confused noise broke over Maura—cries of pain, angry shouts in the Hanish tongue, the alarming clash of metal against metal.

With trembling fingers she shoved the queensbalm into her apron, then fumbled in the pockets of Langbard's sash until she found what she was looking for—clippings from the feather of a cuddybird, famed for its ability to blend with its surroundings.

Murmuring the ritual words that would invoke the bird's special powers, Maura sprinkled a liberal pinch of the cuttings over her head. Then she waved her hand in front of her face. She could still see it if she looked hard enough, but the edges blurred and her flesh took on the hues of the underbrush, in a strange transparency like softly rippling water. For most purposes, the spell rendered invisible whoever it was cast upon.

Thus protected from hostile eyes, Maura turned to flee.

The cries of pain reached out and caught her by the heart. Perhaps she could steal a quick look from the cover of the trees. Just long enough to prove to herself that this was none of her concern. That way the cries might not haunt her dreams tonight…if she managed to get to sleep.

As Maura crawled through the underbrush to the edge of the forest, the caution Langbard had drummed into her from her youngest years battled an insistent urge to help. No one had taught her that.

Peering out from behind a low thicket of mothbroom, she

saw what she had expected. The ground sloped downward from the eaves of the forest into a hollow from which many trees had been cut, providing her with a clear view. A large troop of Hanish soldiers, probably from the Windleford garrison, appeared to have ambushed a gang of outlaws.

One of the outlaws was trying to keep the others in a tight clutch, back-to-back, their blades bristling as they retreated toward the cover of the trees. When a Hanish arrow struck one outlaw in the shoulder, the men to his left and right locked their arms through his to carry him with the group. Hanish soldiers circled around the thorny knot of outlaws just out of blade reach, bellowing what sounded like taunts or curses.

Suddenly one outlaw broke from the group, bolting toward the forest through a slender gap in the surrounding ring of enemies. He did not get more than ten yards when the soldiers fell on him and hacked him to pieces.

Maura raised her hand to stifle a scream, but instead she retched up every crumb of the lunch she'd eaten with Langbard.

When she was able to glance up again, the cluster of outlaws had broken and scattered. The men were running in all directions, scrambling to reach cover before swarms of Hanish soldiers overtook and butchered them.

One of the outlaws, the man who had struggled to hold the others together, looked as if he alone might escape. He ran swiftly, now crouching, now leaping over a fallen tree or small boulder that lay in his path. Ducking and dodging, he never held to the same course for long, but ran in a weaving, erratic fashion. Often, Hanish arrows struck the ground where he had been only an instant before.

Against her will, Maura found herself hoping this man

would get away. Silently she cheered every inch of distance he put between himself and his pursuers. Her breath caught at each near miss of an arrow, then hissed out in relief when he kept running. Her muscles tensed as if trying to bestow any speed or strength she possessed upon him.

Closer and closer he came, through the clear-cut hollow that gouged a deep wedge into the western border of Betchwood. The Han had dispatched all the others. Now they joined in pursuit of this one last outlaw…whose endurance was beginning to fade.

No one could keep up such a pace, running uphill, unless aided by powerful magic, which Maura sensed the outlaw did not possess. She could almost feel the air rasping down his throat, scouring his lungs. The hard strength of his leg muscles dwindling, until they would soon be weak and yielding as suet, unable to lift feet that grew heavier with every step.

He stumbled. She gasped.

He rolled with the fall, staggering onto his feet again with renewed desperation.

Then a Hanish arrow struck him in the left arm.

It would all be over soon.

She must not watch, must not care. He was only an outlaw, after all. Langbard's recent account of her parents had not penetrated as deep as the fear and loathing Maura had harbored for so many years against this man's kind.

Go to his aid? Unthinkable!

Before such madness could commandeer her will, Maura lurched to her feet and turned to run away.

His shield arm had been hit.

Rath Talward tossed his small buckler aside and wheeled

to face the Han. For the fight he was about to make, he would need no defense. Nor would he want it. This would be a fight to the death.

For as long as he could remember, he had lived by a few simple rules: *Stay alive. Stay free. Stay fed.*

Now that it had come to the sharp edge of a blade, he knew freedom must stand first. Even ahead of life itself. Better to die than be taken to the Blood Moon mines and enslaved with Hanish poison. He would give them no choice but to kill him.

The enemy would soon swarm over him. Rath dragged his left hand up to wrap around the hilt of his sword, then covered it with his right and crouched, poised to strike the first Han who came within reach.

A big one raced toward him—a thick, curved blade held high, shield raised, and a long plume of flaxen hair streaming from the top of the helmet. If a warrior must meet his death, there was a kind of honor to be found in falling before such a strong, fierce foe.

Rath sucked in a breath and rallied his spent body for one last effort before it could rest…forever.

Amid the pounding advance of the Han, and their harsh blood-bellows, Rath heard the oddest sound. A woman's voice, clear and sweet, raised in a gentle chant that stirred memories of his all-but-forgotten childhood.

It distracted him for a crucial instant. His muscles relaxed and his blade sagged.

The next thing he knew, the big Han plowed into him, hurling him to the ground and driving the arrow deeper into his arm. The Han fell, too, cursing as he stumbled over his fallen foe.

While Rath struggled through a haze of shock and pain to get his feet back under him, the Han lumbered up and kept on running. More Hanish soldiers ran past, their eyes fixed on a point off in the distance.

Had one of his comrades also eluded their swords to make a bolt for freedom? Then why did the rear guard not close in to hew him down?

All but a few of the Han had streamed past Rath without a glance, when something tugged at his sleeve. From out of nowhere, a beguiling voice whispered, "Come this way, quickly! They will soon realize their mistake."

Rath shook his head hard. Perhaps he'd knocked his wits loose when the Han had run over him.

"Now, I said!" The voice hissed in his ear, like the soft, angry buzz of a wasp. The tug on his sleeve grew more insistent.

Rath stumbled in the direction he was being pulled, up the slope toward the trees. "What are you?"

A chill of fear slithered through him such as he had not felt when running from the Han or facing them to meet his end.

"A friend you ill deserve." The voice sounded breathless, and somehow vexed with itself.

Rath had heard that same edge in his own voice often enough to recognize it.

A friend?

"What sorcery is this?" Wrenching his arm free, Rath glanced down to find it...gone.

"Sorcery? How dare you! Please yourself, then, ungrateful lout." The voice grew fainter, moving away from him. "Stay here and let the Han butcher you."

Rath was tempted to do just that.

The soldiers could only kill him once. With luck it might be over quickly. He had tasted the cruel pain Hanish sorcery could inflict. The kind that made strong men plead for death.

Would this not be just the kind of torment in which the Echtroi took cruel pleasure—tempting him with sweet-sounding false hope?

Well, he would not take their tainted bait.

Rath waited for the voice to return and entice him further. It did not.

Barely discernable beneath the clamor of the Han, he could hear the faint patter of footfall, the snap of a twig, the swish of brush. When he looked in the direction of those sounds, he marked the signs of some unseen creature passing. A creature whose invisible movements betrayed no intention of turning back.

Pain blazed in his arm, then, as if to punish him for ignoring it as long as he had. But when he reached to break off the shaft, Rath could see neither the arrow nor his arm. The invisible fingers of his other hand closed around something solid that felt like an arrow shaft. He snapped it off, biting back a groan.

What if he stayed like this, unable to be seen by anyone, himself included? A few benefits raced through his thoughts, chased out by a hoard of drawbacks.

"Wait!" he called in an urgent whisper, staggering after whatever had done this to him. "You cannot leave me like this!"

He stumbled into a tall clump of mothbroom, sending a small cloud of yellow blossoms billowing up as if they were real insects that had only lighted on the branches for a moment.

Something latched on to the front of his leather vest and pulled him to the ground.

"Sit and hush!" ordered the voice. "Invisibility is not much protection if you blunder around making noise and bumping into everything."

That made a simple, workaday kind of sense that Rath did not associate with the Echtroi or any other Han. In fact, it was more the sort of thing he might have said, if he'd had the power to turn people invisible.

Invisible? Rath sank to the ground. His wound must be making him light-headed. Perhaps he was dreaming all of this. For the sake of his fallen comrades, he hoped he'd dreamed the whole horrible day.

"Who are you?" he asked again. "Why did you do this to me?"

"It will not last, if that is what worries you." The answer came from very nearby. "Another hour. Less if you wash."

That was a relief to hear, though it did not answer either of his questions.

"Then should we not get as far away from here as we can before it wears off?" Rath was not certain what had made him say *we,* as if he expected or desired that they should stay together. Experience had taught him that he fared best on his own. Yet he seemed doomed to go through life picking up followers, the way a long cloak picked up troublesome burrs. "First, I must go see if any of the others are still alive."

When Rath tried to rise, the world spun and wobbled around him. He collapsed back onto the ground, jarring his injured arm. The pain that had prowled menacingly around the border of his consciousness bit into him once more. He tried to stifle a cry that rose to his lips and partly succeeded.

"You do not sound in fit condition to go anywhere," said

his unseen companion. "Even if you were, I saw what happened. You would find none of your friends whole, let alone alive."

She whispered a few words Rath did not understand, but which had a strangely familiar sound.

"Fools!" he muttered. "If they had kept together we might have gained the woods and had a chance. I warned them it was likely all a trap in the first place."

Long ago Rath had learned that, to survive, he must treat death with contempt and anger. Draw a warning from whatever mistakes had led to the calamity, then move on. Grief was a heavy, useless luxury he could not afford to carry.

It was just as well if none of the others had survived. If they had, he'd likely have been compelled to risk his fool neck to help them.

"I think the Han are coming back this way," whispered the voice. "That madfern worked well considering how thin I had to spread it."

"What?" Rath understood each word separately, but taken together they made no sense to him.

"Never mind, I was only speaking my thoughts."

Speaking them in Umbrian, too. Not Hanish, or even Comtung. That was another riddle Rath had neither the time nor the patience to untangle.

He could hear the soldiers coming back toward them. A violent rustle of branches told him they were searching the edge of the forest.

"Go," he ordered in an urgent whisper. "The deeper you get into the forest, the safer you'll be. The Han do not like trees, especially a great many together."

"Why did you not tell me sooner? Let us go, then."

Rath shook his head. Then he remembered his invisible companion could not see him, either. "Do not wait for me. You said yourself, I am not fit to go far."

"Chew on this." A small flower floated in the air toward him. Its five outer petals were the color of cream with a faint blush, while the inner ones had a warm rosy hue. "It will ease your pain and give you strength enough to walk a little way."

"What is it?" As Rath spoke, the flower wafted closer and closer to his mouth, until an unseen hand pushed it in. He almost spit it back out. But when his teeth closed on the delicate petals, a fresh sweetness filled his mouth and the pain in his arm lessened. He heard a soft rustle beside him. Then invisible fingers skimmed across his shoulders and something wedged under his right arm, coaxing him to rise.

To his amazement, Rath discovered he could stand. He was still dizzy, a condition made worse by not being able to see his own feet. His arm still hurt, but in a scattered, distant way, and his invisible legs seemed sound enough to hold him up.

With a bit of help.

He could feel the solid warmth of a shoulder braced beneath his arm. He sensed a fragrant, willowy presence moving at his side.

They had not gone far when the Hanish voices grew louder behind them and the bushes began to rustle violently. Rath and his companion froze. For a wild moment he wondered what had become of his sword. Then he remembered he had sheathed it earlier, without thinking or being able to see what he was doing.

Behind them, the soldiers burst into harsh, scornful laughter.

"What are they saying?" asked Rath's companion in a barely audible whisper, almost strangled with fear.

"Something about a puddle of vomit. They say some lowling must have watched their games."

Rath wasn't sure what had him answer so readily. He usually took care to conceal his grasp of Hanish. Long ago, he had learned that every piece of knowledge was a potential weapon. And he lived by the old Hitherland adage, "The most perilous blade is the hidden one."

Did the same not apply to an enemy?

Rath could not deny this creature of sorcery had done him stout service so far. But what had prompted her? What did she want from him?

The creature uttered a curse. But one so mild it sounded altogether foolish under the circumstances. Rath battled a dangerous urge to laugh.

The Hans' next words killed his misplaced mirth.

His alarm must have communicated itself to his companion. "What are they saying now?"

"One asked if they should set the hounds after it...you... us."

She cursed again. A better one this time.

Rath was tempted to teach her some truly powerful profanity. Hanish hounds did not fear forests, like their masters. But they could be every bit as merciless.

What's more, they would not need their eyes to find him. They would smell his blood. And once smelled, they would not rest until they had tasted it.

3

Hanish hounds? Maura's organs twisted themselves into an ice-knot.

She had seen those horrid creatures in the village. All hard muscle, sharp teeth and slick black pelts, snarling on the ends of chains that never seemed strong enough to hold them if they smelled blood or fear. The soldiers of the Windleford garrison might not glance at her when she scurried through the market square, but their hounds were alert to her presence.

Alert and restive.

"Run!" growled the outlaw.

Maura did not wait for a more mannerly invitation. Off in the distance, she could hear the chilling sound of baying.

She repented getting herself mixed up in this dangerous situation. Fate had already thrust enough trouble on her shoulders today. She'd hardly needed to go looking for more.

She and her outlaw made good haste for a while, especially given his wound and the energy he must have consumed running from the Hanish ambush.

He was not *her* outlaw, Maura reminded herself. Saving him from slaughter should not obligate her to this ungrateful ruffian. Yet, in some unjust fashion, it did.

Her legs protested the demands she was making on them. The air she gasped in stung her throat. Every tree they passed seemed to have a low-hanging limb to whip against her face. Or a twisted root hiding in the carpet of last autumn's decaying leaves to catch her foot.

With every step, the outlaw leaned on her more heavily. A chew of fresh queensbalm could provide an astonishing surge of energy and pain relief for one tiny blossom, but the benefits wore off quickly. And it was not safe to consume in larger quantities.

Maura plundered her memory trying to recall the route she had taken to get here. She had been so preoccupied with her worries and doubts, she'd scarcely paid heed to where her feet had been taking her. If she got out of her present misadventure alive, she swore to the Giver, and herself, that she would always mind where she was going from now on.

Just when she doubted she could go another step, a soft, welcome sound beckoned her onward. The sound of moving water.

"This way," she gasped. "Just a little farther."

"What?" The question retched out of the outlaw. "You have…a fortress…of sorcery…where we can take shelter?"

Maura was tempted to drop him right there and let him fend for himself, or not. But those hounds… She could not abandon her worst enemy to them.

"I am...*not*...a sorceress!" They continued to lurch forward, though Maura feared each step might be their last. "I am an...enchantress!"

A tremor ran through the outlaw, then he let out a hoarse, wheezy laugh. "I feel...much safer...now."

Not only an outlaw, but an ignorant one. If he did not know the difference between mortcraft and vitcraft, she wasn't about to waste her dwindling breath explaining it to him. He probably would not have the wit to understand anyway.

"Just keep...moving." She forced the order through clenched teeth. "Or I may...turn you...into...a newt!"

It was an empty threat, of course. The proper ingredients and spell might temporarily lend a person the special abilities of a newt. Whatever they might be.

Maura doubted the Echtroi would bother to cast such a spell even if they knew how. It would not hurt enough to suit them. The Han had convinced most Umbrians that all magic was evil. Much as the notion outraged Maura, at the moment she was desperate enough to turn their slander to her advantage.

Ahead of them, the ground fell away, sloping down to a narrow brook. Coming here a while earlier, Maura had crossed it by scrambling over a pair of stepping stones.

This time she launched herself and the outlaw into the cold, swift-flowing water, instead.

"What are...you doing?" he demanded, but his voice sounded weak. Whatever was keeping him on his feet now, it was no longer the queensbalm.

"Dogs will...follow my scent." She hoped.

That was not her only reason for taking to the water. She

was also counting on it to bear this large man's weight. She would only have to tow him along in the proper direction, and the natural flow of the brook would help with that.

"Just around...that bend," she urged him. "Then rest."

The barking and baying grew louder behind them. Maura knew the brook water would soon wash away her cuddybird spell, making them visible to their enemies again.

Dragging the outlaw out of sight of the stepping stones, she found shelter for them both behind a large, half-submerged tree trunk. No sooner had they drawn a few ragged breaths than the forest upstream erupted in a tumult of thrashing underbrush and blood-chilling howls.

The outlaw's arm had draped over Maura's shoulder while they'd been walking. Now he pulled her toward him. She was too spent and too terrified to resist.

He smelled of leather, sweat and smoke. His chest felt hard as oak and his sound arm pressed her tightly to him. She sensed strength and protectiveness in his hold. Even though she knew he was too badly injured to defend her, she found a curious comfort in his one-armed embrace.

As rapidly and noisily as the hounds had come, they passed by, their baying growing fainter as they followed Maura's old trail. She let out a quivering sigh and thanked the Giver with all her heart for their narrow escape.

Much of the tension in the outlaw seemed to slacken, too. "That was good thinking, just now. You have the makings of a fine..."

"Outlaw?" Maura drenched the word in scorn as she pulled away from him, cursing her weakness for accepting comfort from such a man.

"Considering the present *law* of this land, I think better of myself for being outside it than in." His indignant reply cut through the air like a birch switch. "And many folk you would disdain as outlaws still know how to accept a word of praise with good grace."

"I do not need praise from the likes of you."

"Good, for you will get no more! Just say what payment you want and we can part company. Be warned, I have little of value. Despite what you may have heard, men like me do not often live long enough to accumulate riches."

The bitterness in his voice took Maura aback, as did the word "payment."

"I want nothing from you...outlaw. Perhaps in the life you lead no one ever does a good turn without expecting some reward. Where I come from, people do it all the time."

She remembered her childhood lessons at Langbard's knee. Before she'd been taught the simplest spell, he had provided more important instruction.

"Remember, child, the Giver is a spirit. Though its will is powerful and can work wonders, it still must use our hands, our lips and our hearts to work its special grace in the world."

With that fond memory came a twinge of shame. She had not let the Giver speak through her, just now. She opened her mouth to apologize, searching for the right words, struggling to subdue her old bitterness to force them out.

"I entreat your pardon." That was what she'd meant to say, but she had not spoken yet. Instead those words came from the outlaw, now perfectly visible below the waist, with his upper body growing clearer by the moment.

"You do?"

He made the traditional gesture of respect, somewhere between a nod and a bow. "You saved my life, twice at least, and I have not yet offered you a word of thanks. Whether you ask reward of me or not, I am in your debt."

Maura almost wished he had stayed invisible. His presence was not quite so threatening then.

He towered above her, dressed in sinister black from head to heels. Shaggy, unkempt hair the color of ripe acorns fell almost to his shoulders. An angry scar slashed crosswise down his left cheek and his nose looked as though it had been broken at least once. Deep-set eyes, dark as a moonless night, appeared to take much in, but give little out. His large hands looked capable of snapping any bone in her body with almost no effort.

She shivered. Not for the world would she let this fellow know he had provoked it.

"We cannot stay here." She glanced up at the sky. "It will grow even colder as it gets dark."

And she had to get home. Langbard would be frantic, especially if he heard the hounds baying from Betchwood.

"Go, then. I will rest here a moment more, then look for somewhere I can go to ground for a while." The outlaw glanced down at his injured arm, now quite visible.

From his black sleeve it was impossible to tell how much the wound had bled. How was he going to remove the head of that Hanish arrow?

"Have you a camp or friends I can take you to?" she asked.

His gaze snapped back to her, as if he'd been lost in his own plans and had forgotten she was still there. Perhaps he'd also been wondering what to do about his injury.

"I have no friends." He jerked his head back toward the hollow where the outlaws had been ambushed. "No comrades anymore, either. Do not fret yourself, I will manage on my own. I always have."

Perhaps. But had he ever been this badly off before?

It was none of her concern, Maura told herself. She'd already done far more than he had any right to ask of her. Not that he had asked.

Everything she'd done for him so far had been the result of her own decisions. He was where he was now because she had intervened. Was it so much better to escape a swift Hanish sword stoke, only to bleed or starve to death, alone in the forest, freezing and in pain?

What could she do to appease the daft sense of responsibility she felt for this fellow? Fetch him home to Langbard's cottage? It might put her and her guardian in terrible danger.

Besides, the cottage was still a long way off. She had barely managed to bring the outlaw from the edge of the forest. Now they were cold and wet, his strength would be less than ever. What if they ran into more hounds or Hanish patrols on their way?

"You are not staying here in the woods to die like some poor beast." Maura did not stop to ask herself how she would compel him to come if he refused. "I am taking you home with me. Just long enough to dry out, eat and have your wound tended, mind."

The outlaw did not answer.

Did he spurn her help? Or did he guess the suspicion and reluctance behind her offer?

She glanced up to find his head slumped onto his shoulder. Maura barely stifled a shriek of frustration.

It had been difficult enough bringing the man this short distance. How would she ever get him all the way back to the cottage now? It all would have been much easier if she *had* been able to turn him into a nice pocketable newt.

That preposterous notion sparked an idea that might truly work. Maura was not anxious to undertake it, though.

Glancing down at Langbard's sash, she winced. "I hope none of these things will come to harm from a little water."

She rummaged in the topmost pocket, making a face as she pulled out a disgusting wad of finely cut fur held together by bear fat.

Plugging her nose, she jammed the glob of hair and fat into her mouth. Bad enough she had to eat such stuff, but to inflict it on a stomach that had already taken some abuse that day was almost too much. She tried not to think about that as she chewed and swallowed, then struggled to hold her gorge.

He must have died. That was Rath's first thought when he began to wake.

His second was that foolish old Ganny Oddbody had been right after all. She had always stubbornly maintained that the spirits of living folk went on to some good place after the trials of this world.

That world.

He surely must have left that world behind, for he had never felt such warmth, peace and comfort when he'd been alive. If he'd known such good things awaited him, he might not have exerted himself so hard to stay alive. Nor imposed on the pretty little sorceress to help him.

Rath wondered what had become of her. If this was death, then he hoped she had died, too. Yet such a wish did not seem right, somehow.

He recalled the brief, faint glimpse he had got of her before he died. She'd been a beauty, with her rich vibrant hair and eyes that held the innocent promise of springtime.

Innocent promise of springtime? He must be dead. Rath had a silent mocking laugh at his own expense. He'd never indulge in such fanciful sentiments if he were alive.

Nearby, a soft, familiar voice asked, "Is he going to live?"

The lady sounded a good deal more concerned about the possibility than Rath felt just then. It provoked an unfamiliar sensation in his heart to hear someone speak as though his living or dying mattered to them.

He couldn't decide whether he liked it or not.

"Live?" a deep masculine voice replied. "I should say so. He appears to be a hardy fellow, this outlaw of yours. If his scars are anything to judge by, he's survived worse than a Hanish arrow in the arm."

Rath took an instant dislike to the speaker. He had reconciled himself to the notion of being dead and finally at peace. He did not welcome the news that he would live, or the reminder of his wound, which began to throb with pain the instant he turned his thoughts to it.

"I told you, Uncle, he is not *my* outlaw. He is not *my* anything. I regret that I ever let myself get mixed up with him. It is the last thing we need just now, with what we have to do."

And what might that be? Rath wondered. It was only the first of many questions to plague him. Where was he? And how had such a slender lass managed to shift him any distance from that brook? Just because she was comely and had helped him get out of a tight spot did not mean he dared trust her.

"Do not be too hasty, my dear," said the man she'd called "Uncle." "The Giver's will often manifests itself in ways we may not understand at first. I believe this rugged character may be of use to us."

There! He'd known it. They wanted something from him. While the thought made Rath rally his defenses, it also gave him a harsh sense of reassurance that the rules of life he'd always lived by were still in effect.

He considered opening his eyes and demanding answers to his questions. Instead he left them shut and concentrated on keeping his breath slow and deep. He might discover far more about this pair, and what they intended to do with him, by listening while they talked together.

"Of most valuable use," the man repeated in a reflective, secretive tone. Then he added, briskly, "Not with that arrow barb still in him, though."

Rath felt a touch on his arm and heard a murmur of words that had no meaning for him. Then a white-hot lance of pain shot through his flesh. He had only felt its like once before, and he had sworn never to suffer it again.

With a bellow of pain and rage, he wrenched his eyes open and thrust his right hand up to coil in a death grip around the throat of his tormentor.

The sorcerer gazed into Rath's eyes with a look far too calm and curious for a fellow having the life squeezed out of him.

Rath fought an urge to release the old man, for fear that merciful impulse might not be his own will, but the volition of some foul magic.

The woman screamed. "Let him go, you beast!"

She was a fine one to throw insults around.

"First tell me where I am and what you want with me!"

"You're in a better place than you deserve!" she cried. "And I want *nothing* to do with you!"

She swung the side of her hand down on his wounded arm like the chop of an ax. Rath doubted an ax blow could have hurt worse. Instinct made him release the sorcerer to shield himself from further attack.

The old man stumbled back, gasping for breath. Meanwhile the woman opened her other hand and blew a wisp of something toward Rath. When he tried to swat it away, it clung to the fine hairs on his arm. He tried to pluck it off with his other hand, but that arm seemed incapable of anything but pulsing with pain.

While he struggled to rid himself of whatever she'd beset him with, the witch uttered a singsong of strange words that wrapped around Rath, binding him to the bed.

"There! That should keep you from doing any more harm for a while." Her green eyes flashed pure malice.

Where had the "fresh innocence of springtime" gone? Likely he'd only imagined it.

She turned to the old sorcerer, whose face was beginning to pale from the livid shade it had been when Rath first released him. "Uncle, are you all right? I told you we should have bound the ruffian before he woke up."

The old sorcerer pushed away her worried attentions. "Don't fuss, Maura."

So that was the hillcat's name? Not that Rath cared, but it gave him something to call her if he had to.

He did not like the way Maura's uncle was staring at him. Not that the old man's gaze held any blatant hostility—quite the opposite. That was what bothered Rath. He expected hostility, and perhaps fear, from a man he had just throttled.

Nothing else made sense, and Rath liked events to make sense, no matter how harsh.

The sorcerer looked neither frightened nor angry. Rather his gaze held a faint sparkle of curiosity—even admiration.

He approached the bed without the least sign of concern for his safety. "I must entreat your pardon, young man. I had hoped being unconscious would buffer you against the discomfort of my ministrations."

"What did you do to me?" Rath looked from the old man to Maura and back again. "What do you want with me?"

"As to the first—" The old man stooped and retrieved a small object from the floor, which he held up between his thumb and forefinger. "I fear it was necessary to get that arrow barb out of your arm before it did any more damage."

Rath's jaw fell slack as he stared at the small shard of metal, still slick with his blood. He had never ceased to marvel how so tiny a thing could be so deadly.

"Impossible." He shook his head. "It hurt, true enough, but only for an instant. Never long enough for you to dig that thing out."

"Dig it out?" The old man winced. "I would never maim a man that way." He stared at the arrow barb in his hand. "The Han put those sharp fins on the back end, so they do even more damage if a body tries to pull one out."

"If you didn't dig it out, then how…?"

"I regret, it was necessary to push the thing through the rest of the way. It was so deeply imbedded, it did not have far to come."

"But…?" Pushed? How?

"Enough questions for the moment." The sorcerer handed the arrow barb to Maura. "Dispose of that for me, if you please, my dear. And when you come back, bring clean linens and hot water. And the herbs, of course. You know what to fetch as well as I."

He turned back to Rath. "We must bind your wound now that it has bled enough to rinse out the lifebane."

Rath craned his neck so he could see his arm. It had bled surprisingly little for what the old sorcerer claimed to have done. There was only a tiny puncture where the barb must have come out, almost as if the flesh had parted to let it pass, then sealed itself after. Now that the echoes of pain had ebbed from Maura's blow, his arm hurt far less than it should have.

Rath's gaze strayed back to the old man, who was tilting his neck from side to side while rubbing his jaw.

"I am sorry if I hurt you." His apology sounded gruff and grudging, but he could not help it.

He had very little practice of such niceties. Most men he'd ever harmed had done plenty to deserve it. It was partly his own fault, he acknowledged, that the pain from the old man's treatment had taken him unawares, since he had given no sign of being awake.

"No lasting harm done." The old fellow chuckled softly, as if at some private jest. "You are very strong. Quick, too."

"When you live as I do, you have to be."

"I suppose so."

Rath glanced around the room. It was small with a low, gently sloped ceiling. The window shutters had been thrown open and a mild night breeze drifted in, tempering the pungent aroma of herbs that pervaded the place. A little bit of a fire crackled in the stone hearth by the door. The room had no other furnishings but the bed Rath was lying on. For a moment, he stopped tensing against his invisible restraints and relished the unaccustomed comfort of a feather mattress.

A moment later, he heard a brisk step on the wooden floor outside the room and Maura entered. She held an earthen basin from which wisps of steam rose. Several strips of linen hung over her arm.

"Thank you, my dear." The old sorcerer pointed to the floor beside the bed. "Just set everything down there."

He glanced back at Rath. "My name is Langbard, by the way. Langbard of Westborne. I am a wizard…as you may have guessed by now. And the young woman who brought you here is my ward, Maura Woodbury."

Rath acknowledged their names and relationship with a curt nod. "And just how did you bring me here, Mistress Woodbury? Did you have a pack animal tethered nearby, or did you float me down that brook?"

She did not bother to look up from the floor where she was setting the hot water and cloths. "If you must know, I carried you on my back every step of the way. Not that I expect any thanks from the likes of—"

"Maura." The wizard interrupted her in a rising tone of warning, then his steady blue gaze fixed on Rath again. "Your name, young man?"

"Rath Talward. Some call me Rath the Wolf."

"Rath?" Maura muttered. "What kind of people give a child such a name?"

"It suits me well enough." With the fierceness of his voice he dared her to look at him. "And no one *gave* it to me. Like everything else I've ever wanted in life, I *took* it."

"As long as you are content with it," said Langbard in the calming tone of a peacemaker, "that is what matters, surely."

He knelt beside the bed, gently edging his ward aside. "Maura, I am surprised at you. I have never known you to be ungracious to a guest in our home."

Maura jumped to her feet. "No guest in our home ever tried to strangle you before today. Fine thanks for our aid, that!"

"I never asked for your aid," Rath growled.

Part of him protested that it could be dangerous to antagonize his captors. Another part felt so foolish and vulnerable being bound by a force with less substance than cobweb. It compelled him to lash out with the only weapons at his disposal—his words and his attitude.

"Perhaps you did not." Langbard began to wash Rath's wound with the warm water. "But I hope you will have the sense to accept it with good grace."

Rath could never remember being addressed in quite that tone of exasperation tempered with forbearance. It made his conscience tingle just as the herb-strewn water made his torn flesh tingle. He knew both must be cleansing and healing, but he could not bring himself to trust the strange sensations.

"Where I come from, no man does a good turn for another unless he wants something in return."

"I regret it is the same everywhere, Master Talward." Langbard smeared the wound with what looked like a paste of crushed fresh leaves. "The only difference is that the people you have known make no secret of the exchange. Will it ease your mind if I tell you plainly there *is* something I want from you?"

"Perhaps." Rath considered. "What is it?"

Langbard wrapped a wide strip of linen around Rath's upper arm. "If you give your word you will do no violence to Maura or me, I will have the binding spell that holds you removed."

"You would believe the word of someone like me?"

"Trust must begin somewhere, young man." The old wizard looked up suddenly, catching Rath in his discerning gaze. "Since I believe it comes more easily to me than to you, I am willing to make the first overture."

While her guardian tended Rath's wound, Maura had wandered over to the hearth and added another stick to the fire. Now she rose and stood watching the two men with ill-disguised wariness. She probably had some other innocent-looking leaf or feather or bit of ash in the pocket of her apron with which to subdue Rath again if he did not mind his manners.

"I will do neither of you any further harm." He flung the promise at her. "You have my word…which is worth far more than the lady may believe."

She narrowed her eyes as if to say he presumed a great deal to speculate about what she did or did not believe.

"Very well then." Langbard grappled onto the bedpost to hoist himself to his feet. "Maura, if you would be so good?"

"Are you certain about this, Uncle?"

"Quite certain. Go ahead."

With the air of someone compelled to act against her better judgment, Maura intoned yet another string of words Rath did not understand. When he tried to raise his sound arm, it jerked up, pushing against a restraint that was no longer there.

Removed by a girl's garbled singsong? The old wizard might be content to trust *him,* but Rath doubted he could return the compliment. His suspicion of magic ran too deep.

He slid up, so his shoulders rested on the pillow. It felt a little less vulnerable than being flat on his back. His wounded arm protested the movement, though not as painfully as he expected.

"You never answered my second question, old man. What is it you want with me?"

"All in good time," the wizard replied. "Once you've rested and had something to eat."

"Those can wait." Rath's stomach disagreed loudly. "I'd prefer to know what you would have me do before I accept any more help from you."

"Fair enough." Langbard settled himself on the edge of the bed. "It is fortunate, your appearance in our lives at just this time. Maura and I must set out on a journey soon. About the time you should have your strength back, I believe."

"Uncle!" Maura cried.

Clearly she had not known what her guardian meant to ask of him. Now that she understood, she did not approve of the idea. For some perverse reason, her resistance eased Rath's suspicions.

The wizard raised his hand to bid her be silent. "An old aunt of Maura's wishes to see her. She lives to the south, in a little town called Prum. You have probably never heard of it."

"Prum?" Rath heard himself say, in spite of his usual reluctance to reveal what he knew. "On the edge of the Southmark steppes? They have a fine cattle fair there in the fall."

"You do know it!" Langbard rewarded him with a broad smile.

"I have been there a time or two." He glanced at Maura, narrowing his eyes and flashing his wickedest grin. "Good pickings at cattle fairs."

She rewarded his baiting with an indignant huff that made her attractively shaped bosom rise and fall beneath her tunic. Rath could not recall the last time he'd had such amusing sport.

"Maura and I are not so well traveled," said Langbard. "The way is long, I understand, and the roads not as safe as they might be. We could use a guide and guard to escort us, if you would be willing to oblige us in exchange for healing and hiding you? It occurs to me you might like to make yourself scarce from this part of the kingdom for a while."

So he might. Much as he loathed the Han, Rath had a grudging respect for their thoroughness. They hated to leave a job unfinished, and he was the unfinished part of their duty to root out the fugitives making camp in Betchwood. He could do worse with his time than steal away to someplace safer in the innocent-looking company of an old man and a pretty girl.

He held out his right hand, palm up, in the customary sign of good faith. "I hear the Southmark steppes are pretty in the spring. I believe we have a bargain, old man."

Before the wizard could slide his hand over Rath's to seal their agreement, Maura cried, "Never!"

4

"Maura," Langbard rumbled in a more ominous tone than she could ever recall him using with her, "you and I can talk about this later. At the moment, I am discussing the matter with Master Talward."

The wizard's thick brows lowered over his piercing blue eyes as he fixed her with a look that would have made most folk cower.

What had come over him? He'd been mild as a sheep after Rath Talward had throttled him. Now he rebuked her for giving him a warning he would be a fool to ignore?

Maura had no intention of being silenced by his stern stare. Not with their safety at stake. "Have you gone daft, Uncle? Journey all the way to Prum in the company of this outlaw?"

She stabbed her forefinger in his direction. "It makes no

sense, if you fear for our safety, to tote a brimming basket load of trouble along with us."

Rath Talward *was* trouble. Maura had no doubt of that. The air of it hung about him like a potent, pungent musk.

Moreover, he relished having everyone know it, too. Eyeing her with such gleeful impudence and grinning when he spoke of good pickings at cattle fairs. Boasting of taking anything he wanted in life, including that ridiculous name. She had to admit, it did suit him.

As if to confirm her thoughts, Rath Talward gave a lazy stretch with his good arm, bringing it to rest behind his head. The bed linens slid down, by design, no doubt, to reveal more of his muscular bare chest, its rippling flesh seamed with more than one battle scar.

"If a party hires a bodyguard for his meekness and good manners, they are begging to have their throats slit in their sleep before they ever get where they are going." He spoke with impudent ease, and his voice seemed to linger lovingly on the violent words.

Maura wanted to hustle him off to the Windleford garrison, where he clearly belonged. What had she imagined she'd seen in him earlier, to stir a flicker of admiration and sympathy?

"We have ways of protecting ourselves, in case you have not noticed." She directed her next words to Langbard. "Those ways will be of little use guarding against one who travels with us. I tell you, we have more to fear from him than from any dangers we might encounter on the road to Prum."

The wizard shook his head. "We do not have an unlimited

supply of cuddybird feathers, my dear. You know how hard they are to come by."

She did, all too well. Ever since Langbard's sight had begun to fail, she'd had to gather the pesky things, which were only visible against a background of snow. Since cuddybirds wintered in the Southmark steppes, the only time one could hope to find any in Norest was after an early or late snowfall.

"Spells are all very well," Langbard continued. "But sometimes there is no substitute for a swift application of physical force."

"Well said, wizard!" Rath Talward extended his hand once again. "Have we a bargain, then?"

"We have." Langbard laid his hand on the outlaw's, palm to palm. Then they reversed, with his hand on the bottom.

"Men!" Maura glared at the pair of them.

Sorsha had often complained about this vexing tendency for male creatures to side with one another against a woman. Especially if they were in the wrong.

It did not surprise her that an outlaw would do such a thing. She had thought better of Langbard, though. "I am sure I will not get a wink of sleep the whole journey for fear of what he may be plotting."

"Tush, my dear." Langbard rose from his perch on the edge of the bed. "After all that has happened to him today, young Rath is likely as frightened of us as you are of him."

The outlaw gave a hiss of contemptuous laughter, yet a subtle tightening of his rugged features told Maura that Langbard's guess might not have strayed too wide of the mark.

"Now—" Langbard strode toward the door "—we must let our bodyguard rest and recover his strength while we make preparations for our journey. Come below and make the man some food, Maura, if you please."

Her nerves were badly frayed by all that had happened. When she'd woken that morning, it had been to the relative safety and peace of her familiar world. She would go to bed, exhausted but probably unable to sleep, facing a bewildering and perilous future. At the moment, Rath Talward embodied all her worst fears, sheltered under her own roof.

She shot Langbard a reproachful glance. "If you like him so well, *you* cook for him!"

With that she swept out of the room.

A moment later she heard Langbard's footsteps on the stairs behind her. "Your pardon, my dear! After the day you've had, I should have bid you rest rather than put you to work. Get yourself to bed while I make food for both you and Talward."

At the foot of the stairs, Maura stopped and turned into the comforting embrace she knew would be waiting for her.

"I do love you, Uncle." She gave a sniffle, followed by a weary chuckle. "But you are a terrible cook. If you fix a meal for this Talward fellow, he may think you are trying to poison him and cancel your bargain."

Still holding her close, Langbard threw back his head and laughed. "So that explains why you took over the kitchen when you were barely high enough to reach the kettle!"

Maura glanced up to see a mist of unshed tears in his eyes.

His voice fell to a broken whisper. "I always tried to do my best for you."

Her vexation with him melted into a warm puddle. "Of course you did. No one could have done better. I have had such a happy life here, can you blame me if I am loathe to leave it?"

Langbard raised his hand and passed it over her hair. "I know there will be dark and dangerous days ahead for you, my dear. But I hope fond memories of our time here will sustain you until you win your way to an even happier future."

He pressed a soft kiss to her forehead. "I know you think I am being a willful old fool to insist on taking young Rath with us. Truth to tell, he is exactly the sort of escort I had hoped the Giver might send."

"You believe *that* is my birthday present from the Giver?" Maura rolled an aggravated gaze in the direction of the gable room upstairs...or perhaps toward heaven.

"Now, now." Langbard shook his head. "He is just the kind of companion we need. The man knows his way around the kingdom. He is strong, swift and resourceful. He must be, to have lived the kind of life he has and evaded the Han for so many years."

"But, Uncle..." It was probably pointless to protest, but Maura could not give in without trying.

As she'd expected, Langbard refused to heed her. "I believe there is more good in him than you...or he may suspect. The years since the Han invaded have not been kind to your generation, Maura. Give him a chance, won't you, for my sake? He is not nearly as fierce as he likes to pretend."

"Oh, very well." Maura grumbled as she stepped out of his embrace and headed for the kitchen. "Against my better judgment, I assure you. And on condition that you will teach me that trick with your voice."

"Trick?"

She turned to look back at him. "Do not play innocent with me. You know what I mean. The tone that makes people do whatever you ask them, no matter how much they might protest."

"I hate to disappoint you, my dear, but there is no magic in that." Langbard thought for a moment. "Apart from love, I suppose, which is the most potent kind of magic."

Would she find love with the Waiting King? Maura wondered as she puttered in the pantry. If they were destined to wed and reign, neither of them would have much choice in the matter. No more choice than she had about starting off her quest in the company of the last Umbrian she would have chosen as an escort.

Had he lost all sense, accepting the old wizard's offer? Though Rath Talward had never lain in so comfortable a bed, in so snug a room, he could not sleep.

Perhaps because it *was* so warm and cozy. He was not accustomed to comfort. He mistrusted it. More often than not, anything that looked, sounded, felt, smelled or tasted too good was apt to be bait for a trap.

A number of those suspicious attributes applied to Maura Woodbury. Rath hadn't tasted her, yet, but he did not doubt he'd be able to add that to the list. The only thing that eased his wariness somewhat, was her opposition to her guardian's plan. If she grew friendly, *then* he would worry.

He heard the muted patter of footsteps on the stairs just as a savory aroma wafted into the room. His mouth watered so hard and so fast, he was obliged to swipe the back of his hand over his lips to keep the moisture from dribbling down his chin.

A soft tap sounded on the door. Rath was not sure how to respond. It had been a long while since he'd lived under a proper roof. Even then, folk had come and gone as they pleased.

"Are you awake?" Maura called softly. "May I come in?"

"Aye, come. It is your house."

She eased the door open, then entered, bearing a wooden tray. The appetizing scent grew stronger.

Rath's belly let out a shrill squeal. When had he eaten last? After all that had happened today, his last meal felt like a distant memory.

"Well," said Maura in a tone of dry amusement, "that answers my next question."

Rath cocked his brow.

"I was going to ask if you were hungry."

He gave a harsh chuckle. "Been hungry most of my life."

The moment the words were out of his mouth, he wished he'd swallowed them, instead.

Maura's face blanched. Something unfamiliar flickered in her eyes. Could it be pity? If so, he wanted none of it.

"Where is Langbard?" he asked in an impudent tone that he hoped might get a rise out of her. "When you left a while ago, you didn't sound very anxious to cook for me."

"Do not provoke me," she snapped, "or you *will* find yourself eating Langbard's cooking! Then you'll be sorry."

He doubted it, after some of the things he'd eaten over the years. For a moment, he considered telling Maura a few of them, just to relish her disgust. Then he decided against it. He did not want her treating him to another look like the last one.

She started to set the tray of food on his lap.

Rath tried to sit fully upright, but his head spun and his arm gave a queer tingle that alarmed him more than the ordinary kind of pain he was used to. He sank back down.

"Lie still then." Maura lowered the tray to the floor. "I will feed you."

By the sound of it, she suspected his dizziness might be a ploy to rile her. Rath decided he would rather have her think that than guess the truth.

"Never been waited on before." At the risk of getting whatever was in that bowl upended on top of his head, he settled back with a brazen grin. "And by such a beauty, too. I could get to like this."

"You will not get the chance, outlaw." She thrust the spoon toward him with a movement so swift and forceful it might have broken a tooth if he had not jerked his mouth open in time. "I promised Langbard I would see you fed, tonight. Tomorrow, you can feed yourself…or starve. I do not care which."

She settled herself on the edge of the bed, with a bowl of generous proportions in one hand. With the other, she pulled the wooden spoon out of Rath's mouth, leaving behind some hot, soft-textured food of hearty flavor. It was all he could do to keep from groaning his enjoyment.

It tasted so good…too good.

He tried to spit it out, but his mouth mutinied. The food slid down into his stomach with a soothing sensation that promised to tame his gnawing hunger.

"What is this?" He averted his head as Maura brought another spoonful toward him. "Not loaded with sorcery is it?"

"As a matter of fact—" Maura made no effort to cram the spoon into his mouth, but waved it beneath his nose, tantalizing him "—this barleymush does contain some herbs that will speed the healing of your wound. If such *sorcery* is too vile for you to take into your fine body, I can always fetch it away and tell that wicked old wizard you do not wish to eat."

A very few times that he could recall, Rath had tasted honey. Maura's tone reminded him of it—sweet, yet cloying. The little vixen was amusing herself at his expense.

"You are sure that is all?" he growled, then snatched another bite before she could withdraw the spoon. "Herbs to make me heal faster?"

She heaped the spoon again. "If I was the kind of person who would poison you, do you suppose I would be truthful enough to admit it?"

Rath chewed on her words as he chewed on the barley-mush, though the latter hardly needed it. When and how had she turned everything around, baiting him when he had started out trying to fluster her?

"True enough." This time, he did not even pretend any reluctance to eat what she offered him. "It would be too late now, anyway. Might as well die with a full belly."

She bent over to set the bowl and spoon back on the tray.

Rath tried to ignore the gentle swoop of her bosom when she leaned forward. He would only need to nudge his hand a few inches and he could touch her there. His palm and fingertips felt as though a colony of wood ants were swarming over them.

Before he succumbed to temptation, Maura sat up again, lifting a mug from which tendrils of steam rose. "Thirsty?"

For more than he'd find in that cup, though Rath did not dare say so in case she splashed it in his face or flounced off without giving him a drink.

"What is it?" he asked instead.

"Just dreamweed tea. It has a mild taste, I promise. It will help you sleep." Her voice betrayed her weariness. With her free hand, Maura reached over to knead her shoulder.

Her pretty features tightened in a grimace of pain. "Will I have to answer these questions for everything I feed you?"

A strange, sour ache nagged deep in Rath's belly. If it had not been for her, Hanish hounds would be gnawing on his dead flesh by now. She had far better cause to be wary of him than he of her.

He shook his head, as he raised it to take a deep sip of the tea. When he lapsed back onto the pillows again, he tried to infuse his tone with an apology he found it hard to put into words. "Feed me what you will, and I'll be grateful for it."

Another thought occurred to him—something she had said earlier. In the confusion of the moment, he had not heeded it properly. "Did you…carry me here, truly?"

Maura gave a slow nod, as if the movement hurt her neck. "Dragged you the last bit, when the spell started to wear off."

"How far?"

"It seemed like a hundred miles at the time." She held out the mug again and Rath drank. "In truth, probably not more than five."

"Five miles?" Rath almost choked on his mouthful of tea. "You could not have!"

The withering look she shot him said she wished she hadn't. "If you could exchange backs with me, you'd believe it soon enough, I promise you."

Something in her tone assured Rath she was telling the

truth. Yet when he tried to picture it… "What did you mean about the spell wearing off?"

She told him about the spell of strength. Even after some of the things he'd eaten, the thought of bear fur and grease made his gorge rise. He wasn't certain he'd have been able to swallow such stuff to save his own life, let alone someone else's.

"The trouble is, you pay for it afterward." Maura twisted one arm behind her to rub her back. "Langbard is brewing me up a liniment to ease the worst of it."

That did it. Rath felt lower than a marsh mole's burrow!

He tried to make a wry jest of it. "That will teach you to go wandering around Betchwood saving outlaws."

A bewildering sense of ease began to steal over him. It lulled the heightened caution and defense he'd spent a lifetime building and arming. Maura's dreamweed tea must be working.

"Go rub yourself with some of that liniment." He nodded toward the door. "Leave the food and tea where they are. I can reach down to feed myself the rest."

Something made him add, "You have done me more than enough good turns for one day."

For a moment, Maura looked as though she might insist on staying. Rath could not risk that with his guard crumbling so rapidly.

Then a wide yawn overtook her and she flexed her back. "Now that you mention it, I have, haven't I?"

With stiff movements, she rose from her perch on the side of the bed, then shuffled toward the door. She did not move fast enough to outstrip Rath's faltering vigilance.

"Why did you bother with me?" He'd assumed she must want something from him, yet she seemed fiercely resistant to Langbard's plan of employing him as a bodyguard.

The question made her hesitate. But she did not turn to look at him. Instead she stood poised for a moment, her hand on the door latch.

Then she left Rath with an answer to ponder until the dreamweed tea finally overpowered him. "I cannot tell you. For I do not know, myself."

Rath cursed himself for a vulnerable fool when the pounding on Langbard's cottage door shook him out of a heavy sleep.

A man like him could not afford to sleep soundly. An outlaw must be ready and able to spring into a fighting stance at the faintest sound of trouble. Anything less put him at grave risk.

Over the years, he had perfected the skill of keeping some of his senses alert even while he slumbered. Last night, when he'd had every reason to be extra vigilant, he had succumbed to the perilous luxury of a deep, defenseless sleep.

One that might have cost him his life, or his freedom.

When the racket from the door roused him, Rath feared he might have to pay that high a price for his reckless negligence. He scrambled from the bed to find himself without a scrap of clothes apart from his loin linen. Neither did he have a single weapon apart from his hands, feet and teeth. The room provided no place to hide and a poor avenue for escape, since the only window overlooked the cottage door. If Hanish soldiers had come in search of him, he would be at their mercy.

At least he could stand up without a great wave of dizziness knocking him back down again. His legs still felt a little weak and his wounded arm still hurt, but he had endured worse.

Not wanting to betray his presence to those below, he took care to keep his steps light and stealthy as he moved toward the one spot in the room that afforded him a slight advantage—behind the door.

Once in place, he stood poised and waiting. The minutes crawled by, stretching longer and longer. Rath's patience and uncertainty stretched with them to a tense, quivering pitch. After the first burst of noise, it had grown quiet downstairs. Too quiet. Rath was certain it boded no good.

He could hear the murmur of voices but no words. What was happening down there? Were Maura and Langbard being questioned? They had done a great deal for him at risk to themselves, but he had no illusions. If the cottage was surrounded and a quick search certain to expose him, they would have to betray him in hope of being spared themselves. They did not need his services as a guide and bodyguard *that* urgently.

At last the voices died away. Rath thought he heard the cottage door open and shut, but that might only be a ruse to lure him down. If so, he was not about to take the bait. Let them walk into his ambush, instead, pitiful as it was.

So he skulked behind the door with his skin prickling in gooseflesh and his belly growling to be fed, his ears alert for the most furtive sound of movement that might signal they were coming for him.

At last he heard it—the tread deliberately muted in a bid to take him unawares. Slowly and softly, the door swung open.

Rath tensed to spring.

* * *

The loud knocking on the cottage door set Maura's heart knocking hard against her ribs.

Pulling a shawl around her, she flew to answer the insistent summons. She hoped Rath Talward would be stirred from his sleep by the noise, and that he would have the wit to hide while she stalled a search.

As she unbolted the door and pulled it open a crack, she called, "Is so much racket necessary at this hour of the—"

Before she could finish, whoever was on the other side of the door pushed it fully open and swooped down on her. The instant before she recognized her friend Sorsha, Maura instinctively raised her arms to fend off an attack.

"Thank the Giver you are all right!" Sorsha wrapped her in a forceful embrace. "I was so worried last night, after hearing what went on in Betchwood yesterday."

Her poor friend looked so distraught, Maura felt compelled to reassure her...even if it meant palming off a half truth. "Langbard and I are both fine, I promise you."

Now that the shock of Sorsha's arrival was beginning to wear off, Maura's back reminded her of how she had abused it yesterday. She hoped her friend would not notice the reek of liniment or try to guess why she might need it.

She summoned a smile that she hoped was bright enough to ease Sorsha's concern, but not so bright as to arouse fresh suspicions. "We did not stay long. Did something happen in Betchwood after we left?"

She beckoned her friend inside and shut the door behind her. Sorsha would know something was amiss if she came over to Langbard's cottage at this hour and Maura did not invite her in for a cup of icemint tea.

"Did you not hear the commotion and those filthy hounds baying for blood last eve?" Sorsha shuddered as she took her usual seat at the small kitchen table.

Maura shrugged. "You know how Langbard is. We try not to pay trouble any heed and hope it will return the favor."

Checking that there was still water in the kettle, she lit the fire under it.

"That sounds all very well," said Sorsha, "but often enough trouble comes hunting for you. Those cursed hounds took three of our lambs before Newlyn fought them off."

Guilt stabbed Maura deep in the belly. She fumbled the tea crock and almost dropped it. "Is Newlyn all right?"

She'd been so relieved yesterday when the hounds had passed her and Rath by to follow her old scent. She'd forgotten it would lead them toward Hoghill Farm.

"Only a wee burn or two on his hands." Sorsha sounded vastly relieved. "That was getting off light, I told him."

"Burns?"

Sorsha gave a grim chuckle. "Newlyn fought them off with lit brands. Gave them a little taste of pitch and fire. Enough to send them yelping away, the demons!"

Maura's admiration for Newlyn Swinley rose to new heights. If anything worse had happened to him or to his family, she would never have forgiven herself.

"Before you go I will give you some merthorn salve to ease his burns." She spooned a measure of tea into the pot, then settled down at the table with Sorsha to wait for the water to boil. "And the queensbalm for Prin Howen's boy."

While her friend recounted more details of the attack and heaped curses on the heads of the Hanish garrison, Maura kept one ear alert for sounds of movement from the room overhead. She recanted her earlier hope that the knocking had roused Rath Talward. Now she wished with all her heart he would sleep soundly until after Sorsha left.

"Newlyn said it did him good to give those vicious beasts a taste of their own poison, at last." Sorsha's mild eyes flashed with righteous wrath. "After some of the dreadful goings-on he witnessed in the mines, poor fellow."

A high-pitched whistle from the boiling kettle made Maura start. For five years Sorsha's husband had made a quiet but vital place for himself around Hoghill. It was easy to forget that he'd come here a desperate, broken fugitive from the mines.

Fragrant steam rose from the teapot as Maura poured boiling water over the dried icemint leaves. She inhaled a deep draft of the calming aroma, trying in vain to regain her shattered illusion of security. "I hope none of the soldiers will come around asking questions."

"So do I." Sorsha gnawed at her lower lip. "They might wonder about that black vest and breeches hanging on your clothesline. Not the sort of thing I've ever seen Langbard wear."

At Sorsha's probing remark, the teapot bucked in Maura's hand. A steaming wave sloshed over the brim of Sorsha's cup.

"Your pardon!" Maura gasped. "I am all sausage fingers this morning."

She set the teapot on the table then grabbed a cloth to wipe up the spill. All the while, her thoughts churned and spun.

"*Those* clothes!" She forced a chuckle. "They belong to…Langbard's nephew. He is visiting from…Tarsh. That is why we did not stay long in Betchwood yesterday. We met him on his way here."

"A lucky meeting." Sorsha's eyes narrowed as she lifted her cup and took a cautious sip. "Not often travelers from Tarsh come overland."

"H-he gets seasick." Maura forced her hand to stay steady as she poured her own tea. This lying business was tricky. She would have to practice the unsavory skill, though. She might need it in the days ahead.

"I never heard of Langbard having any family but you. Besides, is he not from Westborne?"

"What? Oh…yes, of course." To buy herself time to think, Maura took a long drink of tea and nearly scalded her mouth. "But his sister…his half sister…much younger half sister… lives in Tarsh with her family. Her son decided to study the Elderways…so he came looking for Langbard."

"Well, I'm sure Langbard will be happy." Sorsha nodded over the information as if she believed every word without question. "The Han have made the Elderways so unpopular, I hear there's hardly a body over the mountains can speak *twara* or minds about the Giver. I shall look forward to meeting… What is his name?"

"Ra-Ralf." Maura congratulated herself on coming up with a name that sounded quite commonplace, yet close enough to the truth. "Langbard *is* very pleased to have him here."

"But you are not?" Sorsha aimed a shrewd look at her friend. "The bother of another man to look after, I suppose. Do not let the two of them put upon you, whatever you do. What is he like, this Ralf fellow? A strapping lad, if the size of his clothes are anything to judge by."

"He is big." Her poor back had reason to know it!

"And?" Sorsha prompted her. "Dark? Fair? Good-looking? Ill-favored? Obliging?"

Maura was not certain she liked the peculiar interest in her friend's face and voice. This sounded like more than mild, neighborly curiosity about a visiting relative. "Not dark. And not ill-favored if he made an effort to tidy himself up. His manners are…a little rustic."

"From Tarsh?" Sorsha laughed. "I should think so! Rustic or not, I expect Newlyn would like to meet him. Come over for supper on market day. Tell Langbard I will make his favorite pork and dumplings."

Would they still be here come next market day? The dismaying question caught Maura by the throat.

"I will ask Langbard and let you know what he says." She was not certain which would be harder to bear—a farewell meal with her friends, or slipping away without any special leave-taking.

Sorsha drained the last of her tea. "Now that I know you are safe, I must get home before Newlyn starts to fret that something has happened to me."

Maura fetched a little crock of salve for Newlyn's burns and another of queensbalm ointment for Noll Howen. Before she went back into the house after waving Sorsha goodbye, she lifted Rath's clothes from the line. They were not altogether dry, but she decided to take them in just the same.

Hanish soldiers had never yet visited Langbard's cottage, but the previous day's experience had taught Maura she could not count on life to continue its safe, familiar pattern.

Musing about the drastic changes she would soon face,

Maura wandered back into the cottage and up the stairs. She decided to hang Rath's clothes from the mantel in the spare room. That way, they would be dry and waiting for him when he felt like getting up.

Hoping he would still be heavily asleep, she decided not to knock. With luck, she might be able to slip in and out without disturbing him. Or perhaps she was more worried about letting *him* disturb *her*. He had proven himself far too skilful at it.

Her arms full of clothing, she nudged the door open with her shoulder, then tiptoed in. A passing glance at the bed made her freeze in place.

Rath Talward was gone.

As she opened her mouth to call for Langbard, a powerful arm snaked around her, pinning her own arms to her sides and pulling her back against Rath Talward's broad chest. His left hand clamped over her mouth as he demanded in a soft growl, "What have you done with my weapons, witch?"

By the time Rath recognized Maura Woodbury, it was too late to stop.

Besides, the Han might be using her as a decoy. If nothing else, it was she who had rendered him so vulnerable by giving him that sleeping potion and taking away his gear.

In a swift, fluid motion, he wrapped his right arm around her, just below her bosom, pinning her arms to her sides and pulling her back against him. To his injured arm, he left the simple task of clapping a hand over her mouth.

The lass fell into his ambush as easily as ripe fruit from a tree. Before Rath could congratulate himself, his body succumbed to an ambush of desire mounted by the slender, womanly curves wriggling against him.

Men who plied his trade did not get enough chances for feminine company unless they took it at the point of a blade.

Rath had always been reluctant to pursue that course. Foolishly reluctant, he'd sometimes chided himself. Until now, he'd never let his unappeased lust put him at a disadvantage. Cursing under his breath, he tried desperately to think something loathsome or tedious that might break the grip of his unwelcome arousal.

The moment he seized her, Maura dropped his clothes on the floor. She made some muffled noises, her mouth moving against the palm of his hand as she continued to writhe in his grasp, pummeling his shins with her feet. Suddenly her resistance slackened. Against every rule of combat he'd ever learned, Rath let his hold slacken, too.

Swift as the strike of a coiled rock snake, her left arm flexed at the elbow, sending her fist pounding against his wound. The burst of pain made him lose his grip on her mouth. She parted her lips wide enough to bite down hard on the base of his middle finger.

Rath jerked his palm away from those sharp little teeth before they could inflict any more damage.

Expecting her to yell for the Han or perhaps scream for Langbard's help, he was surprised to hear her hiss, "Why ask me a question then stifle me so I cannot answer? Now, let me go or I shall make you very sorry!"

She had turned him invisible, carried him five miles on her back and bound him so he could scarcely move a muscle. Rath had enough disadvantages at the moment—he did not need to add a bothersome hex to the rest.

He thrust Maura away from him with such force she staggered and almost tripped over his clothes.

"Who is downstairs?" he demanded. "I heard the pounding on the door. I thought you might be a Hanish soldier."

As he spoke, he swiped his clothes from the floor and held them in front of him so Maura would not see what manner of sorcery she worked on his body without even trying.

She rounded on him in a half-crouched stance as if preparing to fend off an attack. Rath was torn between alarm and admiration at how she had exploited his weaknesses to break free.

"There is no one down there now, unless Langbard has woken." She glared at Rath. "The pounding was our neighbor. She came to make sure we were all right."

Maura's gaze fell to the leather breeches and vest in his arms. "She saw your clothes hanging on the line. I told her you are Langbard's nephew, Ralf, visiting from Tarsh."

"Well, well." Langbard bustled in. "I always fancied having a nephew. Though there is not much of a family resemblance between us, I will admit."

He directed a warm smile at Maura. "That was quick thinking, my dear. I hope Sorsha will not make too free with the information around the market."

Then he looked Rath up and down. "You seem a good deal better than you did when Maura fetched you from Betchwood yesterday. Still, you had better rest while you can. It is quite a journey to Prum. I want you fit to protect us if the need arises."

"I cannot just lie about, unclothed and unarmed," Rath protested. "What if that had been soldiers at the door, rather than a neighbor woman. I'd have been done for."

"Go ahead and dress, then!" cried Maura before her guardian could answer. "But your weapons stay outside. I will not bide under the same roof as those tools of pain and death."

Rath could not let such a slur pass. "My blades deal a far faster, more merciful death than most sorcery! I'll wager this cottage is crammed to the eaves with tools of that kind."

"How dare you?" Maura headed for the door, keeping Langbard between her and Rath. "Uncle, I do not know how you can think of traveling with such a witless lout, danger or no danger!"

When she had descended the stairs with a far heavier tread than she'd used to climb them, Langbard broke into the kind of smile Rath had only ever seen on young children or simpleminded folk. "Mark me, lad, she will come to like you, yet!"

Rath scowled. "Let the wench like me or loathe me as she will. I do not care."

He spoke the words with such force, he almost made himself believe them.

Langbard kept Maura so busy for the next several days she scarcely had a thought to spare for Rath Talward except when he was in her direct line of sight. Fortunately for her, and perhaps for him, the outlaw did not stray her way very often.

She suspected Langbard might be responsible for that, as well—an effort to forestall domestic mutiny.

Much to Maura's surprise, it worked. Almost against her will, and certainly against her better judgment, she found herself growing accustomed to Rath Talward's lurking presence around the cottage.

After that first morning, when he had scared her half to death, he'd done nothing further to frighten her. Still, she kept remembering the harsh power of his grip and the heat of his bare skin when he'd held her against him. If she pondered on it very long, her own flesh grew too warm for comfort.

Now, for instance.

Hearing the two men entering the cottage, Maura quickly bent near the hearth to give the stew a stir. That would explain away her flushed cheeks.

Behind her, Rath sniffed the air. "Smells good! I cannot recall the last time I ate so well for so many days at a time."

Maura did not want that careless scrap of praise to please her as much as it did. She tried to dismiss it with a tart answer. "You have been working hard. They say a sharp appetite makes anything taste good."

The outlaw gave a dry grunt of laughter. "Whoever says so has never had to eat some of the things I have."

His tone rasped against Maura's composure, which, of late, had rubbed too thin for her liking. She turned to confront him, her gaze drifting over his shaggy, rangy form. Why could Langbard not see the danger this man posed?

To her peace of mind as much as anything else.

"Perhaps if you had settled down to a bit of honest work before this, you would not have had to eat such things."

His lip curled. "Be careful who you condemn, my lady, and for what. The day may yet come when you will be that hungry and have to choose between unlawful survival or honest starvation."

Langbard had been watching them with a look of fond amusement that vexed Maura almost as much as the outlaw's mocking insolence. Now he interrupted before she could work up a suitably scathing retort. "Come, you two! Have pity on my tired old ears and speak a little more gently if you please."

He dropped onto his accustomed chair. "Besides, we have

more important matters to talk over. I have decided we must set out for Prum no later than the day after tomorrow."

"So soon, Uncle?" Maura's stomach felt as if it were falling out of her body into a deep pit.

Often during the past few days she had lapsed into familiar routines, savoring a fleeting pretense that nothing had changed—that nothing *would* change. It suddenly occurred to her that the root of her annoyance with Rath Talward might be the bothersome reminder he represented that her whole world was about to turn upside down.

With stubborn resolve, she clung to her last tattered remnants of habit, serving supper at her familiar table with her familiar crockery. Langbard murmured the ritual blessing of the food while Rath sat with a self-conscious scowl on his face.

"We cannot tarry, my dear," said Langbard after he had finished the blessing. He patted the back of Maura's hand in what felt like a gesture of apology. "Your aunt will be waiting for us. I would have gone before now, but I wanted young Rath to regain his strength for the journey."

So the outlaw had done her a favor. Maura took a bite of her stew and found she had little appetite for it.

"I can be ready to go whenever you give the word." Rath stopped eating long enough to tap his fist against the arm that had been wounded. "You'd never know I had a fly bite there, much less a Hanish arrow clean through."

"I am gratified it has healed so well. Though you may thank Maura for that since she compounded the poultices."

From the opposite side of the table, Rath made a deep nod of acknowledgment. "Once again, I am in your debt, my lady."

"Do not call me that!" Maura did not mean to snap at the

man, but his words reminded her too forcefully of what she would soon face. "And take care you don't get hair in your stew, bending over it like that."

The possibility of getting stew on his hair concerned her less. It would take a great deal more than that to make him look any more unkempt.

Perhaps fearing further hostilities might break out over the supper table, Langbard quickly changed the subject. "I want the two of you to go in to Windleford tomorrow and buy supplies for our journey."

Maura fumbled her spoon. "Prance into Windleford in the company of a wanted outlaw? What if the soldiers spot him?"

Rath nodded, for once in agreement with her.

Langbard waved away Maura's objections. "I have a wee spell to take care of that."

"You said we oughtn't squander our cuddybird feathers."

"It is something else entirely," said Langbard. "It makes a body blend in with the herd…crowd. Especially to the eyes of predators. Umbrians will be able to see and hear you as plain as can be. But the Han will not notice you at all as long as you do nothing to draw attention to yourselves."

"Hundredflower." Maura rolled the name around on her tongue. "I should have known."

From the time she'd been a child, Langbard had always sprinkled a little of it over her before she left home. He had claimed it would protect her from catching any sicknesses going around the village. It gave her a strange, breathless feeling to look back over her life and recognize all the subtle preparations Langbard had been making for the time that had finally arrived.

"I do not see why we both have to go." Maura pushed a large chunk of carrot around her bowl with her spoon. "I have done our marketing for years on my own without any complaint from you."

This would be her last visit to Windleford. She did not want Rath Talward dogging her footsteps, needing to be introduced and explained with a tangled litany of falsehoods.

"Of course I had no complaint," said Langbard. "Nor do I now. But a long journey south requires provisions you might not consider. Rath will know what we need and may be able to direct you in your purchases."

"Very well. He may come with me. But on one condition."

Two sets of thick brows, one gray, the other tawny, rose in a wordless query.

Maura looked from her guardian to the outlaw, forcing herself to meet his piercing, truculent gaze with a bold challenge of her own. "Wash…your…hair. I refuse to be seen in the company of such an unkempt ruffian. Even if the Han take no notice of us, the village folk may remark about you in some soldier's hearing."

When Rath made a face, she asked, "Why do you balk at a little soap and water when you would not quail before a blade?"

"Would you have me primped like some Hanish court-boy?" The look of horror on his face made Maura fear he might spit on the table for emphasis.

Though she had no idea what "a Hanish court-boy" might be, she had noticed that even the soldiers of the provincial garrison seemed vain about their flowing flaxen manes.

"No, but—"

"Fancy grooming is no boon to an outlaw." Rath gave his

shaggy head a defiant shake. "His friends tend not to respect him nor do his enemies fear him as they ought."

"Fine, then." Maura pushed her chair away from the table. "Stay at home and rub a little more dirt into your hair while I am gone. If I see a nice patch of burrs by the side of the road, I will fetch some back for you."

Barely resisting the urge to upend the rest of her stew over Rath Talward's untidy head, she strode off to the preparing room. At least this meant she would not have to suffer his company in the market tomorrow.

Maura wished the prospect brought her a greater sense of satisfaction.

"I would have preferred the burrs," Rath grumbled the next day as he and Maura led Langbard's pack pony along the road to Windleford.

He plowed his fingers through his newly washed and shorn hair. "What did you put in that rinse water?" He wrinkled his nose. "I smell like a Venardi bed-girl!"

Rath could not decide which vexed him worse—that the old wizard had bewitched him into getting his hair properly washed for the first time in years, or that he had not been able to muster enough strength of will to resist.

What vexed him more than either was the pert little smile of triumph Maura Woodbury made only a token effort to hide. "I do not know what you are complaining about. It was only a little fleawort to kill vermin."

When Rath began to sputter, she darted close enough to ruffle his hair. "And honeygrass to make it shine. You look like a different man, altogether—almost handsome."

Before she could dance out of reach, he grabbed her by one ridiculously delicate wrist and pulled her toward him. Part of him wanted to rage at her teasing, while another part secretly enjoyed it far more than he dared let himself.

"You grow too bold, wench." He chased away her provocative little smile with a wolfish grin. "Is there nothing about me you fear?"

Maura's great green eyes widened until they looked as vast and turbulent as the Sea of Dawn during a storm. Their beauty made him almost reckless enough to cast himself adrift in their bewitching currents, knowing full well he might wreck and drown.

"Aye!" she cried. "Your breath. It reeks. You should chew on a leaf of icemint."

He leaned closer. "If I sweeten my breath, will you give me a kiss?"

The most inviting pair of lips he had ever seen parted…but not to honor his request. "I'd sooner kiss a musk-pig! Take your hands off me, Rath Talward, before I turn you into a…"

"Save your threats!" Rath laughed as he swooped in and pressed a kiss on Maura's neck, just below her ear. "Langbard told me the difference between your harmless vitcraft and the mortcraft of the Echtroi. You can do no worse than put me to sleep or befuddle me like you did the soldiers in Betchwood."

"Rogue!" She squirmed out of his arms.

"At your service, my lady." Rath bowed. "And let me give you a priceless piece of advice, at no cost."

Maura's eyes narrowed and her hands hovered over the many-pocketed sash Langbard had made her wear. "What advice?"

Rath ruffled the pony's dark mane in a mocking imitation of what Maura had done to him. "Do not flirt with a man unless you wish him to collect on your offer."

"I? Flirt with you? You must be daft!"

Rath shot her a dubious look. "I grant you may have been raised too sheltered to know about flirting. That *is* what you were doing, all the same. It could land you in a great deal of trouble if you try it with a man who respects women less than I."

"If this is your notion of respect, the Giver save me from a brazen fellow!" All the while she glared at him, Maura did not seem aware that she was rubbing her fingers over and over the spot on her neck where he'd left his kiss.

Rath was not certain what that meant…if anything.

"Someone had better save you if you have not learned a bit more caution by the time we reach Prum." He dropped the taunting note from his voice. He did not want Maura to dismiss his warning as a jest. "A good many cattle drivers pass in and out of that little town. Compared to some of them, I am a perfect flower of honor."

He expected her to huff, or protest more, perhaps even slap his face. But she did none of those.

For an instant Maura's gaze faltered before his, then she lifted her chin and looked him square in the eye. "Consider your warning heeded. Now, let us buy our supplies and get home as soon as we can. I still have a great deal to do around the cottage if we are to leave tomorrow."

"Fair enough." Rath tugged on the pony's rope halter.

They walked the rest of the way to the village in awkward silence.

As they came within sight of the garrison, Rath muttered, "I hope that flower spell of Langbard's works."

"It does." Maura sounded as though she took offense at his doubt, yet Rath noticed she moved to put the pony between her and the garrison. "I have been coming and going in Windleford for years and never had a single Hanish soldier glance at me."

Her claim reassured Rath. The Han were still men, after all. If they had been aware of a comely lass like Maura moving about the village without an escort, no doubt one of them would have approached her.

"Besides," she added, "in that old robe of Langbard's and with your hair tidied up, you look almost respectable."

"But you know better?" Hard as he tried, Rath could not keep a teasing note out of his voice.

He had no more business flirting with Maura than she had with him. He did not want to encourage her in dangerous habits.

"I know better." Maura slid him a sidelong glance. "But your secret is safe with me. Just remember what Langbard said. Keep your eyes downcast. Do nothing to draw their notice."

"Easily said."

Rath glanced ahead at a young soldier marching down the narrow road toward them. By his side, a black hound strained on its short chain, dense muscle rippling beneath its dark pelt.

With all his will, Rath battled his urge to draw the sword concealed beneath Langbard's robe. Pulling the pony closer to the gutter, he did his best to give the soldier and the dog a wide berth. He made an effort to look servile, but it was not easy. Living outside society in the company of desperate men, he'd had to adopt a bold, swaggering manner. Any sign of meekness might have invited a dangerous challenge.

The dog gave a menacing growl as it passed them, but the soldier only snarled a Hanish curse and gave the beast a hard cuff on the ear to silence it. He did not even glance in Rath and Maura's direction.

"Well, well," Rath muttered once they were out of earshot.

This vitcraft of old Langbard's might lack the fearsome power of Hanish mortcraft, but it had its uses, just the same. Especially for a man in his trade. Perhaps, if he kept his eyes and ears open on the road to Prum, he'd be able to pick up a few more handy little spells like this one.

He and Maura continued on their way to the village square, where they set about purchasing supplies for their journey.

The first merchant they approached looked Rath up and down. "We heard ye and Langbard had a visitor, Mistress Woodbury."

The simple statement implied a question and demanded an introduction.

A faint sigh escaped Maura's lips ahead of her answer. "You heard right, Master Starbow. This is Langbard's nephew, Ralf, from Tarsh."

"Tarsh, is it? My grandsire on my mother's side was born in Bagno. What part do ye hale from, Master Ralf?"

By the look on Maura's face, Rath could tell she was worried that he might say or do something to make the villagers doubt her story. He would give her a surprise.

Letting his features fall a trifle slack, he affected a broad Tarshite accent. "Honored to meet 'e, sire. I comes from the West Shore. Good fishin', there, the West Shore."

"So I've heard." The merchant failed to smother a grin as he turned his attention back to Maura. "And what can I get for ye today, mistress?"

When she rattled off a number of items, including rope, flints and canvas, Master Starbow's eyes grew round. "Going on a journey, are ye? Odd, that, with a visitor newly come."

Before Maura could answer, Rath spoke up. "I's a-fetchin' Uncle and the missy back to the West Shore for a spell."

"I don't suppose ye'd be fetching her home for yer bride?" The merchant gave Maura a broad wink as he set about collecting the items she'd requested.

"Say, I guess that'd be right fine!" Rath cried.

Maura punished him with a sharp elbow in his ribs the moment the merchant's back was turned.

A short while later, when the merchant went to fetch three leather drink-skins from his storeroom, she hissed, "What possessed you to say those things? Do you tell falsehoods for the pleasure of it?"

"No. I tell falsehoods for the same reason I do most everything—to survive. Did you never think that having the whole town know your business might not be the safest course?"

He braced for a stinging reply that they were only going to Prum to visit her old aunt. Instead her face turned pale.

Before he could ask her what was wrong, the merchant returned and he was obliged to slip back into the character of Langbard's oafish nephew.

They made several more stops that afternoon, all lengthened by the need to introduce "Ralf," and receive the villagers' best wishes for their journey. As Rath watched Maura take her leave, a vague ache settled in his heart.

What must it be like to live all one's life in the same place, having neighbors to care about your business, perhaps lend a hand in times of trouble? What must it be like to return to a place at the end of the day and feel that was where you belonged?

He had turned to crime when he'd been too young to survive any other way. It was a life for the young and hardy— lads with a taste for violence and danger. Lads with a daft certainty they would live forever, always one step ahead of the next blade or arrow.

Perhaps the time had come to consider a change. He'd already grown accustomed to the modest luxuries of a snug roof over his head, a soft bed to sleep on and hot, filling meals at regular times. Even the opportunity to do an honest day's labor in exchange for his bed and board had given him a sense of satisfaction and accomplishment unlike any he'd known.

He wondered how long Langbard and Maura intended to stay in Prum? They'd need a dependable escort for their return journey. Perhaps if he proved himself reliable, the wizard might consider making him a permanent part of their household. In these perilous times, it wasn't safe for an old man and a young woman to live alone on the fringe of town— even with their magical means of defense.

It would probably mean spending the years to come playing "Simple Ralf" from Tarsh for the benefit of the villagers. Though the role had already ceased to be amusing, Rath reckoned he could do worse.

After a final stop at the butcher's shop to purchase a quantity of dried, smoked meat for their journey, Rath and Maura headed back to Langbard's cottage leading the well-laden pony. The spring sun had already begun to set behind the distant Blood Moon Mountains, and a chill breeze whistled down from the north.

A breeze that carried the faint reek of smoke.

Years of experience made Rath tug up the hem of Langbard's old robe and unsheathe the blade concealed beneath it.

He turned to Maura. "Stay here! Better yet, take the pony into the trees and keep out of sight until I come back for you."

She drew back, staring at the blade in his hand with a look of revulsion. "What is it?"

"Nothing, I hope." Rath darted ahead, then called back in an urgent whisper. "But you might want to dig out some of those bird feathers, just in case."

Behind him, Rath heard the pony give a nervous whinny as Maura cried, "I smell smoke! Wait, I am coming with you!"

6

Fire! The cottage was burning!

Maura tugged on the pony's halter rope, but it moved ever more slowly until finally it refused to budge another step.

"Uncle!" Maura dropped the rope, not caring if the fool beast bolted all the way to Southmark.

As she ran toward the flaming cottage, the north wind blew smoke into her face. Every breath slashed into her lungs, while a cold blade of fear threatened to disembowel her.

What could have happened? Could a stray spark from one of the hearths have landed on something flammable? Might some of the plants hanging to dry in the preparing room have caught fire from the candle over which she distilled potions? She would never have left it burning, would she?

A hundred questions roiled in her mind, together with possibilities, blame and sickening fear. Her gaze roved frantically about the property, desperate for a glimpse of Langbard. Though their cottage was the only home she had ever known, she would cheerfully watch it burn to the ground as long as he remained safe.

But she saw no sign of him. Surely if he'd escaped the burning building, he would be rushing to and fro with buckets from the well, or conjuring some powerful spell to extinguish the blaze. That could only mean…

She screamed his name, rushing toward the door, through which a great cloud of smoke billowed.

"Maura, no!" Rath reared suddenly in front of her, blocking her path to the cottage.

She struggled against his powerful grip, flailing at him with fists and feet. "Let me go! I must find Langbard!"

"He is not in there, I promise you."

"Oh, thank the Giver!" Maura went limp with relief. "Where is he, then?"

Rath did not loosen his hold on her. In the sweet elation of the moment, Maura savored the strength and warmth she discovered in his arms.

"I…found him," Rath gasped, "out back."

His tone set a fresh chill through her. "Found? Is he all right? I must go to him. Uncle!"

Once again, she tried to tear herself away from Rath. He fell back a little. Enough to take them out of the path of the smoke that poured through the cottage door, and the waves of intense heat that rippled in the cool spring air.

"Do not bother to call for him." The harsh tone of Rath's voice belied a curious gentleness in the way he held her. "He cannot hear you now."

"He is unconscious?" As Maura pushed her way forward, Rath retreated, slowly giving ground.

What was he doing? Did he not understand Langbard needed her? Silently, she blessed the Giver that she had Langbard's sash. It contained enough of the ingredients she would need for healing most injuries.

Now that she and Rath were out of the worst of the smoke, she could smell the aroma of burning herbs from the preparing room. Breathing it eased the sting in her lungs and muffled her panic with a false sense of peace.

"I wish he were only unconscious," Rath murmured. His grasp softened from one of restraint to an embrace of comfort. "There is nothing you can do for him now, unless this vitcraft of yours is powerful enough to raise the dead."

"Dead?" He could not be. Not Langbard.

Rath heaved a great sigh. "I am sorry, lass."

"No! You are lying!" Maura tore herself out of Rath's arms and dashed past the well to the little garden behind the cottage. She found Langbard lying there, solid and unblemished, as if in denial of Rath Talward's dire pronouncement. His robe bore a few scorch marks and there was a little smudge of soot on one cheek, but no burns that Maura could see. No wounds. No blood.

"Quick!" she called to Rath. "Fetch me some water. There should be a dipper by the well."

She pressed her hand over Langbard's chest and thought she felt a faint, erratic beat.

"Uncle?" She struck him lightly on the cheek, trying to rouse him. "Can you hear me? Can you open your eyes?"

If I could open them, do you not think I would? If Langbard had parted his lips and spoken the words, Maura could not have heard them more distinctly in his familiar voice.

"That's all right, then. Just keep them closed if you would rather." Maura fumbled in the pockets of his sash for quickfoil, a rare herb prized for its properties as a stimulant and restorative. "I am here now. You will be fine. I am sure Sorsha and Newlyn will not mind letting us stay at Hoghill until you are well enough to travel."

She forced a thin, shaky laugh. "What a shame the fire could not have waited another day."

"Here is that water." Rath knelt beside her, holding out the earthen dipper. "I think it will do you more good, now, than him, poor fellow. I wish there was aught we *could* do for him."

While Maura took the dipper and scattered a generous measure of quickfoil into the water, Rath reached toward Langbard's cheek. His hand hovered there, not quite touching, as if he craved some contact, but did not know how.

"I only knew him a short time, but no man treated me better in all my years."

Much as it vexed her to hear him talk as if Langbard was beyond their aid, the wistful edge in his voice and the awkward tenderness of his gesture called to her heart.

"Langbard thinks well of you, too." Perhaps that should have been enough for her. But the big outlaw stirred up too many long-held fears and too many long-denied desires. "He will be grateful you were here to help us. Can you fetch me a hot coal?"

The flames reflected in Rath's dark eyes as he stared at her, his thick brows bunched. "A coal? Whatever for, lass?"

"To mull the tonic, of course." Maura held out the dipper.

"The quickfoil will work faster if the water is hot. I have no time to heat it any other way."

"Oh...yes...fine." The expression on Rath's face told Maura he did not understand.

But he staggered to his feet and returned a moment later with a half-charred stick, one end of which glowed an angry red. He thrust it into the dipper Maura lifted toward him. The water bubbled and a cloud of steam hissed up, redolent with the odors of burnt wood and potent herbs.

As she inhaled, Maura felt her heart beat stronger and faster. Surely this would revive Langbard.

"Can you support his shoulders?" she bid Rath. "Lift his head so I can get this into him?"

"Maura—"

"Just do it!"

Rath withdrew the steaming stick from the dipper and tossed it away. "It is no use. Can you not see?"

"I said, do it!" The shrill pitch of madness in her voice chilled Maura.

Do not be too hard on the lad. Langbard's words, in Langbard's voice.

"Did you hear that?"

"I heard you," Rath growled. "Hold his head. Now you hear *me*. It will do no good."

Despite his protest, he moved to do her bidding.

He is right, you know. Listen to him. He has seen far more of death than you have, my dear.

"Be quiet and drink this!" Maura snapped. Even half-dead, men took one another's part.

"He *is* quiet," said Rath in a hushed but firm voice. "And he cannot drink."

As if to confirm his words, the quickfoil tonic dribbled out of Langbard's mouth as fast as Maura could pour it in.

I am sorry, my dear. I wish I'd done better for you.

"But you did!" Casting the dipper aside, Maura threw her arms around Langbard's neck and cradled his head, her cheek pressed to his. "No one could have done better!"

A bristle of whisker rasped against her skin. Langbard's flesh felt cold...lifeless.

"Oh, Uncle!" Sob after sob shuddered through her and tears flooded her eyes—more tears than she had shed in her whole life until now. Yet they could not begin to moisten the parched wilderness of her grief.

She was scarcely aware of Rath Talward, moving away to let her mourn in private. After what seemed a very long time, she felt his hand giving her shoulder a firm shake.

"Leave us be!" she cried.

"No!" His voice sounded as urgent as his touch had felt. "I cannot. Look at this."

She looked. Not because she cared but because, if she did as he bid, Rath Talward might leave her alone.

Between the smoke and the weeping, her eyes were almost swollen shut. A few unshed tears still lingered, blurring her vision further. In the livid light of the fire, Maura could make out a long slender shape in Rath's hand.

"Do you know what this is?" he demanded. "Do you know what it means?"

Though she could not see it well, Maura sensed it. Something dark and oppressive beating down on her spirit with the combined weight of fear, grief, guilt, rage and bone-shattering loneliness.

She shrank from it. "I do not know what it is, nor do I care. It is evil. Take it away!"

"It is evil, though it is spent of its power." Rath tensed. Then, with a release of coiled, violent power, he hurled the thing into the fire. "That was a bronze wand with a blood-gem imbedded in its tip. It means the Echtroi have been here. It must have been they who did this."

The Echtroi. Maura shuddered.

This was the first she had ever heard of the Hanish death-mages venturing over the Blood Moon Mountains. But she knew of their terrible power as well as if she had lived under their shadow every day of her life. Their dark robes were the fabric of her nightmares.

"They cannot have gone far." Rath's large hand closed over Maura's upper arm, ready to hoist her to her feet. "And they may return. We must get as far away as we can before they do!"

Rage burst and crackled in Maura, as hot as the blaze that had consumed her home and her past. "This is *your* fault! Sheltering you brought danger upon us. I should have stayed clear of trouble as Langbard always bid me. I should have left you to the Han!"

Rath Talward had long since ceased to care what anyone said to, or about, him. In his early years he'd suffered a knock or two for challenging a slur on his character or ancestry. Having made up his mind such taunts were not worth his trouble, he had cultivated a deaf ear and an impervious heart.

The bitter accusation Maura flung at him gnawed through

all his carefully constructed defenses. To his surprise and dismay, it inflicted a stinging wound.

Perhaps because it confirmed his own daft sense of blame?

"You are right." He did not flinch from Maura's accusing glare. "You should have left me be. But there is no changing that now."

Like grief, regret was a luxury beyond his means.

He latched on to Maura's arm, intending to hoist her to her feet. "We cannot linger here. If the Echtroi get hold of us, we will wish the blackhounds had torn us to pieces that day in the woods."

She jerked her arm out of his grasp. "Go, then. I will be glad to see the last of you."

If only he could. Obligations were a dangerous extravagance for a man like him. By saving his life from the Han, Maura had laid a claim on him—one he did not like or want, but which he could not ignore. Langbard's kindness to him and his responsibility for the old wizard's death only intensified that claim.

Rath dropped to his haunches. "If I was certain they would follow me and do you no harm, I would strike out on my own." He nodded back toward the burning cottage, then down at the dead wizard. "But I know better than to rely on their neglect. Come. Langbard would not want you to fall into their clutches."

His words finally reached her. Rath could see it. Though he had hoped invoking Langbard's wishes might sway her, he had not expected so intense a response.

Maura's eyes widened. She seemed to struggle for breath. Finally she was able to inhale enough to fuel a high-pitched whimper. For some reason, his warning seemed to have distressed her even worse than Langbard's death or the evidence that the Echtroi were behind it.

Rath put aside his puzzlement. He did not have time to indulge it now. Whatever the reason for Maura's terror, he must use it to get her away from there.

"It will be all right," he promised—a blatant lie. "I will stand by my bargain with Langbard to deliver you to your aunt. But we must go now."

A bewildering succession of thoughts and emotions flickered in the depths of her eyes until her gaze fell back to Langbard.

Shaking her head, she spoke in a halting, sorrowful murmur. "I cannot leave him. Not like this. He must be properly buried. We must share the ritual of passing."

"There is no time!" Rath longed to shake her out of her folly. "Who will bury *us* if the Echtroi catch us here? The ritual of passing is only a daft bit of superstition. Langbard is past caring what happens to him now. If you do not want the Echtroi to have his body, let me throw it on the fire."

Even as he made the offer, Rath knew it would be one of the most difficult tasks he had ever set himself.

"No!" Maura spread her arms over the old wizard's body in a protective gesture that warned Rath she would fight him to the death to prevent it. "He will be decently buried if I have to dig the grave with my bare hands. And he will have the ritual of passing, for his sake and for mine. I will not suffer him to be lost."

Lost? Rath tried to recall what he had heard about the ritual of passing. Something about shepherding the spirit of the dead into the afterworld? And was there supposed to be some passing of memories from the dead to the mourner? Such beliefs had been in decline even before the coming of the Han.

He had two choices, Rath decided. Sling Maura Woodbury over his shoulder and hope her screams of protest did not attract dangerous attention. Or leave now and let the foolish creature fend for herself.

As self-preservation warred with obligation, Rath's mouth opened and the most outrageous question came out. "How long would you need for this passing business?"

Maura groped for one of Langbard's hands. "How long can you give us?"

Hard as he tried to resist the plea that ached in her voice and eyes, Rath could not. "An hour. No more. I might be able to scratch out a shallow hole by then."

"An hour." Maura exhaled the words on a shaky breath. Then she pointed to a small shed at the bottom of the garden. "You will find a spade there."

With a curt nod, Rath headed for the shed. If he had something to occupy his energies, perhaps he would not drive himself mad imagining a death-mage behind every tree for the next hour.

"Wait!" Maura called.

Rath glanced back.

She held out her hand to him. What did she want? A clasp for reassurance…some help with the passing ritual? He had no time for such dawdling if they were to bury the old wizard and escape with their lives.

But she looked so forlorn, kneeling there on the cold ground over the dead body of her guardian, with their home burning behind her. Whatever she wanted, Rath could not deny her.

"What is it?" He approached her with faltering steps.

The walk to the village and back had tired him more than he cared to admit, and his wounded arm gave a twinge as he thought of the digging he would have to do.

As he drew closer, he could make out a small object resting in the palm of her hand.

"Swallow it," Maura urged him, "if you can bear to. It will give you strength to dig faster."

Rath felt his features twist into a look of disgust. It was more than the prospect of eating something so revolting. This was magic—powerful, unpredictable, dangerous. He'd just as soon have tried to swallow his sword. At least he knew what that would do to him.

But how could he refuse after Maura had been willing to consume the wretched stuff on his account?

Gingerly he took it between his thumb and forefinger. It felt like a fat, furry caterpillar. He had not eaten one of those in quite a while. But he had managed to choke them down when there had been nothing else to eat.

He forced his mouth open.

Maura picked up the dipper she had dropped earlier and offered it to him. "You might as well wash it down with what is left in this. The essence of bear will give you strength. The quickfoil potion will give you vigor."

"Sounds grand." Rath bolted the wad of bear fur and fat, which tasted every bit as vile as he'd expected.

He followed it with a deep draft of the potion. Fortunately it tasted a good deal better than he'd expected, despite a faint seasoning of charred wood. It kept him from gagging on the other.

"Now, repeat these words," said Maura. Then she spoke a strange phrase Rath vaguely recognized as Old Umbrian.

"Can you not say it?" he asked. "Like you did when you turned me invisible?"

"I can, but the effect will be more potent if you pronounce the spell yourself. Come now, it is neither long nor difficult."

He did not have time to argue with her. So he muttered the strange words reluctantly, wondering what they meant and hoping some misspeech on his part would not throw the spell awry...making him shrink or go deaf.

"I do not feel any different," he announced when the incantation was done.

Maura did not reply.

"Is there anything you need?" he asked. "Anything I can do...before I...set to work."

Offering help felt awkward and unnatural to him. Until now, it had taken every bit of his energy and concentration to look out for himself. He'd had none to spare for anyone else. Rath was not sure he had, now. He felt compelled to ask, anyway.

"You could refill the dipper," Maura replied. "I will need water for the ritual, to wash away the cares of this world so they do not weigh on his spirit."

She stared down at Langbard as she spoke. Sorrow seemed to have settled over her like a heavy mantle.

Rath headed for the well, remembering another death long ago—the last one he had allowed to maul his heart. Deep personal attachments like this were a liability he dared not risk. It troubled him to remember how, only a few hours ago, he had pondered the daft notion of attaching himself to the old wizard's household.

The life of an outlaw might present greater physical hardships and dangers as a man grew older. But settling down, forming ties with folk, held perils of a different kind that might prove even more lethal to someone like him.

When he tugged at the rope to raise the heavy, water-filled bucket from the depths of the well, Rath gave a start at how quickly he was able to hoist it up. He realized his weariness had eased, too, and his arm no longer pained. Otherwise, he felt nothing out of the ordinary.

That did not allay his wariness of magic.

He hurried back to Maura and thrust the dipper into her hands. "The spell is working. If the tools will hold, I should be able to delve Langbard a decent resting place in an hour."

Her gaze searched his face, looking for...what?

"Why are you doing this? I know you do not believe in the passing ritual."

"No, I do not." That part of his answer came readily enough. As to the rest, Rath knew no more than she did. Only one explanation rang true, though it made little sense to him. "But you do."

Because the admission made him feel weak and fanciful, he added a harsh order. "So get on with it."

Maura had studied the ritual of passing, along with all the other rituals, spells, language and legends that belonged to the Elderways. She knew what she was supposed to do. She knew what was supposed to happen. That did not stop her from feeling overwhelmed and unprepared.

It galled her having to accept Rath Talward's help after he had brought this calamity upon them. But Langbard's death had made it even more imperative she take up her quest for the Waiting King.

Her guardian had sacrificed all his plans and ambitions to play his part in preparing her for her destiny. Though the scope and risk of all that lay ahead still confounded Maura, she knew she must honor his memory by doing what he would have wanted her to do. Which would mean relying on Rath Talward, at least for a little longer.

Forcing her thoughts away from the outlaw and the sound of his digging, Maura wet a corner of her shawl and washed the smudge of soot off Langbard's cheek. Then she anointed him after the fashion he had taught her.

On the brow to purify his thoughts. On the lips to purify his words. On the hands to purify his actions. All the while crooning the Litany of Passing that would release his spirit from his body and guide it back to the Giver from whence it had come.

The ritual words served another purpose, too, freeing her spirit to journey part of the way with Langbard. Along the path to the next world, he would unburden himself, bequeathing to her any memories, skills or knowledge he wished to leave behind.

Come, my dear, said Langbard, *we have not much time. I set the Echtroi chasing a false trail, but I fear they will not be fooled for long. By the time they return, you must be as far from here as you can get. And mind you cover your tracks well. I expect Master Talward knows all about that. Bless the Giver for sending him to us.*

Bless the Giver? Had dying addled Langbard's wits? If not for Rath Talward…

No, Maura, Langbard chided her. *It is we who brought this danger upon him, not the other way. The Echtroi have discovered there is something afoot that threatens them. They do not know what the threat is or how it will come about, but somehow they learned of my involvement and my whereabouts.*

That meant...

You must be very careful. The forces arrayed against you are powerful and vigilant. They will do anything to hold what they have taken...and what has taken them.

If only he could come with her.

I will. In my own way.

With that, a swift-flowing stream of memories swirled in Maura's mind and heart. She saw the Oracle of Margyle, felt the sense of thwarted ambition that the seeress's long-ago prophesy had provoked in a young scholar. She saw another woman look up from a scroll. A slow half-wary smile spread across the woman's face as she met a new look in the eyes of the man she had despaired of ever caring for her.

Maura's heart gave a lurch as she beheld a young woman cradling an infant, with an air of wistful joy shadowed by deep anguish. Langbard's unacknowledged love ached within Maura as she watched her beautiful, doomed mother and absorbed a few of the memories *she* had passed to him.

With the sensation of her hand clasped in Langbard's, Maura wandered farther abroad in spirit than she ever had in body. Together, they crested Pronel's Pass under the looming shadow of the Three Castle Mountains. They waded through the tall waving grass of the Southmark steppes as a great cloud of star moths fluttered into the air to begin their northern migration. They stood on the sandy western shore of Galene, watching the sun set beyond the horizon of the Sea of Twilight.

Bits of lore. Spells he had meant to teach her. Properties of plants not native to Norest, but which she might encounter on her travels. All these now became part of her, as if she had experienced every one firsthand. Much as the passing ritual enriched her, Maura dreaded the moment it must come to an end. Then all she would have left of Langbard was this part of himself with which he had endowed her.

"Maura!" Rath's urgent whisper accompanied by his rough grip on her shoulder wrenched her spirit from its wanderings.

Suddenly she was back in the garden behind the burning cottage, kneeling beside Langbard's lifeless body, with Rath hovering over her.

She resented him intruding so abruptly on her final farewell. "Are you finished already?"

"Almost." His hold on her arm slackened. "But that is not why I roused you. There is someone skulking about."

An unnatural edge of fear in his voice made Maura's blood freeze. Anything that unnerved a dangerous man like Rath Talward must be menacing, indeed.

7

Whatever stalked them was still out there. Every one of Rath's quivering senses told him so. Why did they not strike and be done with it?

Had Langbard put up enough of a fight to weaken them or at least make them hesitate to attack again? Or did they want to toy with their next victims, relishing the fear they inspired? Whatever the reason, he must seize this meager opportunity and turn it to his advantage.

Clutching the hilt of his sword tight, he brought his lips close to Maura's ear. "Have you anything in your sash that might bind or befuddle them long enough for me to strike?"

It galled him to beg her help. He would have preferred to slip off into the night and pretend the past few days had never happened. He yearned to reclaim his old straightforward life in which nothing mattered beyond keeping himself alive, free and fed.

But he had made a bargain with Langbard. Now Rath discovered that having given his word meant something to him after all. The old wizard's death did not release him from his pledge. If anything, it bound him more firmly than ever...to Maura Woodbury.

Somehow, he must get the wizard's ward safely to her aunt in Prum. Whether she wanted his company or not. The first step on that journey would be to escape from Windleford with their lives. For that, he needed her help.

Maura gave a barely perceptible nod in response to his question. "What good will it do? In the time it will take me to recite the spell you could strike...or they could."

Her lips hardly moved as she whispered the words. Rath had seen small animals paralyzed with terror—Maura reminded him of them.

"What if you say the words before you do...whatever it is you do? Would the spell still work?"

Maura turned her face toward him. "I s-suppose it might."

She looked so vulnerable, so steeped in sorrow and fear, a compulsion to protect her took possession of Rath. One that had nothing to do with his promise to Langbard.

"Even if you said the words very quietly—whispered them under your breath?"

"Perhaps. I've never tried it. I've never had to."

"Well, you do now." He rested a hand on her shoulder. "In a moment, I want you to stand up and walk toward the bottom of the garden. When you pass that bramble bush, recite your spell, then turn and cast it."

He doubted whatever she did would hold or daze one of the Echtroi for long. He had no illusions that her gentle, capricious vitcraft was any match for their powerful dark sorcery. "I will come along behind you to finish the job."

"Very well." She stared into his eyes with a fierce concentration, as though she feared her resolve would shatter if she looked away.

All her life, she had been sheltered from the harshness and dangers of life he knew too well. Little wonder if the violent swiftness of recent events had overwhelmed her.

"If they are watching," he said, "I do not want them to suspect anything. In a moment, I am going to hold you close, to make it look like I am trying to comfort you. Use that as cover to get whatever you need from your sash. Do you understand?"

She nodded. Her eyes were no longer so swollen from crying. But they were wide with alarm. Was she more frightened of the Echtroi? Rath wondered. Or of him?

Not that he cared.

He kept telling himself that as he gathered Maura into his arms. Or rather, his arm.

Since he dared not release his sword, he settled for wrapping his left arm around her shoulders and pulling her toward him. Maura did not resist, but bowed her head until her brow rested against the hollow of his shoulder.

For a moment, Rath forgot the true purpose of what he was doing. Nothing seemed as important, just then, as holding Maura—imparting with the warmth and strength of his embrace what he could not put into words.

His regret over Langbard's death, and his lost opportunity to know the old wizard better. His determination to fulfill the promise he had made. A strange but powerful connection between the two of them that he had been loathe to acknowledge.

From the moment they'd met, he and Maura had rubbed each other the wrong way. Just as two pieces of flint scraping together struck sparks. Mishandled, sparks could ignite the kind of blaze now consuming Langbard's cottage. Tended properly, they could kindle valuable light and warmth.

Scarcely aware of what he was doing, Rath let his head cant sideways, until his cheek rested against the crown of Maura's head and the smooth, chestnut tendrils of her hair. Her nearness made him yearn for so many things he'd convinced himself he did not want.

Maura began to fumble in the pockets of the sash. That subtle movement stirred Rath from his seductive, risky musings.

Lifting his head, he clutched his sword tighter and swept the area with an alert gaze. He dared not let his guard down the way he'd just done. Not with danger so near at hand and poised to strike. It shook him to realize how exposed he had left himself to attack.

"Ready?" he asked in a sharp whisper.

Maura nodded, her head rubbing against his shoulder in a precarious caress.

"Good. Let's go, then, while we still have a chance." It cost him such an effort to release her, that when the force of his will overcame the resistance of his inclination, he fairly jerked Maura to her feet and shoved her toward the foot of the garden.

Giving her several steps' lead, he followed, hoping whoever was watching them would have as much trouble keeping their eyes off her as he did. For then they might not notice him following, blade in hand.

As she took those final steps past the bramble bush, Rath noted the subtle change in her movement, gathering itself to pivot so she could cast her spell. His own muscles tensed to smite a killing blow with his sword. He knew better than to hope for a second chance if he fumbled the first.

Maura whirled around. Something left her hand to fly through the air. Rath swung his sword.

A cry rose from behind the bramble bush.

"No!" Maura threw herself toward the sound.

Rath's sword whistled through thin air, over the heads of Maura and whoever she had knocked to the ground.

He growled an oath—the vilest one that came to mind. Raising his sword, he barked at Maura, "Get out of the way, blast you!"

Her head snapped around. The way the fire reflected in her eyes made Rath fear she might strike him dead with her glare. "Put that thing down! It is only Newlyn…our neighbor from Hoghill Farm."

She rolled off the man who lay motionless beneath her. "I am so sorry, Newlyn! We were afraid you might be…someone else."

She began to intone the spell that would unbind him.

The farmer struggled against his invisible bonds. "Sorsha sent me to find out if you were all right. We could see the fire. What happened?"

Rath did not give Maura time to answer. He had a few questions of his own that demanded answers. No man provoked his fighting instincts to their present raging pitch without paying a price.

"If you meant us no harm, why were you skulking behind the bushes?"

"Trying to reckon if you might do *me* any harm." The man shot Rath a black look as he sat up. "I reckon I know the answer to that, now, Master Ralf from Tarsh."

The bite of mockery in the fellow's voice told Rath he saw through that ruse.

Scrambling up from the ground, Maura offered Newlyn Swinley her hand. "We would never have tried to hurt you, if we had known it was you. We are not certain what happened, either. When we got back from the village, the cottage was burning and Langbard—"

Her voice choked off.

Newlyn nodded toward the wizard's body. "I was afraid of that. I'm sorry, Maura. He was a good man. Dunno what would have become of me without him and Sorsha."

Maura made an obvious effort to regain her composure. "Langbard had every confidence in you, Newlyn. I know he admired the way you were able to put the past behind you and start a fresh life. You and Sorsha have repaid any help he gave you many times over."

"Was it the fire killed him, then?" Newlyn's heavy dark brows knit in puzzlement. "The smoke?"

Rath shook his head. "I think it was more than that. I found a metal wand with a spent blood gem."

Newlyn shrank from the words as if from a threatened blow. Whatever "old life" he'd left behind, it must have involved some contact with the Echtroi. Rath wondered if he pushed aside the farmer's long dark hair whether he would find a telltale brand from the Blood Moon mines on the back of his neck.

"That is why Maura and I ambushed you." He made no apology for their actions.

If this man had escaped the mines, Rath knew he would not grudge their caution, even if it might have cost him his head.

"We must get away from here," added Maura, "in case whoever did this comes back."

"Your pony is tethered at our house." Newlyn looked from her to Rath and back again. "From the look of his pack, I would say you were planning a journey before any of this happened."

"We were," Rath answered when Maura looked torn about what and how much to tell her friend. What he had guessed about Newlyn's background stirred a sense of kinship in him, as well as a feeling of admiration...and a little envy. "For your own safety, it is best if we tell you no more."

"Maybe you should let me be the judge of what is and is not safe for me to know." Newlyn's eyes narrowed and the muscles of his face tightened as he stared at Rath. The man took a step nearer Maura, as if to establish his claim of longer acquaintance.

"He is right, Newlyn." Maura reached for the farmer's hand. "If it were only your safety at risk, I might give you the choice of how much you wanted to know. But there is Sorsha to think of, and the children, too. I cannot put them in danger."

Her words puzzled Rath. She made it sound as if whoever had killed Langbard might be after her, when only a little while ago she'd insisted he had brought this calamity upon them.

That *was* the only explanation that made sense...wasn't it?

"This does not make any sense," said Sorsha a while later, as she bustled about her kitchen serving Maura and Rath a late supper.

They had both protested they were too upset to eat, but Sorsha had not heeded them. Her first instinct when confronted with any manner of trouble was to feed someone.

"Why would anyone want to do away with a peaceable old fellow like Langbard?" She paused in the middle of carving a loaf of bread into thick slabs. "I cannot believe it yet. I keep expecting to look up and see him coming through the door, looking for a bite to eat."

Setting aside her knife, she lifted the corner of her apron and wiped away the fresh tears.

"I know how you feel." Maura spoke in a bemused murmur. She could not seem to take it in, either. Though she had helped Rath and Newlyn bury Langbard not an hour ago, she could not keep from wondering when he would be joining them at the table.

Perhaps not wanting to upset her further, Sorsha quit sniffling and recovered her manner of brisk efficiency. In no time, she had a plate of bread on the table, together with a crock of fresh butter and heaping bowls of soup.

"Something else that does not make any sense is your going off so sudden like. Can you not at least stay here till the morning? It is not safe to be traveling in the dead of night."

Despite his claim not to be hungry, Rath reached for a slice of bread. "It would be even less safe to stay here. For your sake as well as for ours, Mistress Swinley. Mark me, there will be Han swarming all over Langbard's property by tomorrow."

He glanced toward Newlyn. "Your husband might want to make himself scarce if they come to Hoghill asking questions."

"Oh, my." For the first time in all the years Maura had known her, Sorsha sounded thoroughly intimidated.

Rath took a second slice of bread, buttered it, then shoved it toward Maura. "You may not feel like it, but you must eat, just the same. To keep up your strength."

Beneath his gruff words and offhand manner, Maura sensed an attitude of concern he did not find easy to express. Perhaps because it came so hard for him, it warmed her all the more.

He had put himself at risk so she could have time to share the passing ritual with Langbard. He appeared ready to honor his promise to escort her south, when he might have used Langbard's death as excuse to back out. Might Langbard have been right about Rath Talward, after all?

Forcing herself to pick up her spoon, Maura made herself eat the soup, which tasted vaguely of all the smoke she had breathed during the past few hours. She tried to think of nothing beyond her next bite of food. If she let herself dwell on Langbard's death or her parting from Sorsha, or the long, dangerous road that lay before her, she would curl up into a trembling ball of tears and never stir a step from Hoghill Farm!

While Maura and Rath ate in stunned silence, Sorsha and Newlyn withdrew to the other corner of the big kitchen and talked together in hushed, urgent tones. With all her heart, Maura hoped her coming here would not bring trouble on them.

A week ago, if anyone had told her she could be a dangerous person to know, she would have laughed in their faces. Now she wondered if she was being fair, imposing on Rath Talward's unexpected sense of honor? For the moment, she had no choice.

"See there," said Sorsha when Rath and Maura had finished eating. "You must have been hungrier than you thought. I do hate to see you go, but I will be a little easier in my mind knowing you did not leave on an empty belly."

Those words appeared to spark another thought. "What about clothes? You will only have what is on your backs."

"Come." She took Maura's hand. "I have a few things I can spare so you will have a change. Some of my clothes have gotten a bit too snug since the babies came. Slight as you are, they should fit you fine. A bit on the short side, but that's no bad thing if you're traveling. Less skirt to catch on thorns or drag in the dust."

Maura rose and followed her friend out of the kitchen. Behind her, she heard Newlyn offering Rath whatever supplies they might need for the journey that they had not purchased in town that afternoon. Had it really been such a short time ago?

Plucking a candle from a sconce by the doorway, Sorsha led her friend to her bed chamber off the small parlor.

Once they were out of earshot of the kitchen, she whispered, "Are you sure you want to go away with that man? If he's Langbard's nephew from Tarsh, then I'm the Oracle of Margyle!"

In spite of all her cares, those words brought a faint, fleeting smile to Maura's lips. "No, he is not Ralf from Tarsh. But he is not quite as dangerous as he looks, either. At least...I do not think so."

"I do not like this." Kneeling before the low trunk at the foot of her and Newlyn's bed, Sorsha lifted the lid and began to pull out items of clothing. "Our quiet little bit of country has been in an uproar since that fellow showed up. Handsome as he is, I do not quite like his looks...if you know what I mean. I reckon if he lit out, laying down a nice smelly trail for a few miles, you could hide here with us until things settle down."

If only Sorsha knew how much that plan appealed to her!

Maura made herself shake her head. "There is something important I have to do. Langbard trusted Rath and believed he could help me. I have to believe it, too."

"Rath the Wolf?" cried Sorsha, forgetting the baby asleep in the cradle beside her parents' bed. "Curse me for a fool! I should have known. I heard all about him in town. They say the garrison ambushed his gang of outlaws and did away with them all."

"They did. I saw it." Those sights had haunted her dreams ever since.

Sorsha laid a hand on her bosom as if to slow her hammering heart. "Most folks said they caught the Wolf, too, and killed him. But I had my doubts. Kezia Wintergreen said she heard from one of the soldiers that he vanished right before their eyes."

"I made him vanish. Cuddybird feathers."

"That's that, then." Sorsha shut the trunk lid with a thump that made the baby cry out in her sleep. "You are not going anywhere with that creature, no matter what Langbard thought of him. Imagine what he might do to you out in the middle of nowhere, with nobody to come to your aid!"

Maura forgot that she had said much the same thing recently. She *tried* to forget the way Rath Talward had kissed her neck during their walk to Windleford. "If he wanted to do anything like that, he could have done it any night since we took him in."

"He would not have dared with Langbard there to call."

"The way Langbard sleeps? You must be joking!" The moment those words left Maura's mouth, they turned to smite her heart. "I mean, the way he *slept*."

She jammed her fist against her mouth to stifle a sob.

"There now, I know what you meant." Sorsha wrapped an arm around Maura's shoulders. "I was the same after my mother and father passed. For weeks I kept talking about them as if they were still around."

After a moment she added, "When Ma died, I felt that bad, I kept on doing everything about the farm the way she always liked it done, even though I had a notion or two of my own that might have been better."

Maura remembered. It had been she who'd first suggested Sorsha would not be dishonoring her mother's memory by making a few changes.

"Don't you make that same mistake," said Sorsha. "Don't rush into something dangerous because you think Langbard would have wanted it. Especially not with that man. He is nothing but trouble, I can see that plain as plain."

Part of Maura wanted so much to heed her friend, to use Sorsha's objections and her own fears as an excuse to avoid an enormous task for which she felt so woefully unprepared. But there was so much more at stake than the smooth running of a provincial farm.

She fought to regain her composure. It would not do to have Sorsha think she was too distraught from grief to know what she was doing. If her friend believed her life or virtue were in danger from Rath Talward, Sorsha might do something truly dangerous, like alerting the Hanish garrison.

"I might have said the same thing about Newlyn when you first met him. Come to think of it, I am almost certain I did."

Sorsha puffed up, like a mother hen defending her brood. "That's not the same thing at all and well you know it, Maura Woodbury!"

"Oh, isn't it? He was a pretty dangerous-looking character, then, as I recall, and wanted by the Han."

The look that came over her friend's face told Maura her words were having the desired effect.

"You saw the good in him, though," she reminded Sorsha, "and so did Langbard."

"Have you fallen in love with this Wolf fellow, then?"

"No!" She had no business fancying any man if she was to be the bride of the Waiting King. That notion still left Maura feeling light-headed and far out of her depth. "But I do need someone like him to help me on my way."

"I hope you are right about him," Sorsha grumbled. "I still wish you did not have to go so sudden. You will come back, won't you, once you have done this thing you need to do?"

"Perhaps. I cannot say." If she failed, she might return to Windleford, one day.

But she must not fail. She must find and waken the Waiting King so he could drive out the Han and restore the old throne of Umbria. Then men like Newlyn would no longer need to fear discovery and boys like the dear little ones who slept in the next room would never be rounded up and sent to the horror of the Blood Moon mines.

"If you must, I suppose you must." Sorsha sighed. "Get word to me, if you can, now and then. For I will be thinking of you and wishing you well, asking for the Giver's favor on you."

"And I you!" Maura caught her friend in a swift, fierce embrace. "Now I must not tarry any longer."

For one thing, it could put her dear friends in danger, and for another she might lose this brief spark of resolve.

"Take these, then." Sorsha deposited a pair of laced leather boots in Maura's lap. "Mother had them made for walking to market, but she hardly got to wear them. They are too narrow for me."

While Sorsha packed the other clothes into a bundle, Maura removed her shoes and replaced them with the walking boots.

She had almost finished tying the laces when Newlyn appeared at the bedroom door. "Ralf says you must come at once. He wants to be well away before it gets light."

With a swiftness that caused Maura both dismay and a contrary sense of relief, Rath Talward hustled her through her teary farewell to the Swinleys.

The lights of Hoghill still flickered invitingly in the distance when Maura roused from her rueful reflections to notice which way they were headed. She glanced up into the night sky, toward a cluster of stars known as Menya's Slipper.

"Where are you taking me? This is north. We are supposed to be going to Prum."

Suddenly all Sorsha's warnings, and her own former misgivings reared up to haunt her.

"No," said Rath. "We are *supposed* to be going to Tarsh. That is what the people in the village think. If the Swinleys are questioned, I want them to be able to say they last saw us heading north. It is probably safe to turn south now, though."

"There was no need to waste time going out of our way."

From the hood of the fleece-lined cloak Sorsha had given her, Maura inhaled the comforting scent of her friend. "Even if we had told Sorsha and Newlyn where we're going, they would never breathe a word to anyone else."

"They would not mean to, perhaps." Rath gradually changed course until they were headed southward, skirting Hoghill. "But the Han are no fools. They are good at asking ten different questions whose answers will only tally if a body is telling the truth."

"Indeed?" She knew so little about the Han, except how to avoid them. It occurred to Maura that such ignorance might prove a grave handicap to her in the days and weeks to come.

"This way," said Rath, "your friends can lie or tell the truth, whichever they like, and the Han will still believe we are going north. For a while, at least."

Something in his tone made Maura pull her cloak even tighter. But it did nothing to relieve the chill that crept into her heart.

8

"What now?" Maura's voice betrayed her exhaustion.

An hour's walk had brought them to the banks of the River Windle, a few miles downstream from the village. Rath was not certain how much longer darkness would remain their ally. With all that had happened, this one night already felt many hours longer than usual.

"What do you mean, what now?"

Maura sank to the ground. "I mean, how are we supposed to get across the river? It is too wide, cold and fast to swim at this time of year. Perhaps we can find somewhere to hide until later in the day, then slip into Windleford and cross the bridge."

"Are you daft?" Rath's arms were beginning to ache from the exertion of digging Langbard's grave. His offer to escort Maura Woodbury to Prum seemed more like a fool's errand with every passing moment. "Prance right through Windleford in broad daylight while the Han are looking high and low for us?"

"I still have some hundredflower." Maura spoke in a sharp, antagonistic tone. "We pranced right through Windleford yesterday without attracting a single Hanish glance. Besides, is that not the last place they are apt to look for us—right under their noses?"

The gruff retort he had ready to unleash upon her burst into grudging laughter. "I will say this for you, wench, you have plenty of gall! You would make a fine outlaw."

"I suppose that is your idea of flattery?"

Rath felt it again, the rasp of their very different natures against one another, striking sparks. Was it just his fancy—or did his pulse beat stronger, his senses all grow more alert?

"Take it as you will," he quipped, then he grew serious again. "I will not trust my life to a scattering of flower petals and a few mumbled words of nonsense. Even if that spell of yours did keep the Han from noticing us, there are still those cursed hounds. Or one of the village folk might point us out."

"You have a better idea, I suppose?"

His mouth stretched into a wide grin of anticipation. "We wouldn't be here if I didn't."

"Indeed?" Maura sounded dubious. "And what might that be?"

"You will see." Rath scrambled down the bank. Though he had not slept in almost a day, his weariness had mysteriously abated, as had the ache in his arms.

He groped around the loose dirt of the shoreline, trying to hold back his mounting alarm.

Where was it? He cursed under his breath.

"Well?" Maura's question wafted down to taunt him.

"I cannot make out anything down here." This was the right spot, wasn't it? "Can you strike a light?"

"Are you not afraid someone might see it?"

"I am more afraid they will see *us*," Rath snapped, "if we do not get across the river before the sun rises."

He heard her muttering quietly to herself. No doubt she was fumbling through the pony's packs looking for flint, all the while questioning his judgment, his morals, his trustworthiness and anything else she could think of.

He glanced up to see a strange, soft green glow descending toward him. The eeriness of it made him jump back and trip over a stick of driftwood, landing hard on his backside.

The light began to dance then. Rath could make out Maura's face behind it.

"Do not worry," she called softly. "It's just a bit of green-fire. It should shed enough light for you to find what you are looking for, but it is hard to see from a distance."

"Sounds useful." Rath grunted as he picked himself up and reached for the slender stick with the glowing tip.

"It is." Maura handed him the stick. "It does not last very long, though, so be quick."

That did not surprise Rath. From all he had seen, this vitcraft was fickle stuff with very definite limitations. Handy enough in a pinch, but laughably feeble compared to the dread power of Hanish mortcraft. Much as he feared the latter, he respected its power.

"Aha!" In the queer green light, Rath found what he was seeking.

He pushed back a screen of long grass that hung down from the bank, and high reeds that grew at the water's edge. Then, taking the light stick between his teeth, he used both hands to tug the small, crudely made raft out of its hiding place.

"Ah!" The muted sound of Maura's astonished understanding contained a hint of admiration.

A ridiculous sense of satisfaction swelled within Rath. He tried to subdue it by issuing her a brisk order.

"What did you say?" she asked.

Removing the stick from his mouth, Rath tried again. "Unpack the pony. We must lash the packs to the raft."

In the fading gleam of greenfire, with the ebbing power of the strength spell, Rath hauled the crude frame of lashed logs to the edge of the water. He had just given it a last heave when Maura appeared beside him, struggling under the weight of one of the packs.

Recalling everything that had happened to her that day, something deep in his gut gave a sharp twist. At the same time a grudging sense of respect flickered within him. In spite of everything, the lass was still on her feet, still bearing her part.

"I will take that." He seized the pack from her. "You should sit back down and rest a moment."

"Not until we are out of danger." Her answer gusted out on a ragged breath. "Besides, if I do not keep moving I may start thinking."

"Please yourself then." Rath dug a length of rope from the pack and used that to tie it down.

By the time he had finished, Maura was back with the second one. "How did you know where to find this raft?"

"I was the one who put it here." He lashed down the second pack, hoping it would balance with the other one. "Over the years, I have discovered a body can never have too many escape routes. Can you look about on the bank for a long pole to help shift this thing?"

While she was busy looking, Rath led the reluctant pony down to the water. There he fashioned a harness from the last of the rope and tethered the skittish creature to the makeshift barge.

"I found one." Maura climbed aboard, handing Rath the pole. He handed it right back to her. "I need you to push while I try to convince this stubborn beast to pull. Do not waste your strength, though. Wait until I give you the signal."

The pony did not seem to approve of Rath's plan at all, but at last it responded to his tugs on the harness by wading into the water.

"Now!" Rath called to Maura. "Push!"

The raft did not budge.

"Here." He thrust the rope into Maura's hands while taking the pole from her. "See if you can coax the beast to pull harder."

He dug the pole into the silt of the riverbed and pushed until his muscles fairly groaned in protest. Still the raft did not move.

Rath cursed. He did not want the morning sun to catch them on this side of the Windle. If it did, there was far too great a likelihood the Han would also catch them.

Maura's voice rang out. Was she cursing, too? Perhaps. Rath did not understand any of the words.

"What does that mean?" he asked.

"I do not know. It is something I heard Langbard say to the pony by times. I thought it might be a beast charm."

"Beast charm?" Rath scoffed as he tried to rally his dwindling strength for one last push. "Why do you not just summon the fenfolk while you are at it, or whistle for the Waiting King and ask if he will lend us a hand."

Preposterous stories all of them—fit for no one but fools and little children.

Maura did not reply, but the raft gave a slight lurch.

"Whatever you said—" Rath jammed the pole deeper and strained until he feared his joints might pop "—say it again!"

At his urgent bidding, Maura gasped the strange words, louder this time.

Perhaps they had nothing to do with it. Perhaps the pony sensed his only way out of that cold water was to make for the far bank with all speed.

Between the animal's efforts and Rath's, the crude barge began to ease away from the shore. Just when he'd decided he could not muster another jot of effort, even if the whole Hanish army had been arrayed along the riverbank bellowing for his blood, the raft slid far enough for the current to catch.

It pitched forward, throwing Rath off balance. The pole slipped from his grasp.

He lunged for it. If it remained sticking up out of the water, it might tell the wrong people more than he wanted them to know about where he and Maura were going. As well, it might be his only means of nudging the raft to the far bank before the Windle carried them toward the Winding Rapids.

Flailing to recover his balance, Rath braced to slam into the relentless cold and deadly swiftness of the river. Then

Maura caught a fistful of his robe and pulled him back. With a sucking, scraping noise, the pole came free of the riverbed and Rath tumbled backward onto the packs.

"Hang on!" He only had breath enough to gasp those two words, though he hardly needed to.

If Maura Woodbury had any sense, she'd grab something solid and cling to it for dear life.

Once the little barge finally scraped free of the shallows, it soon made up for lost time, racing downstream, propelled by the river's turbulent springtime flow. The pony no longer had to worry about pulling the raft. It was now being dragged behind.

The poor beast's terrified whinnies stirred Rath to action. If they drifted too many more miles east, they would tumble over the Winding Rapids. He did not fancy their chances of reaching the other side undrowned...Maura's especially.

"I wish I had taken my chances with the Han." Her voice was tight with fear.

Had she never been on the water before?

"Just hold tight," Rath tried to reassure her, though he was far from confident himself. "We will be across and back on dry land soon."

"Not soon enough for me!" Maura gave a squeal as the raft bobbed high, then fell again, flinging up a great spray of cold water.

Rath braced the pole between their two packs, using it as a crude rudder to edge their barge toward the far shore. At least, that's what he *hoped* it was doing.

"We are slowing," said Maura after a few moments. "What does that mean?"

"It may mean your pony has found a foothold," Rath answered between clenched teeth. His arms felt ready to fall off, and he would be happily rid of the pain they were causing him. "Perhaps you should ask him and find out."

He thought he heard her mutter something about being vastly amusing for a man whose corpse might soon be fish food, but he had more important things to do at the moment than trade quips. "Grab on to my robe in case I start to slip."

One thing he could say for her, she was quick to follow orders.

Rath pushed the long stick deep into the water. A surge of relief buoyed him when it struck solid bottom. Giving a quick push, he lifted the pole free again and sought a fresh bit of leverage for his next thrust. Each time he lowered the pole, more and more of it reared above the surface of the water until the bottom of the barge finally struck ground.

"Untether the pony and lead it ashore," he bid Maura. "I will get the packs. Quickly, before the raft works free again."

Once they had unloaded, he pushed the raft back out until the current caught it. Now the Winding Rapids could dash the thing to pieces, with his blessing.

Rath gazed eastward. The first tentative light of dawn was beginning to glimmer in the distance. When he scrambled ashore, he could see Maura rubbing the pony down with her cloak.

He tossed the packs over the beast's back.

"Come on." He took Maura's arm. "Let us find somewhere we can hide and sleep until nightfall."

"Sleep," she murmured, listing against him until her head rested against his shoulder.

Perhaps it was only the giddiness of exhaustion, but a bewildering sense of satisfaction engulfed him. Not only because he had wriggled out of yet another tight spot, but because he had helped Maura out of one, too.

Waking overwhelmed Maura like a vicious attack. She started up from the pile of straw where she had been sleeping. For the first time in her life, she woke somewhere other than her own cozy little chamber in Langbard's cottage.

She had never seen this place before. It looked like a small barn, with a rough-hewn wooden frame and shafts of sunlight piercing narrow gaps between the wall boards.

Where was she? Her heart pounded and she struggled for breath as the memories assailed her.

Her room was gone. The cottage was gone. Langbard was gone. Everything familiar and beloved had been violently ripped from her life. And her heart along with them.

Grief gnawed at her, its teeth sharpened by guilt that she had let herself sleep and forget.

A ragged sob escaped her...followed by a gasp as Rath Talward sprang to his feet, sword in hand, between her and the half-open barn door.

When the attack he clearly expected did not come, he whirled around to confront her. "What is it? I heard you cry out."

Maura averted her face to hide her tears. She felt far too vulnerable around this man at the best of times. "Wh-when I woke up, I did not know where I was."

She heard Rath sheathe his sword. "I don't wonder at that. Your feet were still moving when we reached here this morning, but you were not awake."

The direction of his voice changed slightly. When Maura

stole a glance at him, she found him crouched before her, balancing on the balls of his feet. "It is good you were able to sleep."

"I wish I had not." With the back of her hand, Maura dashed away the tears that blurred her vision. The tears a man like Rath Talward must surely despise. "Last night, I had gotten used to it all…in a way. When I woke, it hit me all over again."

"Weep, then, if you want to." He looked rather awkward suggesting it. Endearingly awkward. "You have cause enough and we cannot go anywhere until it gets darker."

"What, are feelings something you pack away when they are inconvenient, then bring out later to air when you have time for them?"

"You make that sound like a bad thing." He pulled a droll face, then immediately grew serious again. "When you live as I have, that is what you must do to survive. If it helps, I know how you are feeling."

A strange softness in his voice and his dark eyes made her crave his sympathy with an intensity to which she dared not surrender.

"What?" she asked. "Was the person *you* cared for most in the world murdered? And the only home *you* ever knew put to the torch?" It made her gorge rise to speak of what had happened to her in such bald terms.

"No."

She had thought not.

"It was a fever took Ganny, not the Echtroi. She was too humble a soul for them to bother with. Either way, she was just as dead."

Rath's features remained impassive as he spoke, but Maura sensed the turbulence in his heart. "Her little hovel may still be standing for all I know. Without her there, it might as well have burned to the ground, for I could not stay. You would have found that too, I daresay, if Langbard's cottage had been spared and we had not needed to be off."

He was right. Maura did not have to stretch her imagination far to recognize it. She wondered if Rath Talward had ever known the luxury of peace to unpack those feelings and air them properly. Or had he buried them too deep for that?

"Your grandmother?" she asked.

Strangely it did ease her to know he had endured something similar and survived. Thinking about his situation provided her with a welcome distraction.

"Maybe." Rath jumped to his feet. "Or maybe just some daft old woman who took in an orphan babe."

He headed to where the packs lay in the straw. Nearby, the pony stood, looking as if it would be content never to budge again.

"Hungry?" Rath pulled one of Sorsha's hard-boiled eggs from the pack and tossed it to Maura before she could answer.

He took another for himself, crushing the shell in his fist, then peeling it off. Tossing the peeled egg up in the air, he caught it in his mouth and wolfed it down in three bites.

Maura glanced down at the egg in her hand. She and Rath had walked far and crossed the river after Sorsha's late supper of soup and bread. Now hunger gnawed at her belly. But so did grief, making her feel too queasy to eat.

"Bread to go with that?" Rath took out a small loaf, more

bounty from Hoghill Farm. He broke it in half, then offered one of the pieces to her.

"How did you come to be with Langbard?" he asked. "I know you called him uncle, but he said you were his ward."

"He took my mother in, before I was born. After she died, he looked after me."

Maura forced herself to peel her egg. No doubt she and Rath would have another long walk tonight, and many more in the days and nights to come. A part of her understood what he meant about putting feelings aside to survive. You could carry them in your heart, just not let them hinder you from eating or sleeping. Not let tears blind you when you needed to see, or regrets distract you when you needed to concentrate on staying alive.

And if such actions made you seem hard or unfeeling, that might not be a bad thing.

"This Ganny of yours, was she anything like Langbard?"

"No." Rath gave a grunt of laughter at the notion, then seemed to think again. "And yes, in an odd way. She was not learned, like him. Never set foot a mile from home in her life. Hadn't power of any kind. Just a poor, simple, harmless, ignorant old woman…."

He turned his back on Maura, gazing toward the door of the little barn as if he expected to see someone entering. "One who would give an ungrateful beggar the bread out of her own mouth."

The ache in his voice made a morsel of egg catch in Maura's throat.

Abruptly he spun around to face her again, his tone as hard and sharp as the blade he wielded. "Do that once too often, you sicken and die. And the world's still just as full of beggars."

Maura understood. "She followed the Elderways, you mean? She believed in the Giver?"

"Aye." Rath spat in the straw. "The Giver and the Waiting King and every other fool's tale you ever heard! Mumbling daft blessings over food so foul it did not deserve to be blessed."

Part of Maura bristled at Rath's dismissal of the Giver and the Waiting King. But another part saw past his anger and bitterness to the hurt and regret. Her belief in all things good and magical had grown easily, nurtured by Langbard's steadfast, loving presence, free from the kind of fear and want Rath Talward had known from too early an age.

"I am sorry."

"For me?" Rath stabbed his thumb toward his chest and forced his features into a look of derisive amusement that did not fool Maura for an instant. "You need not be, my lady. I learned early to fend for myself, and those lessons have served me well ever since."

He glanced toward the door, clearly eager to cut short their talk about his past. "I wonder what hour of the day it is? I should go check the sun."

With that he swung about and strode to the barn door.

"Would you like me to turn you invisible?" Maura called after him.

"Save your feathers." Rath did not look back. "I heard Langbard say they are hard to come by. We may need them worse before we reach Prum. Besides, I have a few tricks of my own for keeping out of sight that do not require magic. I would sooner rely on my own skills. I know they will not let me down."

With that, he slipped out of the barn, leaving Maura to choke down her food and to digest what he had told her about his past. She did not trust this peculiar feeling of sympathy for him that was taking root in her heart, any more than he trusted magic or the Elderways. Wariness and antagonism were a good deal safer.

He had not thought about old Ganny in years, Rath mused as he and Maura and the pony continued their journey that night.

At least, not *often*. And he had never spoken of her to another person. He had not meant to tell Maura about her. The words had just tumbled out. He had better learn to curb his tongue.

What had stirred up all those old, useless memories? he asked himself. Until they felt as raw as when he was ten years old and turned out on the streets to fend for himself?

The wizard and his ward, no doubt, with all their gabble about the Elderways and all the daft little rituals he had done his best to forget. Langbard's death, too, perhaps, and watching Maura grieve in a way he had never been able to let himself do.

Rath glanced sidelong at her moonlit shadow, wrapped in a pensive hush as she walked. He had to admit a grudging respect for how she carried on, doing what needed to be done, yet not denying the deep sorrow of her loss.

One moment she stirred his sympathy, the next moment she vexed him. Either way, she claimed far too much of his attention. This was too dangerous a time for distractions.

As if to reinforce that notion, something stirred in a clump of bushes ahead of them. If he had been as alert as usual, rather than wrapped in disturbing thoughts, he might have had an earlier warning of possible danger.

Cursing his inattention, Rath froze, pulling the pony to a halt.

"What is it?" Maura whispered.

Had she not heard? If not for him, she might have blundered into peril.

"Wait here." He handed her the pony's rope halter.

With a soft metallic hiss, his blade slid free of its scabbard.

Maura let loose her own soft hiss of reproach. "Is that how you meet every situation—with force of arms?"

"Yes!" *How else?* his tone demanded.

Every situation was a potential threat. The only way to counter a threat was with a more dire threat. This sheltered flower had better learn both those harsh truths soon unless she wanted to end up dead or worse.

Though he knew he should keep his attention fixed on the possible threat ahead of them, Rath could not resist calling softly over his shoulder, "If it will make you feel better, you can dig something out of that sash of yours."

Another rustle from the bushes roused his caution back to its proper height. He approached with slow, wary steps, senses on alert for the slightest sound or movement.

When he was within striking distance, he tensed his knees and leapt into the air, crying, "Who goes there?"

Immediately he dropped into a crouch and swung his blade, expecting to hear his enemy's whistling above his head. This trick had worked well for him before in darkness.

His blade whipped through the thin branches, but failed to make the solid contact he had expected. At the same instant, something broke from the bushes, traveling low and fast. It struck one of his legs with enough force to topple him onto his backside, cursing.

The pony gave a frightened whinny and skittered back until Maura spoke to it in a tone of firm but gentle reassurance.

The next thing Rath heard was a soft chuckle and quiet footsteps approaching.

"Well done." Maura's hand groped for his to help him up. "You saved us from an attack by that vicious creature. A woodhare, I guess, by its size and the speed it was running."

Rath scrambled up, letting go of her hand the instant he got his feet under him. "I would rather flush a hare by mistake than risk strolling into an ambush!"

"A shame you could not have caught it," replied Maura, ignoring his gruff tone. "A bit of stewed rabbit is very nourishing."

Rath sheathed his blade then groped for the pony's lead rope and marched away.

Maura fell into step with him, keeping the pony safely between them. "Do you suppose you could snare a rabbit—on purpose I mean?"

"Of course I can!" Was she *trying* to get a rise out of him? "Lived most of my life on little else but fish and small game. It is a wonder I have not sprouted fur or gills by now."

"Good," said Maura. "Then, wherever we make camp in the morning you'll set a snare or two? The fresh food Sorsha gave us is running out and I want to save the dried provisions until we have no other choice."

"You make it sound as if we were going on a long trek beyond the Great South Desert. It should not take us more than three weeks to reach Prum, unless we both break our legs and this fellow runs off on us." He patted the pony's broad rump.

"Besides," he continued after a moment, "we are well away from the Windle with no sign of anyone following us. Once we get some rest tomorrow, I think it will be safe to start traveling by day. We will be able to move even faster then."

Maura took a while to answer. "I still think it makes sense to live off the land as much as we can. It is like what you said about never having too many escape routes."

Rath could not shake the feeling that she had some secret motive behind her desire to conserve their supplies. Or perhaps his healthy sense of suspicion was running away with him?

He laughed, partly at her and partly at himself. "You are sounding more and more like an outlaw, my lady. I had better get you to your old auntie in Prum before you are thoroughly corrupted!"

Even as he spoke, his feet seemed to slow, as if he was reluctant to hasten their parting.

9

"Can we stop and rest for a while?" Maura's gaze lingered on the small lake as they passed it on their second full day of walking. "It looks so pretty and peaceful here."

Tall reeds swayed in the mild breeze and spring sunlight danced on the water between flat green leaves of pondflowers. The place entranced Maura with its beauty.

When Rath did not appear to have heard her, she raised her voice. "You will probably think this is nonsense, but I have never seen a lake before."

"Never seen a lake?" Rath cast her a dubious look. "Truly?"

Maura shook her head. "Nor an island, nor the sea. Not even a mountain, except far in the distance. That spot in Betchwood where we first met was the farthest I had ever been from Langbard's cottage."

Her grief for Langbard struck her afresh when she spoke his name. As it did every time she woke, and often after some activity or talk or other thought temporarily pushed it from her mind. Foremost among those distracting thoughts was the nagging worry of where she must go and what she must do once she had found the wise woman, Exilda, and the map.

Yet, between her sorrow for the past and her fear for the future, Maura's present journey offered surprising moments of discovery and diversion…even delight. Knowing how fleeting they could be, she treasured them all the more.

Rath turned his gaze toward the lake, as if he had not noticed it before she spoke. "Might as well stop here as anyplace, I suppose. We are not being pursued that I can tell, and we have made good speed. There is no hurry to reach this aunt of yours, unless she might have heard news about Langbard and be worried for you?"

His words reminded Maura that she *did* have a reason to get to Prum as quickly as possible. Langbard had told her the Waiting King must be woken by Solsticetide. Until she saw Exilda's map, she would have no way of knowing how much farther she must go to find him.

"That may well be." Swallowing a sigh, Maura cast a longing glance toward the lake. "And I do not want to keep you from your own…business. It was good of you to help me get away from Windleford. I do not want to trespass on your kindness any longer than I can help."

"My kindness?" Rath laughed at the notion. "You would not get very far on that! I made a bargain with Langbard and though I am an outlaw, I do keep my word."

Maura hastened to assure him she no longer doubted that.

Before she could get the words out, Rath spoke again, his voice heavy with regret. "Even if I had not promised, I still would have done what I could for you, to make up for bringing danger on you and Langbard. I did not mean for that to happen."

"No!" Maura circled around in front of the pony, planting herself in Rath Talward's path. "What happened to Langbard was *not* your fault. I know I blamed you at first, and for that I entreat your pardon."

She pointed to a tree near the lake, its branches garlanded with blushing blossoms. "Let us sit and talk a bit while we eat and let the pony graze. An hour or two hardly matters in a journey of this length. Who knows but a little rest now may help us walk all the faster when we set out again."

After a moment's consideration, Rath nodded. "That is another outlaw rule to live by. Rest and eat at the first safe spot you reach, for you may find yourself tired and hungry later when you dare not stop."

The pony had already taken advantage of their brief pause to nibble a mouthful of tender new grass.

Rath tugged the beast toward the tree. "Just a little farther, old fellow. Then you can eat and drink your fill."

"So," he said when he had turned the pony loose to graze and he and Maura had settled in the shade to eat, "how can you be so certain I am not to blame for what happened to Langbard?"

"Because he told me." Maura bit into the last of Sorsha's dried apples. "During the passing ritual. I know you do not believe in it, but I heard his voice in my mind, and shared some of his memories. You cannot imagine what comfort it brings me to have had that time with him. It is as if part of him remains with me and always will."

Out of the corner of her eye, she saw Rath squirm. The man seemed more at ease fending off accusations and insults than accepting apologies or thanks.

"If I did not draw the Echtroi down on you, what did?" His question almost made Maura choke on her apple.

She could not entrust Rath Talward with the truth, could she? He had done her good service in the past few days. Despite Sorsha's warnings and a few half-acknowledged fears of her own, he had not taken the slightest liberty with her. For some reason, his unexpected gallantry did not please her as much as it should have.

For the most part, though, he had fulfilled Langbard's original judgment of him—hardy, brave, resourceful. And, at heart, not nearly as fierce as he liked to pretend. But given his disdain for everything to do with the Elderways, it might not be in her best interest to tell him of her true errand.

Or the true danger that attended it.

At best, he might think her a madwoman and abandon her in the countryside, many miles from Prum. At worst, he might decide to turn her over to the Han in hope of a reward or clemency.

"The Echtroi came for Langbard." With so little practice at telling falsehoods, Maura doubted she had much skill. For that reason she stuck as close to the truth as she dared. "He was more important than he may have seemed to you. He had been in hiding a long while and they finally found him."

Hoping to distract Rath from asking what would make one

old wizard such a threat to the Han, she hurried on. "You could say it was we who brought danger on you."

"No worse than I could have brought on myself." Rath did not sound greatly troubled by what she had told him. Perhaps he was relieved to know that once he parted from her, the Echtroi would not be dogging his heels.

Just then, a fishhawk that had been gliding overhead in slow, graceful arcs plunged out of the sky like an arrow. An instant later, the bird rose back into the air with a triumphant shriek. Its wings pumped hard to lift the burden of a fat fish clutched in its talons.

Rath watched, nodding his approval. "Mind what you said the other night about living off the land?"

"Aye," said Maura. "What of it?"

He had flustered her when he'd questioned why they should conserve their traveling provisions. It had occurred to Maura that she might need those supplies later, when she no longer had a skilled hunter to help her find food.

Rising slowly to his feet, Rath pulled off the robe of Langbard's he had been wearing since leaving Windleford, revealing his own snug leather breeches, dark shirt and padded vest. "This might be a good place to replenish our stores. Do you know how to catch fish, or do you have a spell that will make them jump out of the water into your frying pan?"

"Of course not!" Somehow, she did not mind his teasing as she once had. "Though there is a blessing you should say to thank the Giver for the food you've been provided."

As she had expected, Rath rolled his eyes and shook his head, though he looked more amused than scornful.

"Can you teach me how to catch fish?" Maura asked. She might need any survival skills she could pick up from him.

"Aye." Rath offered his hand to hoist her up. "If we make camp here, I can show you how to set a rabbit snare, too."

After an instant's hesitation, Maura took his hand, and let him help her to her feet. But when it came time to let go again, her hesitation lasted more than an instant.

He had large, well-shaped hands. Though he held her gently, she sensed the restrained power in his grip. True, those hands had wielded weapons and done violence. But somehow she knew it had never been in a careless or remorseless manner, and never without dire cause. For all he might dismiss his old foster mother's beliefs, her example must have laid a worthy foundation that the demands of his later life had not altogether eroded.

Maura felt it in his hands and she glimpsed it in his gaze as both held her for a long, sweet, bewildering moment. The next thing she knew, his lips were drawing closer to hers. She remembered that day on the way to market when he had asked for a kiss and she had refused him. If he asked now, she would still have to refuse...though she found herself wishing otherwise.

Still closer he came. Perhaps he did not mean to ask this time, only to take what he wanted unless she made some move to stop him. How tempted she was to pretend she did not see it coming until too late.

What would Langbard say, though? He had approved of Rath Talward as her bodyguard. But not for these wages!

"P-please," she murmured. If she pursed her lips a trifle more, they might brush against Rath's. How that impulse enticed her! "I must not."

At her tremulous words, his whole body seemed to tense and harden, as though supple plant matter had been transformed into unyielding metal.

"Of course, you must not!" He released her so abruptly, she almost stumbled. "A virtuous follower of the Giver should never consort with a vile outlaw. Think how you might be corrupted."

"I think nothing of the sort!" Maura backed away, wondering if her regret for that aborted kiss blazed on her face as it ached on her lips.

"Do you not?" Rath's lip curled. "Ever since we met, you have called me nothing but lout and ruffian. Said you would rather kiss a musk-pig."

Beneath his gruff tone he sounded genuinely aggrieved. Did he *care* what she called him or how she thought of him? Most of the time, he seemed to relish shocking her with his menacing pose.

"I only called you a lout when you acted like one," Maura protested. "Which you have often gone out of your way to do."

She hesitated for a moment, wanting to tell him the truth about why she could not kiss him. At least, as much of the truth as she dared. Before she could decide how much that might be, another fishhawk plunged out of the sky, quite near.

Ignoring her reproach, Rath bent over and picked up a pebble. Then, with a sudden release of tightly coiled strength, he sent it skipping over the still surface of the lake with a succession of soft splashes, each coming quicker than the last.

Maura needed something to do with her hands, lest they reach for Rath Talward. She needed something to do with the restless energy his nearness had kindled within her.

Spotting a small stone nestled in the grass, she picked it

up and tried to copy Rath's swift, fluid release. Her pebble hit the water and sank with a loud, clumsy gulp that seemed to shatter the brittle tension between them.

Rath laughed, with only a hint of mockery. "Well, that was truly pitiful."

He made a quick search nearer the shore, then handed Maura a flat, smooth stone that looked like a coin with a bulging middle.

"Hold it like this." He demonstrated the proper grip with another pebble he had picked up.

When she could not duplicate it, exactly, he nudged her thumb and forefinger into the proper positions. "Now watch me."

For the next hour he tutored her in this amusing but useless art as if both their lives depended on it. When Maura finally made her stone perform three little hops before disappearing into the lake, he thumped her on the back by way of praise.

Then he set about teaching her a few more serviceable skills with surprising thoroughness and patience. Not once did he mention what had almost happened between them. Nor did he try to make it happen again.

Maura told herself she should approve Rath's unexpected show of discretion. Just as she should welcome his new, comradely manner that refused to acknowledge her womanhood or any troublesome spark of attraction between them.

If only she could match his knack for ignoring the potent awareness that prickled beneath her skin, anticipating and savoring his most casual touch.

And the faint sting of shame that followed it.

* * *

"See that?" Rath whispered, pointing toward a faint path in the grass that ran from a small stand of trees down to the lake.

Maura edged closer to him. "What did you say?"

The warm spring light played over her hair, until a scattering of strands shimmered like sunbeams.

Rath tried to ignore it but the subtle pungency of new growth all around stirred his senses, making them far too responsive to every glimpse, murmur and whiff of Maura.

It was a good thing she had stopped him from taking that kiss he would surely have regretted. He knew she was not the kind of woman to embark on a casual, passing frolic with a fellow like him. Though he had flirted with the notion of settling down to a dull but honest life, he had since thought better of it.

If he was not careful, the solitude and tranquility of the lake would lull his deeply ingrained caution. For the past several days, he and Maura had been constantly on the move during their waking hours, with the pack pony providing a safe buffer between them. Their new activities kept him closer to her than was good for his self-control.

"There, where the grass is worn down." He forced his thoughts to the task at hand. Never had they rebelled so stubbornly to his will. "That is a way small creatures come to the water at night. It is where we must set our snare."

He scratched away a clump of grass, then scooped out a handful of soft brown dirt, which he rubbed on his hands.

"What are you doing?" Maura shot him a suspicious look.

"Masking my scent so it will not ward our prey away from the snare." He offered her some dirt. "Rub this onto the string."

Understanding glimmered in her gaze along with something Rath had seen so seldom he did not trust himself to recognize it.

Admiration? No, it could not be.

As he set the snare, Maura hovered close, watching his every move, whispering questions. Rath did his best to answer and to explain each step, though part of him felt daft for bothering.

Once he delivered the lady to Prum, he doubted she would ever need to snare small game. Yet she fixed her attention upon him with the air of a person whose survival might depend upon mastering these skills of rough living.

After the snare was set to his satisfaction, Rath fetched a bit of waxed string from his pack, along with a hook carved from bone. Then he cut a long supple stick to make a fishing rod.

On a narrow finger of land that thrust some distance into the lake, he sank onto the grass and pried off his boots, then rolled his breeches up to his knees. Maura followed his lead, pulling off her walking boots and hitching up her skirts.

When Rath caught a glimpse of her slender bare feet and shapely naked calves, the April sun seemed to shine hot upon his face. He forced himself to concentrate on assembling the fishing rod and showing Maura how to cast the line out into the water.

"Get a good grip on the rod," he warned her. "If a big fish goes for the bait, you do not want it pulled out of your hands."

"Like this?" The murmur of the gentle west wind through the rushes made a delicate music to accompany the beguiling lilt of Maura's voice. She grasped the slender wooden pole near the end with her right hand, then wrapped the fingers of her left hand over the other fist.

"Bring one down more." Keeping his distance, Rath tried to instruct her by pointing. "And the other up a ways to give you more control when you cast."

Maura fumbled with the rod, trying to place her hands the way he had told her.

"Here, let me show you." Against his better judgment, he took up a position behind her, wrapping his hands over hers. "Cast the line out like this. Then pull it through the water this way, so the fish will think that bug on the end of your hook is moving."

"You know," said Maura, "it was not what you thought... the reason I stopped you from kissing me."

What made her bring that up now? It was not a talk they should be having while his arms were wrapped around her. But when Rath tried to pull away from her, he could not. "What makes you think I was going to kiss you?"

"Nothing!" Maura glanced back at him. "And everything! Are you saying you would *not* have kissed me if I had let you?"

Rath thrust out his chin. "Would it have been such a crime if I had? Like rest and food, pleasure is one of those things a body ought to take whenever the chance comes."

She tossed her head, making her thick glossy braid slap against his cheek. "What makes you so certain a kiss from me would bring you pleasure?"

Rath could not let a challenge like that go unanswered, even though he sensed what dangerous combat it might spark.

"There are some things a man just...knows." His tongue caressed every word as he leaned closer to Maura. "What makes you so certain a kiss from me would *not* bring you pleasure? Have you ever been properly kissed by a man? One of the lads from the village, perhaps?"

"A Windleford lad?" Maura laughed and some of the tension eased out of her body. "Between their fear of Langbard and their fear of the Han, there was not a lad in the village brave enough to speak to me, let alone try anything more daring."

What a pack of fools!

"I could not let you kiss me, no matter how pleasant it might be," said Maura, "because…I am promised to another man."

"Of course. The aunt in Prum—I should have known." Rath let go of her and backed away. "You seem to have gotten the knack of angling."

No sooner had he put a safe distance between them than the line went taut and Maura squealed.

"Do not let go!" Rath cried.

It had taken him a while to find a likely looking branch for a rod, and he did not want to lose it in the lake. The next thing he knew, he was standing behind her again, his legs braced and his hands gripping the rod over hers. The power of the pull on the end of the line surprised him.

Maura let out a trill of anxious laughter, followed by another squeal when the rod gave a sudden twitch in her hands and almost tipped her off balance.

"What have you snagged, lass, a lake lizard?" The fish was either very big or a fierce fighter—perhaps both.

"Lake lizard!" Maura's grasp slackened.

She backed away from the water, but had nowhere to go… except to press herself tight against him. Rath almost lost his grip, too. On more than the fishing rod.

"Hang on!" He could barely force the words out, for every breath he inhaled filled his nostrils with the scent of her. "And do not be daft. There is no such thing as lake lizards."

"So you say." Maura did not sound convinced, and she did not budge an inch away from him, but she did clasp the fishing rod tighter.

"So I say." Rath nodded, in part to feel the whisper of her hair against his cheek. "And since I have seen more than one lake in my life, you may take my word. This is a big fish, with plenty of fight in him. If we can land the creature, we will eat well for our trouble. We must tire him out."

For what seemed like a very long time, yet not half as long as Rath would have liked, they nestled together, fighting the fish. Pulling it toward the shore as close as they dared without breaking the rod, then leaning forward and letting the tip of the rod dip beneath the water surface as they allowed the fish to swim away before dragging it back again.

Rath fought a similar battle with his self-control. Until today, he had been able to rely on his will to curb his passions. But how was a man to resist the temptation of a woman in his arms, her hair blowing in his face and the soft curve of her backside pressed against the lap of his breeches? By the time they landed the gasping, writhing fish, Rath was ready to collapse onto the ground, writhing and gasping along with it!

"That should make a fine meal," said Maura, her voice breathless from their long fight with the fish. "A pleasant change from cheese and cold mutton sausage, at least."

Her hands trembled as the fishing rod fell from her grasp.

"You build the fire." Rath pulled his knife from his belt. "I will gut it."

"A moment!" Maura held up one hand to forestall him. The other she reached toward the fish which gave one final violent twitch, then lay still.

"A moment for what?" Rath ran the pad of his thumb over the blade of his knife.

"The blessing I told you about. To thank the Giver and to dispatch the spirit of this creature back to the water."

"Spirit? Of a fish?"

Maura lifted her face to his. Her gaze flashed a challenge, while the slope of her brows conveyed a wistful entreaty. "Do you not believe that all living things have spirits?"

"I am not certain *I* have a spirit, let alone that dead fish." Rath pointed with his knife. "But do what you will. I need to go sharpen my blade."

Before she could reply, he stalked off to find his whetstone. When he returned to clean their catch, his disdain was honed to a fine edge, as well.

"So, is your Giver all thanked and this fat fellow content to be eaten?"

When Maura nodded, Rath thrust the point of his knife into the fish's belly and sliced it open with one fierce slash. As he thrust his bare hand in to wrench out the slimy innards, he glanced up at Maura with narrowed eyes ready to relish her look of disgust.

But she defied his expectations. Her head tilted in a pensive, curious manner. "What did the Giver ever do to harm you, Rath Talward? How can something you claim not to believe in do you harm?"

Such daft questions did not deserve answers. Yet words seemed to form on Rath's tongue without his leave. And they were too bitter not to spit out.

"It *can* do you harm when others believe and act on those beliefs in foolish ways."

He forced his attention back to the fish. He would rather gut and clean a hundred stinking fish than talk about this.

"The old woman who raised you?" Her gentle tone slipped the question beneath his guard. "Was she unkind? You did not make her sound so when you spoke of her before."

"Ganny, unkind?" Rath could not summon words strong enough to denounce the wicked folly of that notion. "She would not have known how to be!"

"Then how did her beliefs harm you?" Maura asked. "Langbard taught me the Way of the Giver is one of peace and respect for all life."

When Rath did not answer, she added, "I do not mean to be contrary. I only want to understand."

Rath found his voice. "Then understand this." He jabbed the air with his knife for emphasis. "Those too-peaceful beliefs were to blame for our hard life and for her death. Always looking out for other folk who never returned the favor. Biding patient and stupid as a sheep for the Waiting King to return, all the while the wolves were circling."

With a fierce slash, he cut the fish's head off, then its tail. "I learned from her folly, though. Since then, I refuse to trust in anything but my own strength and guile. And I refuse to care about anything but my own survival."

He tossed the gutted fish to the ground in front of Maura. "You may not think it a very noble creed, but it has kept me alive all these years. That is more than I can say for Ganny and your Giver!"

In the wake of his rant, a strange sense of relief settled on Rath, the way a seething belly calmed after a violent bout of retching.

No doubt Maura would respond with scolding or argument. He hoped she would. A good battle of words might be just what he needed to cure the sweet ache in his flesh she had inflicted.

He cleaned his blade on the grass, then wiped it with a scrap of oiled cloth before thrusting it back in its sheath. When she did not reply at once, he ventured a wary glance at her.

But she did not glare back at him, or even look toward him. She had picked up the cleaned body of the fish, now nothing more than a piece of fresh food. With an absent air, she gazed down at it, one finger sliding over its smooth skin.

"It kept you alive," she mused softly, more to herself than to him. "I wonder—is that kind of life worth living?"

Her gentle query stung Rath hard, in a place he had thought himself invulnerable. So he did what he'd always done whenever he had been fool enough to wander into an ambush.

He fled.

Maura did not think much of it when Rath stalked off after cleaning their catch. Surely he would return to eat.

For the next little while, she had plenty to occupy her. First she built a small fire, then seasoned the fish with a sprinkle of herbs and wrapped it in several layers of wet pondflower leaves. Finally she buried it in the hot ashes to cook.

With all that, she scarcely spared a thought for Rath until she raked the charred bundle out of the ashes and unwrapped it, sending a subtle but appetizing aroma wafting off on the mild evening air. Still he did not come.

What ailed the man?

She had challenged his unbelief and the merits of a life lived with no thought for anyone but himself. What of it?

When Langbard first took him in, over her objections, she had said any number of things that should have offended him far worse. He had appeared impervious to her insults, often pretending to be flattered by them.

Could he have some other reason for abandoning her? As darkness began to fall with no sign of his return, Maura grew more and more certain that was what Rath Talward had done.

Had their disagreement reminded him of the way he meant to live his life? He had strayed from that self-contained path in recent days—keeping guard while she had attended to Langbard's passing ritual, helping her escape from Windleford, then escorting her this far south. Contrary to his self-serving creed, he had risked much for her.

Perhaps he had recognized it himself and feared he might be sliding down a slippery slope toward the kind of selfless virtues he claimed to despise. Or perhaps he had hoped to receive her favors in payment for his services. Upon discovering she was not prepared to make such a bargain, he might have decided the whole venture was no longer worth his trouble.

At least he'd had the decency to leave her the pony and supplies. As Maura faced the prospect of continuing her journey without him, that provided slight comfort.

In an effort to soothe her mounting alarm, she tried to commune with the Giver. But never had it felt so remote—as though it dwelt far off, among the distant stars that glittered in the night sky, rather than quickening every living thing around her.

Wrapped in her cloak beside the banked fire, she fell into a restless sleep, plagued by fearful dreams. The forces massed against her loomed larger and more menacing than ever. Not just the Han and the Echtroi, but lawless Umbrians, wild animals, distance and terrain. Her own resources were pitiful by comparison, and dwindling.

Against all reason, she had felt safe in Rath Talward's company. It might have been nothing more than an illusion, but it had brought her some comfort and enabled her to carry on.

Later that night, the sound of stealthy footsteps roused her from a fitful doze. All her fretting had been for nothing—Rath Talward had come slinking back at last.

Resentment and relief warred within her.

Suddenly, rough, powerful hands seized her and a large, foul-smelling palm clamped over her mouth. Maura tried to scream, though a curiously detached part of her wondered why she bothered when there was no one to come to her aid. Not that it mattered, for the beefy hand muffled her cries. When she drew breath through her nose to fuel her struggle, the reek of unwashed flesh made her gag.

She tried to use some of the tricks that had proven so effective against Rath, the morning he had made the mistake of grabbing her from behind. But the person who held her had no wounds she could exploit...at least none that she knew of. She writhed in her captor's grip, all the same, pummeling his stout legs with her heels, though she might have been kicking a tree trunk for all the good it did.

From out of the shadows came the voice of another man. "Sounds like you have bagged yourself a hissing hillcat, Orl. Think it needs to learn some manners?"

The man who held Maura gave a garbled grunt.

An instant later, another hand lunged out of the darkness

to clout her on the side of the face. The shock of the blow stunned her. Pain thundered through her head.

"Another peep and I will hit you *hard* next time," growled her assailant in a tone of harsh satisfaction that warned Maura he would welcome the opportunity.

Clenching her teeth, Maura managed to mute a sob into a faint whimper. She prayed it would slip beneath the threshold for more punishment.

It must have, for the man who had struck her moved away and spoke to someone else. "Just her?"

"Looks like." To Maura's ringing ears, the pitch of the answering voice suggested a younger or smaller man.

"Is she daft, coming here alone?" asked the first man.

Both the other fellow and the one holding Maura replied with scornful sniggers.

What would they do to her? If they'd meant to kill her outright, she would not be alive now. A warning of Rath's sent a deathly chill of panic through Maura.

"Compared to some...I am a perfect flower of honor."

She was not quite as innocent as he'd believed her. She might have little experience of men, but she had some information that Sorsha had relayed from Newlyn about the ways a woman could be mistreated. The last thing in the world she wanted was to learn about them firsthand.

10

"Has the wench got anything worth taking?" asked the fellow who seemed to be in command, the one who had struck Maura.

"Just food and such in the packs, Turgen. But there is a pony."

So they were outlaws...not that Maura had been in much doubt. The question about anything worth taking made her remember her sash. She might be able to reach one of the lower pockets without squirming too much and risking another cuff from Turgen. But what could she reach that would be of any use to her?

Cuddybird feathers would be wasted in the dead of night. Spidersilk was really only effective against a single enemy. Madfern, perhaps, or dreamweed? With those, she ran the risk of dazing or drowsing herself along with the outlaws, unless she could get upwind to cast the spells. Then there was the matter of getting her mouth free to speak the incantation.

"Not a bad night's takings," muttered Turgen. "Been a while since we got a woman."

The leer in his voice sent a chill through Maura.

But it was nothing to the dread that engulfed her when the other outlaw replied, "Hope she lasts longer'n the last one."

That decided her. She must act the instant she got a chance. Until then, she must find some way to master her panic, so she would not be too flustered or too numb to take advantage of her first decent opportunity.

In case it proved to be her last.

Rath returned to the lakeshore in the waning hours of the night, resolved to put as much distance as he could between himself and Maura Woodbury. As soon as he could.

While he still could.

The quarrelsome exchange between them that had set him to flight had made him face the truth he'd been struggling to ignore. His brief alliance with her had already begun to change him in subtle ways he could not abide. If he let her get any tighter hold on him, those changes might threaten his survival.

How had she gained so much influence over him in such a short time? True, she was a fine-looking lass and he regretted that they had not been able to take enjoyment in one another. But he had long since discovered the danger in letting the transient pleasure of a woman mean anything more.

Was it possible the wizard's ward had worked some kind of enchantment over him? He did feel strangely at odds with himself, and less in control of his own actions than he had been in a great while. Perhaps his original suspicion of Maura had not been groundless after all.

He had returned to her, hadn't he, when cold reason warned him to keep on walking and forget he had ever met her?

The force of his obligation had drawn him back the way a rod and line snared a squirming fish, the odor of which still hung in the air around the campsite.

But Maura, the pony and the packs had all disappeared.

Rath tried to dismiss the uneasy chill that seeped into his bones on that mild spring night. He should get some rest. Whether Maura had gone looking for him or decided to part ways, he had no way of knowing. Nor had he any hope of finding her until he had some light to see. Until then, the least wasteful use of his time would be to sleep.

Determined to do just that, Rath slid his sword from its scabbard. Then he pulled his cloak around him and settled himself in a sitting position, with his back to the oak's broad trunk. Taking the hilt of his sword in his right hand, he drew his dagger with his left and held them crossed in front of him, ready to lash out in defense the instant he stirred. Woe to any fool who blundered upon him before the sun rose!

Thus armed and determined to snatch an hour's sleep, Rath found he could not rest no matter how hard he tried. In fact, the harder he tried, the worse sleep eluded him.

Maura was probably not in any danger. She had plenty of vitcraft tricks at her disposal to keep her from harm. He had seen firsthand how effective they could be. Even if she were in danger, it was no concern of his, much less his responsibility.

Was that what she had told herself, he wondered, when she

had seen the Han closing in to slaughter him? Or when they had called their hounds? Or when he had swooned in the brook, miles from Langbard's cottage?

If she had, she'd been right. His fate should not have mattered to her. Certainly not enough to risk her own safety as she had. Not once, but three times. She'd known nothing about him, except that he was an outlaw. If anything, that should have disposed her against him.

Though he was not sorry to have escaped, Rath wished his deliverance had come by some other means. Not since he was a motherless babe had anyone done so much for him, asking so little in return. He could not fathom it. It made him feel both highly privileged and deeply unworthy. He could not decide which of the two unsettled him worst.

Slowly his weariness began to overcome his disquiet, until there were only two questions left that it could not subdue. Around and around in his mind they chased one another, demanding answers but finding none. Where had Maura gone? And why?

Rath told himself he did not care. When that failed he told himself he *should not* care.

The lass belonged to another man, after all. And even if she had not, there could be nothing lasting between a woman like her and a man like him. He should not care what became of her. But Rath had knocked around the kingdom long enough and hard enough to know that people did not always oblige a body by doing what they should.

At last, just when he should have begun to stir, he fell asleep. Not long, yet long enough and deep enough that he woke with a start of alarm to find the sun a finger's width above the low eastern horizon.

Rath shook himself awake and leapt to his feet, cursing. His gaze swept the campsite looking for answers to his questions.

The fire appeared to have died out on its own. A blackened bundle rested against the circle of stones that had contained the small blaze. Sheathing his sword, Rath stooped to examine it more closely. It turned out to be a packet of overlapping pondflower leaves wrapped around a generous portion of seasoned fish.

Had Maura saved this for him to eat when he returned? A spasm of shame clenched his belly. Or had she kept it to break her own fast this morning? If so, why had she left it behind?

He checked the surrounding grass, searching for more clues. A wide swath around the fire had been trodden down, but he and Maura might have done all that. A narrower trail led to where the pony had been tethered...though not as narrow as Rath would have expected.

It appeared more than two people had gone that way, though Rath was quick to admit Maura might have made several trips back and forth from the fire. As he followed the pony's trail away from the lake, he became convinced that more than one person had gone with it.

Soon Rath found evidence that he'd been right...though he would far rather have been proven wrong. In a place where the ground was soft and the grass scant, he spied a clear footprint—one a good deal larger than Maura's.

When he stepped on the spot with his own boot, the other print spread out longer and wider. All Rath's conflicting feelings about Maura fell away, then, mown down by an urgent drive to find her and make certain she was safe.

He started to follow the trail at a crouching run, but before he had gone far, his stomach gave an empty gurgle. Remembering the packet of fish in his hand, he stripped off the burnt outer leaves and began wolfing down the food as he ran.

He tried to keep from fretting too much over Maura's disappearance. Imagining her in danger would only distract him. Perhaps the fellow with the huge feet meant her no harm. Perhaps she had gone with him willingly, exchanging one protector for another. Hard as Rath tried to convince himself that there might be nothing sinister behind her leaving, all his instincts and all his experience urged him to make haste after her.

Do not fret. Do not fret!

Over and over Maura repeated those words to herself as the outlaws bore her farther away from the lake. After a time, the litany ran through her head like an enchantment.

Except, this enchantment was not working.

Her heart continued to hammer. Her belly churned. And it felt as though an unuttered scream had lodged in her throat, choking off her breath. Her cheek ached where Turgen had hit her and her ear still stung from the blow.

Men who struck a woman with such casual violence or handled her the way Orl did, as if she were a sack of vegetables rather than a living creature, would not hesitate to degrade and abuse her for their pleasure until she died of their ill treatment or did away with herself from despair. Tears prickled her eyes and that voiceless sob edged a little higher in her throat.

Keep thinking like that and you will not stand a chance in the world. She heard Rath's words as clearly in her mind as she had heard Langbard's the night of the fire, when he had been past communicating with her any other way.

The tone was blunt and faintly scornful. It made Maura clench her teeth and swallow her tears, even if they did choke her. She would show Rath Talward! Just because he had abandoned her did not mean she would curl into a quivering ball of fright. She would not give him the satisfaction.

Indeed, my lady? Then what are you going to do?

Just what she had planned from the beginning, of course. She would conserve her strength and wait for the first moment her hands and feet were free.

She had rescued Rath from the Han, hadn't she? When he had tried to throttle Langbard, she had put a stop to it. And when he had grabbed her from behind that first morning at the cottage, she had fought her way free. She would show *these* ruffians their error accosting defenseless women in the dead of night!

The night began to wane. Off to Maura's right, the sky had taken on a soft glow, the color of queensbalm petals. That must mean they were heading south, for which Maura was grateful. Once she escaped—she savored that reassuring thought—at least she would not need to double back to reach Prum.

The turf that lurched and swayed beneath her looked like heath, with many moss-covered outcroppings of broken rock and scattered clusters of low scrub. The ground appeared to be rising. Maura wondered if Rath would think any of that significant.

Not that she cared whether he would or not. She wished she could get him and his disparaging comments out of her mind and keep them out. Though she had to admit, they'd shaken her out of her crippling panic. For that she was grudgingly grateful.

Just then, Orl broke the silence of their march with a garbled grunt that ended in the rising tone of a question.

"I don't care!" snapped Turgen, as if he had understood. "Set the wench on her feet and let her walk the rest of the way. It is not far to camp."

Then he added, in a tone that made Maura's stomach plunge, "Aye, set her down. I would not mind getting a look at her now that there is light to see."

Quick to do as he was bidden, Orl stopped and unloaded Maura off his beefy shoulder.

This was it—her chance to escape. Before they got her back to their camp where she might be surrounded by too many people to subdue with a single spell. Or where someone might recognize the significance of her sash and take it away from her. Then she would truly be at their mercy.

In the short time it took for Orl to set her on the ground, Maura's mind raced. Sleep, daze or invisibility? Which spell should she use?

Sleep, she decided with barely a heartbeat to deliberate. The pocket that held the dreamweed would be easiest of the three to reach. And unlike the precious cuddybird feathers, dreamweed flourished in most eastern woods, readily available to someone like her who knew what to look for. Besides, her captors must be tired after a night stalking the countryside. That would make them vulnerable to a sleep spell.

As Orl eased his tight grip on her arms, she reached toward her sash. But her fingers felt so wooden and clumsy, she feared she would not be able to fumble the pocket open or dig out a pinch of the powdered weed if she tried.

Do not waste your chance. Rath's voice whispered in her thoughts. This time he did not sound scornful. *Play for time.*

Though her hand prickled with the fierce urge to strike back at her captors and her legs ached to run the moment they came to rest on solid ground, she sensed that neither would be able to do what she demanded of them just then.

"Can you believe our luck, lads? We have snared a beauty." Turgen's voice came from so nearby, Maura shrank back in dismay.

A good thing she had not reached for her dreamweed or he could have caught her before she had a chance to use it. If she acted very docile, now, perhaps the bandits might let down their guards, giving her a better opportunity.

Good lass! That's using your head.

When a shiver ran through her, she did not try to hide it. Instead she pulled her cloak tighter around her as if she were cold or fearful of being touched. Both were true. But more important than either, Maura needed to keep her sash hidden and to conceal her hands as she rummaged in the pockets

Adopting an air of timidity that was only a little exaggerated, she lifted her gaze to observe her captors. There were three of them. She'd been right about that much. Even before any of them spoke again, she had no trouble figuring out who was who.

The fellow whose name she did not know led the pony. As she had guessed, he was shorter and slighter than his companions. The patch of downy whiskers on his chin confirmed his age. If she could bind the other two with a spell, she might be able to fight or flee this stripling.

Orl, the one who had seized and carried her this far, stood a head taller than any man she had ever seen. His blunt fingers were each nearly as thick as her wrists. The roundness of his big face, and the fact that he was missing three front teeth, gave him the appearance of an overgrown child. That did not make Maura fear him any less.

Though not half so much as she feared their leader, Turgen. In some ways, he reminded her of Rath. The two men had a similar hard build and battered features. Turgen appeared to hold with Rath's opinions about proper outlaw grooming. His dark hair looked as though it had been hacked to its present shoulder length with a dull knife by a blind barber.

There, all similarity ended.

While Rath had a hard, dangerous look and manner, seasoned with a dash of mocking impudence, Turgen had a truly sinister, predatory air.

When he raised his hand, Maura flinched. But he only ran his fingers over her hair as if perfectly entitled to do it...or anything else he might wish to do to his prisoner. The excessive delicacy of his touch still managed to suggest lurking violence that could erupt without warning.

"Seems a shame to let Vang have her first, after we went to all the trouble of finding her, now, doesn't it, lads?" With his forefinger, Turgen traced her features—the tilt of her nose, the curve of her mouth.

Meanwhile, Maura's fingers edged toward her sash and the pocket that contained the ground dreamweed leaves. Let the knave touch her face as though it were his to admire or punish as he wished. Let him believe he had her even more terrified than he did. It clearly amused him and kept him from doing anything worse while her hands and feet recovered.

Out of the corner of her eye, Maura spied the younger outlaw scuffing the heath with the toe of his boot.

"I want no part of it," he muttered. "Vang won't like it."

Turgen's fingertip froze on Maura's chin. She closed her eyes, expecting a blow. Some instinct told her when this man was crossed, he could lash out at whoever was nearest.

When Turgen spun about to confront his younger comrade, Maura opened her eyes again and heaved a soft sigh of relief.

"You know your trouble, you whining whelp?" Turgen took a menacing step toward him. "You spend too much time worrying what Vang will like and what he won't."

He let fly a backhand cuff that would have lifted the young fellow off his feet. But the lad ducked and danced back a step.

Don't just stand there gaping, lass! The thought jolted Maura. She would never get a better opportunity.

The younger outlaw had drawn Turgen several steps away. Orl's attention was fixed on his comrades, as Maura's had been.

Whispering the words of the incantation, she reached into a large pocket on her sash and pulled out a generous pinch of dreamweed. Then she skipped a few steps to her left, to put the west wind behind her.

Her sudden movement made the trio of outlaws turn toward her, their differences forgotten. As they swarmed after her, Maura opened her hand and blew the powdered dreamweed at them. The delicate little cloud of herb powder wafted on the air.

It looked so pitifully inadequate to stop the three men lumbering toward her. Orl, least of all. A man his size would probably bathe in a vat of dreamweed tea without raising a yawn.

Hitching up her skirts with one hand, Maura turned to run. With her other hand, she fumbled at her sash. Perhaps the dreamweed would slow the outlaws long enough for her to reach the cuddybird feathers. She could hear the outlaws coming behind her, but she dared not spare the time to glance back.

Then something made her cloak catch tight around her throat, choking her and jerking her backward. Dazed, gasping for breath, she fell back, colliding with something large, solid and malodorous. Orl, no doubt.

Her fall must have knocked him off balance, too. For before Maura could catch her breath, they both began to tumble down the gentle slope. When they finally came to rest, Maura struggled to her knees, trying desperately to muster her rattled wits.

Orl sprawled nearby in a great senseless lump.

Had the sleep spell finally taken effect? Or had he bashed his head against an outcropping of rock during their fall? It did not matter, Maura told herself. As long it kept him from following her, she would consider it a blessing.

She tried to rise and run, but her head went into a dizzy spin that brought her to her knees. Unable to stand, she crawled toward a small thorn thicket. By the time she reached it, her dizziness had lifted enough to see the three outlaws lying about on the heath, sound asleep.

How she longed to join them—but she must not! If she succumbed to the sleep spell, she would be worse off than ever, and her efforts would all have been in vain.

What to do? A few moments ago, thoughts had raced through her mind. Now they felt bloated and cumbersome. It took all her dwindling strength to budge them. Where was Rath Talward's mocking advice when she most needed it?

Somehow, Maura knew it would have goaded her to action. But, like the man himself, it had deserted her.

No! She fought to keep her eyes open. Rath's advice could not leave her if she refused to let it go. What would he say if he were here?

She let all her other sluggish thoughts slumber to concentrate on that one. Just when she feared sleep would claim her, she imagined, or perhaps dreamed, Rath standing over her. What was he saying?

You put everyone to sleep with your sorcery. Can you not use it to revive yourself?

"I have told you." She spoke the words aloud. "It is *not* sorcery!"

The force of her anger went some way toward rousing her. Rath's answer did the rest. Of course, she had something to rouse her—in her sash. She had not used all her supply of quickfoil in the futile effort to revive Langbard.

She tried several pockets before she found the herb, and she had no hot water to brew a tea. Instead she placed a few crumbs of dried leaf on her tongue and let the sharp tang quicken her torpid thoughts. As she had rummaged through the sash for quickfoil, now she plundered her memory for the incantation. At last she remembered the first few words. By the time she said those she was beginning to feel more alert. Other words came to her until she had spoken them all.

A tide of energy and renewed confidence surged within her. She knew just what she must do next. Staggering to her feet, Maura resolved to unload everything from the pony but a little food. Then she would climb onto the beast's back and ride as far from here as it would carry her.

Before she could fully savor the heady draft of hope, a sharp, resonant voice rang out behind her. "Blade and blood, witch! What did you do to Turgen and his lads?"

Before she could reach her small hoard of cuddybird feathers, rough hands seized her arms and she was spun about to face a hulking man whose left eyelid had been crudely stitched shut over an empty socket.

As the sweet wine of hope turned to vinegar on her tongue, desperation made her defiant. "Who are you to care?"

The monstrous man gave a gust of harsh laughter and pounded his massive chest with his thumb. "I am their leader. Vang Spear of Heaven."

Why had she even asked? The moment the daft question left her lips, she'd known who he must be.

In three swift strides, the bandit leader reached her. "I can wait to learn your name, witch…"

As she quailed before the ferocity of his one-eyed glare, Vang reached beneath her cloak. "Until I take this."

One massive hand closed around her sash and yanked hard. Maura gave a gasp of surprise and pain as the stitching ripped over her shoulder and the bandit leader robbed her of her only defense.

11

As he followed her trail south, Rath wished he had Maura's sash with him. He could do with a drink of that potion she'd given him to wash down the bear fur on the night of the fire—something to keep him alert and give him fresh energy. Stopping for a moment to catch his breath, he took a quick sip from his drink skin, but it was not the same.

Gazing around from the wooded ridge of a low hill, Rath took his bearings, trying to figure out where Maura might be bound. She, and the man or men with her, appeared to be headed due south, which puzzled him. Most folk would have gone west to Long Vale, a wide strip of fertile farming land in the lee of the Blood Moon Mountains. Travel and trade between Norest and Southmark flowed through the vale.

A less popular choice might be to make east for the coast,

then hire passage on boat in one of the harbor villages. It made no sense for Maura to do that, since Prum was far inland.

Straight south lay Aldwood and beyond that Lost Lake, where few dared venture and from which fewer ever returned. Between there and the Sea of Dawn, the Unnamed River oozed through the Far Fens. Apart from the bowels of the Blood Moon Mountains themselves, there were few parts of the kingdom Rath had less inclination to explore.

For all that, once he had recovered a crumb of energy, he set off south at a quiet steady lope, like a tawny wolf tracking its prey. Like a wolf, too, he kept his senses alert for any subtle warnings of danger.

The sun had risen quite high behind thick banks of cloud by the time he reached Battle Heath, north of Aldwood.

"What's all this?" he muttered to himself, puzzling the riddle of tracks on the turf.

Maura and her companion had stopped here, long enough for the pony to forage on a small patch of grass and relieve itself. The party had spread out, too, by the look of it, though why, Rath could not guess. At least, not until he examined the terrain more closely.

In one spot a wide path of bracken had been flattened, as if something large had rolled or slid over it. Whatever it was had gouged the turf in two spots and...

Rath peered closer at a jagged spur of rock. Was that blood? He had seen enough of the stuff in his life to be tolerably certain.

With renewed urgency he scoured the area. A tiny flash of color caught his eye from a clump of bushes. When Rath checked it, he found a long thread of green wool fluttering in the breeze. He would wager good coin it had come from Maura's cloak.

While he knelt there staring at the thread, his nose twitched, smelling something that did not belong. The faint tang of herbs reminded him of Langbard's cottage.

How did all these small clues fit together to explain what had happened here? Scores of possibilities clamored in his thoughts. Some quite innocent. Others too alarming to dwell on. Rath forced them all from his mind.

Whatever had happened, Maura was no longer here, so he must waste no more time here, either. He must pick up the trail again and follow it until he found her. Then she could satisfy his curiosity with the whole story.

After making a rapid circuit of the area, Rath picked up some clear tracks again, still pointing south. Unless he was much mistaken, more people had joined the party.

The clouds began to spit fat drops of rain. Rath hoped it would not turn into a full-fledged storm and wash away the tracks he was following.

Slightly rested from his short pause, he set off, torn between the conflicting needs for haste and stealth. If only he had a few of those feathers Maura had used to make him invisible to the Han. And might there be some herb that lent a man the ability to run faster and farther?

Giving a wry shake of his head, he muttered under his breath, "Never thought I'd live to see myself hankering after sorcery!"

A chuckle froze in his throat. He dove to the ground.

He had just mounted the crest of a low ridge that overlooked Aldwood. The great forest stretched off to the east as far as he could see and for some distance to the west, as well. Around the fringe of the wood, Rath could make out several men coming and going. He hoped they had not marked his presence.

From some distance within the borders of the forest, slender plumes of smoke rose above the tree tops. Rath guessed they came from the cook fires of a large and well-organized camp.

But whose?

The sound of voices behind him sent Rath scrambling for cover. If the two men who strode into view a few moments later had been more alert, he might have found himself in a vat of boiling trouble. Luckily they were deep in talk and never spared a glance his way.

"That will have Turgen in a temper, no mistake!" said the taller of the pair, who carried a short bow over his shoulder. "I'll wager Vang had a fine laugh over it, the three of 'em laid out cold like that."

"I'd have paid good coin to see it," replied the other fellow. "How do ye reckon she did it?"

The bowman shrugged. "Witchery of some sort. I would not meddle with her but Vang is bound to get to the bottom of it. Mark me, he is looking over his shoulder these days. Anything that bids fair to help him hang on, he will use it."

"Aye, he's a cunning one."

Those were the last words Rath could make out as the two men moved out of earshot.

Crouching in the thicket, staring toward the ancient towering pines of Aldwood, he tried to make sense of what he had just overheard. It seemed his worst fears had proven true.

Somehow, Maura had fallen into the clutches of the notorious outlaw lord, Vang Spear of Heaven.

For many years, Vang and his men had operated out of the Blood Moon foothills, sweeping down to prey on farmers and travelers in the Long Vale. Rath wondered what had brought them this far east.

By the sound of it, Maura had not come willingly with Vang's men. A brief flicker of amusement and pride stirred within him, imagining her bewitching three of her captors. That would explain the strange signs he had read upon the heath.

The swift flash of levity quickly burnt itself out, leaving behind dregs of bitter ash. Maura's valiant defense had not been enough, after all. She was now Vang's prisoner.

How could he free her? Rath asked himself as he gazed toward the vast forest, as forbidding as the man who now ruled it.

Did he even dare to try?

So much for oracles and legends!

Maura paced the small stone cell into which she'd been thrown, trying *not* to think about what Vang and his men would do to her and how soon they would begin.

The damp stone walls seemed to close in on her with the suffocating tightness of despair. Being captured by outlaws had long been one of her worst fears. Now it had come to pass.

If she lived to be as old as Langbard, which at the moment seemed unlikely, she would never forget the leering looks she'd received from Vang's men as she'd been marched into his camp. Hard as she had tried not to let them see her naked terror, she doubted they'd been fooled.

Once again Maura made a circuit of the cell, searching in

vain for any possible means of escape. But it looked no more promising than it had before. The stone walls were as stout and unyielding as they could be.

What business did a stone castle have in the middle of a forest in the first place?

If she were the size of a hare, she might be able to wriggle through the narrow slit of a window that let in a small amount of light and air. There would still remain the problem of reaching it, though, since it was set high in the wall, just below the ceiling. From outside, the tiny window opened at ground level. At the moment Maura could see two pairs of booted feet wandering past. There could be no escape that way.

Given the right tools and enough time, she might be able to gouge a useful-sized hole in the sturdy timbers of the door. But she had neither. There was a small slot at the bottom, probably for pushing food and water through. But its dimensions were even smaller than the window's.

Heaving a sigh of defeat, Maura sank to the floor. If she were ever to get out of here, it would not be by her own efforts.

"Giver," she whispered. "I cannot do your will without your help."

Outside her cell door she heard footsteps approaching. They halted outside her door. Then Maura heard the scrape of a heavy bar being lifted.

Inhaling a deep breath, she rose to her feet and adopted a stance of poised stillness completely at odds with the stew of feelings churning inside her.

The door swung open. A short but burly outlaw entered with a length of rope in his hands. Behind him, two others crowded in the doorway, training short bows on her.

All three moved in an awkward, jerky manner as if they had the palsy. Their gazes faltered before hers. Were *they* afraid of *her?* That preposterous notion made Maura give a burst of nervous laughter.

"There now, what is so funny?" demanded the man with the rope. "Vang wants to see you and that is no laughing matter."

Maura had never supposed it might be.

"Turn around," ordered the outlaw. "If you please," he added in an uncertain tone that suggested he would not know what to do if she refused. "Your hands are to be bound behind your back. Vang's orders."

So even the Spear of Heaven himself considered her dangerous. That absurd possibility gave Maura the tiniest crumb of confidence. She clung to it.

"Very well." She feigned a haughty assurance. "If your leader is so wary of a single defenseless woman, I will humor him."

Imagining herself a regal lady from one of Langbard's stories, she turned slowly, holding her wrists behind her for the outlaw guard to bind.

The rope rasped against her skin, making her feel more vulnerable than ever. But the poor man's fumbling fingers and stammered apology fed her tenuous sense of power. And something else, too, that she had not expected.

A sense that these men were also creations of the Giver, no matter how badly the ills of the world had marred them.

"There you go, my lady." Where Rath had gently mocked her with that title, this fellow sounded sincere. "That rope is not too tight on you, is it? I might be able to loosen it. Just a bit, mind, or Vang will have my head."

"Do not fret yourself." As she turned around, Maura caught

the man's eye and smiled. "I know you are only obeying the orders you were given."

The man's rough features softened and his squinty eyes seemed to glow. How long had it been since anyone had spoken a kind or forbearing word to him?

"W-will you come, then, my lady?" He made a sweeping gesture toward the cell door with an air of awkward courtliness.

"I will." She inclined her head in the way she imagined a queen might do to acknowledge a respected courtier. "Thank you."

The bowmen drew apart to let her pass, while the other guard scurried ahead to show her the way.

"What is this place?" Maura gazed around her as she walked down a long hallway lit by flickering torches. She had been too overcome with fear to take much notice when she'd first been brought here.

"Some old ruin of a castle," replied her guard. "Vang found it and brought us here from out of the hills. Some of it's fallen down but parts are still good. Even the worst of it is better than living out-of-doors or in caves."

Maura recalled some things Rath Talward had said in bitter jest. "Your life is not an easy one, I know."

What tragedy or ill chance had brought him here?

Maura did not get a chance to ask, for they now entered a large room that might once have served as a royal banquet hall. Its vaulted stone roof had fallen over the centuries, but the outlaws had made shift a crude replacement of timber. Though it looked out of place atop the fine stonework of the walls, no doubt it kept the rain out just as well.

Rough-hewn trestle tables and benches lined the sides of

the hall, at which sat a small host of the most desperate-looking men Maura had ever seen. While the sight of them still struck fear in her heart, it did not provoke the swooning panic it might have done an hour ago. For she saw each man as the Giver might—an individual with vices and virtues, regrets and fears.

At the head of the room, sat their leader, Vang. The bandit chief rested on a chair that had been carved from a huge tree stump. Some of the roots spread out beneath it, like tentacles. Across his lap rested the sash that held all Maura's spell ingredients.

He beckoned her. "Come, witch, and give an account of yourself."

Maura willed her voice not to tremble as she walked up the aisle between the tables. "You mistake me, sir. I am no witch, only a traveler who means you no harm and begs leave to be allowed on her way."

Vang paused for a moment and appeared to ponder her request, then he shook his head. "You give yourself too little credit."

He held up her sash. "Tell me, what is all this?"

Part of her was tempted to bluff about her powers, so the outlaws might be too frightened to keep her. Yet she heard herself reply, "Nothing that will do any harm. Herbs, mostly, for treating wounds and sickness. Shall I show you?"

"Like you showed Turgen and his lads?" Vang clutched the sash as if he expected Maura to wrest it from him by force. "It was more than a few herbs struck them all down."

To either side of her, Vang's men began to mutter feverishly among themselves.

"I did nothing to hurt them." Maura turned her head to show her bruised cheek. "I fear they cannot say the same for me."

"My men only did as they were bidden. Watching out for anyone who trespasses on our territory and bringing them here for questioning."

Maura seized on an elusive wisp of hope. "If you find such travelers pose no threat to you, do you send them on their way?"

Again Vang appeared to consider the notion. "Not often, no. Where were you bound when my men found you?"

A warning of Rath's flashed in Maura's mind. Claiming she was headed for Tarsh would be too obvious a falsehood, and she did not know the names of any towns in the Long Vale.

So she answered, "My destination is my own business."

Vang leapt to his feet and marched toward her, shaking the sash in his fist. "Since you are here and I am asking, that makes it *my* business, too, witch."

As he bore down on her, Maura struggled to hold her ground.

"Now, leave off toying with me," Vang roared. "Else I will give you a matching bruise on the other side of your pretty face! And a few other places that show less but hurt worse!"

As the outlaw loomed over her, his breath hot on her face, Maura discovered there were depths of fear she had not yet begun to plumb. Her knees began to tremble and her insides seemed to collapse into a bottomless void.

Then from behind her came the most welcome sound in the world—Rath Talward's impudent, mocking voice. "Have a little respect for the lady, Vang. If she has to look at a face as ugly as yours, she deserves fair words to make up for it."

Vang's hulking head snapped up to stare past Maura. The

whispering around them rose like the menacing buzz of a shaken wasp's nest.

"It has been a long time since we have seen you in these parts, Wolf." Vang's voice took on a note of baiting banter. "Who let you in?"

"Why? Am I not welcome?" Maura could picture Rath's look of feigned surprise. "No one tried to stop me from coming here…at least not enough for me to take seriously."

A muted crunch followed, that sounded like the cracking of knuckles.

Vang seemed to forget Maura altogether. "You have tidied up since we last met, Wolf. Getting soft?"

"Try me."

The audacity of the challenge made Maura catch her breath.

To her surprise, Vang did not press it. "What brings you here? Come to join us at last? I heard you had some trouble with the white heads. Heard they chopped you in little pieces and fed you to their hounds."

Maura risked a backward glance. Even if she had known Vang would flatten her for it, she would not have been able to resist.

A strange, sweet spasm gripped her heart when her gaze fastened on Rath. His wet hair was short, but by no means *tidy*. A stumble of whisker bristled on his chin. Beneath that brazen grin, his face looked drawn, as though he had gone too long without sleep. Was that a drop of blood trickling from the corner of his mouth?

Never in her life had Maura been happier to see anyone. She could barely keep from running to throw herself into his arms.

"My flesh must not have agreed with their delicate bellies."
Rath swaggered deeper into the hall, toward Maura and the
outlaw chief. "And when did Vang Spear of Heaven start paying any heed to Hanish boasts?"

"I did not say I believed them." Vang shrugged. "I was only
telling you what I heard."

"As for what brings me here, I did not come to join you."
Rath swept a glance around the hall. "Though your new quar-
ters are a vast improvement over the old."

"It suits me." Though Vang's tone sounded indifferent,
Maura could see his chest puff out under his thick fur vest.

Rath strode toward Maura then wrapped his hand around
her upper arm. "I came because you filched something of
mine and I want it back."

The instant he caught a good look at her face, outrage
flashed in his eyes. He was quick to conceal it from the outlaws, but Maura recognized it and it warmed her.

Tilting her chin with his fingers, Rath inspected her bruises.
He clucked his tongue. "And you have damaged it."

A few days ago, Maura might have bridled at such casual
handling. Not to mention being spoken of as if she were his
possession. Now she knew he was only doing what needed to
be done to win her release.

When their gazes met, she sensed a plea for patience and
responded with a wordless assurance that she understood.

"Turgen struck the wench." Vang pointed toward his lieu-
tenant, who glowered at Rath and Maura. "If you have a complaint, take it up with him."

Rath glowered back. "I may do that."

"How were my men to know she was yours?" Vang strolled

back to his rustic throne. "If you wanted to keep her, you should have kept a closer eye on her."

"A man can only do so many things at once," said Rath. "I doubt even the mighty Spear of Heaven could hunt and stand guard at the same time."

"That is why I keep this lot around." Vang made a sweeping gesture that took in all the men sitting at the tables. "So I do not need to hunt *or* keep watch. But enough bandying words. We hold the wench now. That makes her ours. Have you forgotten the outlaw code? What I take and can hold belongs to me."

Maura tried to keep silent, but the words burst out of her. "If you ask me, that sounds more Hanish than Umbrian."

Vang looked from Maura to Rath. "You have not taught her proper meekness, Wolf." His gaze flicked back to Maura. "No one did ask your thoughts, wench. Nor ever will as long as you remain here."

"She does know how to scold." Rath gave an exaggerated sigh. "I would be doing you a favor to unburden you of her company."

"Never fear, I can cure her of that quick enough." Vang kneaded his fist into the palm of his other hand. "Besides, I judge she could be of use to me, if she can do to my enemies what she did to Turgen, Orl and young Jaro."

"That kind of power is like a blade with two edges, Vang. A man must always be on guard that it does not turn and do him an injury."

Vang rose from his chair again and marched toward them. "The trick with such blades is to keep a good firm grip."

With those last words, he reached for Maura's other arm,

clenching his fist around it with such brutal force that she cried out in pain.

"Unhand her!" Rath threw himself between the bandit lord and Maura, driving the edge of his hand against Vang's arm, just behind the elbow.

At once the cruel pressure of Vang's grip broke and Maura was able to pull her arm away.

"You will pay for that!" Vang snarled.

Rath shoved his way farther between Maura and the bandit lord. "Take care it does not cost you more to collect than the debt is worth, Vang. Since you will not give the lady up, I will fight you for her!"

"You? Challenge me?" Vang laughed. "Very well, then. I have not had much sport of late. An hour from now?"

Before Rath could answer, Maura cried, "No!"

"Curb your tongue, witch!" Vang fixed her with a fierce, one-eyed glare that would probably have silenced any man in the room. "This is none of your concern."

Maura ignored the pleading look Rath directed at her. "Since I am the one being fought over, I cannot think whom it concerns more. What satisfaction is there in besting a foe who labors under a disadvantage? Or do you fear to fight fair with Rath the Wolf?"

The bandit lord shook his fist in Rath's face and his voice thundered through the hall to echo off the stone walls. "Vang Spear of Heaven fears *no* foe!"

Rath did not flinch before Vang's noisy fury.

Maura tried not to either. "Then you will want to allow your challenger a good night's sleep and a full belly before you fight him?"

"So I will! No one will dare say Vang Spear of Heaven must starve his opponents to beat them. Tomorrow, then, Wolf, after you have slept long and eaten full."

Rath nodded his agreement. "You are a worthy foe."

A wave of relief threatened to overwhelm Maura. At least this way *if* Rath fought the bandit lord, he would not be at quite so great a disadvantage. More important, though, her challenge to Vang's outlaw code of honor had bought her some precious time. Time to dissuade Rath Talward from risking his life for her.

Though it warmed her heart to know that he was willing, she could not let him make that kind of sacrifice for her. Langbard's death already weighed far too heavy on her conscience.

"What do you mean, *not fight Vang?*" Rath struggled to keep his voice to a whisper as he lay in the rain-soaked grass at the base of the ruined castle, his face pressed to the tiny window of Maura's cell. "I have no choice if you want to get out of here. And you *do* want to get out of here, believe me!"

"Of course I do!" Maura's urgent whisper floated up to him. "More than you can possibly know. But not at the cost of your life. Surely there must be some other way."

"I tried to find another way. Did you not hear me? I tried to call on my past acquaintance with Vang. Tried to convince him you would be more bother than you were worth. We are lucky he accepted my challenge rather than just tossing me into one of these cells and doing as he pleased with you afterward."

"Why are you doing this?" Her question wafted out of the darkness to pierce his heart. "What happened to caring about nothing beyond your own survival?"

What *had* happened to it? Rath was not certain. Perhaps it was only submerged in a passing wave of madness. Surely once he got Maura safely to Prum and out of his life, everything would go back to what it had been.

Rath tried to believe that. He tried even harder to convince himself it was what he wanted.

"You were the one who told me such a life was not worth living."

"No. I *asked* you to look into your heart and discover if *you* thought it was."

Rath did not reply straightaway, but held himself still, scarcely breathing, listening for footsteps of a guard on patrol. All he heard was the patter of falling rain and the ghostly rustle of the wind high up in the ancient, towering pines. Perhaps in so isolated a spot, Vang thought such precautions unnecessary.

Rath would have been more cautious. Especially after what his recent lack of caution had cost Maura.

"I did not come here to quibble with you," he said at last. "We do not have time for it."

Some compulsion he did not understand made Rath slide his arm through the tiny opening, extending his hand down to Maura. "You risked your life for me that day in Betchwood. Like it or not, that put me in your debt. Last night I failed you. You are in this cell now, because I let you down. I need to make up for that, though damned if I understand why."

Maura must have seen or sensed him reaching toward her, for her hand found his and clung. "You did not ask for my aid that day. Twice you told me to leave you. No harm came to me on account of what I did. At least nothing worse than a sore back. I cannot bear the thought of having your blood on my conscience. Whatever debt you owe me, or think you owe me, I deem it canceled."

"But…" It did not work that way. A debt of that kind had more to do with him than with her. It blighted his solitary independence. To free himself, *he* must be satisfied that he had done enough to repay it.

"I know if you try you can find some other way out of this than fighting Vang." Her grip tightened on his hand, conveying the urgency of her plea and her confidence in him. "Even if you defeat him, how do you know he will honor his promise to let us go? Your wits are sharper and more powerful than your blade, Rath Talward. For my sake and your own, use them."

He tried to muster a halfway persuasive argument, but he could not shift his stubborn thoughts from the sensation of her hand in his. Her skin was so smooth, her bones so delicate yet perversely strong. His fingers moved over hers in a restless caress, far more intimate and provocative than a simple joining of hands ought to be.

Kneading the tender pads of flesh at the base of each finger. Lightly gliding his thumbnail over the warm, creased valley of her palm. Circling her dainty wrist with his thumb and forefinger.

Maura's hand did not remain passive beneath his touch, but roved with a will of its own. When she innocently stroked his middle finger the way a woman might fondle a man to rouse him, Rath's body responded as though she had. He bit back a soft groan of wanting that could never hope to be satisfied.

When the sounds of approaching footsteps intruded on this strange, sweet moment of communion between them, Rath could barely keep from surging up and throttling Vang's men.

"I cannot stay!" he whispered, pulling his hand back with bitter reluctance. "If I am found here it could go ill for us both."

He felt the tension in Maura's flesh as she strained upward, trying to maintain contact with him until the last possible instant. "Promise me you will think about what I said?"

"I promise." Not that it would change anything.

With all the stealth of a wild creature, Rath scrambled up from the base of the tower and disappeared into the rain-drenched shadows.

He could not do what Maura asked and still win her freedom...could he? After what had just passed between them, he wanted to, more than ever. And not only to repay a debt.

12

With everything at stake, had she been a fool to press Rath for a less violent solution to her predicament?

Maura pondered that question from the moment she woke after a nightmare-plagued sleep, until the moment Vang sent his guards to fetch her so she could watch the fight. She wished she had been spared that honor.

If Rath's challenge to Vang was going ahead, that could only mean he had not been able to devise another plan…if he had even tried. It also meant she had failed to convince him that he owed her no further obligation.

Could that be because her intrepid words had communicated one thing while her clinging hand had told quite a different story? Her hand tingled as the guard bound it behind her. She had slept all night with it pressed to her cheek and her lips, convinced it still carried a whiff of Rath's scent, however faint.

She could not escape the feeling it also carried an echo of his touch. If she ran her fingers through her hair, it would be as though he had done it from a distance. If she cupped her cheek with her palm, it was easy to imagine his hand in place of her own.

"That too tight?" asked the guard.

Shaken from her musings, Maura murmured, "It is not uncomfortable, thank you."

"Let's go, then, if you please, my lady."

The guard's use of that courtesy title shook Maura. She had no business entertaining tender thoughts about Rath Talward. No business touching his hand the way she had last night, or allowing hers to be touched. The darkness, their jeopardy, and the impossibility of it going beyond hand-holding, all had lulled her sense of right and wrong.

If she believed Langbard, which she must, she had a destiny to fulfill. Beyond getting her to Prum, Rath Talward could have no part in that destiny, nor would he want to. If they both escaped Vang's clutches, which seemed unlikely at the moment, Maura vowed she would do nothing further to confuse Rath about her feelings.

If only those feelings did not confuse her so badly!

The guard led her through the half-ruined castle to a large courtyard. Sometime during the night it had stopped raining, but the ground in the courtyard was still muddy.

Vang's outlaws lounged around the walls, clustered in small groups, talking together. The loud murmur of their voices quieted as Maura entered and was led toward a small, backless bench that stood to one side of a wide, arched entranceway. Though she kept her gaze fixed forward, she sensed heads turning as she passed.

Out of the corner of her eye, she spotted Turgen watching her intently. The bruises he had inflicted on her face began to ache as if on some wordless signal. A similar malevolent energy urged her to turn and look at him, but Maura refused to surrender to it. Instead she tilted her chin a little higher, straightened her shoulders and kept walking. When she reached the stool, she slowly lowered herself onto the seat.

No sooner had she done so than Vang strode into the courtyard through the entrance beside her. Somehow he looked even bigger than he had the previous day. He wore about him an air of confidence, bordering on smugness that sent a quiver of dread through Maura.

When Rath arrived a moment later, ducking under the archway through which Maura had entered, he appeared preoccupied, not even sparing a glance in her direction. Certainly he did not look as though he had benefited from the sleep she'd secured for him. Had she destroyed any slight advantage he might have gained by selfishly keeping him talking late into the night?

Once he'd left her, had he tossed and turned until daybreak, trying to contrive a means of escape other than fighting Vang? The result of her well-intended meddling would likely be Rath beaten bloody or worse.

Rage and despair at her own helplessness seethed inside her. If only she still had her sash and her hands free, she would show Vang and his outlaws a thing or two! On the heels of that thought came a twinge of shame. Did she rely too much on magic, the way she had accused Rath of overrelying on his blade? Whatever happened in the next little while, she must find some way to help Rath and herself.

Behind her back, Maura flexed her wrists against the rope that held them, then strained to lift one middle finger so she could probe her bonds for weakness. The knot felt tight and solid. She doubted she could have worked it apart with her hands free.

But, wait…the cord had been looped several times around each wrist and not too snug. Perhaps if she pulled it very tight on one side, the rope would loosen enough on the other for her to wriggle that hand free. Then, if a chance came for her to aid Rath or create a distraction, she would be ready to seize it.

"Rath the Wolf!" Vang's deep raspy voice boomed out, hushing all the others and making Maura give a guilty start as she struggled against her bonds. "You challenge me for the freedom of your woman, who is my prisoner?"

The rope squeezed tighter and tighter around Maura's left arm, until her fingers tingled and began to go numb. But still she could not work her right hand through the bottom loop.

"I do not!" cried Rath.

For a moment, Maura forgot her bonds, bewildered by Rath's answer. Had he found a way to do what she'd asked? The possibility made her blood course faster and a rush of swift, urgent energy surge through her, as if she had drained a draft of potent quickfoil elixir.

Rath's words sent a drone of muted muttering around the fringe of the courtyard. All the outlaws sounded as surprised by this new development as Maura felt.

Except, perhaps, Vang?

Maura waited for him to question Rath or bid him be gone, even have him seized and bound. Instead the outlaw chief seemed to hesitate, as if waiting for an explanation.

He did not have to wait long.

"After thinking on it," Rath announced, "I realized my quarrel lies not with you, but with the fellow who stole and mistreated my woman in the first place."

His gaze raked the crowd until he found the man he sought. "I challenge Turgen to reclaim her!"

The noise in the courtyard swelled as the outlaws set up a feverish mutter. Maura's fragile optimism flattened as quickly as the froth on cheap ale.

The prospect of Rath fighting Vang for her had been bad enough. But Vang had only the one eye—that must be counted an advantage for his opponent. Though he was a big, powerful man, he looked less nimble than the swift, lean Wolf.

Turgen, on the other hand, appeared far too well matched for Rath in both size and agility. He had also proven his ruthlessness. If Rath *must* fight one of the outlaws, Maura would have favored Vang.

Just then her left arm throbbed, reminding Maura of her own modest, and possibly futile, plan. With the outlaws around her all distracted, she redoubled her efforts to work her hands free.

"To the Pit with you and your challenge, Wolf!" Turgen snarled. "I took the woman under orders. We spied the smoke from your camp and were sent to fetch whoever we found. I gave her a warning smack to quiet her." His lip curled. "It worked well. You should try it…if you ever get another chance."

Rath chuckled as if he found the scornful quip amusing. "I believe I will."

The next instant his hand flew up, clouting Turgen with a blow to the head that rocked the outlaw sideways. Those standing near him jumped away as a great gasp went up from all the onlookers. Maura flinched back with a sudden jolt that tore her right hand free of the bottom loop of rope.

Turgen recovered quickly from the shock of Rath's blow. "I will have your hide for that, Wolf!"

He lunged at Rath, who danced aside from his onrush at the last instant, leaving only an out-thrust foot to send Turgen sprawling onto the muddy earth of the courtyard.

Loud shouts went up from the crowd. Some sounded hostile to Rath, but most rang with amusement at Turgen's expense and admiration for Rath's skill. Maura worked her hand free of the second loop.

Turgen scrambled to his feet and went for Rath again with a swift swinging fist.

Twisting into a crouch, Rath caught Turgen's wrist and jerked the outlaw over his shoulder. When Turgen staggered back up, bright blood steamed from his nose and his eyes blazed with murderous hate.

He made a flying tackle at Rath, who took only a glancing blow on the shoulder, then tumbled out of Turgen's way, rolling to a stop at Maura's feet. Leaping up, he checked for any immediate danger from Turgen. Apparently satisfied that he was safe for the instant, he swooped in to plant a kiss on Maura's cheek.

At least that was how it must have looked to Vang's men. As his lips skidded over her face approaching her ear, he whispered, "Next time I roll this way, say the cuddybird spell!"

Had she heard right? Had she imagined it?

When Rath danced back into the middle of the courtyard, Maura caught his eye and nodded. Then she twisted her hand out of the third loop of rope and felt it fall slack. Blood rushed back into her left hand, making the flesh burn and sting. Maura bit her lip to keep from crying out.

Out in the middle of the courtyard, Turgen closed with Rath again. He feigned to pounce right, then made a quick shift left, catching a handful of Rath's padded leather vest. This time Rath was caught moving the wrong way. Before he could dodge, Turgen landed a solid blow to his jaw that rocked him back.

Before Rath could recover, Turgen charged with his head down, plowing Rath back into the courtyard wall and driving his head into Rath's belly. Maura jammed her eyes shut, but not in time to miss the grimace of pain that twisted Rath's features.

Would he get the opportunity to roll this way, as he'd planned? Maura feared he might not.

Rath surprised her, though. And Turgen, too.

Perhaps he had exaggerated how badly the blow hurt and winded him. For when Turgen pulled back, Rath moved after him with a deft pivot. Locking the outlaw's head in the crook of his elbow, he threw himself back against the wall, battering Turgen's pate against the stones.

Once. Twice. Thrice.

When Rath finally let him go, Turgen collapsed to his knees.

The other outlaws roared their approval. Maura wondered if Turgen's cruelty had made him enemies even among such hardened characters. Or perhaps Vang's men simply enjoyed watching a fight between two well-matched foes.

Rath gave a jaunty wave to acknowledge their cheers as he made his way toward Maura. But she sensed his pain in the stiff way he walked.

His hand moved toward a pocket of his vest. His gaze found hers and he gave a barely detectable nod. Grateful for the tumult around her that drowned out her words, Maura began to chant the invisibility spell.

A blur of swift motion behind Rath drew her horrified gaze. Turgen lunged toward him, a dagger raised to strike.

She tried to cry a warning, but her tongue got tangled between Old and New Umbrian, and her breath stuck in her throat.

Perhaps her face flashed a wordless warning, or the sudden hush of the outlaw audience might have put Rath on his guard. Without a twitch of warning he dove to the ground, legs churning until they struck Turgen just below the knee.

Turgen's lethal rush swept him forward, though this time he had the presence of mind to tuck in his head and roll with the fall. Landing at Maura's feet, he sprang back up in a menacing crouch.

Now! Maura's whole body seemed to vibrate with the need to act. Leaping from the stool, she whipped the rope that had bound her hands around Turgen's throat and pulled with all her might. She did not want to kill him, only hold him…for as long as it took.

"Now, Rath!" She cried the incantation at the top of her voice, as time stretched taut and thin.

With one hand, Turgen tore at the rope around his neck.

With the other, he swiped his dagger back at Maura. They ended up in a wild dizzying whirl, Turgen trying to strike Maura with his blade while she kept jumping sideways to avoid it.

She was too occupied with keeping one step ahead of Turgen's slashing dagger to notice what Rath or Vang's men were up to. Then, all of a sudden, she could no longer see Turgen, though she felt the rope in her hands and the powerful movements of his body. A quick glance assured her that she was invisible, too.

Letting go of the rope, she dropped to the ground and rolled away. Only then did she notice Vang's outlaws rushing toward her. One tripped over her, crashing to the ground nearby.

For a moment Maura feared she would be caught in the crush of milling bodies. But Vang's men had been thrown into confusion by the invisible, thrashing Turgen and his lethal, unseen blade. Blood gushed, pain stabbed from out of nowhere, spreading panic among the outlaws. In the midst of such confusion, no one paid much mind if they tripped over or bumped into her unseen form.

Slowly, Maura fought her way to the courtyard wall where the turmoil was least. She cast a glance about for some sign of Rath's passing, but saw none. What would they do now? How would they find one another in such a vast place, with both of them invisible?

They must not waste time trying, she decided reluctantly. If they did not get as far out of the reach of Vang's men as possible before they became visible again, everything they had done and risked would be in vain.

She must head toward the Long Vale and follow it to Prum. If she and Rath met up later on the road, she could thank him then. She had no great hopes that would happen, however. Now that he had provided her with this means of escape, surely Rath would consider his debt to her paid and return to his old life.

Edging her way toward one of the courtyard entrance arches, Maura told herself that would be best...for both of them.

She took another step toward the entryway...or tried to. But some force held her back. A large, warm force. One that smelled of leather, sweat and smoke.

"Rath?" she whispered, raising her invisible hand to his invisible face.

"Who else?" The jaunty murmur of his voice reached out of nowhere and wrapped around her.

Tears flooded Maura's eyes. Some shred of sense warned her to blink them back so they did not wash away the cuddybird spell. But she was too overcome with joy and relief to heed it.

Before she had time to think what she was doing, her hand followed the rugged edge of Rath's jaw to slip around his neck and pull his face toward hers. They blundered together with only touch to guide them, until her lips found his.

They pressed together...parted...tasted...clung, while stifled sobs quaked through Maura. His arms wrapped around her, pulling her tight to him for what seemed the longest, sweetest time. At last his lips left hers, roving over her cheek until they reached her ear.

"This will have to wait." His regretful whisper was not much louder than a breath. "There is something I must do. Get away from here. Make your way west. Visible or not, I will be able to track you."

Maura angled her face to bring her lips close to his ear. "Can I not stay with you? You may need me."

Though he did not speak or make any movement, she sensed his refusal.

"I helped you just now," she reminded him, "against Turgen."

She felt his hand on the back of her head, stroking her hair, and his brow pressed to hers. "So you did, and well, too. But two of us together are twice as likely to be noticed around here, even if we are invisible. Besides, even when I cannot see you, you distract me worse than I can afford."

He clutched her in one final fierce embrace then pushed her toward the nearest archway which was, for the moment, empty of outlaws. "Go!"

Maura did not wait for a more mannerly invitation. She slipped through the arch and cautiously made her way out of the bandits' lair. Then she ran as fast as her legs would carry her in what she desperately hoped was the right direction.

"So tell me," said Maura when she and Rath stopped to rest that evening and they were both fully visible again, "how did you come by the cuddybird feathers? And why did you insist on fighting Turgen instead of Vang?"

They'd had little opportunity or energy for explanations after fleeing Aldwood on a horse Rath had taken from the outlaws. He'd assured Maura the beast was not stolen, only traded for their pack pony. He wondered what she would say when he showed her what he'd *traded* for their pilfered supplies?

"The feathers? From your sash, of course." Rath knelt at the edge of a narrow brook and refilled his drink skin.

After a quick swig, he handed it to Maura. "That was part of the bargain I made with Vang."

He leaned back on the grass and rubbed his jaw where Turgen had struck him. Though it ached fiercely, it did not feel broken. His back and belly pained, too, where Turgen had butted him into the wall.

Once Maura had drunk her fill, she poured some of the water on her hand and splashed it on her face. "What bargain?"

Before Rath could answer, she glanced at his face and winced. "Let me look at that. Where else are you hurt?"

While she knelt beside him, examining his bruised face with a tender touch, Rath tried to make light of it. "Don't fret yourself. I have come off far worse than this in fights over the years. Who knows what kind of a bloody pulp I would be now if I had fought Vang? And I would have fought him, if it had not been for you."

He retrieved the water flask from Maura and took another, longer drink. "After you bid me use my wits instead of my blade, I did some thinking. It came to me that if I beat Vang, I'd have to take his place, which wasn't what I wanted. So I had a little talk with the Spear of Heaven, this morn. I told him he might well trounce me, but not without taking a fair beating that would leave him weakened for another challenge."

Maura had listened to him with her brow furrowed. Now those creases smoothed out and her eyes widened. "From... Turgen?"

"Aye, from Turgen." Rath grinned. "I had overheard a thing or two about him, and I have seen plenty of his ilk over the years. Biding his time to oust the chief. He must have rubbed his hands with glee after I challenged Vang."

"So you told Vang you would fight Turgen, instead? I won-dered why he did not look more surprised when you switched your challenge."

Rath nodded. "Vang is no fool. He knows he is not getting any younger, and I think he has been wary of Turgen for a while. In exchange for teaching Turgen a lesson, I made Vang give me a little something from that sash of yours, though I did not tell him what it would do."

"That *was* clever." Maura's eyes shone with such transpar-ent admiration, it made Rath squirm. "I knew you could think of something if you put your mind to it."

Against hostility or scorn he was on firm ground, armed and ready to give as good as he got. He had almost no expe-rience of honor and respect. Like so many other pleasant, un-familiar things, they put him on his guard.

"Just do not expect me to find a sly solution for every bit of trouble we meet between here and Prum."

She gave a little start. "You still mean to come with me?"

"Unless you do not want me." Rath tried to sound as if it did not matter a great deal either way. "I don't reckon I will be any more welcome in Aldwood, for a while, than I am in Norest. Might as well push south, and since you are headed that way, too, it makes sense for us to travel together."

For a moment, Maura pressed her lips together, thinking. Then she nodded. "It does make sense. And I have no objec-tion—quite the contrary. I only hope you do not still feel ob-ligated to me."

"Rest easy." Rath flexed his jaw then made a wry face. "I count my debt paid to the last copper."

In spite of that, his compulsion to go with Maura had not

diminished. Rath understood it less than ever. Perhaps it was no more than what he had told her—the prudence of two people traveling in the same direction to stick together. The lass had proven herself handy to have around in a pinch.

"What are you chuckling about?" Maura asked.

Rath had not realized he was chuckling. "Just recollecting how you jumped up and slung that rope around Turgen's neck. I do not know who you took more by surprise, him or me. I almost forgot to toss those feathers."

He laughed harder just thinking of it, then let out a hiss of pain as his stomach muscles protested.

Maura reached to pull open his vest. When Rath tried to slap her hand away, she slapped his back. "Let me see! There is not much I can do without my sash, but perhaps I can find some fresh herbs hereabouts to make you a poultice."

"Who says you do not have your sash?" Rath pulled his vest open to reveal the wide, pocketed strip of leather. "I think I should get one made for myself, to hold extra weapons, flint and such. It could be quite useful."

"You have it!" Maura cried, running her hand over the sash as if to prove to herself it was real. "Was this what you went back for?

"It's even been repaired where Vang tore it!" A sob ripped through her excited laughter. "Thank you."

She hid her face with her hand for a moment until she had composed herself.

Rath battled the urge to take her in his arms. If he did, he feared he would also surrender to the impulse to kiss her again. And that would be a mistake.

"I am sorry." Maura wiped her eyes with the sleeve of her

tunic. "I did not mean to blubber. I do not know what came over me. It is like having a bit of Langbard back, somehow."

So much had happened in the past week, Windleford and Langbard's death seemed far in the past. Yet hearing Maura speak his name made Rath recall how fresh her bereavement was. Since he had forgotten anything Ganny might have taught him about offering comfort, he settled for trying to lighten the moment.

"Did you think I would leave something so valuable in Vang's possession?" He pretended to look severe. "Especially since he would not have the first notion how to use it."

"Since you went to the trouble of recovering my sash," said Maura, "you had better let me use what is in it to tend your injuries. Off with your vest and shirt now, like a good fellow. I want to see what I'm doing and the light is fading fast."

She soon had him stretched out flat on the grass, stripped of the sash and his upper garments while she probed his badly bruised abdomen with a gentle touch that tormented Rath equally between pain and pleasure.

"Your pardon!" she cried when he clenched his teeth and sweat broke out on his brow. "I did not mean to hurt you."

No more than she meant to rouse him!

"Whatever you're doing," he grumbled, "do it quick and be done before I freeze." Small fear of *that!*

"You need a poultice of winterwort to draw the bruises." Maura spoke in the cool, practical tone of a woman who never guessed the effect she had on him. "Then a brew of laceweed to work from the inside in case of bleeding."

She took some dried herbs from one of the sash pockets, then mixed them in her palm with a bit of water from the brook. Rath flinched when she smeared the cold compound on the flesh of his belly. After she bound it with a roll of linen from another pocket of the sash, she helped him back into his shirt and vest.

"I wish we could make a fire to mull the tonic." Maura rummaged in her sash again. "But I suppose we dare not."

Rath shook his head. "No more fires until we get safely to Prum."

"It will not be a pleasant journey." Maura put a pinch of three different herbs into Rath's drink skin, then shook it. "We have a horse with no saddle or harness, a sash with a fast-dwindling stock of magical ingredients, no food, and no fire."

She heaved a sigh as she handed the flask to Rath. He took a great swig, then battled to keep from spewing it out again. A few moments later, his pain began to ease enough to make him brave another taste. Prepared, this time, for the strong, strange flavor, he found it more tolerable. By the time he'd drained the flask, he thought it jolly fine stuff.

"Do not fret." He clapped a heavy hand on Maura's shoulder. His tongue felt thick and lazy. He had to work hard to keep his words from slurring. "Once we reach the Long Vale, we will be fine."

He fumbled on his belt for a small pouch. When he shook it, the coins inside jingled. "A parting gift from Vang Spear of Heaven."

The sky had grown too dark and his eyes too heavy for him to make out the expression on Maura's face. Would it be a stern frown, he wondered, heralding an equally stern lecture on the evils of thievery? Well, what did she expect? He was an outlaw. What was more he had never claimed to be anything else.

To his surprise, Maura only chuckled. "Langbard said you were resourceful."

The unexpected approval in her voice, and the endorsement of the old wizard brought Rath closer to tears than he had ever been since Ganny's death. Or perhaps it was that potion of Maura's that made him maudlin.

"Well," said Maura when he did not reply, "since we cannot have a fire, may I at least curl up near you to sleep?"

He wanted to tell her it might be better for both of them if she kept her distance. Instead he heard himself say, "Do as you like."

Perhaps his tone betrayed his misgivings. For when Maura nestled close to him, she whispered, "Just for warmth, truly! That…kiss…after you fought Turgen. I did not mean…"

"Nor I!" Rath shook his head vigorously. "I have seen such things before, after danger passes. There comes a moment of relief so fierce, it is like madness. Once, after I outran a Hanish patrol, I jumped off the edge of a waterfall."

"You did?" Maura's tone held a hint of doubtful amusement. The tension in her body eased and she edged closer to him.

"Truly. I could have done myself more harm than the Han might ever have done me. Folk are not responsible for the fool things they do or say at times like that."

"I suppose not." Rath could picture Maura smiling over his old folly and their recent one.

"So you need not fret that I will say anything about it to… your bridegroom when we reach Prum."

What sort of man had Maura's aunt contracted for her? Rath wondered as a warm, wholesome drowsiness stole over him. Young? Old? Poor? Prosperous? A wizard, perhaps, or a scholar of the Elderways?

One thing Rath knew for certain about this unknown fellow. He was a very lucky man.

13

"You were lucky to escape with no worse injuries," said Maura the next morning as she applied a fresh poultice to Rath's bruised belly. "How does it feel?"

He glanced down at the angry purple marks on his abdomen. "Not as bad as it looks, luckily. The emptiness inside pains me almost as bad. I wish I had thought to steal some food along with your sash and the coins."

Maura finished binding the fresh poultice in place. "I will make us up a little draft to drink before we start on our way. It will not be the same as a filling meal, but it should refresh us until we can find somewhere to buy food."

"If my reckoning is right, a steady day's ride should bring us to the Long Vale." Rath put his shirt and vest back on and wrapped his cloak tight against the cool morning air that promised to warm as the sun rose higher. "Can you not put

some of that poultice on your face? I do not want folks who
see us to think I...did that."

Beneath his gruff tone, Maura detected a hint of tenderness.
"It is hard to bind a poultice on the face." She chuckled. "Besides, if folks see the bruises on your jaw, they may think I
gave you back worse than you gave me."

After sharing the draft she had prepared, they scrambled
onto the mare's broad back and continued westward. True to
Rath's prediction, they reached the Long Vale before sunset.
Soon after, they came to a village that made Maura homesick
for Windleford.

They stopped at a small inn on the edge of town where they
ordered a meal. It was plain fare, but plentiful and tasty—fresh
bread, a mild sweet cheese for which the Long Vale was
famed, and a hot, filling dish of ham and red cabbage with
dumplings.

"This was almost worth going hungry for." Maura sat back
from her empty bowl with a contented sigh. "It is so good to
eat at a proper table again."

Working his way through his second large helping of ham
and cabbage, Rath shrugged. "To me, eating at a table seems
odd. Though I reckon I could get to like it."

While he continued to eat with single-minded diligence,
Maura watched him with an oddly possessive curiosity. For
many years he had lived and thrived on the kind of existence
they had shared during the past week. The danger, the hardship, and the constant movement had quickly lost all charm
for her—not that they had held much to begin with.

More than ever, she admired Rath Talward for holding on

to his courage, his humor and the decency of character he tried so hard to hide from a world that might exploit it as weakness.

When the innkeeper came to present their bill, Rath asked, "Where might we find a saddler in your fine village?"

"A saddler, goodmaster?" The innkeeper scratched his prominent chin. "Why, there is none nearer than Folkin's Mills, a good many miles south through the Vale. Is it tack you're wanting? For I have a pair of saddles and some stray bits of harness I could make you a good price on."

When Rath and Maura exchanged a look, he hastened to explain. "Now and then, folks stop here without the coin for food and lodgings, so I take whatever they have in trade."

His bushy brows knit together. "How do you come to have a horse, but no saddle or harness?"

Maura braced herself for whatever clever story Rath would invent to explain their situation. While their safety might well depend upon such convincing falsehoods, it troubled her to pave her path to the Waiting King with lies.

"Now, there is a tale." Rath flashed the innkeeper his most roguish grin. "I reckon you have heard of the outlaw, Vang?"

The innkeeper's eyes widened. "Few folk 'round these parts who have not, goodmaster. Did his men make off with your gear?"

"Not quite. We stole the horse from them!" Rath slapped his palm on the table and let out a bellow of laughter, in which the innkeeper joined. "We did not think it wise to hang about their camp searching for a saddle."

"I should think not." The innkeeper laughed until Maura feared he would burst his apron.

When Rath paid for their dinner the man jingled the coins

in his hand, still chortling. "I suppose you lifted this lot from Vang, too, and got your bruises from his men?"

"So we did." Rath winked. "Though we left them in worse shape than they left us. Now if you will oblige us with a look at those saddles, I shall be pleased to put more of Vang's hoard into your hands."

The innkeeper wiped tears of mirth from his eyes. "A tale like that is almost worth the price of a saddle, young master."

"Tale?" Rath gave a comical pretense of outrage. "Every word is the truth, I swear it."

"Aye, and my brother-in-law's the Waiting King!" quipped the innkeeper as he led them off to inspect the tack he had for sale.

Maura wondered if he gave them such a good price on the saddle and harness because Rath had amused him so well.

"Perhaps so." Rath chuckled when she suggested it later. "I do not know what made me do it. I had a good story all ready, then this strange urge came over me to tell the truth."

He glanced back at her as they climbed the winding stairs to the room they had hired for the night. "If I am not careful, you will soon have me tamed with your witchery."

"Do not fret." She gave him a playful slap on the back. "I am no beast charmer."

Would she *want* to tame him, even if she could? Maura wondered. As with most of her feelings about Rath Talward, she could not be certain. Only one thing she knew without doubt, just then. She would be glad of an excuse to cling to him for the next several days as they rode through the Long Vale.

They had not been long on the road the following morning when Maura tapped on Rath's shoulder. "Stop a moment, will you?"

"Aye." He reined the mare to a halt. "What for?"

"You will see." She slid off the horse's flank and jumped the ditch to a small meadow.

The land looked like it had once been cultivated, but now it lay fallow, yielding only tall grass and a bountiful crop of hundredflowers. Maura picked as many as she could stuff into the wide pocket of her apron.

"Good thinking," said Rath when she returned to the road. "We have been fortunate not to meet any Han since we reached the Long Vale, but I do not expect such luck to hold."

As they set off again, Maura pulled a great handful of petals from some of the flowers she had gathered. Then she scattered them over herself, Rath and the mare.

"Repeat the spell after me," she bid Rath. "That will make it more potent."

"Talk fast," said Rath. "I think I hear something on the road ahead."

Now that he'd mentioned it, Maura heard the sounds, too—the swift, hard tramp of metal-shod feet and the harsh jabber of Hanish voices. Her own voice a trifle breathless, she spoke the spell in short phrases for Rath to repeat.

He slowed the mare to delay their encounter. They had barely finished reciting the spell when they rounded a bend in the road and saw a small troop of Hanish soldiers ahead. From what Maura could tell, peering out around Rath, they had stopped marching and were clustered around a donkey cart.

"Hang on," Rath muttered over his shoulder.

He urged the mare to a brisk trot, then made her jump the

ditch. The landing jolted Maura but she managed to keep her seat. When they drew even with the Han, she understood why Rath had left the road. There would have been no room for them to pass without attracting unwelcome notice to themselves.

At the moment, all the soldiers' attention was directed toward the donkey cart and its elderly owner. Some of them were pushing him back and forth between them, bellowing what sounded like questions and orders, while others watched and laughed.

"What are they saying?" she whispered to Rath. "Why are they harassing him?"

He turned his head to watch the soldiers, and to whisper an answer back to her. "They are berating him for kicking up dust on the road that they will have to walk through. It might dirty their precious hair! By the sound of it, the old one does not know much Comtung. Some of them are taking that as an insult."

"Metalmongers!" Maura fumed. "A great show of courage, that, picking on a defenseless old man."

"Do not be fooled, the Han are brave enough in battle."

"When they have their enemies outnumbered ten to one, perhaps," Maura muttered through clenched teeth. "I would like to see one of *them* have the courage to march into Vang's lair, all alone!"

The old man looked from soldier to soldier, trying in vain to find one who might show the faintest spark of compassion or decency.

"Please, good masters," he cried in Umbrian. "I mean you no harm!" He tried to bow. "I entreat your pardon if I have offended!"

One of the soldiers pushed the old man away, imitating his words in a tone of mocking contempt. When he staggered, another of the soldiers thrust out an iron-soled boot to send him sprawling onto the dusty road.

A third soldier fetched him a hard kick as he bellowed an order in Hanish. When the old man tried to stagger to his feet, Maura saw a single tear dribble down his wrinkled, dust-smudged cheek.

The intensity of her outrage made Maura's whole body tremble. She did not notice herself sliding off the mare's flank until Rath caught her arm.

"What do you think you are doing?"

"I do not know." She struggled to break free. "Something. I must do something!"

"No!" Rath twisted halfway around in his saddle to catch her by the waist. "They will only go harder on the old man if you do. Believe me, I have seen it a hundred times."

Maura knew he was talking sense and yet… "Is there *nothing* we can do?"

Rath made a sound deep in his throat, like a vexed sigh wed to a growl. "Wait here." He eased her to the ground. "Do nothing until I have drawn the Han off. You mind me?"

She nodded.

"Good." Rath pointed to a nearby clump of bushes. "Get the old man off the road and keep going on to the nearest village. I will catch up with you there."

Before she could answer, he rode off.

What was he planning? Maura wondered. Would it place him in danger? She almost wished she had not gotten him involved.

Meanwhile the soldiers continued to bully the old man

who was now weeping openly, begging them to let him be. Those signs of weakness seemed to goad the Han further, making them ever more vicious in their taunts.

Then, suddenly, there was a loud clang. One of the Han flinched and cried out. Another clang. Another cry. More, until the soldiers forgot their victim, drawing their weapons and peering around to locate the source of this brazen attack upon them.

They did not need to look for long.

A familiar voice roared down from a gentle incline on the opposite side of the road, along with a fresh hail of well-aimed stones. Though Maura did not understand the Hanish words Rath shouted, his jeering tone and the soldiers' furious reaction convinced her they were grievous slurs.

Her gaze flew to a sparse clump of trees partway up the low hill. She caught a fleeting glimpse of Rath as he lunged out from behind one of the trees to hurl another small rock and another huge insult.

One of the soldiers raised his bow and sent an arrow flying. Rath ducked back behind the tree before it whistled past.

The Han with the most elaborate helmet plume bawled an order, sending the whole troop racing up the slope brandishing their blades.

"Don't you dare get yourself killed, Rath Talward," Maura muttered under her breath as she watched him flee up the hill ahead of the charging soldiers. "May the Giver go with you."

She forced her attention back to the old man, who cowered beside his donkey cart.

Stealing out from her hiding place, she knelt beside him. "Come, Oldfather. We must get you away from here while the Han are busy elsewhere."

He raised his arm to shield his face. "They will be angry if they come back and find me gone."

Maura made a gesture of respect, then took his arm with a gentle but urgent touch. "If they do return to this spot, I am certain they will have forgotten all about you. And you will be far away."

When fear and confusion still made him balk, she pleaded, "A good man has risked much to help you. Do not let his brave deed be for nothing."

Perhaps her words convinced the old man, for he leaned heavily upon her to heave himself to his feet. Once in motion, he proved surprisingly nimble. Scrambling into the cart, he motioned for Maura to pass him the donkey's reins.

When she did, he beckoned her to climb onto the seat beside him. "It is not safe for a pretty young lass to linger here, either. I can take you a ways toward Folkin's Mills, if that is where you are bound."

"Thank you, Oldfather."

Once Maura had taken a seat beside him, he slapped the reins hard against the donkey's hindquarters. The beast protested with a shrill bray, but set off at a smart pace down the road.

Remembering the hundredflowers she had thrust into her apron pocket, Maura pulled off a handful of petals and tossed them in the air to fall over the cart, the old man, the donkey and herself. Then she spoke the words of the spell.

The old man stared at her, his eyes wide and his jaw slack. "Is that *twara* you speak, lass?"

"It is. A spell to keep the Han from paying us any mind." She explained about the hundredflowers and made him repeat the words of the incantation until she was certain he would remember them. "From now on, I want you to use this spell whenever you venture from home and might meet up with any Han."

At last the old man seemed to rouse from his frightened bewilderment. "When I was a boy, my mother had a few little spells she used, the Giver rest her spirit. To make the hens lay and to patch up we younglings when we hurt ourselves. Nowadays, folks say that is all foolishness or wickedness, but I know different."

Maura patted his hand. "I hope you will try to remember your mother's spells, and use them…teach them to your grandkin. Tell them all the old stories you can recall. All the blessings and rituals. The Han have robbed Umbria of so much else, we must not let them take our greatest riches."

A tremor quaked through Maura when she finished speaking. Those words had not been her own. Someone or something had used her tongue to speak.

The old man stared at her, his sparse white brows knit together. In a voice hushed with wonder he asked, "Who *are* you, lass?"

Once again the words seemed to come from outside her, or perhaps from a deep place within her that she had never explored.

She raised her fingertips to brush against the old man's forehead, then down to his lips, his chest and the palm of his hand in an ancient blessing. "I am the Destined Queen, Oldfather. Keep hope. I am on my way to find the Waiting King."

"Here you are," cried Rath when he finally overtook Maura many hours later on the outskirts of a good-sized town. "I was afraid I had lost you!"

"*You* were afraid?" Maura raised her arm to shield her eyes from the setting sun as she gazed up at him. "After you set a whole troop of Hanish soldiers on your tail? I have been frantic with worry, wondering if you managed to outrun them. What happened to your creed of looking out for no one but yourself?"

"Did I not say you were having a dangerously wholesome influence on me?" A burst of hearty, refreshing laughter shook Rath as he extended his hand to hoist Maura up behind him.

He had no right to feel so absurdly pleased with himself and the whole world! He had just done something dangerously daft for an old man he had never met in his life. An old man who could not possibly do anything to repay him for the foolish risk he had taken.

"If they had caught you—" Maura shuddered, her arms tightening around him.

"If they had caught me," Rath replied with witless good cheer, "I would be *lucky* to be dead by now. But they did not catch me."

Perhaps it was his narrow escape that had left him with such a dizzying sense of freedom and power. Some untrustworthy instinct told him it was more than that.

"How is the old man?"

"Shaken," replied Maura, "and confused, but not badly hurt, thanks to you. He told me to give you his thanks…and his blessing."

"I hope you told him to give the Han a good wide berth from now on, supposing it means driving that cart of his in the ditch. They are hardest on the weak and the old. I think such folk remind them of what they will become one day and it terrifies them to the marrow of their bones."

Where had that notion come from? Rath wondered. It had never occurred to him before he heard the words coming out of his mouth. Yet it had a ring of truth.

"I thought the Han were not afraid of anything." Maura sounded as if she were talking to herself. "Everyone in Windleford was afraid of *them,* but I never saw them harass ordinary law-abiding folk as bad as they did that man."

"Windleford is a haven compared to most places." Rath did not like to dwell on memories of some places and things he'd seen. "And this side of the mountains is a hundredfold better than the other. I hope you never have to see—"

The words caught in Rath's throat and he almost gagged on them. The fleeting elation he'd felt after escaping the Han soured into something vile, even poisonous.

At first he had not recognized the contorted shapes in the large tree ahead of them. Then he had wondered if they might be children, climbing in the branches. But the forms were too large to be children. And they were not moving.

"Don't look, Maura!" The instant those futile words left his lips, Rath wished he could recall them. He had never yet met a person who heeded such a warning. Curiosity ran too strong in most folk.

"At what?" Maura shifted her perch to peer around him.

She gave a strangled cry, then pressed her face against his back…too late to shut out the gruesome sight.

Rath struggled to keep his last meal from coming back up.

Those things in the tree had once been men. Now their mangled corpses hung from the branches as a brutal warning.

"From the mines."

Buffered by the layers of cloak, vest and shirt, Rath still felt Maura's head move against his back as she nodded. "That could have been Newlyn."

He plundered his mind for anything he could say to comfort her—to comfort himself. "They are better off now than when they were alive, poor devils."

There was no question of Rath and Maura eating after that. But he insisted they take a room at the town's small inn.

"The horse needs to rest and feed," said Rath. "I rode her hard to get away from the Han. And, spell or no spell, I do not fancy being caught on the road after dark."

This time he did not jest with the innkeeper or draw attention to Maura or himself in any way.

Once they were safely inside their room he slid to the floor with his back propped against the door and his dagger drawn.

Catching Maura's eye he nodded toward the bed. "Sleep if you can. Prum is still a good way off. I mean to travel as far as we can every day until we get there."

"Very well." Maura removed her boots, then lay down on the bed, her face toward the door.

For a time, the only sounds in the little room were the muted voices and rattle of crockery from the kitchen below. Then Maura sat up. "It would make more sense if you take the bed. I can always sleep tomorrow while we ride. You will need to have your wits about you."

"I am fine here." Rath yawned. "I have slept in far worse."

"I cannot sleep," said Maura. "So I might as well sit guard while you get a proper rest."

"Sit guard?" Rath could not keep a hint of amusement

from his voice. "Do you mean you would use my dagger if you had to?"

"N-no," she admitted after a moment's hesitation. "But I would have my spidersilk ready, or dreamweed."

"Why not use that dreamweed on yourself, then?" Why was he resisting. If Maura did not want the bed, who was he to argue?

"I cannot bear to close my eyes. I keep seeing those bodies in the tree. One had his eyes gouged out, and a crow was—"

"I warned you not to look! Have you nothing in that sash of yours to purge such evil memories?"

If she did, he might beg her for a dram to soothe his mind. Maura shook her head. "If I did, I would not use it."

"Are you daft?"

"Perhaps." She rose from the bed and walked to the window where she stared out into the night. "I do not expect you to understand, but it feels wrong for me to forget."

She was right about one thing at least. He did not understand. "Why make yourself unhappy when there is nothing you can do to change it?"

In the luminous dusting of moonlight through the tiny window, Rath saw her turn. Two strides brought her to the door, where she knelt before him and clasped his hand in both of hers.

"We did change it, though." She spoke in a rushed, eager whisper. "Today. You and I. For one old man. If we can, others can, too. And if enough do…"

Her newfound zeal might seduce him, if he let it. But he must not. Maura had only the barest notion of what the Han had done to Umbria. Rath wanted to keep it that way.

"That is all well and good, lass. But your new husband may

have different ideas. I doubt he will want you risking your neck or attracting the wrong sort of attention from the local garrison."

Rath hoped the fellow would be capable of protecting Maura, the way Langbard had. "The best thing you can do for yourself and for Umbria is to lead a quiet life in Prum. Sow your door yard with hundredflowers and herbs. Teach your children vitcraft and the Elderways. Make your home like a tinderbox that keeps an ember glowing until the day comes when it may kindle a fresh fire."

Who was he trying to fool, her or himself? The Han would only get stronger in the years ahead while Umbrians sank deeper into bondage. Any hope of resistance had been squandered years ago.

"I thought you mistrusted vitcraft and despised the Elderways." Maura's words exposed a vulnerable spot within him.

"I thought so, too."

In another week, he and Maura would part company. And not a moment too soon, if he ever hoped to get his old life back. The question Rath asked himself many times through that long, dark, silent night was—did he *want* it back?

Their next days' journeys were longer, but less eventful. For several of them, a soft, gray mist shrouded the countryside, muffling sounds and limiting vision to a few yards in any direction. What brutal sights was it protecting her from? Maura wondered, not truly wanting to know.

Though she was grateful for the respite, another part of her felt sick with shame for shrinking from the harsh reality that most Umbrians could not escape. Those were not the only contrary feelings and inclinations that warred within Maura every mile they traveled southward.

Since that fateful talk with Langbard, which now seemed so long ago, everything she had seen and experienced urged her to pursue her quest with true fervor. The night when Rath had said there was nothing she could do, a small but potent voice inside her had insisted otherwise.

Her destiny was not the burden she had first thought it. Now she saw it as a precious opportunity to do something which most Umbrians despaired—driving out the Han, restoring peace and freedom. Reaching Prum, meeting with the wise woman, Exilda, and finding the map to the Secret Glade would be a major step toward that goal.

A step that would take her away from Rath Talward.

Three weeks ago, she would never have guessed how much the prospect of parting from him would dismay her now. How had he come to make such a large place for himself, so deep in her heart, in such a short time? That was a question she could not answer...or dared not.

Perhaps it was only because she had become so dependent upon his help to reach Prum.

"I shall be sorry to bid you goodbye, Rath Talward." It was all she could do to keep from clutching tighter to his waist as they rode toward Prum in the pouring rain. "I do not know how I would have managed without you. You have been everything Langbard said you would be, and better."

But if she were to accomplish the task she had been set, she must learn to rely on herself alone.

"Do not slight yourself, lass." Though he spoke in a hearty tone, Rath's voice sounded strangely husky. "You have taken

your own part…and mine, by times. We do things differ-
ently, you and I, but our ways seem to mesh well enough."

"So they do."

Was it possible she could entreat him to continue as her escort for the rest of her journey? "Where will you go after we
reach Prum? What will you do with yourself?"

His shoulders lifted and fell in an expressive shrug. "I have
not thought much about it. A man like me does not plan too
far ahead. I watch what happens and see if I can turn it to my
advantage. Or steer clear if I smell trouble on the wind."

It did not seem right, somehow, for a man of his abilities
to be living from day to day, with no aim beyond survival.

"I might hide the summer in Southmark." His voice fell to
a musing murmur. "Earn an honest coin herding cattle, maybe,
or riding guard on the drive to market."

True, it would be honest work, a positive step up from
thieving. Still, Rath Talward as a cattle herder or drive guard
seemed a waste to Maura.

He glanced back over his shoulder, water dripping from the
raised hood of his cloak. "If I find myself back in Prum for the
cattle fair, would I be welcome for a meal in your new home?"

"Of course!" The words had barely left her mouth before
Maura remembered the truth. "That is…you would. I do not
know a great deal about the man my aunt intends for me. He
may not live in Prum at all."

"How do you feel about wedding a man you have never
met?"

That at least Maura could answer truthfully. "A little anxious, if you must know. But I trust he is good man. And I know
Langbard wanted this for me. It will be well."

"I hope it will."

They met a few Hanish soldiers on the road that day, and saw others as they passed checkpoints. Fortunately the hundredflower spell proved resistant to the rain.

It was dark by the time they crested a low ridge and saw the lights of Prum, a faint glow off in the mist.

Maura tapped Rath on the shoulder. "It is late. You must stay the night at my aunt's house, I owe you that at least."

She hesitated to extend an invitation on behalf of a woman she had never met. Once Exilda understood how much they owed Rath Talward, surely she would not grudge him a night under her roof. If the woman was a friend of Langbard's she must follow the Giver and the hospitable customs of the Elderways. She would not turn away a weary traveler on a wet night.

"You owe me nothing," said Rath. "Besides, I have coin enough for an inn."

Perhaps it would be better if they parted tonight, Maura tried to convince herself. The darkness and the mist would swallow Rath up, as though he had never been. And tomorrow she would waken to a new day and new life, in which he would play no part.

"Which way to your aunt's house?" Rath asked as they rode into town.

"I cannot tell you, for I have never been here. Langbard did not tell me the way…since he meant to come with me."

"Luckily Prum is not a very big place." Rath turned their mount off the main road onto a narrower street. "I will head toward the inn, if we do not meet one of the townsfolk to ask along the way, surely we can get directions there."

They had not gone far when they overtook a stooped figure, with a bulky bundle slung over her shoulder.

Rath slowed the mare. "Your pardon, goodame. Can you tell us the way to the house of Dame Exilda?"

Without slowing her pace or even glancing up, the woman grunted, "Who are you to ask, stranger?"

Rath laughed. "You are a woman after my own heart, goodame. You give away nothing until you know where it is going."

"If you aim to flatter it out of me, save your breath, boy."

Maura smothered a chuckle. At last Rath had come up against someone as wary as himself.

"I will use my breath," said Rath, "to tell you why I ask. I have brought Exilda's niece all the way from Norest for a visit. Since the hour is so late, we would be obliged to you for directions. No doubt Dame Exilda would, too."

"Rubbish!" snapped the woman. "Everyone in Prum knows Exilda had no living kin."

Maura felt Rath's body tense at the woman's words. "There must be some mistake…"

The woman rounded on them, then. In the faint light of a nearby window, her wrinkled face looked like a grotesque mask. "There is a mistake, sure enough, and you have made it, boy! Asking after she who has been dead a month and bringing a *niece* I will swear is no kin of hers. Now, be off before I report you to the garrison!"

The person she had come all this way to find was dead?

A pit of seething doubt gaped in Maura's belly, but she mastered it long enough to call after the woman, "Please, can you at least direct us to wherever Exilda lived before she…died?"

"I could." The woman's voice rang with grim satisfaction. "But there is no use you looking for lodgings, there. It burned to the ground the night Exilda died."

14

A tempest churned inside Rath Talward as he thrust Maura through the open doorway, into the cramped little closet of a room tucked under the eaves of Prum's oldest and smallest inn. He strode in behind her bearing a stubby candle, the flame of which flickered wildly.

"Now, then…" Rath shut and bolted the door behind him. "Out with your story, and make it a good one."

Ignoring her woeful look, he stooped to light a small fire laid in the hearth, then set the candle on the narrow stone mantel.

"Well…?" He peeled off his wet cloak and hung it on a high peg beside the door. "Have you nothing to say for yourself? Or are you too grieved by the news of your *dear aunt's* death to speak?"

"I am grieved." Maura's whispered answer trembled in the air. Her face was pale as whey.

As far as Rath was concerned, her pose of distress was only a different kind of weapon, dangerous in its subtlety.

Maura heaved a deep, shuddering sigh. "But not because Exilda was my aunt."

"What *did* bring you here, then? Why did you lie to me?"

His anger seemed to strike an answering spark in her, for the line of her mouth tightened and one delicate brow arched. "Who are you to condemn *me* for one harmless falsehood? The reasons for my coming here are nothing to you."

"Who says they are not?" He needed to move, but the room was so small Rath could do no more than circle Maura while he spoke. "Langbard was killed and his cottage burned on the eve of our departure. Now I hear the woman you came to meet was also killed and her house burnt. Strange chance, that."

Maura flinched at the stinging sharpness of his tone. "I doubt it was chance. But you knew coming with me would be dangerous. My true reason for coming did not make it any more so."

Though her words sounded positive, even defiant, her faltering gaze told Rath she did not fully believe what she was telling him.

"As for what right I have to condemn your falsehood," he growled, "I *never* claimed to be a model of truth or virtue. Now, tell me why you came to Prum so I can reckon how deep a snare you have lured me into."

"If this is a trap, then I am the prey, not you." She nodded toward the door. "Go, if you fear for your safety. I will not stop you."

Fear for his safety? Was she trying to shame him into staying? He *should* go. Whatever she might tell him, true or false, would make no difference now. Except to the vexing itch of curiosity within him.

"The truth first," he demanded. "Or do I not deserve it?"

His question to Maura raised another in Rath's mind. Was the truth such a valuable commodity that the right to it must be deserved or earned? Until lately, he had not thought so. Then Maura had made him believe otherwise…all the while she had been lying to him.

"If it is a matter of deserving," said Maura, "then of course you do. I have not forgotten all I owe you for bringing me here, even if things have not turned out as I'd hoped."

Did she mean to chide him? Perhaps he deserved it. Whatever her reasons for coming to Prum, they did not lessen the help she had given him when he'd needed it.

"Take off that cloak," he bade her in a gruff mutter, "before you are soaked to the bone."

Maura glanced down at her cloak, as if she had just remembered it was wet.

"I do not grudge you the truth." She fumbled with the tie at her neck.

Rath's fingers tingled with the urge to help her, but he ignored the sensation.

At last she worked the stubborn knot loose. "But I fear you will be like that innkeeper when you told him about stealing Vang's horse. The lies I told you were far easier to believe than the truth."

She hung her cloak beside Rath's, while he settled himself on the edge of the bed. "This man you were supposed to marry—is he real, or was he just an excuse to keep me at bay?"

That was the only part he cared about, Rath admitted to himself, not that Exilda woman or Maura's reasons for coming to Prum. But he could not decide what answer he wanted to hear.

Slowly Maura turned to face him again. After a moment searching for the right words, she said, "There is a man I am meant for. Though not some match made by an aunt for her niece."

She inhaled a deep breath. "I came to Prum in search of an ancient map that shows the way to the Secret Glade...of the Waiting King."

Then she fell silent, like the expectant hush after a crash of thunder. She held herself so still, she might have been a statue carved of wood, or stone...or ice. Except her eyes. They roved restlessly over Rath's face, watching and waiting for his response.

What response, though? Rath's first urge was to slap the bed and roar with laughter, but Maura had warned him he might. Suddenly it felt vital to not behave as she expected.

"You have wasted your time, then, and mine. There cannot be a map, for there is no Waiting King. He is the biggest lie of all—a story for simple souls who are so starved for a scrap of hope they will swallow anything."

"I did not expect you would believe." Maura sighed. "That is why I did not tell you sooner. A part of *me* still has doubts. Not about the Waiting King...about myself...that I could be his Destined Queen."

That was the one part of the story Rath might have been tempted to accept. "I have often wondered if the Han did not spread the tale of the Waiting King. To keep Umbrians idle, biding their time for deliverance by some great figure of legend, rather than rising up in rebellion themselves!"

For as long as he could recall, the myth of the Waiting King had riled him. Perhaps because Ganny had believed in it with her whole simple, trusting heart. And it had betrayed her faith. If the Waiting King truly existed—if he woke tomorrow and fulfilled every daft prophesy about his return—it would be twenty years too late.

Now Maura had risked her neck, and his, in the cause of that despised fantasy. Rath ached to draw his blade and lash out. At what, though?

"It hardly matters, now." Maura sank to the floor in front of the hearth and chafed her hands before the fire. "Whether you believe, whether I believe, whether the Waiting King is real or just a story. With Exilda dead and her house gone, there is no map for me to find the Secret Glade. I have barely begun this quest and already I have failed."

Rath tried to hold on to his anger. Without it, he felt unarmed and vulnerable. Yet the tighter he clutched it to him, the faster it seemed to dissolve. Maura needed him, now, as much as she had needed him back in Vang's stronghold. More, perhaps, and not just for this one night.

What would she do? Where would she go? Those questions mattered to him far more than he wanted them to.

He knelt beside her in front of the fire. "Lie down and get some rest, why don't you? Things are bound to look better in the morning."

Maura cast him a sidelong glance. The ghost of a smile hovered on her lips. "When did you become such a hopeful fellow, Rath Talward?"

He made a droll face. "I did not say they would look *much* better. But some, surely?"

"Will they?" Maura's gaze strayed back to the fire's dancing flames. "With Langbard's death, I lost my past. Now I have lost my future and my purpose. I have nothing."

"You still have me." Rath's heart had not knocked this hard against his ribs when he'd challenged Vang to fight. "If that is worth anything to you."

Slowly Maura turned toward him. Slowly she raised her hand to his cheek.

Rath fought the urge to nuzzle into that touch, for fear she would see how he hungered for it.

"Having you still here is worth *everything* to me. In fairness, though, I cannot ask you to linger. Any claim I had on you lapsed days ago. I only continued to impose upon your generosity for the sake of a worthy cause. Now that cause has miscarried, I must set you at liberty, with my deepest thanks."

Her hand climbed higher until her fingers played through his hair. "You have sat guard while I slept, too many of the past nights. Tonight, let me do this last small favor for you. I doubt we are in any immediate danger, and I need time and quiet to think."

Suddenly Rath's eyelids felt too heavy to lift. He fought an urge to yawn, but lost the fight. Had Maura cast a dreamweed spell without him knowing it? "I reckon I could sleep, at that."

Enveloped in a weary haze, he rose from the floor to perch on the edge of the bed. Maura pried off his boots, then reached for his waist.

"What are you doing?" he roused himself enough to ask.

"Unbuckling your blade belt—what do you think?"

Rath was still master enough of his wits not to answer that.

Maura ungirded his blade and his dagger. "I will lay them beside the bed, within easy reach. Though I doubt you will need them."

She twitched the bedcovers down. Then once Rath stretched out, she tugged them back up over him. "Rest well."

Rath mumbled a vague reply.

It did not take long for sleep to overcome him, but in that short time he mulled over what Maura had said. She was alone now, with nothing and no one. He recalled that feeling with bitter clarity. Many years had passed since it had first befallen him. It had persisted until a short while ago, when Maura Woodbury found her way into his life.

If they parted company tomorrow, Rath sensed he would be every bit as bereft as she.

In some strange way Maura could not begin to fathom, the soft, sonorous buzz of Rath's breathing comforted her through the long, bleak hours of that night.

What now? Over and over the question tumbled in her thoughts until it made her quite dizzy, but never coming closer to an answer.

Should she make her way back to Windleford? To Sorsha and Newlyn—the only people who might offer her a home she would be tempted to accept?

Someday, perhaps. But when she thought of Hoghill Farm, Maura remembered the menacing shadow under which she and Rath had fled. After all that had happened since then, that night seemed long ago, but it had not been. If she returned to Windleford too soon, she might place her friends in danger.

Could she stay here in Prum? Work for her keep? Her heart quailed at the prospect of trying to make a place for herself so far from everyone and everything she had ever known. Besides, danger might lurk here, too, if the same forces that had destroyed Langbard had also slain Exilda.

What choices did that leave her? Continue her journey in search of a safe haven? North to Tarsh, or the wilds of the Hitherland? Search for a ship willing to sail the dangerous passage to the Vestan Islands?

For all her uncertainty about the future dismayed her, Maura was forced to confront a secret shame. Part of her was relieved to be spared the burden of her quest. What would Langbard think of that, if he knew?

Langbard…? Giver…? Anyone…? What am I to do?

No fond, exasperated voice came to her from the afterworld, only the muted crackle of the dying fire and the unlikely reassurance of Rath's steady breathing. No sense of calm certainty enveloped her, as it had in Vang's dungeon and when she had told the old man that she was the Destined Queen.

Could Rath be right about the Waiting King? Was he at best a fantasy and at worst a lie? To accept that would free her of responsibility.

How tempting she found *that* notion.

But she had made a promise, of sorts, to that old man on the road…and to Sorsha…and to Langbard.

By the time the first feeble rays of daybreak light had begun to steal in the tiny window, Maura had made her decision. Not easily or without many misgivings, but one she could live with.

Quietly she rose, then stood for a moment staring at Rath, his rugged features softened in sleep. Langbard had believed he'd been sent by the Giver to aid her. Though he had seemed a strange choice at first, Maura was now inclined to agree.

No doubt he would scoff, even take offense, at the idea that he was employed by a power in which he did not believe, for a cause he disdained. One day he might come to see the truth—but she and her quest could not wait for that day.

A chill of dismay rippled through her at the thought of going on alone, without being able to draw on Rath's well-honed survival skills. But memories of what she had learned from him, and all she had faced and overcome so far on her journey, stoked her waning courage.

Though she longed to bestow one last caress of silent thanks for all his help, she did not dare wake him. For he would surely try to discourage her from what she meant to do. And her newborn resolve might be too weak to resist.

With an effort of will, she turned away and tiptoed toward the door, where she lifted her cloak off the hook.

"Going to fetch me breakfast?" Rath's voice rumbled behind her.

Maura did not turn to face him, but she heard him yawn and stretch. She could picture the ripple of his lean muscles.

"I knew I should have sprinkled some dreamweed over you so you would not wake."

"Too late now." The wooden bed frame creaked as Rath sat up. "If not to fetch breakfast, where are you bound for at this hour? Or is that none of my business?"

Though she told herself not to, Maura looked back. "What does it matter where I am bound or what I mean to do? The time has come for us to part ways. I will be no further burden on you."

He raked a hand through his hair. "I never claimed you were a burden."

"No." Maura twitched her cloak over her shoulders. "You did say you refused to care for anything but your own survival. My company has put you in danger too often."

"Aye…well…" His hand roamed over the crown of his head to scratch the back of his neck. "A body can grow used to a change quick enough, and I have got…used to…minding that you are all right."

He looked so awkward and earnest—the opposite of his usual cockiness. Maura found it strangely endearing.

"Are you saying you will worry about me?" The thought made her smile.

"Perhaps I am." Rath scowled. Did he think she was laughing at him for a show of weakness? "Nothing wrong in that, is there?"

Maura shook her head. "Nothing at all. Though I have faith in your ability to look after yourself, I shall wonder about you, too, and how you are faring."

"Then do not be so mysterious." Rath perched on the edge of the bed and pulled on his boots. "Ease my mind by telling me what you mean to do."

He would give her no peace until she did, Maura could see that. The sooner she confessed, the sooner she could be on her way. She could not afford to waste time.

"Very well. I am going to search for the Waiting King, map or no map. Langbard told me I have until Solsticetide. I will not give up until that time, if it means combing every inch of forest I can find between now and then."

"Are you mad?" Rath retrieved his blade belt from the floor, then rose from the bed to gird it on. "You would be lucky to search the whole of Aldwood in that time and it is only one of many forests in Umbria. Why, the Hitherland has little *but* trees!"

"I knew you would try to discourage me." Maura headed for the door. "That was why I did not want to tell you. That was why I tried to steal away before you woke. Farewell, Rath. May the Giver go with you, whether you wish it to or not."

She unbarred the door and tried to pull it open, only to find it would not budge. After tugging on the handle without success, she glanced up to see Rath's hand holding it shut. She could feel him hovering behind her.

"Heed me, Maura. If you had years to comb every forest in the kingdom, it would not matter. There is no one for you to find. You would be wasting your time."

Part of her wanted very much to heed him…but not all. She spun about to find him looming over her, close and compelling.

"It is mine to waste, if I choose!" Her back pressed against the door as she tilted her head to meet his gaze. "What better way would I spend it? Every moment working and planning to keep bread in my mouth and avoid notice of the Han?"

"That would be a good start!" Rath leaned closer. A few inches more and his face would be pressed against hers. "How are you to search the country without food to keep you on your feet? Without any means of protection?"

She had to escape the bewildering force that drew her toward him! "I did not expect you to understand." She squeezed between Rath and the door, retreating toward the bed. "Part of me wants to think as you do. Then I could abandon my task without reproach."

Rath turned, keeping himself between Maura and the door. His brow furrowed as if to ask what prevented her from following the sensible course.

"It is something I must do." She tried to explain in a way he might understand. That proved difficult since she was not certain she understood herself. "Just as you felt you must see me safe to Prum. Even after you had no further obligation to me. If there is the smallest chance I can find the Waiting King, I must pursue it…for the people of Umbria and for myself."

She reached into a pocket of her sash and pulled out a tiny ball of spidersilk. "Now, will you move away from the door and let me get on with what I have to do? Or must I put a binding spell on you?"

"Save your cobweb." Rath stepped away from the door, crossing his arms over his chest. "If you are that set on your folly, go. I will not stand in your way."

"It may be folly," said Maura. "But I *am* set on it."

Somehow, Rath's opposition had strengthened her resolve—another favor he'd done her, even if he had not meant to.

She walked the few steps to the door quickly, half fearing Rath might change his mind at the last moment and try to stop her after all. But he did not.

Relief and disappointment battled within her as she pulled open the door and strode through into the narrow hallway.

She was closing it behind her when Rath's voice rang out. "Hold a moment."

"What now?"

"A suggestion, if you will stay long enough to listen."

It vexed her to realize how much she wanted an excuse to linger in his company. "If this is some trick to detain me…"

"No trick…I swear." Rath crossed back to the bed and sat down, holding up his hands. "But step this way and close the door, so the whole inn does not hear what I have to say."

If he had meant to stop her, he could have done it before this, Maura decided. But if he truly had some advice to offer, she would be foolish not to listen.

She reentered the room, shutting the door firmly but quietly, "What is this *suggestion* you have to offer?"

"Just this—if you are looking for one special leaf, it will be easier to find by concentrating on a single tree than by combing the whole forest."

"You might have a brilliant future as an oracle, Rath Talward. Would you care to tell me what this leaf riddle means?"

"Think for a moment," he snapped. "If there *was* a map, which I still do not believe, who is to say it was destroyed? If this Exilda creature was a wise woman in more than name, I doubt she would have left something so important lying around her cottage."

That made sense. Maura chided herself for not considering the possibility. "You think Exilda might have told someone if she hid the map elsewhere?"

"It hardly matters. Even if you have to search every inch of Prum, it will be quicker to find a map hidden in one small town than a grove hidden in a large kingdom. Less dangerous, too."

Maura mulled over his advice. "You are saying this to keep me out of trouble."

"What if I am?" Rath acknowledged her charge by thrusting out his lower lip. "That does not make it any less true."

"Perhaps not," said Maura. "Either way, it may not matter. But it does make sense to exhaust all possibilities here, first. Have you any other wise words to share before I go?"

"Only two." Rath rose from the bed and made the gesture of parting, touching the tips of his fingers to his chest, then sweeping his arm outward. "Be careful."

"I will." Maura returned the gesture of parting. "I always am."

As she hurried away, she whispered to herself, "Too careful, sometimes."

In that spirit of caution, she sprinkled herself liberally with hundredflower petals and chanted the spell before crossing the threshold of the inn onto the street.

Now that she no longer had to keep up a determined front before Rath, Maura had to admit her bones ached and her head felt as if a cold fog had penetrated it. Her stomach squealed and rumbled in protest at having gone empty so long. Commitment to her cause would not take her far if her body failed from hunger, exhaustion or the illness they were sure to breed.

She must eat, Maura decided, setting off down a cramped, crooked lane toward the village square. And to eat she must work, beg or steal.

The scent of fresh bread lured her to a small bakeshop.

"Is there work I could do here in exchange for food?" she asked the stout motherly-looking woman behind the counting bench.

"Bless me, no, love!" replied the woman. "I have more younglings than I can keep in work. But if it's hungry you are, go 'round to the ovens and tell the lass there I sent you. We have a loaf or two burnt on the bottom you'd be welcome to."

Maura opened her mouth to thank the woman and to ask if she knew of anyone else in Prum who might be looking to hire. Before she could get the words out, however, several customers crowded in and began talking.

Stealing back out of the shop, Maura followed a narrow alley that took her to the ovens. When she peeped in through the open top of the half door, she spied a girl tossing sticks into the oven. The girl worked awkwardly, using her left hand. Her right was bound with a strip of linen.

"Excuse me," called Maura. "I am newcomer in town, looking for work. The woman out front told me I might have one of your burnt loaves for the asking."

"So you may if you want it." The girl fished one out of a basket in the corner and handed it to Maura.

Despite the charred odor, Maura's mouth watered. She wanted to grab the loaf and tear into it, but the bakers had done her a kindness.

"Did you burn your hand?" she asked. "If you have a bit of fat handy, I can make you a salve to soothe it."

"Could you?" The girl threw open the bottom half of the door and beckoned Maura in. "Be obliged, I would. We get so many burns around this place, we've used up all our last batch of salve. With Exilda gone, there's nobody to make more."

The mention of Exilda almost made Maura forget the bread in her hand.

"Gone?" She tried to make her tone sound as guileless as Rath Talward's when he was lying through his teeth. "Will she be coming back soon?"

The girl pressed her hand to her mouth and glanced over her shoulder. Apparently satisfied that no one had overheard her, she lowered her fingers enough to whisper, "I forgot. Mam said not to speak of Exilda anymore."

She pointed to a pair of crocks on a high table beside the door. "We have lard and tallow, whichever you fancy for salve-making. I'll fetch you a bowl and spoon."

With some difficulty, Maura stifled a sigh. She had stumbled upon a potential rich source of information, only to find the door shut in her face.

"What brings you to Prum?" The girl set a tiny clay bowl and small wooden spoon on the table by the fat crocks. "We get strange men passing through all the time looking for work, but not often women."

Maura spooned some tallow into the bowl, then mixed in a pinch of merthorn from her sash. "My uncle died and I have no other family, so I thought I would see a bit of the kingdom."

The girl stared at Maura's sash. "You are a healer? Why, you could earn your living that way."

"Perhaps." Maura took the girl's hand and removed the wrapping. She winced at the raw, red flesh. "Do you reckon I would be welcome in Prum? The Han do not hold with such things. This Exilda you are not to speak of...was she a healer?"

After an instant's hesitation, the girl nodded.

A smile tugged at the corner of Maura's lips. Here might be a way to get the information she needed, without making the girl disobey her mother.

"Did the people of Prum drive Exilda out of town?" With a gentle touch, Maura rubbed a dollop of salve onto the burn.

"I would not want that to happen to me if I began dispensing cures."

The girl shook her head so forcefully her white cap fell askew.

"Then she left of her own accord?" Maura wound the linen back around the girl's hand in a way that would make the bandage less apt to move and chafe the healing skin.

Again the girl shook her head. When Maura feigned confusion, she cast another anxious glance around the oven room then whispered, "She died. Her cottage burnt."

"Oh, dear!" Maura did not have to feign her dismay. "What a horrible way to die!"

The girl leaned close to Maura. In a barely audible voice she whispered, "I do not think Exilda died *in* the fire."

"Whereabouts would I find her cottage?" Maura tried to sound no more than vaguely interested. "There…might…be some herbs still growing on her property that I could use."

"No!" The girl's gaze seemed to fix on someone behind Maura. "I have said more than I ought, already. If Mam finds out, she'll thump me! You'd best go."

Maura whirled about to see what had frightened the girl. All she glimpsed through the open top of the door was a flying wisp of black. When she blinked and looked again, it was gone. If it had ever been there, except in her fancy.

"Do not forget this." The girl picked up the loaf of bread where Maura had left it. Then she grabbed the whole basket of burnt bread from the corner and thrust it into Maura's arms. "Take it all and do not come back."

Maura staggered into the alley. Both halves of the door slammed behind her, followed by the ugly rasp of metal bolts being slid shut.

"Oh, well," she muttered under her breath as she followed the alley back out to the street, "at least I will not go hungry for a while."

She paused for a moment to take her bearings and decide where to go next.

The street bustled with villagers going about their business. A tall, raw-boned woman strode past with a basket of eggs in one hand. Two boys ran by, chasing a third. A swarthy man wearing the broad-brimmed hat of a herdsman led a lame horse toward the smithy. Not one of them so much as glanced her way.

Yet Maura's neck still rippled with gooseflesh.

And the certainty that someone was watching her.

15

The sense that she was being watched haunted Maura as she roamed around Prum that day. Was it only her imagination, fueled by her fears?

When she sat beneath a flowering sunfruit tree on the outskirts of the village to eat some of her bread, a nearby clump of bushes rustled. Was someone crouching there, spying on her? Or was it only a small animal, waiting for a chance to feast on the crumbs she left?

Later, while she wandered the streets of Prum, trying to learn her way around, she glanced back over her shoulder and thought she saw someone quickly duck into the door of a tavern. She slipped around the corner of a small tannery across the road. From there, she could keep an eye on the tavern.

Quite some time passed before anyone came back out the tavern door, and when they did it was only two village men talking and laughing together, not taking the slightest notice of anyone around them.

Maura let out a shaky chuckle at her overblown fears. Between a lifetime of Langbard's warnings and the recent perils she and Rath had faced, it would be easy to let them run away with her. But if she spent every moment jumping at shadows and looking behind to see if she was being followed, she would have no time to search for the Waiting King.

Determined to rein in her runaway imagination, she looked around to decide which way she should go next.

Then she saw it.

Nestled on a modest plot of land on the fringe of the village, surrounded by a great swath of yellow hundredflowers, stood the gutted frame of Exilda's cottage. It reminded Maura so fiercely of her own ravaged home back in Windleford that an ache of longing gnawed at her heart.

Even the well was situated in the same spot as the one by Langbard's cottage. The sight of it reminded Maura of how thirsty she was after eating all that bread. Grasping the rope, she hauled the heavy wooden bucket up from the cool depths. Then she cupped her hands and took drink after drink. Leaning against the cool, hard rounding of the stones, she listened to the sweet springtime trill of the birds. Her heavy eyelids slid shut, and for a moment she could almost believe herself back in Windleford again, with few responsibilities and even fewer cares.

"You, there!" A shrill voice shattered Maura's sweet reverie. "What are you doing, hanging about here?"

The scolding tone reminded Maura of the woman she and

Rath had overtaken on their way into town. She turned to find the woman bearing down on her.

"Your pardon." She shrank back. "Does this well belong to you? I was thirsty and thought no one would mind if I drank."

The woman's small, close-set eyes fairly snapped with hostility. "If you've drunk your fill, be off!"

"So this *is* your property?" Maura feigned ignorance. "I am sorry about your house."

"'Tisn't mine. I live yonder." The woman pointed to a house up the road from the tannery.

"If the land does not belong to you," said Maura, "what gives you the right to order me away?"

What had made her say such a thing? she wondered the instant the words left her mouth. It was a fair question, but not one that was apt to win her aid or goodwill.

The woman glared at Maura so hard her tiny eyes almost crossed. "Keep a respectful tongue in your mouth, stranger-miss!" She hesitated a moment. "Stranger? Are you the one rode into town last night claiming to be Exilda's kin?"

"I did arrive here last night," Maura admitted, though she wondered if it was safe to do so. "But I made no claims of kinship. I came to Prum looking for Exilda. She was a friend of my guardian. Did you know her well?"

"Just lived near is all." The woman backed off, as though Maura's innocent question were a threat. "I've never had no truck with her sort!"

Those words reminded Maura of Windleford, but not in a good way. What a lonely life Exilda must have led—shunned by her neighbors except when they needed healing, with neither spouse nor ward for company. All to protect a map she'd believed would one day lead the Destined Queen to the Waiting King.

Thoughts of what Exilda had sacrificed in her cause emboldened Maura. Fixing the querulous woman with a forceful gaze, she tried to echo Langbard's tone of authority. "Did you see what happened the night of the fire? Did any of Exilda's neighbors come to her aid?"

"Too many strangers!" The woman went into full retreat. "Too many dangerous folk abroad. She brought it on herself— and on us, curse her!"

"What dangerous folk? Did you see someone here that night...or since?" Maura called her last question after the woman as she scurried away, her elbows flapping like a fowl in panic.

With a sigh, Maura turned back toward the cottage, pushing her homesickness into a deep corner of her heart and locking it there. She could take it out and wallow in it at her leisure, once she accomplished her task...or her time ran out. For now, there were things she must do.

Searching the property for a start, noting anything out of the ordinary that might provide a clue to the whereabouts of the map. Only there *was* nothing out of the ordinary.

In a small vegetable patch much like the one Maura and Langbard had kept, green sprouts pushed their way out of the moist spring earth. Exilda's garden was overgrown with weeds, though, and the tender young shoots had been nibbled by animals. Maura took the opportunity to refill a few of the pouches on her sash with fresh herbs, including the rare but precious quickfoil.

Near the garden patch, she discovered a mound of earth sparsely stubbled with young grass. Though Maura knew it was weeks too late, something made her drop to her knees beside Exilda's grave.

"If you can hear me," she whispered, "I have come for your map. If it still exists, please help me find it…in time."

A soft fluttering sound made Maura start. She opened her eyes to see a tiny brown pinefinch perched atop the mound of earth, its head cocked at a quizzical angle.

Maura smiled. For a moment the twin burdens of danger and duty weighed lighter upon her shoulders. "I do not suppose *you* have anything useful to tell me?"

The bird gave a jaunty chirp, as if laughing at her foolish question. Then it flew to light on what was left of Exilda's garden shed. The fire that had destroyed the cottage had not touched the small structure. But something else had.

Something even more violent than flames. The boards had been splintered, as if smashed by a giant fist. Some had been hurled a great distance. Rakes, hoes and spades lay strewn about—one spade driven so deep into the ground that only its long handle showed.

The pinefinch flew up to perch on the end of the spade handle, all the while keeping a curious eye on Maura.

"Someone buried her." Maura looked from the spade handle to the mound and back again. "I wonder who?"

She recalled the night Rath had dug Langbard's grave, while she had observed the passing ritual. "Whoever it was, perhaps they can help me find the map."

Perhaps they *could* help…but would they?

The sound of hurrying footsteps made Maura turn.

"Your pardon, mistress." A stooped, grizzled man beckoned her. "You'd best come away from here, 'fore night falls."

Another villager intent on running her off. Maura fought to curb her temper. "What harm am I doing anyone by being here?"

Her sharp tone seemed to take the man aback. "Why, none at all, mistress…except to yourself if they catch you here."

"They?" The breeze had shifted to the northeast. It whispered over Maura's skin redolent with the scent of danger.

"Them as came that night," said the man, "and have been keeping watch on the place since. I marvel you have escaped their notice this long."

So someone had been watching her…trying to penetrate the subtle but potent protection of the hundredflower spell.

More of the man's warning penetrated Maura's alarm. "*That night?* Do you mean the night…" She nodded toward the black skeleton of the cottage then at the mound of earth under which Exilda's body lay.

"Aye, that night." The man backed off as if hoping she might follow him. "Now, come away before worse happens to you."

Curiosity drew Maura with a greater power than fear. "Did you see what happened that night?"

"Some." The man kept walking in the direction of the tannery. "After it was too late to do aught but dig."

"You dug Exilda's grave?" Maura walked faster to keep up with him. "Did you sit with her, too?"

"For the ritual, you mean?" The man shook his head. "I had my work cut out just to get her buried."

He answered Maura's next question before she got it asked. "I bid old Gristel Maldwin come sit with her, but I don't reckon Gristel saw to any rites. Her and Exilda never had much use for one another."

"Where might I find this Gristel person?" Maura asked.

Even if she had not been on good terms with her neighbor, the woman might be worth talking to. Langbard had taught Maura that, if a passing spirit had enough power, it could still convey messages without the ritual. Exilda might have left some hint of the map's whereabouts.

"She lives yonder." The man pointed to the last in a row of dwellings that backed onto Exilda's little plot of land.

The narrow house looked too tall for its base. A number of stout trees crowded around it with outstretched branches, as if ready to catch it in the event a strong wind knocked it over. That house had already been pointed out to Maura once that day. By the disagreeable woman who had tried to chase her away from Exilda's well.

"If you mean to call on her," added the man, "mind you do not look for a civil welcome. Old Gristel has a disposition sour enough to curdle new milk."

Maura cast him a wry look. "We have met."

The prospect of a third encounter with such an obnoxious person dismayed Maura. Still, she thanked the man for his warning and the information he had given her. Then she mustered her resolve and headed for Gristel Maldwin's house.

Off to the west, the sun sank nearer the tall, jagged peaks of the Blood Moon Mountains, which thrust up like fangs to devour their evening meal. With every step Maura took in the direction of the tree-girt house, the walking boots Sorsha had given her seemed to grow heavier. The cloak fastened around her neck seemed to grow tighter.

There was danger nearby, and no ordinary danger, either. Maura recalled how the Hanish arrow had whistled over her head the day she had rescued Rath. And how the outlaws had grabbed her in the middle of the night. Neither had stirred this chill of approaching peril.

From the pockets of her sash she pulled a handful of fresh dreamweed she had collected from Exilda's garden. With the herbs in one hand and the last of her spidersilk in the other, Maura approached the house with the soft, cautious tread she had so often seen Rath use.

She was still a few steps away when she heard the voice. Though not loud, it had an unsettling resonance unlike any Maura had heard before. As she moved closer, in spite of every instinct that urged her to turn and run, she could tell the words were not Umbrian.

Then she heard Gristel Maldwin reply in Comtung. Out of the rapid, high-pitched gabble, Maura recognized the word *no*. She could guess what must be going on inside, but she needed to see for certain. The only window on this side of the house was half-shuttered, and too high for her to peek in. Perhaps if she climbed the tall bristlenut tree that grew nearby, she could get a better look.

Knowing she would need her hands free to climb, Maura reluctantly returned the dreamweed and spidersilk to the pockets of her sash. Then she sank to the ground and pulled off her boots and stockings. Long ago she had discovered bare feet were best for tree climbing.

Once back on her feet, she hoisted herself onto the lowest

branch. From there, she was able to scramble higher until she could peer in through the unshuttered half of the window. What she saw confirmed her fears.

One Hanish soldier held Gristel Maldwin's scrawny arms behind her back. The angle of the woman's shoulders told Maura they were being stretched painfully far. Though she could not see whoever was questioning Gristel, Maura did catch a glimpse of a second soldier farther back in the room.

How many of them were in there?

The strange voice asked another question, in a tone so quiet Maura could barely hear. The words made Gristel flinch. Her answer came pouring out in a jabber of Comtung and Umbrian while she shook her head with frantic haste. The torrent of words grew ever more shrill and fast, until the frenzy of it penetrated Maura's chest and set everything inside her churning.

Then Gristel's words all merged into a tight, desperate mewl of pain and she twitched as if her head and limbs were trying to tear themselves from her body. Maura clenched her eyes shut and her mouth, lest she surrender to the urge to cry out in sympathy.

After a moment that stretched on and on with no hope of relief, the wailing subsided into a spent, terrified whimper. Maura forced her eyes open to see Gristel slumped forward, her arms still pinned by the Hanish soldier who showed no sign of being moved by her torment.

The interrogator spoke again as he moved into Maura's line of vision. She swallowed a gasp and clung to her perch in the tree branch. This was the first time she had ever seen a member of the Echtroi with her own eyes. If she never saw another as long as she lived, she would be grateful.

The death-mage wore a dark robe and billowing black cloak. A close-fitted black cowl covered his head and the upper part of his face, with two narrow slits behind which his eyes roved restlessly. The lower part of his face was unnaturally pale, with skin pulled taut over sharp bones and a tight, cruel mouth.

In his gloved hand he clutched a wand of burnished copper set with a fire gem. Bending over the whimpering woman, the Echtroi thrust the tip of his wand beneath her chin and tilted her face toward him.

Maura could watch no more. Gristel Maldwin was an ill-tempered busybody and she had been no friend to Exilda. It galled Maura to think of putting herself in peril for such a person. If their places had been reversed, she doubted Gristel would lift a finger to help her. And if, by some slim chance, Gristel knew a scrap of useful information about Exilda's map, she would have told her Echtroi inquisitor long before this.

For all that, Maura could no more leave the woman to her fate than she had been able to leave Rath Talward to his.

Slowly, so as not to rustle any branches against the house, she crawled back along the bough of the tree until she reached the trunk. All the while her thoughts spun with possibilities. The dwindling supply of plant and animal matter in her sash were a pitiful match for the malignant power of the Echtroi and his copper wand.

But they were all she had. She must find a way to put them to their best use. And soon. The Echtroi were notorious for many things, but patience was not one of them.

Any moment the death-mage might decide to give his victim a more lingering taste of the fire gem's hungry power. Or perhaps he would have her hauled down to the garrison for a more thorough interrogation. Maura's best chance was now, while they were inside the house.

Best chance for what, though?

As Maura considered her prospects, her gaze roved over what she could see of the house, from bottom to top. At last it came to rest upon the narrow chimney from which a feeble wisp of smoke rose. Maura recalled a story Langbard had once told her, about an enchantress dropping magical gifts down a chimney.

Well, she had a magical *gift* for the Han!

Staying close to the thick trunk of the tree, Maura began to climb from bough to bough. When the screams began again, she battled to maintain her concentration and keep climbing. At last she reached the proper height and found a branch that stretched out over part of the roof.

She hoped it would be sturdy enough to bear her weight.

The evening grew darker as Maura inched her way toward the roof. The wind began to gather force, making the branch beneath her sway. Was it too late to think of another plan— one that carried less risk of breaking her neck?

A sudden hard gust of wind shook the tree. Behind her, Maura heard a crack and her branch drooped. Clenching her lips to keep from crying out, she sent a silent plea winging through the night for the Giver's help.

As abruptly as it had begun to fall, the branch came to rest and Maura felt the reassuring bulk of the roof beneath her. The frantic hammering of her heart eased, but only a little, as she crept toward the chimney. She rummaged in her sash for every scrap of dreamweed she could find.

Warm air caressed her hand when she held it above the chimney. Sounds rose upon that air, echoing off the hard interior of the tall stone column.

Gristel's shrill keening had subsided and the death-mage was speaking again, in Hanish this time, words that sounded like an order to the soldiers. Was he telling them to investigate suspicious sounds on the roof?

Murmuring the sleep spell, Maura opened her hand to let the dreamweed leaves flutter down the chimney. The last particle had just left her palm when doubt began to prickle in her mind. What if the spell-laden smoke all wafted back up the chimney without making the Han do more than yawn?

Finding nothing else handy to stop the chimney, Maura scrambled up and sat on it. Then she pulled a quickfoil leaf from her sash and chewed on it while chanting the stimulant spell.

It took effect at once, lifting the weight of fatigue that had burdened her all day. It sped her pulse—not in the shallow, erratic flutter of fear, but strong and steady. It sharpened her senses.

But the quickfoil also made it a struggle for her to sit still and wait. Her limbs itched to move. Her thoughts raced with questions and plans.

Maura made herself count to a hundred. Whenever the numbers began tumbling too fast, she forced herself to begin again. By the time she reached the end of her count and rose from her perch, her body was trembling with stifled movement.

Pulling the edge of her cloak over her nose and mouth, she inclined an ear to the chimney opening and listened. All was quiet below. Now, if only she could get back to the ground with all her bones in their proper places!

With the mountains so much closer to Prum than they were to Windleford, the sun seemed to set more quickly here. As Maura tried to find her way off Gristel Maldwin's roof, she had just enough light to make out the vague shapes of branches.

She did not dare use the one that had cracked. But out near the eaves she found a pair of boughs, the lower on which she could walk, while she held on to the higher one for balance and to bear some of her weight. As quickly as she dared, Maura scrambled down.

When she climbed past the window, she glanced inside. Though the room was dimly lit, Maura could see no one stirring.

With only one more branch between her and the ground, she took a wisp of spidersilk from her sash, just in case. Then she dropped the last few feet and froze, her binding spell ready in case someone reached out of the darkness to grab her. No one did, but that only soothed Maura's fears a little.

She groped about for her boots and stocking and pulled them back on with fumble-fingered haste. Then, pressing herself close to the wall of Gristel's house, she crept to the corner and peered around it, expecting to find one of the Hanish soldiers standing guard at the door. Instead the front of the house appeared deserted.

Maura inched forward. Upon reaching the door unhindered, she eased it open and peered inside.

All was quiet and still in the house. At least five people slumped in different parts of the main room, not moving. The scent of dreamweed hung in the air like the warm, soft pungency of fleece on a winter night.

The tightness in Maura's muscles began to ease. Her breathing grew deeper. The beat of her heart slowed.

The time for caution had passed.

Pulling the edge of her cloak back up to cover her nose and mouth, she charged into the room, pausing only long enough to cast the binding spell on each of the Han. Hopefully it would buy her a little time if they woke before she got away.

Finally she turned her attention to Gristel Maldwin, lying on the floor beside the Hanish soldier who had held her arms. At least the poor woman was no longer in pain. Looking down at her limp, slumbering form, Maura realized she had given no thought to how she would get Gristel out of the house.

"Drag her, I suppose," Maura muttered to herself.

If only she had not used up all her essence of bear. It would have come in handy just now. As would some means of keeping her nose and mouth covered when she needed both hands to shift the sleeping woman. Since she could contrive nothing at short notice, Maura resolved to hold her breath for as long as possible. She hoped it would be long enough.

Stooping, she wedged her hands under Gristel's arms and hauled the unconscious woman toward the open door. Fortunately it was not a long distance, for the scrawny creature was heavier than she looked.

A gust of night wind blew into the house, whipping Maura's cloak. She turned her face toward it and sucked in a deep breath. The scent of dreamweed was making her dizzy and awkward in her movements. But the fresh air, her earlier dose of quickfoil and her determination to resist the sleep spell all combined to keep her awake and moving.

She almost tripped over the outstretched legs of the bound, slumbering soldier nearest the door, but she managed to right herself and drag Gristel over him. Staggering backward, Maura gave one last heave to haul her burden out into the night.

Then a vast, black shadow reared up. The faint, flickering light that spilled out the door glinted off a raised blade.

The cry that rose in her throat began as fright, but quickly exploded into defiant anger. Escape had been snatched away from her at the last instant, before, by the bandit lord, Vang. Damned if she would let it happen again tonight!

In a rush of desperate strength, she heaved Gristel up and pushed her toward the bladesman. He uttered a hoarse grunt of surprise as the dead weight of the village woman toppled against him.

That instant was all Maura needed. She turned and darted back around the corner of the house, her fingers fumbling in her sash. Please let it be there! The tiniest wisp would do.

Once she had rounded the corner, Maura dove down, listening for the footfall of her pursuer. It did not follow as quickly as she had expected. That gave her an extra moment to probe the depths of her sash pocket and come up with a few delicate strands. And to begin a breathless chant of the binding spell.

By the time she heard the approaching tread, gathering momentum with every step, she was ready. Pinching the precious threads of spidersilk between her thumb and forefinger, she lunged out, tackling her pursuer around the ankles. His blade whistled through the air above her head as he flailed to keep his balance. But the speed of his own headlong charge sent him pitching to the ground.

Planting the cobweb fibers on his clothes, Maura gasped out the final words of the binding spell.

"Slag!" As he hit the earth with a muted thud, the blades-man gasped a curse. "Fuming, sucking slag!"

Maura recognized the voice.

"Rath?" She staggered to her feet. "Is that you?"

"Who were you expecting—the Kyrythe of Dun Derhan?"

A bubble of panic had been swelling in Maura ever since she glimpsed the death-mage. Now it shattered in a burst of frenzied laughter.

She lunged at Rath again, giving him a cuff on the head so light it was more like a fond ruffle of his hair. "Not the Ky-rythe, perhaps, but one of his servants, you rogue! What are you doing here? You are lucky I did no worse to you."

His hair felt so good beneath her fingers, his voice sounded so sweet to her ears, even when he was spewing curses. His familiar, welcome scent rose to beguile her. They had only parted that morning, yet it seemed much longer.

Far too long.

Before she realized what she was doing or could begin to stop herself, Maura kissed him. Not once but over and over—on his brow, his cheek, his nose, his chin. Some feeble scrap of prudence kept her from straying too near his lips.

Perhaps it was only her overwound emotions breaking free, as they had back in the bandit's lair after they had fought Tur-gen. Or perhaps she needed to convince herself beyond any doubt this *was* Rath Talward on the ground beneath her. If something more than either of those compelled her, she dared not acknowledge it.

One day, perhaps, but not now.

"What are you about, you daft wench!" Rath growled, but his lips whispered over her face as he spoke. "Tie me up and have your way with me—I'll be willing enough, but not with the stench of Han in my nose."

Though his tone conveyed more fond exasperation than true displeasure, Rath's words brought Maura to her senses all the same.

"Your pardon!" she gasped. "I did not mean to… Here, let me unbind you."

"That would be a fair start," said Rath as Maura chanted the spell of release. "I do not fancy the Han finding me all trussed up like this."

"Do not fret too much." In the darkness, Maura fumbled for Rath's arm and helped him to his feet. "They are all trussed up, themselves, and still fast asleep, I hope. Still, neither of us had better linger here."

In the darkness, she fumbled for Rath's arm and helped him to his feet.

"Agreed." Rath reached for her hand. "Let's go!"

Maura froze. "Wait. We cannot leave Gristel behind."

"You mean that body you heaved at me? It was alive?"

"The sleep spell is still on her." Maura tugged him back toward the house. "What good fortune you are here. *You* can carry her."

"Carry her where? And why? Who is this Gristel creature that you and the Han have all taken such an interest in her?"

"She is the woman we asked directions from last night when we rode into town. She was Exilda's neighbor and she is…"

She grasped for an explanation of how Gristel Maldwin

might know about the map to the Secret Glade. An explanation Rath might stand a chance of believing.

"Gone," said Rath.

"Gone?" Maura shook her head. "What gone? Where?"

"How should I know where?" Rath pointed toward the ground near Gristel's doorstep where they had left her lying.

He had spoken the truth. The woman was gone.

16

Rath's face still tingled from the drizzle of kisses Maura had rained upon him. A rain as welcome as any unexpected shower after a long drought. It had taken him as much by surprise as the rest of her ambush. Though he doubted she'd meant anything by it, at least it showed she was not displeased by his sudden reappearance.

That pleased him…far more than he cared to admit.

Now he wanted to get them both to a place of relative safety where they could talk. But Maura had other priorities, the highest of which seemed to be the village woman who had disappeared.

"She cannot have gone far." Maura peered about, but the shadows were too thick to penetrate. "Do you suppose she got confused and went back inside?"

She started for the door, but Rath grasped her by the arm to stop her.

"I will check." Not for anything did he want Maura going back into that house, no matter what kind of spells she had cast on the Han. "You search out here. Start from this point and walk in widening circles. It is the best way to search in the dark for something that may be near at hand."

"Very well, but do not stay inside long or the dreamweed smoke may overcome you, too." Maura pressed something small, smooth and cool into his hand. "Chew on this quickfoil. I picked it fresh from Exilda's garden. It will help keep you awake. And pull your cloak over your nose and mouth."

Rath popped the leaf into his mouth. As the invigorating tang tickled his tongue, he marveled at how readily he had come to trust Maura's brand of magic.

"Can you whistle like a willow-wing?" he asked her.

"I reckon so. Why?"

"To find each other again. We cannot waste time blundering around in the dark, and it could be dangerous to call out."

"Clever thinking." Maura gave his hand a squeeze, then set off on her search. "Take care!"

"I always do." Rath drew his dagger and charged into the house.

The mellow, soothing aroma of dreamweed enveloped him the moment he crossed the threshold. Remembering Maura's advice, he drew up the edge of his cloak to muffle himself against the seductive lure of sleep.

A quick glance around the room revealed no sign of the woman. But three Hanish soldiers and one black-robed deathmage lay where they had fallen.

"Bravely done, lass," Rath whispered.

His excuse of looking for the missing woman had been just that—an excuse. Rath's true intent was to finish what Maura had started so well.

He bent toward the unconscious Han nearest the door, his dagger whetted and ready to warm with Hanish blood.

The soldier's helmet had fallen back when he'd swooned from the sleep spell. Rath's throat tightened as he stared at the smooth, full face of a youth. Suddenly his blade hand felt as if it were in the thrall of Maura's binding spell.

He told himself the boy would not hesitate to slit *his* throat, or worse, if their positions were reversed. He reminded himself of the old Hitherland adage that only a fool ever walked away from a wounded foe. The thought that any mercy he showed this young viper might endanger Maura almost freed Rath from his daft hesitation.

Almost.

Maura would not thank him for such *help*. He could picture the look in her eyes. A mixture of revulsion and disillusionment that should not trouble him one whit, much less put his survival at risk to avoid it.

Fie! If he stayed there much longer the sleep spell would overcome him. He must do what he had come to do, or move on. With a convulsive movement, Rath pounced and his sharphoned dagger slashed.

Then he snatched up his trophy—a long plume of pale hair he had cut from the helmet of the bound, sleeping young warrior. One day, perhaps, they would meet on a field of battle, and Rath would show no mercy, nor would he expect any. But that would be a fair fight, not cold murder. His decision made,

Rath strode around to the other two soldiers and swiftly claimed his prizes.

When he came to the Echtroi, Rath hesitated again. He had heard the old woman's screams. To take pity on a fiend like this would be more than softness, more than folly. It would be a kind of wickedness.

To convince himself this was no youth he should spare, Rath twitched off the mage's black hood. What he saw made the bile rise in his throat.

Apart from the proper placement of features, the Echtroi's face hardly looked human. The skin was pale as ash, except for dark smudges beneath the eyes. And that skin was stretched so tight over the skull, it looked little better than a clean-picked corpse. The death-mage was perfectly naked of hair, not only on top of his head. He had no brows, no lashes, not even the feeblest thread of a whisker to suggest that a beard *could* grow.

It looked less like the face of one who inflicted torture on others than one who had suffered torture day after day, for time beyond reckoning. To kill it might be mercy after all.

Just then, Rath heard a faint noise overhead.

His gaze flew to a steep, narrow set of stairs that ran up the left-hand wall of the room. Might the woman Maura was seeking have had wit enough to hide under the very noses of her captors...or above their heads?

Thrusting the long coils of Hanish hair into the death-mage's black hood, Rath tucked it into his belt and made for the stairs. His foot knocked against something. He glanced down to see a copper wand with a fire-gem flickering on its tip.

"Well, well."

With only the briefest hesitation to touch an object of such menacing power, Rath snatched the wand from the floor and thrust it into his belt as well. How fearsome would the death-mage be now, without his weapon?

When he straightened up again from stooping to retrieve the wand, Rath's head spun. If there was anyone or anything upstairs, he had better find out quickly and flee the house before he ended up on the floor, snoring beside his enemies.

He galloped up the stairs, three at a time. Then he groped about in the darkened room. He hit his head more than once on the low ceiling and tripped over several pieces of furniture before he decided he must have imagined the noise that had drawn him up there.

Fumbling his way back to the head of the stairs, he tripped yet again. Rath cursed.

Then the thing he had tripped over stirred and groaned.

A rush of excitement overcame his growing weariness long enough to grapple onto one scrawny arm and hoist who-ever he had found over his shoulder. Somehow, he managed to stumble down the steep stairs without breaking his neck or dropping his burden.

He found the young Hanish soldier nearest the door waking from the sleep spell, too. The boy struggled against his invisible bonds the way Rath had when Maura cast that same spell on him. When the youth heard Rath coming down the stairs, he craned his neck to shoot a glare of icy outrage.

"Release me at once, lowling!" He barked the order in Comtung.

Rath glared back. To think he had taken pity on this young lout!

He raised one booted foot and brought it to rest on the boy's neck. "Take care who you order about, whelp, or I will cut off more than your pretty hair next time!"

The whelp's eyes widened in dismay, though whether on account of the foot poised to crush his throat or his lost hair, Rath could not tell.

Convinced he'd made his point, Rath withdrew his foot and headed for the door. Then something made him turn and fling a final threat at the arrogant pup and the whole arrogant empire of which he was a willing tool.

"Do not fret about your hair, boy. You will not need it when the Waiting King sends you and all your kind packing from our shores." A hollower boast Rath Talward had never uttered in his life. But how sweet that lie tasted on his tongue!

Well nigh intoxicating.

He had the satisfaction of seeing a flicker of fear in Hanish eyes. That alone was almost worth the folly of letting the young slag-spawn live.

"So you have heard of the Waiting King, have you? Well, his patience is waning. He will not wait much longer. And when he wakes, mind, the Hanish Empire will tremble."

For a priceless, fleeting instant, as he spoke those words, Rath felt himself swell in size. His weariness fell away and his body grew stronger. His senses sharpened and something quickened in his spirit that might have been his lost nobility.

As quickly as it came, the bewildering power deserted him, leaving him smaller, weaker and more disreputable than ever. He swung about, hoping the young Han would not glimpse the change. Then he strode out into the night, pursed his lips and blew the distinctive, swooping whistle of the willow-wing.

* * *

When Maura heard Rath's bird call, she ran toward it. Hot on her heels scurried the kind neighborman who had buried Exilda.

Maura had blundered into him during her search for Gristel. Fortunately she'd recognized his voice before she'd had time to cast a spell. She'd just begun to explain what had happened when Rath's willow-wing call trilled through the night air.

After giving an answering whistle, she caught the man's hand. "Come. That's a friend of mine. I hope he has had better luck than I, finding Gristel."

She doubted it, though. No matter how confused Gristel might have been when she'd woken from the sleep spell, Maura could not imagine her willingly going back into that house with the Han. Still, it relieved her to hear Rath's signal. He had been inside for quite a while. She'd begun to worry the dreamweed might have overcome him, too.

Another whistle sounded, from very nearby. Maura heard footsteps approaching.

She slowed so they would not collide in the dark. "Rath?"

A large shadow detached itself from the surrounding ones. Large and strangely misshapen for a man.

"I found her," said Rath in a loud whisper. "The wily old bird." In a few terse words he explained how Gristel had sought to hide on the upper floor of her house.

Maura could not help admire the woman's quick thinking, and Rath's cleverness at finding her.

"I have someone here who may be able to help us." She hesitated, realizing she did not know the man's name.

He seemed to understand. "Boyd, mistress. Boyd Tanner.

My shop's just down this way a piece. You're welcome to bring Gristel there. I heard someone crying out from her house a bit ago. Fair gave me the chills, it did. After things quieted, I came to see if I could help."

"Many thanks for your aid, Goodman Tanner," said Maura. "A place to bide awhile would be most welcome. Pray lead the way."

Rath muttered his thanks, too. He sounded as though he would welcome a chance to lay down his burden.

Now that the most immediate danger had passed, Maura wondered what she and Rath would do next. Go their separate ways again? It would be even harder to walk away from him this time.

Fortunately the Han had not seen who'd put them to sleep, then trussed them up with invisible bonds. Still, after what had happened tonight, Maura knew Prum would not be a safe place for strangers in the coming days. If Gristel Maldwin could not or would not provide her with some clue to the whereabouts of Exilda's map, she would no longer have the luxury of roaming around town in search of it.

"Through here." The tanner pushed open a wide door at the rear of his premises. "And up the stairs."

The pungent smells of hides, smoke and animal oils made Maura's nose twitch.

"I have a little room where I sometimes hide folk who run afoul of the Han." The tanner plucked a small candle from a sconce just inside the door. "The smells around this place throw their cursed hounds off."

Once they reached the top of the stairs, he hurried past Maura to what looked like a blank wall. He slipped his forefinger into a knot in one of the boards. A hollow click sounded from behind the wall, then a section of it pivoted inward.

The tanner slipped through the secret door.

Maura motioned Rath to go next. "I will close up behind us."

After pushing the door shut and refastening the clever little latch above the knothole, Maura followed the others past a heavy dark curtain into a tiny, windowless room with a straw mattress on the floor. Rath eased Gristel Maldwin off his shoulder to lie on it.

Maura squeezed past him to kneel beside the woman who was beginning to rouse from the sleep spell again.

Gristel's eyes flew open wide. "Where am I?" She cowered on the mattress, raising her hands as if to fend off a blow. "Where are *they?* Who are you?"

"Hush," said Maura. "We mean you no harm. You are somewhere safe. Are you in any pain, still?"

"Some." The woman looked from Maura to the familiar face of the tanner. When her gaze strayed to Rath Talward, a fresh look of fear twisted her sharp features.

She grabbed Maura's hand and squeezed it tight. "Do not let them find me again! I do not know the things they want to find out about Exilda. They will hurt me again."

A violent trembling shook her.

"Shh." Maura made no move to retract her hand from Gristel Maldwin's desperate grip. "We will not let anyone harm you."

She glanced up at the tanner. "Can you fetch me a cup of hot water? I will make a draft to soothe her."

He bobbed his head. "Aye, mistress. Kettle's on the hob. I'll not be a moment."

True to his word, he returned quickly with the water, into which Maura drizzled a pinch of summerslip. Gristel Maldwin sniffed the brew with a suspicious look, but after a tentative sip or two she drank the rest readily.

When she had finished, Maura took the empty cup and handed it to the tanner. "Now, Goodame Maldwin, we will not hurt you, but I need to know…what manner of questions did the Han ask you about Exilda?"

Her gentle query brought an anxious look to the woman's face again. "I didn't rightly understand half what they asked. I only know enough Comtung to get by. What I could make out was something about a *place paper.*"

Behind Maura, Rath murmured, "A map?"

Gristel cast him a wary glance.

"It is all right," said Maura. "This man found you after you went back into your house to hide. He brought you here. You have nothing to fear from him. Now, they asked about a map?"

"I…reckon that might be what they meant. They wanted to know if Exilda had any visitors…wizardfolk. I tried to tell 'em she kept to herself but…"

In spite of the draft, the woman grew agitated again, and Maura spent several minutes soothing her. If her questions had not been so urgent, she would have left Gristel to rest, but the protection of darkness would slip away with the passing hours. And the spells she had put on the Han would weaken.

"Your pardon, goodame, but I must ask you a question or two about Exilda. I promise I will not harm you, no matter what your answers. Though it will be a great boon to me if you can remember."

"I'd like to oblige you folk, but Exilda and me did not get

on. She kept to herself. Ask Goodman Tanner if you do not believe me."

Under his breath the tanner muttered, "Private folk have no use for busybodies."

"I understand," Maura assured the woman, "but you sat with her body the night she died, while Goodman Tanner dug her grave."

"Aye. It is ill luck to leave an unburied corpse alone, or do they not know that where you come from? The ghost may linger to haunt folks."

It grieved Maura that the rituals of the Elderways had fallen into such ignorant superstition, but this was not the time to quibble over it. "Tell me, when you sat with her, did her voice speak to you?"

"Nah! She were dead, weren't she?"

A sigh of bitter disappointment rose in Maura's throat.

"Her lips never moved," Gristel added.

Maura swallowed that stillborn sigh. It tingled in her belly like a potent tonic. "But did you *fancy* you heard her? In your mind?"

"Aye," Gristel looked embarrassed by her confession. "It were naught but nonsense. On account of I was wrought up about the fire and all."

"Please." Maura clutched Gristel's hand almost as tightly as Gristel had clutched hers a while before. "This could be very important. Can you recall what Exilda's voice said?"

"Prattle. Naught but daft prattle. It cannot be important to you."

If Maura had possessed a death-mage's wand, she would have been sorely tempted to threaten the woman. "Tell me, please. What sounded like prattle to you might have meaning for me."

A special incantation, perhaps, that would reveal the site of the map. Or some clue to its location in Old Umbrian words.

"Pickles."

Expecting the rich, musical cadence of Old Umbrian, Maura could not make sense of the simple word. "Your pardon?"

"Pickles," Gristel repeated in a wry tone that said she had warned them. "Pickles, preserves, jellies. On and on till I thought I must be running mad. Even if she had been alive and speaking the words, who would care about such things at a time like that?"

Who, indeed? Maura dropped Gristel Maldwin's hand.

It sounded as though Exilda had tried to communicate something as she'd passed into the afterworld. Perhaps the message had gotten garbled.

Or perhaps...?

"Your pardon!" Maura leapt to her feet. "I must go."

She turned to Goodman Tanner. "My thanks for your aid. It was unlooked for, and all the more welcome for that. I hope someday I may have the means to better show my gratitude."

A change came over the tanner's craggy face. "You're the one, aren't you? The visitor Exilda waited for all these years?"

"She told you about me?"

"Not in so many words, mistress. But now and then she would say, 'She'll come yet, Boyd Tanner.' When I asked her who, she would say no more. I am sorry you were too late for her, and she for you."

"So am I, goodman." Maura scarcely dared acknowledge

the tiny ember of hope inside her. "Perhaps someday I will return to Prum and you can tell me more about Exilda."

The tanner nodded. "This little hidey-hole will be here if ever you need it, mistress."

"My thanks." Maura glanced down at the mattress where Gristel Maldwin was dozing once again. "Can she stay here?"

"As long as needs." The tanner did not look happy about the arrangement, but resigned to his obligation. "Wherever you are bound, may the Giver go with you."

Maura acknowledged the traditional blessing with a tired smile. "And remain with you."

"What was that all about?" Rath stepped aside to let Maura pass, then fell in behind her. "Where do you need to go in such a hurry?"

"I must go back to Exilda's house to check something," said Maura, as they let themselves out of Boyd Tanner's hidey-hole, then picked their way down the stairs in the dim light cast by the hearth fire. "It may be a vain hope, but I have nothing better to pursue just now."

At the foot of the stairs, she turned to him. "Can I impose on you for a while longer? I may need your help."

Rath shrugged. "It is no bother. To tell the truth, I have followed you all day to make sure you did not come to any harm. At least I *did* until you gave me the slip outside the tavern."

"So that was you!" cried Maura, torn between wanting to clout him and wanting to kiss him again. "You might have said something. I was afraid I had the Echtroi on my trail."

Even in the dim light of the tannery, she could see Rath's face take on a look of grave urgency.

"You did. You do."

"What?"

Rath nodded. "After you got away from me at the tavern, I did some poking about the town. I overheard a few of the Han talking amongst themselves. Seems they're swarming the Long Vale rooting out wizards and healers and folk like that. The Lord Governor has sent Echtroi over the mountains to take charge of the search."

A shiver went through Maura. If her guess about Exilda's map proved false, it would be all but impossible for her to return home to Norest.

"I cannot think about that now." Though she spoke the words aloud to Rath, they were addressed as much to herself. "If you will lend me your aid for a few hours more, I will be greatly in your debt."

She pulled open the back door to the tannery and stepped out into the night. Apart from the wind, all was quiet outside. That would soon change once her spells on the Han wore off.

"This way," she whispered to Rath. "Exilda's cottage is not far. What is left of it, at least."

"We dare not stay long," Rath warned her, "if this notion of yours does not yield."

"I know."

A twig snapped beneath her foot. As she stooped to pick it up, Maura chanted the greenfire spell. By the time she moved forward again, the twig in her hand had begun to give off a soft, verdant glow—just enough for her and Rath to see a few feet in front of them.

"Now," said Rath when they reached the charred shell of Exilda's cottage, "what are we looking for?"

Maura scrambled among the burnt timbers, her glowing

twig lowered. "Can you fetch a spade? There's one stuck in the ground at the bottom of the garden."

"A spade? Are you daft, lass? Do you imagine a map survived that fire? Why, there is nothing left of this cottage but a heap of ash."

"There should be one thing left." Maura pushed away the blackened remains of a fallen beam. "The cold hatch under the cottage floor—where folk store pickles and such. I hope that is what Exilda's message to her neighbor meant. I think I know where to find the door that leads down to it, but we will need to shift some of this ash and rubble away first."

"The cold hatch." Rath seemed to ponder the idea. "You may be on to something. Let me fetch the spade."

It took a good hour of hard, dirty labor between them to excavate the cottage floor, often casting harried glances toward Gristel Maldwin's house.

"I think I see it!" Maura cried at last, sweeping away a final layer of soot with a pine branch. "How odd, the boards look as if they have hardly been singed. I wonder if Exilda put a spell of fire resistance on them?"

The possibility lofted her slender hopes higher.

"Is there such a thing?" Rath coughed from all the ash and soot they had stirred up. "Then why did she not put it on the rest of the cottage, and Langbard on yours?"

"The ingredients for it are difficult to come by in large quantities." Maura passed him the greenfire twig to hold while she groped for the latch to lift the trap door. "A wizard would only use it to protect small, valuable items from fire."

Her hand closed over the rope latch. She pulled the trap door open and scrambled down the ladder.

"Pass me down the light!" she called back to Rath.

Instead she had to scoot out of the way when he clambered down after her, pulling the trap door shut behind him.

"What are you doing?" she demanded. "There's hardly room enough for me down here, let alone both of us."

"I had no choice." The greenfire played over Rath's rugged features caked with soot. "I heard some commotion from Exilda's house. I reckon our *friends* have woken from their nap."

Maura bit back a curse. "There is no help for it, I suppose. Thank the Giver we were able to find this place in time. Oh, look! Here's a candle. Light it, will you, before this greenfire goes out?"

Once Rath had obliged, and not a moment too soon, Maura lifted the flickering candle to take a good look around them.

Rath gave a low whistle. "If we have to stay down here awhile, at least we will not starve." He tapped the toe of his boot against one of several stone jugs arrayed on the lowest shelf. "Or go thirsty."

"Exilda was an industrious housekeeper," Maura agreed, looking around the small space lined with shelves on three sides.

Every shelf held regular rows of crocks, jars and jugs. There must be hundreds! And Maura's weariness was rapidly catching up with her.

"The map could be underneath any of these, or inside one, perhaps." She tried to keep a plaintive note from her voice. "If you will start on that side at the top, I will start over here at the bottom. That will keep us out of each other's way for a while, at least."

"Fair enough." Rath set the candle back where they had

found it, tucked in a little hollow high on the fourth wall. "Can we eat as we go? I have scarce stopped for a bite all day."

"I do not reckon Exilda would mind." Maura removed the stopper from a small jug, sniffed, then took a sip followed by a deep draft. She passed it to Rath. "Cherry cider."

For the next several hours they worked, opening lid after lid and stopper after stopper of pickled vegetables, meats and eggs, preserved fruits, cider, ale and wine.

But they found no map to the Secret Glade or anywhere else.

As her hopes waned, Maura's eyelids grew heavier and heavier. Her yawns grew more frequent and deeper.

"Enough!" said Rath at last. "I reckon the sun is up by now and Prum crawling with Han. We cannot go anywhere until nightfall, so why not rest, then finish up later?"

Not waiting for Maura's permission, he removed his cloak and spread it beneath him on the packed dirt floor. Then he settled himself with his back against the one empty wall. There was just room enough for Maura to tuck in between him and the ladder, which she did.

Her head listed against his arm. "I was so sure I would find the map down here."

"We haven't opened *every* jar," Rath reminded her. He reached for a crock on the shelf beside him. "Pickled eggs—my favorite. But only the one container of them that I could find."

"Go ahead and eat them, by all means." Maura closed her eyes, savoring the warmth and strength of him beside her. "We might as well get something for our labor. And thank you for the encouragement, even if you do not mean a word of it."

His arm twitched in a shrug. "I admit, you had me going,

just finding this place after that gabble about pickles. Then the trap door not burnt."

Maura gave a drowsy, dispirited nod. Everything had conspired to raise her hopes. But each jug and jar they'd opened to find only the most ordinary contents had eroded those hopes. Now fatigue began to take its toll as well.

Was it foolish of her to believe she might find the way to the Waiting King here, among pickled rooties and marshberry jam? Was it foolish to believe in any of this?

In truth, she felt more at home in a cold hatch full of preserves than she could imagine feeling in a grand castle. More at ease in the company of a partially reformed outlaw than she could imagine feeling in the company of a legendary king.

Beside her, she could hear Rath eating his pickled eggs with obvious enjoyment. She could smell him, too.

"Ow! Slag!" Rath jumped, spewing a litany of curses in between exclamations of pain. The egg crock shattered on the floor with a pungent splash of vinegar and pickling herbs.

"What's wrong?" cried Maura, jarred from her light doze. "You are hurt." That much was clear. "But how?"

"This! Filthy bit of slag!" Rath hurled a pickled egg at the floor. "So hard it nearly cracked my tooth."

True to his word, the egg did not smash into a mushy mess when it hit the hard packed earth, as several others in the crock had done. Instead it bounced, then split neatly in two.

"This is no egg." Maura scooped up both the perfectly identical halves. Her finger slid over the smooth, rounded surface. "I think it might be a kind of ivory."

She turned the object's flat sides toward her. For a moment she stared in a daze at the fine dark markings etched there.

"Rath, look." She thrust one toward him.

His dark mutter of curses trailed off as he peered at the object in her hand. "Of all the… Well, I never… So there *is* a map, after all!"

There was a map, two as it happened, etched into the ivory of this cunningly wrought object disguised as an egg.

Maura wilted back to her place on the floor, her heart so full she dared not answer for fear of bursting into tears like some overtired, overexcited child.

She had found the map. Her quest could continue with some hope of success. What was more, the very existence of this map bolstered her faith in this unbelievable destiny of hers.

It might even make Rath rethink his doubts.

17

"I am going with you," said Rath, "and that is final, so do not waste your breath arguing."

He had been sitting there for what felt like hours, wrestling with his decision. By the time Maura gave the slightest hint of waking, he could not wait another moment to tell her. Once he had said it aloud, there could be no turning back.

"Hmm?" A yawn stretched Maura's pretty mouth wide. Then she rubbed her eyes with sooty fists, leaving dark shadows around them. "Go where? What are you talking about, Rath?"

"Go here." He held up one half of the ivory "egg." He had been staring at the tiny map etched on it for so long his eyes felt as though they'd been burnt by pain spikes. "To Everwood. According to this, it is where you will find the Secret Glade. This half shows all of Umbria. The other half is a map of the wood itself."

"Everwood?" Maura stretched her arms high, then peered toward the fine etching. "How can you tell?"

"See that crescent in the middle?" Rath pointed. "Those have to be the mountains."

His fingertip was not much smaller than the map itself. It made him wonder what sort of deft fingers had wrought such delicate work. Or had the markings been put there by magic?

"The mountains." Maura yawned again. "I guessed that much."

"Those two spots above the upper tip of the crescent must be the North Lakes," Rath continued. "So that mark just south of Great Forest Lake has to be Everwood. I grew up not far from there. It is wild country and few folk venture far into the forest. There's a daft old tale that…"

"That what?"

The memory made the back of Rath's neck prickle. "Nothing. Just a yarn the oldlings would tell to keep foolhardy lads from wandering into the forest and getting lost."

"What sort of yarn?" Maura pulled a slender jug from the nearest shelf and removed the stopper.

"Foolishness," Rath insisted. "I hardly recollect it."

"Try." Maura took a long drink followed by a sigh of enjoyment. "After last night, I could use a laugh."

"Oh, very well. Ganny and some of the other old folk used to say there were parts of the wood where time stopped. They claimed there was once a lad from the village who strayed too far into the forest. Everyone gave him up for dead until he strolled back home twenty years later, not aged a day. He thought he'd only been gone an hour."

"Oh, my," whispered Maura. She took another drink. "That would explain a great deal."

"If it was true."

She turned to stare at him. "After all that has happened, can you still doubt?"

"I doubt everything." Rath tossed one half of the egg-map up in the air, then caught it in his hand. "It is my nature."

"Then why do you insist on going with me?"

He had asked himself that same question many times during the past several hours. And he had not been very satisfied with the possible answers.

"Perhaps because I have a taste for adventure." That was true enough. "Perhaps because anything that sets the Han in such a stew is worth doing."

Maura made her own guess. "Perhaps because you think I cannot manage without your help."

"No." Rath dropped the two halves of the map onto the lap of her apron, then reached for her hand. "I may not be certain what my reasons are, but I know what they are *not*. Any woman who can do what you did to three Hanish soldiers and a death-mage does not need some ill-bred outlaw to take her where she wants to go."

With her free hand, Maura patted her sash. "The credit belongs here, not with me. Only the Giver knows what will become of me once I have emptied its pockets. I used up all my spidersilk last night, but I do have a fresh supply of quickfoil and dreamweed from Exilda's garden."

"Then you should make an effort to restock your supply whenever you get the chance." Rath pointed toward the ceiling of the cold hatch. "There's a nice bit of cobweb, for a start."

Maura picked up the map of Umbria. "Is it a very long way to this Everwood place? What is the quickest route to get there?"

"That depends," said Rath. "If we were a pair of sunhawks, we could fly over the mountains, then head north. Have you a spell that can make us fly?"

Maura chuckled at the notion.

"A shame we had to come all this way to find the map," said Rath. "If we had headed west from Windleford instead of south, we might already be there by now."

He pointed to Windleford, then traced their route to Prum.

"And Everwood is way up there?" Maura asked, a plaintive note in her voice.

Rath gave a rueful nod. "I am sorry to bear ill news."

"So we must go back the way we came, then travel that much farther again to the west?"

She had said *we*, not *I*. That pleasant surprise distracted Rath from the rest of her words for a moment.

Then they sank in. "We cannot go the way we came. It is too dangerous with the Han on alert in the Long Vale. And I would not fancy meeting up with Vang or any of his crowd."

Maura shuddered. "Neither would I. But what other choice do we have? Surely you cannot mean to…"

"Go through Westborne?" Rath completed her question. "That is just what I mean. It is a straighter route and, say what you will about the Han, they keep up roads well."

"But there will be twice as many Han in Westborne as in the Long Vale…five times…perhaps ten!"

"True, but they will not be expecting us to march right under their noses."

"With good reason—it is folly!"

Part of him agreed with her. Long ago, Rath had sworn that he would never again set foot west of the Blood Moon Mountains. It *was* the quickest way to Everwood from Prum, but what did haste matter if he did not believe in Maura's Waiting King?

"I will not let any harm come to you," he promised.

A country-bred lass like her, with scant knowledge of Comtung or Westborne ways, would need to rely on him. Was that what compelled him to insist on traveling through the heart of Umbria, where Hanish control was strongest?

Or was it something else that made even less sense?

"I cannot believe I let you talk me into this," said Maura two days later, as she and Rath rode up into the foothills of the Blood Moon Mountains.

"Into what?" Rath glanced back over his shoulder. "Taking this route to Everwood, or letting me come with you?"

"Both." She gave a chuckle to show she did not mean it… at least not entirely.

True, she quailed at the thought of passing through Westborne. But it seemed there was no *easy* or *safe* way to get where she needed to go. At least this route offered them a little respite from danger while they traveled through the barren lands of the Waste.

As for letting Rath come with her, she was grateful he had insisted. Too grateful, perhaps. She sensed his presence posed a different kind of danger to her quest. A potent danger to her heart.

"Is it safe to stop yet?" she asked. "My backside is aching something fierce from this long ride."

They had stolen out of Exilda's cold hatch just after sunset two days ago. Then they had sneaked back through town to the inn, where they retrieved their horse and a few supplies. Twice they'd had close brushes with Hanish patrols, but Rath had managed to avoid them both. Once out of town, they had gone as quickly as they dared in the darkness. At times, Rath had dismounted and led the horse with Maura on its back.

When the sun had risen again, they'd hidden and slept until dusk, then struck off toward the high country. They had been riding ever since, with only brief pauses to snatch a little food and drink.

"Just a bit farther." Rath shifted in his saddle. Perhaps he had a sore backside, too. "I know a place where we should be safe to stop for the night. A great many plants grow around there. I thought you might want to replenish your supplies."

Maura nodded. The emptier the pockets of her sash grew, the more vulnerable she felt. "Would there be any water around this place, by chance? After grubbing through all that soot at Exilda's cottage, I am so dirty I can scarcely stand myself."

"And I." Rath gave a growl of wry laughter. "A few weeks ago, a little soot would not have bothered me. I am going soft, I tell you, and you are to blame for it."

"There is nothing *soft* about you, Rath Talward." Maura batted at his hair, on the pretense of knocking some of the soot out of it.

"There had better not be, if I am to get us through Westborne safely." Rath ducked his head to dodge her touch. "And to answer your question, there is plenty of water where we are headed. A warm spring pool, as it happens."

"Warm spring? What is that?"

"Just what it sounds—a spring of water that comes out of the ground warm. I do not know why, but there are several of them here in the foothills."

"Warm water?" Maura tried to imagine it. "Without hauling it from the well and heating it on the hob? I fear I shall never want to leave."

She feared it even more once she saw the place.

Nestled in the hills, surrounded by great swaths of green fern and sheltering trees, it was a tiny paradise.

"I cannot decide what to do first." Inhaling a deep breath of the faintly pungent air that rose from the surface of the pool, Maura dipped her hand in to confirm that the water was warm. "Should I do some gathering, wash my clothes or bathe?"

"I know what I *want* to do first," Rath said as he heaved the saddle off the horse and tethered the beast to graze. "But perhaps we should look for plants while we still have light to find them."

"Duty before pleasure?" Maura directed a teasing grin his way. "That does not sound like the outlaw code."

"*Necessity* before pleasure," Rath corrected her. "If my blades needed sharpening, I would do that before I sat to eat. Our lives might depend on these plants of yours. Besides, I would just as soon bathe after dark."

"Indeed? And why is that?" She had to admit, the notion of soaking in a warm pool under the stars appealed to her.

"Because I think it unwise to tempt myself with more than

a glimpse of what I cannot have." As he spoke, a hot hunger shimmered in his eyes.

How could he possibly find her the least bit appealing, all sooty and sweaty? It sent a delicious yet frightening tingle through Maura's flesh. She tried to suppress it, and when that did not work, she tried to ignore it.

That was no great success, either.

"Your pardon, Rath. You know I cannot. And you know why."

"Aye to both." He made a visible effort to subdue his desire. "Let us get to work, then. What should I look for?"

"I can always use more queensbalm." Maura forced her mind to their task. "I have plenty of dreamweed and quickfoil from Exilda's garden. I could use more madfern, though."

She described what it looked like. "You will probably find it near the pool."

"Madfern?" Rath seemed to savor the word. "I know what it looks like. What does it do?"

Maura had spotted a tiny patch of summerslip. She stooped to pick some of the pale blue flowerlets. "Remember the day I turned you invisible in Betchwood?"

"It is not one I am likely to forget." Rath moved off to search around the pool. "Why?"

"I used powdered madfern to confuse the Han. It made them think they saw you still running ahead of them after you had disappeared."

"Aha!" Rath held up a delicate frond. "It sounds like handy stuff."

Maura nodded her approval. "It is, though you have to be careful with it. You cannot always predict what way the confusion will work on a person's mind."

They continued gathering in silence for a while, then Rath brought Maura several madfern fronds.

"Does it ever feel strange to you, using magic?" He glanced from the lacy green fern to her face and back again. "I mean, my blade has a sharp edge. I swing it and what it hits, it cuts. The larger the blade, the harder the swing, the better the aim, the worse damage I inflict on my foe."

His description made Maura's stomach clench. "What has that to do with vitcraft?"

Rath shrugged, as if he found it difficult to put into words. "You sprinkle a little pinch of fern or feather or web and people disappear, or fall asleep against their will, or cannot move. Is it never hard for you to believe such small things could have so much power?"

"Langbard taught me that everything has power, however small. It is all a matter of finding out what form that power takes and how best to release it."

Rath nodded, but his brow furrowed as though he still did not grasp her meaning.

When the light had become too dim for Maura to tell candleflax from moonmallow, she and Rath agreed that they had earned a rest and a good long soak in the pool.

Pulling off her stout boots and thick stockings, Maura eased her hot, itchy feet into the warm water with a sigh. "Oh, my! Every home in Umbria should have its own warm spring."

Rath ungirded his blade belt and let it drop onto the grass with a muted clatter. Then he pulled off his padded leather vest. The light had grown too dim for Maura to see more than a vague shadow. But even that unsettled her. Rath had been right about the wisdom of waiting until dark to bathe.

Over his shoulder he tossed a jaunty quip. "Is that a royal decree, Your Grace? A warm spring in every home? It would make you a most popular queen."

Maura shrugged out of her tunic. "You may not believe in what I am doing, but you need not make fun of me."

Beneath a layer of soot, her cheeks stung. It did sound ridiculous—her, a queen.

She had only the faintest rustle of the grass to warn her of Rath's approach. Suddenly he was there before her, on his knees reaching for her hand. "Your pardon, Maura. I mock many things, myself included. I swear, I never meant to mock you."

He had shed his shirt. The stars twinkling in the clear, dark sky overhead cast enough light to show Maura that. The force of his masculinity seemed to give off an aura of its own—one that drew her with all the power of a spell. How easy it would be, and how pleasant, to surrender to the pull of her desire for this man.

But how wrong, for both of them.

"The Waiting King is real." She wanted to speak the words in Old Umbrian, as if they were a counterspell to protect her from the potent enchantment of Rath's nearness and her own yearnings. "You will see."

"Perhaps." Rath tilted his face to press his cheek against the back of her hand. "But tell me, if you were to discover he is not, and that you are free from this great destiny, would you...?"

She waited for him to finish, torn already as to how she would answer.

Did she dare confess how urgently she wanted to be in his arms? Lying beneath him? Learning the most powerful kind of life-magic that needed no ingredients but a man and a woman. No incantation but the endearments of lovers and the wordless enchantment of kiss and touch.

He was a strong, masterful man. If he knew the true extent of her weakness for him, might he exploit that frailty, as he did in battle, to force her surrender?

Yet how could she deny the truest feelings of her heart?

"Would I...what?" she asked at last, willing her voice not to quaver.

She could feel the tightness in the muscles of his hand and face. And something more. A strange energy beyond her physical senses perceived his heart and will pulled taut as a rope in the hands of two intense conflicting forces.

Then the cord snapped. Maura felt it so surely, she could almost hear the soundless rending.

Part of her wished he would take her, using his physical strength and the edge of her own hunger to lift from her the harsh weight of choice. Then she could have what she secretly coveted without the blame of consciously betraying her destiny.

"Nothing." That word crackled with the release of pent-up pressure as Rath let go of her hand. "Forget I ever started to ask such a daft question."

He leapt to his feet and disappeared into the shadows. A moment later Maura heard a splash from the pool as he plunged into the water. The breath she had been holding hissed out of her and her body felt limp and spent.

The soft trickle of water into the pool could not begin to fill the awkward gulf of silence between them. Even the haunting call of a nightbird and the occasional sighing nicker from the horse did little to help.

After a moment, Maura dropped to her knees and began to wash her tunic, with loud splashing and vigorous slaps against a large, smooth rock that helped to vent her frustration. When she had finally pummeled the poor garment as much and as hard as she dared, she hung it over a tree branch to dry.

Then she wriggled out of her undergown and shift. Though she knew Rath could see no more than a faint shadow wrapped in shadows, she found herself bashful of the subtle sounds made by her clothes parting from her body.

The memory of his words—*I think it is unwise to tempt myself with more than a glimpse of what I cannot have*—whispered through her thoughts, heated her flesh in a way the mild night air could not cool.

She eased herself into the wet, concealing embrace of the pool. Slowly the warmth of the water and quiet of the night seeped into her, untying some of the knots in her flesh, soaking her clean…in body, at least.

Untying the bit of ribbon that bound her hair, she unplaited it then tilted her head back to wash it. The majestic beauty of the night sky caught and held her gaze, as though she was seeing it for the first time.

"The stars are brilliant tonight," she whispered to herself, almost forgetting Rath's presence. "How the eye of the Steed sparkles! I can almost believe he will put on a great spurt of speed to bear his master after the Black Beast of Ursind."

Ahead of the Steed with its swirling mane of tiny stars lurked a dark, starless void that reminded Maura of an open mouth, ravenous to consume every spark of light from the sky.

"I know the names of the stars." Rath's voice reached out of the shadows from the other side of the pool. "And how they move through the sky as the year passes. But you make it sound as if they tell stories."

"So they do." As Maura's gaze wandered the night sky, all the star tales Langbard had told her rekindled in her memory, and with them a bittersweet sense of closeness to him. "The Steed bears Lord Velorken, who holds the Sword aloft."

She pointed toward the long straight shaft of bright stars that pointed the way north.

"And I suppose," said Rath, "the Hound runs at his heels while the Hawk wheels above, ready to stoop and strike?"

"Just so."

"And who is this Lord Velorken?" Rath's voice took on a warmer, more relaxed tone, for which Maura was grateful.

This unsettling attraction would always be there between them, like a stew simmering on a low fire, giving off a mouth-watering aroma. It needed only a breath of wind to stir the flames and make it bubble away, threatening to boil over.

"When the world was new—" Maura savored the words that began so many of the old stories "—and the Children of the North and the Children of the South were all one kin, the Black Beast of Ursind tunneled beneath the earth, throwing up these mountains. It shook the ground in its rage, spewing out fire and death. The ancient writings say it was the Beast who poisoned metals and gems with death magic.

"Velorken was Lord of the Greatkin. He climbed the Mountain of Snows and there beseeched the Giver to destroy the Beast and deliver the world from its evil. When he woke the next morning, Velorken found a magical horse, twice the normal size, that could outrun the wind and leap so high it seemed to fly without wings.

"Beside the magical steed, Velorken also found a blade of such sharpness and power it could cleave rocks with the lightest stroke. A hawk with eyes so keen it could see all the way from the shores of Westborne to the Vestan Islands. And a hound with a nose so sharp it could track a fish down a stream."

"A good thing the hounds that tracked us in Betchwood that day were not blessed with such noses!" Rath gave an exaggerated shudder.

Maura reached for her cloak and used the hem of it to rub her hair dry. "Armed with his magical gifts, Velorken harried the Black Beast out from under the mountains, then pursued it from Tarsh to the Waste and back again. As you can imagine, they left havoc in their wake. At last, Lord Velorken entreated the Giver to have mercy on his people. He said he would chase the Beast as long and as far as need be, if only he could be given a hunting place where they would do no one any harm."

"So the Giver put them in the night sky?" Rath's voice rumbled with amused disbelief.

"Is it so very hard for you to accept?" Perhaps it was, given the kind of life he had led. "I sprinkled a few feather cuttings and said some words, then no one could see you—not even yourself. What little power I have is lent me by the Giver. Even if a feather did nothing more than help to keep a bird aloft and make it invisible to predators, would that not still be a marvel?"

Rath's only reply was a vague grumble of agreement.

"Langbard taught me the world is full of wonders." Like *warm* water welling up out of the ground. "But people take them for granted because they are familiar and commonplace."

"What else did Langbard say?"

Maura thought for a moment. Then she remembered something Langbard had told her about the story of Velorken. Something that might make sense to a man like Rath.

"He said the star tales might only be that. Tales—fancies of things that never happened."

"Aha!"

"Save your *aha*, Rath Talward. He also said that the most unlikely tale may still contain a great truth."

"That sounds a proper riddle."

"But it is not, really. Think about the story of Velorken. He asked the Giver to do something for him, but instead the Giver provided him with the tools to do it for himself."

Had the Giver provided her with the tools to fulfill her quest? Was Rath Talward one of those? Might his doubt be a whetstone on which she was meant to sharpen her faith? Her desire for him a test of her fidelity and worthiness?

"And when he was willing to sacrifice himself for his people, the Giver made that possible." As she spoke those words, Maura's voice grew quiet and anxious.

Would she be called to give her life or something she valued almost as much in order to deliver Umbria from the Han? And if she were, would she find the courage to do it?

18

When they set out early the next morning, Rath sensed Maura's reluctance to leave behind the small haven of safety and comfort they had found.

He could hardly blame her. Since leaving Windleford their journey had been little different from his accustomed life of hardship and danger. He tried to imagine how much of a shock it must have come to Maura, after her sheltered years as ward of a powerful wizard. And the worst might be yet to come.

"We can stay another day, if you care to," he offered. "It would not hurt either of us to rest a bit before we go on. You might find more supplies for your sash."

He would not mind lingering here, tasting a sense of peace that was sweet, yet piquant. His outlaw wariness warned him to distrust the ease and contentment he found here. But the convictions by which he had lived for so long were beginning to chafe, like the outgrown clothes he had worn as a child.

Maura looked around the spot, so peaceful and green. "Remember what you said last night, about thinking it unwise to tempt yourself with more than a glimpse of what you cannot have?"

"Aye, what of it?" Rath's face stung. Could he be blushing for the first time in twenty-eight years?

"I dare not tempt myself with any more time here." The wistful look on Maura's face made Rath ache. "Otherwise, I may never be able to make myself leave."

But she *was* leaving a place of serenity she clearly craved, to venture into unknown danger on a quest of which she must have doubts. Perhaps the blood of that Velorken fellow ran in her veins, if such a man had ever truly lived. For she had all his resolve and courage.

More perhaps, for he had been a powerful lord, and she scarcely more than a girl. She had no rock-cleaving sword, only the snippets of plant and animal matter in her sash. No steed who could outrun the wind, only a sturdy mare, twice stolen, which would soon be of little use. No keen-sensed hound or hawk to guide her, only…

Was *he* meant to be what the hawk and hound had been to Lord Velorken? The notion of being used by some great invisible power in which he did not believe gave Rath a cold, clammy feeling. Yet something about the image of the hawk drew him. Proud, predatory bird, fierce and solitary.

"Besides." Maura pulled a rueful face. "We must reach Everwood by Solsticetide. You know the way. Can we afford to linger here if we are to reach the Hitherland in time?"

Rath did the reckoning in his head. Part of him wanted to lie and claim they had plenty of time. Urge her to do what part of her clearly longed to. Every additional hour they spent here would make it easier for him to dissuade her from her well-meant fool's errand.

"No." He forced the word through clenched teeth. "We had better make haste."

If she had the courage to undertake this task, he could not bring himself to undermine her. Instead he would see her through to the end, comfort her in her disappointment and hope she would turn to him afterward.

Climbing into the saddle, he hoisted Maura up behind him. Then, willing himself not to glance back, he pointed the mare southward and jogged the reins.

For a time they rode through the high country, both lost in their thoughts. More than ever, Rath was conscious of Maura seated behind him, clinging to his waist, sometimes resting her head against his back.

Ever since he had grown canny enough and powerful enough to attract followers, he had resented their intrusion on his solitude, their demands upon his skills and loyalty. With Maura it was different—perhaps because, in some odd way, she was his leader, not his follower. Yet he welcomed her reliance upon him.

He glanced back over his shoulder. "We have a few more long days' rides ahead of us. Would you care to tell me another one of your tales to pass the time?"

Her green eyes twinkled like starlight on a dewy leaf. "And give you a chance to laugh at my folly in believing such tales?"

The twinkle faded, replaced by a look of disappointment that made him cringe with shame. "I might laugh if the tale is amusing. Otherwise, no cheek, I promise."

"You mean it?"

"Upon my life." Rath nodded. "You see, I have traveled this country from Southmark to the Hitherland, but hearing your tale last night made me feel like I've been stumbling around half-blind all that time. Where did Bror's Bridge get its name? Who was the Oracle of Margyle?"

"Who *is* the Oracle of Margyle?" Maura corrected him. "As far as I know, she lives yet."

She paused for a moment, perhaps weighing his sincerity. "Would you like to hear about the Choice of Velorken's Children? It is not very amusing, I'm afraid. It tells about how the Great Kin were sundered into the Kin of Han and the Kin of Umbri. If you do not know it, then you are more than *half*-blind to what ails our land, now."

"It sounds like a gripping tale." Her words had set the back of Rath's neck prickling. "Let's hear it."

Maura's voice took on the compelling cadence unique to storytellers. "After Lord Velorken chased the Black Beast into the heavens, the Giver sought to reward his children with a wish. They could have knowledge of the special powers of things that grow upon the earth, or knowledge of the special powers of those things from deep within the earth."

Despite his resolve not to interrupt, Rath could not keep silent. "But they could not agree, could they?"

"No, they could not." Maura sounded grieved by the ancient breach. "Have you heard this story before?"

"Part of it, perhaps," Rath admitted. "Long ago, from Gan.

After she died and I was left on my own, I tried to forget everything she had told me about the Elderways."

He'd had too many other things to occupy his mind, just to survive. Old, outlandish stories had felt like so much useless gear he must abandon to travel light. Now he wondered if he had maimed a part of himself by losing that connection to the past?

Maura picked up the thread of her story. "As you said, they could not agree. Han wished for mastery of metals and gems, Umbri wished to be mistress of growing things. Some of their kin supported Han, others Umbri, until it seemed they would wreak more destruction upon each other than the Black Beast had done. The Giver was grieved by their strife."

As Maura told the tale, Rath felt the miles and the hours slipping away. And a lost piece of himself restored.

During the next several days of hard riding, the land became more rugged with every passing mile. And Rath's hunger for Maura's stories seemed to grow with each fresh one she told him. She could feel something stirring and growing within him. It pleased her to be able to repay him in some small way for the great service he was doing her.

How many other of their country folk might harbor the same nameless craving to know of the past from whence they had come and the vast intricate tapestry of which they were a part?

On the fourth day, they stopped at a small trading post in a secluded valley. There, Rath bartered their horse for stout walking sticks and packs heavy with supplies for the next part of their journey.

While he haggled with the trader for a few more strips of smoked Southmark beef that looked like they should be worn rather than eaten, Maura slipped outside to feed the mare a carrot and say goodbye.

"You have borne us well for many miles." She stroked the horse's neck while it chewed on the carrot. "I hope you will find a better life here than the one you left behind in Aldwood."

The horse whinnied and shook its mane.

"Rath says we cannot take you with us, for the way is too rough and too barren for you to graze." Maura wished she knew beastspeech to reassure the creature. "And I would not wish to take you with us into Westborne for fear we might have to part with you there."

A few moments later, Rath emerged from the trading post looking well pleased with himself. "We have a few more hours of daylight and this time of day is best for traveling through the Waste. I reckon we should be on our way."

He helped Maura shoulder her pack. "Are you sure that is not too heavy? I could take some more gear into mine."

"Never!" Maura strove to keep her breath from sounding labored. And they had not started walking yet! "If you stuff another pound of supplies into that pack, you will tumble backward and never be able to get up again. I can manage."

"You are certain?" Rath did not sound convinced. "Our packs will lighten as we go. Though not too quickly, I hope."

He turned to the horse and gave it an affectionate smack on the rump. "Farewell, old girl. Do not let Croll work you too hard. I told him he will answer to me one day if he does."

For what was left of that day, Maura missed the horse dearly and often found herself wishing they had been able to ride it farther. She and Rath walked almost until sunset, by which time she could scarcely put one foot in front of the other. When she thought of how swiftly the horse could have brought them that same distance, she repented ever complaining of a sore backside.

With a groan she sank onto a large flat rock. "Can we spare a little of our lard supply for me to make a liniment?"

Rath shrugged out of his pack. "Is your back sore?"

Maura gave a weary nod. "I suppose a second warm spring would be too much to ask of the Giver?"

He helped her remove her pack. "If I had the power of your Giver, I would conjure you one on the spot." He gave a rueful shrug. "But I have not, and I do not know of any more around here. We will have to make do with liniment, I fear. I will gladly furnish the lard, if you can make enough for us both."

While Maura compounded the balm, Rath gathered sticks for a fire from some stunted bushes near their campsite.

"Why do you bother with a fire?" Maura glanced up from bruising a mixture of moonmallow and cheeseweed. "We ate well at the trading post. A drink and some dried fruit will do me for supper. This far south, it cannot get very cold at night."

"This is neither for heat nor for cooking." Rath laid a bed of kindling over which he arranged some midsized sticks. "Many wild creatures live here on the fringe of the Waste. Some have a taste for human flesh."

As if summoned by his warning, something howled off in the distance.

Maura glanced over her shoulder, half expecting to see a lank wolf or barren cat skulking behind a nearby bush. "As soon as I have made the balm, I will help you gather more wood."

"Do not fret." Rath struck his flint and soon had a small but steady blaze going. "We have enough to last until morning."

Maura set down the wooden bowl in which she had compounded the liniment. The pungent scent of cheeseweed wafted on the still evening air. "I would like to be *certain* we have plenty."

She managed to gather a few good-sized sticks before all the stooping and lifting became too much for her. Then she hobbled back to the fire like an old granddame with winterache.

"Could you boil some water for a tea, too?" she asked Rath.

"A good thought." He rummaged in his pack for the kettle. "While I am gone to fetch the water, you can undress."

"Undress?" The word came out of Maura in a high squeak. Then she realized what he'd meant. "Oh, for the liniment."

Rath shot her a grin that held something of his old impudence. "It will not do much good rubbed through your clothes, will it?"

"I…suppose not."

Once he was out of sight, Maura puzzled a way to bare her back without baring a great deal more besides. Rath had made no secret that he found her desirable, yet he had behaved toward her in a most honorable way. She trusted he would not try to take by force what she could not give him freely.

But what if her resolve wavered and she surrendered to her desire for him? Rath did not believe in the Waiting King. He would have no reason to refuse anything she offered. Maura did not want to do anything to further tempt either of them.

When Rath returned, she was sitting near the fire, her shift pulled down around her hips, and her tunic modestly held in front of her. Her thick braid of hair hung down over her shoulder so as not to get in the way.

She half expected him to make some comment, but he did not. Instead he rigged a frame of sticks to suspend the kettle above the fire. Then he picked up the bowl of liniment, sniffed it and made such a face that Maura burst into nervous laughter.

"It may not have a sweet perfume," she said, "but you will not grudge the smell when you feel how it eases your back."

Rath gave the liniment a dubious look as he scooped a generous dollop onto his fingers. "One thing I will say for it. Lank wolves and barren cats would never want to eat creatures smeared with this stuff!"

While Maura laughed at the notion, he daubed the balm on her back. She flinched when the cool compound landed on her skin. Or perhaps it was the provocative touch of Rath's fingertips on her bare flesh?

Immediately the liniment began to work, sending delicious loosening, comforting warmth deep into her flesh.

"Down a bit farther if you please," she bid Rath, "then up between my shoulders and on my neck."

He did as she asked with a touch that felt strong and deft, yet deliberately gentle. By some mysterious magic, it provoked delicious sensations in parts of her body beyond his reach. She wondered how much more pleasant it might feel if he did caress those parts.

"How is that?" Rath asked.

Maura searched for a word to describe it. "B-better."

She had started to say *blissful,* then stopped herself.

"My turn, then."

She glanced over her shoulder to see Rath pulling off his vest and shirt. Her breath caught as she glimpsed the hard, lean perfection of his naked torso.

"A moment," she gasped, pulling her tunic over her head.

Then she turned and scooped up a dab of the pungent compound to smear over his back.

"Ah! You were right, lass." Rath chuckled. "This stuff feels so good, I do not care if it stinks clear to the Hitherland."

As good as it felt for her to touch him? Maura rubbed the liniment in deep, making the movement of her hands the kind of caress she would never be able to give him any other way.

"Where did you get this scar?" She ran her finger over a puckered seam below his ribs.

"Oh, that one. Escaping from a Hanish roundup of lads for the mines. Almost did me in, but I wouldn't let that slag-spawn have the satisfaction."

"I'm sorry," Maura whispered.

"Sorry? Whatever for? It is long in the past and hardly your fault."

"Sorry for making you remember." The liniment was well worked in now, but Maura could not bring herself to pull her hands away. "Sorry you've had such a hard life while I had such a sheltered one. Sorry I judged you ill for doing what you needed to do to survive that kind of life."

"No harm done." Without any warning, Rath rose and tossed another stick on the fire, though it was burning well.

He flexed his shoulders. "That is good stuff. I feel like I could walk another five miles." He grinned at Maura. "Well, perhaps not five. There, the water is boiling if you want to brew that tea of yours."

They took turns through the night, keeping watch and tending the fire. Rath gave Maura his dagger in case of attack.

Sometime in the thick darkness before dawn, Maura thought

she heard the faint pad of paws and saw the menacing glow of the firelight reflected off watchful, hungry eyes. She fancied she heard something else, too, a soft distant chant of unintelligible words. Then the eyes disappeared and all was quiet.

She sat there admiring the flicker of firelight over Rath's features, as stark and rugged yet strangely beautiful as the wild land around them. Of its own accord, her hand stretched toward his stubbled cheek for a stolen caress.

Then the sound of deep, fierce growls flared from nearby. The sleek pelts of several large lean beasts gleamed in the firelight.

"Rath!" Maura's hand diverted from his face to his shoulder to shake him awake. "Lank wolves! They are at our packs!"

"Slag!" Rath grabbed his sword and leapt to his feet.

Roaring a rolling thunder of curses, he charged the clutch of beasts. They scattered, but did not flee. Instead they drew back, circling with their teeth bared, threatening growls rumbling from deep in their throats.

Then a large one, perhaps the pack leader, launched itself at Rath. His blade whipped through the air to meet it.

The big beast fled, yelping in pain. But not before it knocked Rath's weapon from his hand. Another of the wolves lunged between Rath and the blade.

While Maura had been watching all this, her heart hammering in her chest, she had begun to fumble in her sash for her spidersilk. Would the spell work on other creatures as well as it did on humans?

"Maura!" Rath cried. "Toss me my dagger!"

His dagger, of course! She was so unused to carrying a weapon, she had forgotten it. Now she hurled the weapon through the air, while silently begging the Giver to let it reach Rath, without taking his hand off when he tried to catch it.

The dagger hissed through the air. A shriek of vexation rose in Maura's throat when she saw it would fall wide.

It landed among a small clutch of wolves. One let out a yelp of pain and bolted off into the night. That left three— the one standing over Rath's sword, snarling, and two that had backed off a little from the packs when the dagger had landed in their midst.

Again Maura wondered if her spells would work on animals. If not, she had better have something else to fall back on.

But what? The wolves had both of Rath's weapons.

The beast standing guard over the sword bared its teeth and growled at her. Its haunches tensed, ready to spring. Maura took a step back, then jumped when her foot hit the fire.

The fire! With her free hand, she reached down and grabbed a burning stick by its end. Then she advanced on the lank wolf, chanting her binding spell.

Out of the corner of her eye, she saw Rath pull something from one of the packs and swing it at the other two wolves, while bellowing a loud cry. The beasts let out a chorus of howls that sent chills down Maura's neck. Then they turned and ran.

The retreat of its pack mates distracted the last lank wolf for the vital instant Maura needed. She lunged forward, planting a wisp of cobweb on the beast's pelt as she spoke the last word on the incantation.

Perhaps she had blundered the words in her haste and panic. Perhaps she had not used enough spidersilk for so large a creature. Or perhaps her spells only worked on humans.

Maura had no time to care about the reasons when the beast sprang toward her.

She thrust the stick from the fire in front of her, but it looked pitifully small to ward off a creature of that size. Besides, the flame had all but died out.

Maura braced to be knocked backward by the animal's charge. Instead she found herself flying sideways as Rath dove to knock her out of the beast's path.

The lank wolf hurdled past them, landing on the fire. Burning sticks flew everywhere as the creature followed the rest of its pack mates, yowling in pain.

Rath and Maura lay where they had sprawled, gasping for breath.

At last Rath hauled himself to his feet. "I doubt that lot will be back tonight. But in case something else decides to try its luck, I had better repair our poor fire."

Maura rose, too, though her knees felt like they were made of jelly. Staggering to where Rath's sword lay, she picked it up. "You had better keep this nearby, too, though that stick you took from your pack did well in a pinch."

Her gaze fixed on Rath as he rebuilt the fire. One tip of the "stick" flickered with an eerie flame of its own. "By the Giver, Rath, where did you get that thing?"

"This?" He glanced down. "Came in handy, didn't it? I—"

Before he got the words out, Maura knew. "You took it from that death-mage when you went looking for Gristel Maldwin?"

Rath nodded. "I picked up a few little keepsakes. Did I not mention it? I thought I had."

"I would have remembered if you'd told me you had that... that...abomination! Get rid of it at once!"

"No."

"Rath Talward, do you know what that thing is?"

"Stop shouting," said Rath. "I am not deaf. And I am not daft, either. Of course I know what it is. A sight better than you do, I'll wager. I have been on the wrong side of one of these things. That scar you saw on my back was like a splinter in my finger compared to the pain I took from this."

"Then why in the Giver's name would you want to keep such a thing around you?"

Rath shrugged. "The same reason I *steal* anything, my lady." He seemed to relish reminding her he was an outlaw. "Because it might come in handy.

"This has." He gave the copper wand a little toss in the air and caught it again. "You said so yourself."

"I said that when I thought it was just a wooden staff."

"A wooden staff would not have sent a pair of lank wolves turning tail like that." He stared up at her and something harsh looked out of his eyes. "I mean to keep it, so save your breath arguing. I have a feeling we may need it again before we reach Everwood."

Maura quivered with indignation. Was it not bad enough the man did not believe in the Giver, the Elderways or the Waiting King? Did he have to embrace the evils of mortcraft, too? Part of her wanted to march off to Westborne on her own. But she knew what madness that would be. Rath Talward had made her dependent upon him—curse his hide!

Her tardy sense of fairness protested. She had not put up any great protest when he'd insisted on guiding her to Everwood.

"In that case…" She said the only thing she could say. "Make certain you keep that vile thing away from me!"

"Fair enough." Rath strode to where their packs rested and planted the copper wand between them with its fire gem pointing to the sky. "It can stand guard over our packs, since wild things seem not to like it any better than you do."

Maura grumbled her reply, but Rath hardly seemed to notice. "Get some sleep if you can. I will finish this watch."

"What? Do you not trust me to keep watch while you sleep?"

"You need not be so prickly." Rath planted himself on a rock near the fire that gave him a good view. "You did well just now, waking me so quickly, then taking your part against those lank wolves. But I am used to going with less sleep than most folk. I know I will not be able to get any more rest, so it is foolish for both of us to stay awake."

Maura wanted to nurse her grudge for a while, but he made it so hard. "I doubt I could sleep, either, after all the excitement."

"There is still some water in the kettle." Rath pointed to it. "Put it back on to heat, then brew yourself a cup of that dreamweed tea. I reckon you will sleep sound until morning."

Why did he have to talk such good sense, the rogue?

As Maura put the kettle on and added more fuel to the fire, the lank wolves prowled the borders of her thoughts, stirring vivid, haunting images of what had happened such a short time ago. Her quarrel with Rath about the copper wand had distracted her. Now it all came back—the latest of too many brushes with danger she had suffered since her fateful birthday.

She began to tremble.

"Maura?" Rath stirred from his perch to kneel beside her. "What is it, love? Are you all right?"

She wrapped her arms around herself. "I will be."

"That is not what I asked." Before she could stop him, Rath gathered her close. "This has all gotten to be too much for a sheltered lass from Windleford, hasn't it?"

That was too close to her own thoughts for Maura to deny. She nodded.

Rath cupped the back of her head with his palm and urged her toward his broad shoulder. "I wish I could promise you it will get better."

Maura gritted her teeth. She would *not* weep.

"There is one thing I can promise you, though."

She trusted her voice just enough to ask, "What is that?"

A gust of his breath, half sigh, half chuckle, whispered through her hair. "I can promise that if the two of us stick together, we will best whatever other dangers we meet between here and Everwood. I almost pity the poor fools who try to stand in our way."

Maura chuckled at the thought of all the Han in Westborne trembling before their advance.

"Rath, will you promise me one other thing?"

"I reckon. Depends what it is."

She doubted he would agree, but she had to ask, for it weighed on her mind. "If anything should…happen to me between here and Everwood. If I should be…killed…."

His arms tightened around her. "That is *not* going to happen. I will not let it."

"But *if* it should," Maura persisted, "I want you to do the passing ritual for me."

"Maura, you know I do not believe in all that foolishness of the afterworld and dead folks talking to the living."

"It is not foolishness!" Maura pushed out of his embrace.

"How would we have ever found the map to the Secret Glade if Gristel Maldwin had not heard Exilda speak to her? And do not try to persuade me she thought up that business about the pickles on her own. Who would think of such things at a time like that? It was *because* it sounded so queer that I knew it must be a true message from Exilda."

"Fortunate chance. Happens all the time." A shadow of doubt lurked in Rath's dark eyes.

About the passing ritual? Maura wondered. Or about his own stubborn refusal to believe in anything he could not see, hear, smell, touch, taste or understand?

"You will not think so when you have a chance to experience it for yourself. I heard Langbard speak to me, that night he died. He told me things and showed me his memories, so that they became a part of me, as if I had experienced them for myself."

"You were in a bad way, that night. Not that I blame you. But a mind that is wrought up plays tricks on a person."

"How is this for a trick?" She described the view of Tarsh from Bror's Bridge on a foggy day. The headland rearing up, dark in the mist. The peculiar keening screech of the dawn-gulls. The rolling drum of the waves as they scooped tiny pebbles off the shore and flung them farther up the strand.

For a moment Rath looked surprised—even haunted. Then his lip curled and he laughed. "I believe Langbard told you about it. But how am I to know it was in the few hours after he died and not some time in all the years before?"

Maura sprang to her feet. "You are to know it because I tell you it is true. If that is not good enough for you after all we have been through together, then I do not know why you have followed me the length of Umbria!"

Rath looked like he might be asking himself the same thing.

"Please?" She had one last appeal to try. "The night Langbard was killed, you gave me time to observe the passing ritual with him, even though it might have put us in danger."

"We all do daft things now and again."

"You told me it did not matter whether *you* believed, so long as I did." From that moment she had begun to fall—that is…to see him in a more favorable light.

Rath's features creased into the scowl of a man beaten with his own weapon. He heaved a put-upon sigh and asked in a sullen tone, "So what is there to this passing ritual, anyway? No dancing or any foolishness like that, I hope?"

"It is not difficult." Maura settled herself down beside him again. "You just sit with me. And you say a few words of *twara*—Old Umbrian—as you anoint parts of my body with a little water. It will wash away the cares of the world and purify my thoughts, words and actions for the afterworld."

"Aye." He sounded leery. "Then what happens?"

"Then you will hear me talking to you and you will see things in your mind that I have experienced." A strange peacefulness wrapped around Maura to think of sharing her memories with Rath. Achieving a kind of closeness that was forbidden to them in this world. Bequeathing him memories of her happy, sheltered childhood with Langbard.

"And we will say goodbye…." Her voice trailed off in a whisper.

"We will not have to," said Rath, "because no harm is going to befall you."

"But—"

"But—just to humor you, mind—you can teach me this ritual of yours. It will pass the time while we walk."

"Thank you, Rath!" Maura started to throw her arms around him, then pulled back awkwardly at the last moment.

There had been too much touching between them tonight already. It only whet her appetite for more.

19

Rath had hoped Maura's insistence on teaching him the passing ritual would ease once day returned and danger no longer stalked the boundary of their fire-light.

But he was wrong.

"You put a drop of water on my brow," said Maura in a voice breathless from the weight of her pack. They had been walking for several hours, mostly uphill. "Then you say…"

"Do not say 'my,'" growled Rath. The weight on his back was not nearly as bothersome as the weight on his mind.

"Your pardon?"

"Do not say 'my' as if you expect to die soon." A cold, slimy force squeezed his entrails whenever she did, the way a lake viper wrapped around its prey. "It is bad luck."

"Rubbish." Maura rested for a moment, leaning on her staff. "It is just a way of talking, nothing more."

She did not look appealing in a womanly way this morning. At least she should not to a man in his right senses. Her face was flushed from exertion and the growing heat. She had dark hollows beneath her eyes from scant sleep the night before. Her lips were parched from the dryness, and the pack she carried gave her a misshapen look. Still, the thought of any harm coming to her made the marrow of his bones ache. He had never felt this way about a woman before and he hated how vulnerable it made him.

Perhaps that weakness showed somehow, for Maura relented, as if taking pity on him.

"Oh, very well, then. The *companion* puts a drop of water on the brow of the *sojourner* and says, 'Wash the cares of this world from your thoughts and let them be made pure for a better life in the next.' Only, it is said in *twara,* of course. *'Guldir quiri shin hon bith shin vethilu bithin anthi gridig aquis a bwitha muir ifnisive.'*"

"How am I supposed to remember all that mouthful, not to mention speak it without putting a kink in my tongue?"

Maura waved away his objections. "A body can remember most anything if they repeat it enough times. Come, it is not that hard and you are a clever fellow. Think of each word as a blow to the Han."

Rath liked the sound of that. This *twara* stuff was the tongue of his ancestors, the kin to whom this land had belonged when they had been proud, free folk. And it was not completely unknown to him. During his childhood, Ganny had used a number of Old Umbrian words for things. He must try to recall them.

"Guldir quiri...shin?" He spoke the words to Maura, like an offering of sorts.

Her radiant smile rewarded him for his first tentative effort. *"Hon bith shin,"* she prompted him.

"Guldir quiri shin hon bith shin...bathlu...?" He wished he did not crave her approval so. It felt like weakness and she already rendered him weak in far too many ways.

"Very close!" Maura's eyes glowed with admiration. "The word is *vethilu.* It means thoughts, though an exact translation is 'the whisper of the bees in your hive.'"

Rath grinned. "That is how it feels sometimes. As though a whole crowd of bees were buzzing around inside your head."

"Making honey?" asked Maura.

Only when he thought about her. "What comes after *vethilu?"*

"Bithin." Maura took no notice that he had ignored her question. "It means 'let it be so' or 'may it come to pass.'"

"Wait. I know that one. Ganny used to say it when she got cross about something. *'Bithin...rafail...'* Oh, what was the rest? *'...thelwa shin!'"*

Maura laughed so hard, Rath was afraid she might tip over.

"Well, what does it mean?"

She patted her chest until she caught her breath. "It means 'May the Beast eat you.'"

"The Beast?" Rath pointed to the sky.

Maura nodded. "Aye, *that* beast. Any other colorful sayings of Ganny's you remember?"

As it happened, there were. As they continued to make their way through the arid high country, Rath dredged those all-but-forgotten words from his memory, then laughed with Maura when she translated them. As they talked, the miles seemed to pass more quickly and he hardly noticed the weight of his pack.

Before midday, they found an overhang of rock that provided some shade to wait out the hottest hours.

"No need to build a fire now." Rath let his pack drop to the ground, then pulled out his drink skin. "At this time of day in the Waste, nothing stirs, so we are safe to sleep."

Maura leaned against the sheltering rock and slowly wilted to the ground. "I will not need any dreamweed tea to put *me* to sleep."

They chewed on their strips of spiced beef and ate some of the nuts and dried fruit they had got from the trading post. But they were careful not to drink too much, since there was no place handy to refill their drink skins.

While Maura settled herself in the shade of the rock, Rath climbed a nearby bluff to scout the terrain ahead of them. It looked as though they had reached the High Flat. For the next several days they could make better time.

He noted a spot or two of green on the pale brown landscape ahead, reckoning the distance and direction of each one. With luck, he and Maura might reach one of those before sunset.

Wiping the sweat from his brow, he stumbled back down to the shaded spot where he found Maura slumbering peacefully. Tired as he was, he sat for a time brooding over her—the soft delicacy of her features, the lush fullness of her lower lip, the vibrant glory of her hair. When he had first met her, she'd cast a spell upon his body. Since then, she had cast a much more potent spell upon...his heart? Did he still have one after all these years and the life he'd led?

It tormented him to be so close to her, yet not permitted to indulge the urges she provoked in him. Yet that very boundary had freed him to know her as a person, not just a pretty object of desire and pleasure. In that knowing, he had come to care for her in a way he had vowed never to care for anyone but himself.

If he continued like this, he asked himself as he curled a stray strand of her hair around his finger, might there come a time when he would care *more* for her life than for his own?

The notion baffled and chilled him.

Their journey through the Waste grew easier by the third day. The land was more level and their packs had grown lighter as they'd consumed their supplies. Rath had marked a few watering places on their route where they had stopped for the night or their midday rest.

Though Maura still wished Rath would find a nice high cliff from which to drop that cursed copper wand, she had to admit it did a good job keeping wild animals at bay. She had seen a few flickers of eyes during her night watches, and once thought she heard a shrill growl that might have been a barren cat. But none of the creatures had ventured near enough to harm them.

"Now that I can recite the passing ritual in *twara*," said Rath as they resumed the journey after their midday rest on the fourth day, "do you not think it is time you practiced your Comtung?"

"I know some." Maura wrinkled her nose. "Which is already more than I care to. Vile stuff!"

"I agree," said Rath. "But that *vile stuff* could be important for your survival once we reach Westborne. Many of the younger folk there do not speak Umbrian at all."

"Not speak their own language—that is a shame!"

"So it is." Rath slammed his walking staff against the hard, parched ground as if he pictured a Hanish head beneath it. "Some day, perhaps, you can do something to remedy that. But not if your quest flounders because you could not make yourself understood."

Strange. He spoke as if he was beginning to believe she would one day rule Umbria.

"Go on, then. What should I know?" She would rinse her mouth out well after their lesson.

"Simple things," said Rath. "Travelers' phrases. How to ask directions to where you are going. How to ask the price of goods. How to tell someone you are hurt and ask for help."

Maura hoped she would never need to use that last one. Rath was right, though. It would be just such times she would most need to make herself understood. Besides, if her lessons in Comtung passed the hours of their march as agreeably as Rath's lessons in *twara*, it would seem like no time until they reached Westborne.

"So," said Rath, "how would you ask what something costs?"

"Referna...takolt...kotarst?" Maura made a face as she spoke the words.

"Refernug," Rath corrected her. "And I would say *pranat* rather that *takolt*...unless you are buying something alive."

"A foul-sounding language," grumbled Maura.

Rath shrugged. "Better than Hanish."

"That is not much of a boast."

"Rosfin kempt!"

"And what does that mean, pray?"

"It means impudent wench." Rath chuckled. "You had better learn more Comtung so you will know when you are being insulted."

"I expect I will know by the tone of voice, *lalump*. And to speak true, I would sooner not know when someone speaks ill to me."

"Now, that is where we differ," said Rath. "I want to know exactly what someone is calling me. So, pray, what is a *lalump?* Ganny sometimes called me that when I was a wee fellow, but she never would say what it meant."

"There are more differences than that between us, Rath Talward." Maura felt the need to remind herself at every opportunity. "As for that word, it might mean 'scamp' or it might mean 'fondheart.'"

When he fixed her with a mock-scowl, she relented. "In truth, it is what someone calls a scamp they are fond of."

Rath was more than a "scamp," Maura reminded herself. She had seen the way he'd fought those wolves. He could be a dangerous man when he chose. There was a ruthlessness about him, but a kind of honor, too. The better she got to know him, the more clearly she saw what life had made of him— the bad and the good. Yet every mile they journeyed together, the bad seemed to fade and the good to strengthen.

He glanced back at her, a gleam in his eyes that warned her he meant to tease. Perhaps even in a flirtatious way. Though she knew she should not encourage it, the prospect set a gentle buzz going in her heart.

Before he could speak the words he intended, his gaze

strayed to something beyond her and the muscles of his face tightened.

"Rath? What is it?" Maura spun about. From habit, her hands moved toward the pockets of her sash.

They were near the crest of a very gentle incline, but the land behind them was so flat, she could see for miles.

Her alarm eased when she spotted nothing threatening. "Did you do that on purpose to throw a scare into me?"

"Come!" Rath clutched her arm in a grip that brooked no delay.

He pulled her the hundred yards or so to the crest of the rise, then dropped to the ground, hauling her down after him.

"What is all this about?" She wrenched her arm from his grip. "You'd better have a very good reason to—"

"Shush!" ordered Rath in a harsh whisper. "Look."

He craned his neck a little to see over the crest of the rise.

"I already looked. There was nothing."

"Well, look again."

Maura propped herself on her elbows and peered back the way they had come. "I still do not—"

Rath raised his hand and pointed. "Over that way."

Those three simple, quiet words made Maura's whole body pucker in gooseflesh. Looking where Rath had bid her, she could make out several small shapes that appeared to be moving in their direction.

"Slag!" Rath pounded the ground. "I should have been more watchful. Whoever they are, they've come down from the mountains. Nobody good ever comes down from the mountains."

He scuttled a ways back from the edge of the rise before

standing up. "They probably spotted us hours ago. No help for it now. Come on."

Maura followed him in a hunched run. "Now that we are out of sight, can we not change course and try to cover our tracks?"

The strained squint of Rath's eyes eased a little and he flashed a fleeting rueful smile. "You have learned well, lass. I wish we could, but we are near Raynor's Rift and there is only one way across that will not take us many, many miles longer."

He began walking at a brisk trot. "By luck it is not far. If we can beat them to it, we should be able to put them off our trail on the other side."

Maura picked up her pace. "Let us waste no time then. The Comtung lessons can resume another day."

"Have you got anything in that sash to lend us speed?"

"I do!" She had forgotten about it until this moment. Now she praised the Giver for her faulty memory. "Hold a moment. It will be worth a short delay."

She turned her back to Rath. "Lift my pack and reach into the middle pocket halfway up."

The weight of her pack eased and through her clothes she felt Rath's fingers moving.

"A fine powder?" he asked. "With a waxy feel?"

"That is it! Powdered stag hoof. Get out as much as you can, then take off your boots and stockings."

"There," said Rath after a moment's digging with his fingers. "I think I have it all."

Maura dropped to the ground, fumbling with her laces, then rolling off her stockings. She wrinkled her nose. They could use a good wash the next time she and Rath found water.

She turned to take her share of the stag hoof from Rath. He sat on the ground, struggling to untie his boot with one hand, while the other was cupped around the precious powder.

"Here, let me help." Clumsy with haste, she pried off Rath's boots and removed his stockings. "Why did you not tell me you have a blister on your heel? I will make you a salve for it tonight."

She held out her open palm, into which Rath shook half the translucent gray powder. Just then, a gust of wind whipped from out of nowhere, sending much of the powder swirling into the air before they could close their hands.

"Slag!" muttered Maura. "Quick, rub what is left onto the soles of your feet. It may still be enough. While you apply it, repeat after me, *'Rodiri...thisbrid...kerew ethro...bithin...en fwan...gen lorfin bryd.'*"

Rath recited the incantation without a single mistake and with just the right lilt. "I know some of those words."

"I expect you do. You seem to have a gift for languages." Maura grabbed her stockings. "Now, let us get our boots back on and see if we can make better haste."

As soon as Rath was shod again, he leapt to his feet and held down a hand to hoist her up.

"That way." He pointed to a line of trees stretched across the horizon.

Keeping a firm grip on her hand, Rath set off toward the trees. Not too quickly at first, but gradually increasing his pace.

"It is a good thing I forgot that stag hoof until now," said Maura, her breath coming only a bit faster than usual, though she was running at a speed greater than she had ever run in her life. "When we needed it most."

"Are you not going to credit your Giver for that lapse of memory?" Rath shot her a teasing grin, but she sensed he was not completely in jest.

After that, they saved their breath and ran even faster. They would pay for it later, Maura knew. The muscles of the legs would cramp in painful spasms, just as back and arm muscles ached after bear essence wore off. She would worry about that later and tend them both with liniment and pain-relieving tea. For now, they needed to put as much distance as possible between themselves and whoever was coming behind them.

The trees loomed up before them. Maura could see a gap in the greenery that looked like a path. They seemed to be headed for it.

She could feel the speed spell beginning to wane. Her heart pumped faster, her feet became harder to lift with every step. Clinging tight to Rath's hand, she managed the final sprint into the wooded area.

Once in cover, they stopped, gasping for breath. Maura sank to the ground and pulled out her drink skin. The last watering hole they stopped at had been shallow and the water brackish. Now she quaffed it as though it was mulled peach cider.

Rath unstopped his drink skin, too, and took a quick swig. But he did not sit down. Instead, he staggered a few steps back to the edge of the trees.

"Can you...see them yet?" asked Maura.

"Not yet," Rath called back, his eyes still on the trail they had run. "That is a boon. We should have time to cross the Rift without them hot on our trail."

"Cross the Rift?" Why did those words give her a hollow feeling in the pit of her belly. "How do we do that?"

"Come." Rath strode past her. "I will show you."

She followed him along a well-trodden path.

After a few moments he came to an abrupt stop. "This is far enough."

Maura peered around him.

A few feet beyond where Rath stood, the earth plunged away in a sharp, sheer drop, the sight of which made Maura's whole body go rigid with terror. Between there and the far side of the rift sagged the feeblest excuse for a bridge Maura had ever seen—nothing but rope and boards.

The hollow in Maura's belly gaped to consume her whole body. She staggered a few steps backward from the precipice.

"Quite a sight, is it not?" Rath asked, over his shoulder.

When he received no reply, he turned. "Maura, what is the matter? Are you hurt?"

"The matter?" Maura asked in a tight, shrill voice. Then she broke into wild laughter. "I am not hurt. I am alive, and mean to stay that way."

"That is good." Rath nodded, but his brows knit in a look of puzzlement and concern. "So do I. Which means we had better waste no time crossing the bridge."

"Cross that?" Maura began to shake her head before Rath even finished speaking. "You must be mad!"

"I am not." He squatted on his haunches before her and took her hand. "I have crossed that bridge twice before and there is nothing to it. Just hold on to the side ropes, keep a steady pace and do not look down. Before you know it, you will be on the other side."

"Easily said!" Every time Maura thought of that sheer

drop, she felt as if she were already falling. "A puff of wind, a rotten board and we could plunge to our—"

Speaking of wind, Maura felt as if the wind had been knocked out of her. She gasped for breath harder than she had when they were running. If she had known what they were running toward, she might have turned and gone in the opposite direction.

"I know it is rather high," said Rath, "but—"

"Rather high?" Maura grabbed the breast of his cloak and pulled him toward her. "Until today, I have never been higher than the top of Hoghill. You could put twenty Hoghills in that…that…"

"Rift."

"Rift indeed! It is deeper than the Black Beast's maw, and just as deadly."

"That may be." Rath removed his cloak from her frenzied grasp. "But we have to get across, so we might as well do it and do it quick."

When she opened her mouth to tell him how impossible that was, Rath charged ahead with his words just as he was apt to do with his actions. "If you think that bridge is dangerous now, imagine a bunch of Han chasing you across it."

"How can you be sure they are Han?" Maura demanded. "They may not even have come this way."

"If they came from the mountains, they are Han." Rath spoke with the implacable authority of someone stating the most basic of proven facts. "And there is no other way to come but this."

"Are you certain? Could we not go…?" She pointed north.

Rath shook his head. "That would take us up into the South Crescent. Mountains where you would find drops like that every mile, and no bridge to take you across them, either."

"Then…?" Maura pointed south.

"Perhaps…" he began, sending Maura's hopes soaring. Then his tone turned harsh. "*If* we had triple the supplies and you did not need to reach Everwood until Harvestide. Is there any herb in your sash that will give you courage?"

Maura shook her head. "Langbard said there is no substitute for true courage."

How disappointed he would be in her if he could see her now.

Leaping to his feet, Rath reached down and grabbed Maura by the arm, hauling her up after him. "Enough of this foolishness! I will not let any harm come to you."

Perhaps she was being foolish. Maura stumbled to her feet. True the bridge was a great height, but other people had crossed it safely—Rath, twice.

"If only it was more substantial." Maura allowed Rath to pull her toward the bridge. "Why could they not have built it of stone, with high sides so a body would not have to see what they were crossing."

"This place does not get enough traffic to merit the work of a stone bridge." Rath did not pull so hard once he realized she meant to come. "Besides, I doubt it would last. The earth trembles around here sometimes and rock has no give to it. Rope can bend or stretch a long way before it breaks."

They had reached the bridge again. Rath thrust Maura in front of him. "Hold on to the ropes. Keep your eyes on the far side, and we will be across before you know it."

Her heart beat so fast and so hard, Maura feared it would crack her ribs. Forcing her gaze to the opposite side of the rift, she groped for the hand ropes and clung to them. Then she stepped out onto the fragile span over the abyss.

It swayed beneath her feet. Maura glanced down.

She had not begun to appreciate the rift's true depth. The steep rock sides plunged down and down in a bottomless drop.

"No!"

She spun about and plowed Rath down in her panic to get solid ground beneath her feet. "I...cannot do it. I cannot! Let us hide until whoever is behind us passes, then turn around and go back to Southmark."

Rath picked himself up and turned to glare at her. "You agreed to come this way. The other way is even more dangerous, and will take too long."

"You did not tell me about...that!" Maura's finger trembled as she pointed back toward the bridge.

"I never reckoned you would balk like this. I do not understand, Maura. You risked Hanish blades and the jaws of their hounds to save me. You trussed up a death-mage. You did your part to win our freedom from Vang. Yet you will not walk across a bridge?"

Everything he said was true. It made no more sense to her than it made to him. She had known fear before, but never this paralyzing terror that defied all reason.

"No." She backed farther away pulling a pinch of dreamweed from her sash. "I will not. Not that one. And if you try to force me again, I will cast a sleep spell on you!"

His features twisted in a look of shock and hurt. As if she had drawn a blade and thrust it into his chest. That look passed quickly, though. Something hard and fierce took its place.

"Stay then, coward! Liar!" Glaring at her, he stepped onto the bridge and began to cross it walking backward.

"Coward I may be, Rath Talward, but I am no liar!"

"You are. A liar and a fraud, with all your empty talk about the Giver and the Waiting King and your quest! If you truly believed that pap you spew, you would trust your Giver to keep you safe from falling. There is no Giver. No afterworld. Just a hard, dirty life a body must wrest what they can from!"

"You are wrong!" Maura lurched to her feet. "The Giver created this world and breathed its spirit into every living thing."

"And stuck heroes up in the sky to chase monsters?" Rath's scorn stung like lye. "Rubbish! Stinking, daft rubbish!"

"No!" Maura barely noticed herself clutching the ropes and stepping onto the bridge again. Her gaze bored into Rath with such intensity, she had eyes for nothing else. "Do not say such things!"

"Stop me then, *Destined Queen!*" His tone made a pitiful mockery of that title. "All your prattle about combing the kingdom for the Secret Glade. I see now you meant only the *safe* and *pleasant* parts of the kingdom."

"How dare you?" When she got her hands on him, he would regret his insulting tongue and his foul blasphemy!

"At least I do dare!" cried Rath, retreating faster. "I dare to live my life without the cripple's crutch of faith in some fraud of a Great Spirit! I dare to fight the Han every chance I get, instead of moping around waiting for some dead king to rise from his grave and do it for me!"

"Why, you...!" Maura could not think of an insult rank enough as she charged after him. "I will make you sorry for every wicked word!"

"Why not let the Waiting King do it?" Rath beckoned, daring her to come at him. "Or pray the Giver to strike me down with its awesome power?"

He had stopped now. His mouth stretched in a wide, triumphant grin.

"Take that back, you scoundrel!" Maura threw herself at him. "Believe or not as you will, but do not mock the Giver or the Waiting King! He is real—you will see!"

Rath latched on to her around the waist and plucked her off the ground.

"I will see, will I?" He spun her around, gasping out words between bouts of wild laughter. "When we get to the Secret Glade, you mean?"

"Yes, then you will see. Now, put me down, before I..."

He put her down, but he did not let her go. "Your pardon, Maura, for saying those things. It was the only way I could think of getting you across that bridge without slinging you over my shoulder and carrying you. And that would have been far too dangerous for us both."

"Across the—?" Maura looked back.

Fortunately Rath was still holding her up, for her legs would not. Her head spun and her belly sluiced down into the toes of her boots. Her eyes stung with tears she refused to shed. Instead, she threw her arms around Rath's broad chest and held on tight as she joined in his laughter.

"You clever scoundrel! I cannot believe you taunted me across. Langbard was right about you!"

She tilted her head and looked into his eyes. Just as it had on the bridge, but for a far different reason, the rest of the world seemed to melt away, leaving only Rath—solid, forceful, full of life.

Slowly he bent forward, bringing his lips closer and closer to hers, and any reason to resist him had melted away with the rest of the world.

Then something hissed past them. Maura remembered having heard that sound before. But where?

Rath jerked his head up to look past her.

"Slag!" he growled, pushing her behind him. "We have company!"

Another arrow hissed by.

"Get down!" Rath pushed Maura behind him. "Find a rock or a thick tree trunk to hide behind!"

He dropped down on one knee, well below the height the arrows were coming at, yet still able to see across the rift.

There were three, that he could see, on the other side of the bridge—two Hanish soldiers and a death-mage. If they were the same ones he had left alive back in Prum, he would never forgive himself.

Nor would he ever make that mistake again.

One of the soldiers was firing off arrows as fast as he could load his bow, not even making a pretense of aiming. He must be providing cover for one or both of the others to come across the bridge.

Maura tugged on Rath's cloak. "What are we waiting for?

We must get away before they cross. This is my fault for balking so long on the other side."

"At least you came and they did not catch us on the other side or while we were crossing."

If either of them was to blame it was he. At first he had thought her fear of crossing the bridge foolish. Then he had realized it was like his fear of the mines—a suffocating terror beyond reason or control.

Once he'd understood, it amazed him that she had been able to break the grip of her fear and focus on something else to get her across the bridge.

As soon as she had crossed, he should have grabbed her hand and fled as though the Black Beast itself were howling at their heels. Not stood there like some love-struck boy clasping her in full view of the bridge, wasting precious time they needed to run or hide.

"Go!" he ordered Maura, his voice harsh with anger at himself. "Run. Get as far from here as you can. I will hold this lot for as long as I can."

"No!" cried Maura. Behind him, Rath could hear the faint rustle of her digging in the pockets of her sash. "We are stronger together than apart."

Rath could not deny that. It brought him a fleeting but very sweet sense of satisfaction. Still, he could not take the chance of Maura falling into the clutches of the Han.

"I do not have time to argue with you now." He wrestled off his pack and tossed it behind him. "Do as I say and get clear of here."

Rath drew his blade, though he did not need it…yet.

Not only did Maura fail to flee as he'd bidden her, the fool wench crept forward until she crouched by his side. "Whatever happened to always looking out for yourself first?"

What *had* happened to it? Had he crossed the line, at last? Past which he counted her life of greater value than his own?

Perhaps the Hanish archer thought he had scared them away. Or perhaps he had been trying to make them return fire, to see if they were armed with bows. Rath heard the fellow call out an order. Then the other soldier scuttled across the bridge, his shield raised before him.

"Can we cut the ropes?" asked Maura.

Rath shook his head. "If we try that, the bowman will skewer us for certain. If you will not leave, at least get out of sight."

He pulled her back behind a bush with thick foliage. "Is there anything you can do about those two on the other side?"

"I need to be closer to get the magic agent on them."

A daft notion blossomed in Rath's mind, when he most needed to keep it free of distractions. What if an arrow could be fitted with a tiny cloth pouch containing one of Maura's *magic agents?* When the arrow hit, it would pierce the pouch and release the agent.

The idea had merit. Rath only hoped it was not destined to die with him. That Hanish soldier was almost across the bridge.

Rath steeled himself to fight when suddenly the strangest compulsion came over him. "Maura?"

"What?"

"If I am killed and you survive, will you perform the passing ritual on me?"

"If you wish, but—"

He knew what her hesitation meant. And he could not leave her without an explanation. If only he could find one to satisfy himself.

But there was no time left. The soldier had reached their side of the rift.

Turning toward her, he whispered, "Just in case."

And since his lips were passing anyway, he dropped a kiss on her ear.

For a moment, Maura sat stunned by Rath's request. The notion that he had made even such a tentative step toward belief made her want to laugh and cry at the same time. The possibility that she might have to speak the words of the passing ritual over his dead body filled her with the same helpless terror as when she'd glanced down from the bridge into Raynor's Rift.

Through the leaves of the bush, she could see the Hanish soldier peering around for an instant after he stepped off the bridge. Something caught his attention and drew him further into the trees.

While his foe was distracted, Rath leapt out from behind the bush, his sword swinging. It struck the soldier's metal armor with a harsh clang.

Maura flinched. But as the two men continued to trade blade thrusts and parries, she could see the soldier's armor was only dented from Rath's blow.

A wail of dismay rose in her throat. With only his padded leather vest for armor, how could Rath prevail against the Han, encased in stout metal?

She must find some way to aid him.

The two men were joined so close in combat and moving

so quickly, she dared not try to cast a spell upon the Han, in case it should strike Rath instead. Neither could she risk distracting Rath when he most needed to keep his wits about him.

As she watched them trade and dodge blows, she realized Rath was not as much at a disadvantage as she had first believed. Without the weight and restriction of stiff armor, he was able to move more freely and quickly. Perhaps the best thing she could do for him just now would be to make certain he had only a single enemy to fight.

She crept around the other side of the bush to a spot where she could see the bridge. Though she knew she would not need to cross the rift again, Maura's insides still quivered and her head spun when she glimpsed its unforgiving depth. Then she saw something else that made a different kind of fear grip her.

The bowman was beginning to make his way across the bridge.

What could she do to stop him? She had no weapon, save her magic, and it would not work at this distance. She tried to dig up a rock to throw but it was buried deeper than it looked and would not loosen. As she tried to think of something, the Han drew closer.

Maura dug a generous pinch of madfern from her sash and stole as near to the bridge as she dared. In a whisper barely even audible to herself, she began to recite the incantation.

The bowman stepped from the bridge. But he did not glance down at Maura crouched in the underbrush.

Perhaps the narrowed vision of his helmet kept him from seeing her out of the corner of his eye. Or perhaps his thoughts were too tightly fixed on joining the fight, which

Maura could hear continuing. The Han paused for an instant to grab his bow.

In that instant, Maura sprang up and hurled the madfern into his face. The Han threw down his weapon and staggered back with a startled cry. Maura hoped the madfern would make him see something that would frighten him into turning and running back across the bridge.

Instead he spun about, spread his arms like wings and leapt into the rift.

When Maura realized what the Han meant to do, she tried to grab hold of him and pull him back. She was only able to reach his long plume of hair, which slipped through her fingers as he fell. That was enough to send her sprawling to the ground at the very lip of the rift.

Too frozen with horror even to close her eyes, she watched him fall.

"Maura!"

The abrupt urgency of the nearby shout and the implacable grip of a hand around her ankle tore a scream from her throat. Yet even as she cried out, she recognized Rath's voice and his touch. Maura jammed her eyes shut to block out the shattering sight before her. She feared she would see it in her nightmares for a very long time to come.

Rath began to pull her back from the lip of the cliff, then suddenly he let her go. A hoarse howl broke from him.

Maura recognized the agony of that cry. She knew what had caused it.

Scuttling back from the edge of the cliff, she forced herself to open her eyes. It was as she had feared.

On the far side of Raynor's Rift, the death-mage had raised

his wand to point directly at Rath, who fell to his knees as spasms of pain gripped his body.

Though she knew little of how mortcraft worked, Maura feared its malevolent power. Would it be enough to get Rath out of the Echtroi's line of sight?

Scrambling to her feet, she clutched the end of his cloak and heaved with all her might. As he tumbled backward, his screaming stilled and his body went limp.

She bent over him, stroking his face and hair. "Rath, are you alive? Can you hear me?"

"Yes…to…both." The words rasped out hard.

"Thank the Giver!" Tears sprang to her eyes as she cradled his head in her arms.

"Later," growled Rath. "Is…he…coming?"

"Is who—? Oh!" Maura let him go, then crept to where she could see the bridge without being too visible from the other side…or so she hoped.

"Yes. He is coming!"

Though clearly still in some residue of pain from the mortcraft attack, Rath tried to pull himself along the ground.

"Wand." He forced the word through clenched teeth.

"No!" cried Maura. "We do not know how to use it, or what it will do."

Even if she did know, she was not certain she could bring herself to wield such a thing.

"Get it!" Rath kept crawling toward his pack, though every move was clearly a struggle.

"Very well, then." She could give it to him to hold, at least. Rath did not look capable of using any other weapon.

Maura ran the few steps to where Rath had dropped his

pack, then fumbled it open to retrieve the wand. Meanwhile, her gaze fell to the body of the Han Rath had fought. Its head tilted at an unnatural angle and an appalling quantity of blood had seeped from a gash on its neck.

Maura's stomach heaved, but she managed to hold her gorge. The death-mage would not find her easy prey, huddled on the ground, vomiting.

Something else on the Han's corpse caught her eye.

First, she pulled the copper wand from Rath's pack. It felt hot in her hands, a heat she sensed could quickly travel to her heart, searing everything in its path.

"Here, take it!" Maura shoved the wand into Rath's hands, then hurried to the body of the dead Han. Gritting her teeth and willing her belly not to revolt, she pulled free the bow slung over his shoulder and plucked an arrow from his quiver.

She had never fired a bow before, but she had seen it done. Even if the arrow did not find its mark, it might be enough to make the death-mage think twice about crossing the bridge. Hopefully that would give Rath time to recover from the mortcraft attack so he could fire the bow himself.

When she reached a spot of cover near the bridgehead, Maura was relieved to discover the death-mage had gotten less than halfway across. Still, her fingers fumbled notching the arrow. It took considerable force to pull back the bowstring. Maura thanked the Giver for every heavy bucket of water she had hauled up from Langbard's well.

Now, to aim. She had seen archers close one eye—but which one? Perhaps it did not matter. She could not hold the taut, quivering bowstring any longer.

The arrow flew. Though it missed the death-mage by several feet, it caught his attention.

He raised his wand in Maura's direction.

She turned to run, but before she got a step, pain ripped through her. As bottomless as Raynor's Rift. Every bit as cruel. Every bit as terrifying. It was a pain of deep, searing cold. Jagged shards of ice driving into her flesh, but never bringing the blessed numbness of natural cold.

Maura heard herself scream, but it brought no release, elicited no pity.

With the tiny morsel of herself not yet too overwhelmed with pain to think, she tried to move her twitching body closer to the edge of the cliff. The pain that waited her below could be no worse than this. It would be over quickly. Then all pain would stop.

"Maura!" Rath's voice came to her as if from a vast distance.

She clung to it. One flickering flame of warmth and comfort in a fierce blizzard of bone-gnawing cold.

"Take this!" When he thrust something into her hands, she realized she had dropped the bow. "Hang on to it!"

At once the pain eased to an almost bearable level. But something else took its place—a heavy, suffocating darkness that pressed down on her, stifling all good, all life from her body and her spirit.

Unless it lifted soon, she knew she would suffer something worse than dying. She would be eaten by the Beast.

What had he done? Rath bent over Maura. The only thing he'd been able to think of to save them both from the death-mage. It had saved him...but had it doomed her?

Pain tore at his heart, not inflicted by any cursed gem, but every bit as intense as if it had been.

He unclenched her hands from around the copper wand, then he pressed his fingers to her throat in search of a pulse.

There it was. Sluggish and erratic but holding on, bless her. He must find some way to revive her.

What was that tonic she had compounded in an effort to bring back Langbard? He did not recall the name of the herb she had used, if he'd ever known it.

But names did not matter. He recalled that night in vivid detail, right down to the smells. He would find the right herb, if he had to sniff in every pocket of her sash.

But first he must heat some water.

The Hanish soldier had nicked his arm, but the bleeding had almost stopped. His ribs hurt from a blow that his padded vest had deflected. And every muscle and joint in his body ached from the mortcraft attack.

Still he made haste to gather some twigs, rifle his pack for flint, kettle and water pouch. He did not have much water left, but perhaps that was just as well—a small amount would heat faster. Once he got a fire started under the kettle, he launched his search for the proper herb.

He cast his thoughts back to the night of the fire at Langbard's cottage. He remembered Maura bending over the old wizard's body, as he was doing now, with her. She had not shifted the sash around to dig something from one of the back pockets, he was certain of that. It made his job only half as difficult.

One by one, he began his search through the front pockets, now and then stopping to call Maura's name or give her face a fleeting caress. Some of the pockets were empty. Others held magical ingredients he had come to recognize—dreamweed, madfern, spidersilk. From each of the others, Rath removed a tiny pinch and held it beneath his nose.

Was this it? Perhaps. He could not be sure.

Or this? No, definitely not. The scent was too acrid.

This? Yes! Without a doubt. This had been the ingredient of Maura's tonic—the one she had bid him chew to keep awake when he searched that house in Prum. With eager, trembling fingers, Rath extracted a larger amount and added it to the water in the kettle.

He probably did not have the herb in its proper measure, and he could not remember the words of the incantation Maura had used, but she had taught him enough Old Umbrian, he hoped he could string together something acceptable...if the Giver would allow him a little leeway.

Rath shook his head hard. The Giver? Had that wand blast shaken his wits loose?

True, the vitcraft incantations were all phrased as petitions to the Giver. But that had no bearing on whether they worked, did it? For all it seemed so baffling, there appeared to be some rules to the practice of life magic. Perhaps one day folk would understand how it all worked and think their ancestors daft for believing some all powerful spirit had cared what happened to the trifling creatures of this world.

Firmly reminding himself that speaking a spell did not concede the existence of the Giver, he poured the hot tonic into a mug. Then he lifted Maura's head and shoulders while he mangled a phrase of Old Umbrian that he hoped would suffice to kindle the spell.

He held the mug to her lips, dribbling a few drops of the hot liquid into her half-open mouth.

Nothing happened.

Had he used the wrong herb, after all? Did spells only work if a body believed in the Giver?

Once again he felt for Maura's pulse. It seemed stronger.

Rath made up his mind he would not abandon hope until he had no choice. He coaxed another trickle of tonic between Maura's lips...and another. Until the mug was almost empty.

At last Maura coughed and her eyelids flickered. "Rath? Are we safe? What happened?"

"We are safe enough for the moment." He choked the words out past an enormous lump in his throat. "If you stay quiet and drink up the rest of this, I will tell you what happened."

Maura gave a weary nod of agreement and took another sip from the mug he held to her lips. "The death-mage?"

"Quiet, I said. The death-mage will not trouble us anymore. That copper wand did something to fight off the power of his. It was as though he had to fight to control it. But I could see it was bad for you to hold the other one."

Maura moved her head in a barely perceptible nod.

Rath hoped he would never find out firsthand what she had suffered. "So while you were keeping him occupied, I grabbed my sword and cut the ropes on one side of the bridge."

"Clever," Maura whispered.

"Thank you for staying with me." Rath set the empty mug down. "I would be dead now, without you."

"I fear where I would be without you." Something dire haunted Maura's eyes, then it lifted a little. "Who made this tonic?"

"I did." It made him feel sheepish to admit it.

"But how—?" Every time she spoke, her voice sounded stronger. The color was returning to her face.

Rath shrugged. "I have picked up more from you than just what you've taught me."

A tender smile curved her lips. "So I see."

Just then something stirred in the underbrush nearby. Rath's heart lurched against his ribs. He could not fight again today.

Before he could do more than feel that alarm, a tree mouse scampered out from among the ferns and dead leaves to climb onto a nearby stump.

Rath's panic vented in a burst of hoarse laughter. "Thank you, Master Tree Mouse, for reminding me it is too dangerous for us to stay here."

Reluctantly he eased Maura to the ground. "Rest while I... make a few preparations. When you feel strong enough to walk, we can go a little way off and make camp."

"What about you?" asked Maura. "Are you all right? Your shirt is torn—there is blood!"

"Not much." Rath glanced down at his wounded arm. "My ribs are sore. And my body feels like someone ripped it apart, then put it back together wrong. Do you have any herbs to cure that?"

"I reckon I can find something."

Rath checked the dead Han for any useful plunder before he disposed of the body. He would have liked to take the sword or the shield, but their distinctive designs would draw all the wrong sort of attention to him and Maura when they reached Westborne. He did take the Han's dagger, though, to replace the one he had lost to the lank wolves. The coins in a pocket of the soldier's belt would come in handy, too.

For the first time he could recall, Rath felt a tiny qualm about picking over a corpse. Then his usual good sense reasserted itself. This fellow would not need his dagger or his coins where he was headed, but they might be vital to Rath and Maura's survival in the days ahead.

Grabbing the corpse by its heels, Rath dragged it toward the edge of the rift. When his aching muscles protested, he reminded himself it had to be done.

After a few steps, he halted for a rest. He glanced over to find Maura watching him.

"Do not look at me like that! What else am I to do with it? We cannot risk someone stumbling upon the corpse or they will soon be combing this bit of forest for us."

"I do not blame you." Maura shook her head slowly, as if it were an effort. "Now that he is dead, what does it matter?"

"Now, *that* is a sensible attitude." Rath tugged the corpse a little farther.

"They left us no choice, did they?"

"How's that?" Rath had pulled the Han's body as far as he dared. Now he got behind and rolled it the last few feet.

"The Han," said Maura. "They gave us no choice but to kill them."

Rath pondered her question briefly. "Not much of one. Kill them or let them kill us. I do not fancy the first, but it beats the second."

With that he gave the corpse a final shove, and over the edge it went. So steep were the cliff faces and so deep was the rift, that the corpse's fall made no more sound than the descent of a snowflake from a winter sky. It seemed strange.

Rath dragged himself back to where Maura lay by the small dying fire.

"Have we any more water?" she asked him.

"Whatever is in *your* drink skin. Why?"

Maura reached toward her sash. "Let us put some of it in the kettle and brew a tonic for you while there is still a little heat in these coals."

"We cannot spare the time." He tried not to sound as bone-tired and aching as he felt. "We need to get away from here."

The look she leveled at him refused to make light of his injuries. "Just put the water in the kettle, Rath. We will get away from here a good deal faster if you do not swoon on your feet. While it heats I will take a look at that 'scratch' on your arm. I reckon by that you mean it is not cut *all* the way to the bone."

With a sigh of surrender, Rath reached for the kettle. "You sound right overbearing for a lass who hardly had a pulse a little while ago."

"Proof of how well the tonic is working on me." Into the palm of her hand, Maura sprinkled the herbs she meant to use. "Think how much better it will work on you when I say the right words…or rather, teach you how to say them."

Rath poured some water in the kettle and set it on the coals to warm. Maura dumped her palmful of herbs in the water, then turned to examine his arm.

"You are lucky it was not any deeper, or it would have bled a good deal more." She pulled a couple of wilted leaves from her sash, popped them in her mouth and began to chew on them.

Rath made a face. "What are you doing?"

She spit the chewed leaves back into her hand. "I am sorry I do not have time to mix these into a proper poultice, but this will work in a pinch."

Then she smeared the warm, wet wad of chewed leaves over his wound and bound it with a small strip of linen. As she worked, Rath sensed something weighing on her mind.

"What is wrong?" he asked. "You have seen for yourself, my wound is not so bad."

"It is not that." Maura tested the water in the kettle, then set it back on the coals to heat longer. "I want to ask your pardon for chiding you so often about your use of arms."

She nodded toward the edge of the rift. "Even vitcraft can be used to kill."

Rath reached for her hand and gave it a reassuring squeeze. "I told you...or perhaps you told me. We had no choice. The Han gave us no choice. If they had not attacked us, we would not have gone seeking to harm them."

"Perhaps not this time." Maura's gaze searched his looking for answers Rath did not have. "But when the Waiting King wakens, how are we to rid Umbria of the Han without attacking them? I do not think I have the stomach for it. Langbard taught me to believe that the power of life and death belong to the Giver. Mortals who take that power into their own hands do so at grave peril to their spirits."

Rath reckoned a rough tally of the men he'd killed in his life. Never wantonly, never taking pleasure in it as the Han seemed to do. But when it had needed to be done, he had not hesitated. Nor would he again. Yet he yearned for the luxury of a little peace.

He shook his head. "I am not the Oracle of Margyle, lass, just a simple outlaw from the Hitherland. Something tells me those are questions a body has to find their own answers to. For now, put them aside and take some rest."

Pondering what lay between them and Everwood, he thought, *You will need all the rest you can get for the days ahead. We both will.*

21

"Shh!" Rath whispered in a tone of harsh urgency as he and Maura prepared to leave the fringe of forest on the western edge of Raynor's Rift. "Did you hear something?"

Maura froze, her heart racing and her senses alert, listening for trouble.

How tired she had grown of these constant threats of danger! The past two days she and Rath had spent resting and recovering their strength had given Maura a bittersweet illusion of peace. But it had proven all too fragile.

She so longed for her old quiet life keeping house for Langbard—gathering and preparing herbs, visiting with Sorsha, studying the Elderways. With one small addition.

Or rather, one *large* addition.

She glanced over at Rath, still tense and alert. Her gaze lingered fondly over his rugged features. Any slight sense of safety she still possessed resided in her nearness to him. She had seen the lengths to which he would go to keep her from harm. But why?

That was a question she dared not ponder too long or it would spawn a host of wistful regrets.

Rath let out his breath and the tight set of his shoulders relaxed a little. "I reckon it was nothing. I am jumping at shadows. The sooner we get on our way, the better. Before somebody comes looking to use that bridge. Then this place will be crawling with Han."

"I wish we could stay a while longer." Maura ran her hand down the stippled bark of a nearby tree in a kind of caress. "Even with all the Comtung we have practiced, I do not feel ready for Westborne."

"It will not be as bad as you think." The slight furrow of Rath's brow belied his reassuring words. "There will be plenty of crowds to get lost in. Proper inns where we can eat and sleep."

"Han thick as fleas," Maura muttered as he helped her shoulder her pack.

Rath gave a grim nod. "It is not only the Han you need to be wary of. Watch out for the *zikary*, too. They are Umbrians who work for the Han, even try to copy their looks and their ways. Bleach their hair!"

He spat.

Casting a pensive glance around, he beckoned Maura and they set off, taking care to stay far west of the path that led to the Rift Bridge.

They walked in silence for a while, then Rath spoke again. "Even among the ordinary folk, take care. Watch your tongue.

Do nothing that will draw attention to us. The yoke of the Han has fallen heaviest on Westborne and for the longest time. Folk do what they must to survive. If that means passing information to the Echtroi in exchange for food or slag, so be it."

"Slag?" said Maura. "I have heard you use that word as a curse. What does it mean?"

Rath shook his head in a way that suggested impatience, and perhaps a scrap of envy. "Langbard did keep you well sheltered, didn't he? Slag is dust…from the mines. A wiser man than me once said it numbs the pained heart but rots the spirit. Some folk are desperate enough to reckon that a fair trade."

Maura's nose wrinkled, as if at a putrid smell. "What do people *do* with this mine dust?"

"The men in the mines have little choice but to breathe the foul stuff." Rath's voice sounded harsher than Maura had ever heard it. "I reckon the Han saw it made them more biddable, so they took to giving them more of it to sniff."

He mimed inhaling something off the back of his hand. "Then somebody got the clever notion of using slag to pay off Echtroi snitches. Then they started selling it to other folks."

"Is this slag really so terrible?" asked Maura. "If it makes people more biddable?" Vang Spear of Heaven and his outlaws could use a dose.

Rath shook his head. "It is not so terrible what the slag does to you when you take it. It's what it does to you when you *cannot get it*. The stuff makes a body its willing slave."

"Did you ever…?"

"Once. For a while." Rath looked off into the distance with a rueful frown. "It is one of the worst feelings in the world when you come off it. Like the pain you feel when you warm frozen toes too fast in the winter, only, it is not your flesh, but your senses."

Just hearing about it made Maura flinch. How many Umbrians had fallen under the thrall of this slow, pitiless poison? Defeating the Han might be the least of the challenges the Waiting King would face when he woke.

"Light is too bright," Rath murmured. "Colors pain your eyes and patterns make you dizzy. Everything looks all jumbled, somehow. Any tiny noise is like a hammer beating against your head. Every smell makes you want to retch. It feels like every inch of skin has been flayed off your body and you're raw."

An echo of that old torment throbbed in his voice.

Maura moved closer to him and slipped her hand into his. It would be little, if any, comfort. But she had nothing else to give. Nothing else she dared give, though she wanted desperately to soothe his distress.

"Newlyn Swinley, you remember him—from Hoghill back in Windleford? I think he must have gone through something like that when Sorsha found him."

"I reckoned he might have been in the mines." Rath gave Maura's hand a little squeeze. Perhaps her clumsy attempt at solace had not been too wide of the mark after all. "It would take quite a man to win his way free of that vile place."

He thought for a moment. "And quite a woman to help him break free of the slag."

Sorsha and Newlyn, remarkable? Maura had never thought of them that way. They had been her neighbors and friends, beloved but familiar. Now Rath's comment made her appreciate them in a new way. And long with all her heart to see them again.

"Langbard helped them, too," she said, "once Sorsha convinced Newlyn to trust him."

She cast her memory back to that time, one of the few brief episodes of turmoil she had known in her quiet life. "There is a weed called freshwort. It grows in the mountains. It helps a person resist the slag. Newlyn must have eaten some after he escaped the mines."

Hearing her own words, Maura gave a little start. "I did not know that."

"How could you not know?" Rath cast her a glance of puzzled amusement. "You just said it, didn't you?"

"Yes. But I did not know it before that. It must be one of the memories Langbard shared with me during his passing ritual."

She braced herself for a scoffing reply from Rath, but none came. Could it be that a tiny seed of belief had begun to take root within him?

He was not daft enough to believe most of the things Maura had told him.

Rath stole a glance at her as they emerged from the forest and walked toward a small trading post very much like the one back in Southmark.

No, he did not believe. But more and more with each passing day, he *wanted* to. The trouble was, a man could not will himself to believe in things like that. Either he accepted them or he could not. No amount of proof could convince him if he doubted. No amount of scoffing could budge his faith if he was lucky enough to believe.

Rath made a sweeping gesture with his hand. "Welcome to Westborne, Mistress Woodbury."

Downhill in the distance, stone fences and hedgerows criss-crossed the gently rolling farmland. A narrow road wound its way north while a river meandered westward to empty into the Sea of Twilight.

Maura stared down at the Great West Plain. "It does not look so dangerous from here."

Even though he knew better, Rath had to agree. From this distance, Westborne looked so fertile and serene. Perhaps it had been that way once. Was it possible the slender young woman beside him had the power to make it that way again? Or was he straying into dangerous delusion?

When Rath recalled some of the improbable things he had seen her do over the past weeks, the notion of her being the Destined Queen did not seem quite so far-fetched.

"Come." He nodded toward the trading post. "Let us see what we can squeeze out of Yorg for some gently-used camping supplies. Yorg is the brother of Croll, the fellow we bought all this from. The Waskin brothers trade back and forth these same few packs and pots, rope and bedrolls to travelers crossing the Waste. Yorg has a weakness for a pretty face. Give him a smile and he'll likely give us a better price."

Between that and what he had taken off the body of the dead Hanish soldier, they might be able to pay their way at least to Deadwood. Rath would figure out some way to get more by then.

A voice rang out. *"Stev retla dar!"*

Rath froze. He reached for Maura's arm, but she had already stopped. Their Comtung lessons practice must be working. Or perhaps she guessed Yorg's meaning from his tone.

From around the side of the small, tumbledown cabin of undressed timber, Yorg Waskin shuffled out with his bow drawn and aimed at Maura.

"Who be you and what be you wanting?" Yorg called in Comtung.

"Travelers from Southmark," Rath called back, "who took a more mannerly leave of your brother Croll, several days ago." As he spoke, he subtly angled his body to deflect any arrow that might fly toward Maura.

"Is this the way you welcome customers?" He glanced around. "No wonder you are not doing very brisk business."

"Oh, customers!" Yorg lowered his bow. "Your pardons, goodfolk! Customers are getting scarcer all the time. Fewer folks crossing the Waste. But I am plagued with cursed *slaggies* coming to steal. I will soon have to sleep with a bow under my pillow. Come in and show me what you have to trade."

When he got a clearer view of Maura, the trader ran a hand over his sparse hair, while he greeted her with a wide smile that exposed a mouthful of broken, rotten and missing teeth.

"Pardon my rude welcome, Beauty." Yorg's eyes gleamed with leering eagerness that made Rath's fist itch. "If I had got a fair look at you first, I would have been more friendly."

Maura replied with a tight, guarded smile as she backed a step away from him.

"Very fine, indeed!" The trader's gaze slid over her.

"She yours, friend?" Yorg asked Rath. "Or did you bring her in for sale?"

Rath wrapped his arm around Maura's shoulder. "She *is* mine."

His heart seemed to swell in his chest as he spoke the words. "And she is *not* for sale at any price."

Yorg shrugged. "I cannot blame you. Pity, though. What a price she would fetch in the flesh market at Venard!"

"Speaking of prices…" Rath battled the urge to throttle the lecherous trader. "What will you give us for our gear?"

Fortunately for Yorg Waskin's thick neck, a question about business diverted him from leering at Maura.

"Let us have a look at what you've got." He beckoned them into the trading post.

The place did not look as though it had seen much business of late. Dust lay over a pile of bedrolls and several coils of rope. Cobwebs clung to a shelf lined with pots and kettles.

Rath wrinkled his nose at the smell of the place. He did not want to think about the food Yorg Waskin might be peddling.

In Comtung, he bid Maura to empty her pack onto the long narrow table that was the cleanest thing in Yorg's cabin.

"We will keep one of the packs," he told the trader.

In fact, he was tempted to hang on to all their gear. But from what he recalled of Westborne, there were few good spots for camping. Most of those were already occupied by the kind of folk he did not want Maura to meet. Besides, they could use the coin Yorg gave them to pay their way north.

The trader swept a calculating eye over their supplies. "Five silvers for the lot," he said at last. "Mind, I am being openhanded on account of your pretty lady."

Five silvers? That and what he'd taken off the Han would not get them far.

"If that is openhanded, I would hate to see you in a stingy mood." Rath began stuffing supplies back into Maura's pack. "We traded your brother a good horse and saddle for all this and our food."

"I told you business is bad." Yorg shook his head. "Croll and me have to make what we can on the few there are. Say, six silvers, then, but I cannot go higher."

"Sorry." Rath stuffed the kettle into his pack. "If we cannot get twenty silvers, they are worth more for us to keep."

"Twenty!" cried Yorg. "You jest! Are you sure you do not want to sell the lady?"

Maura shot Rath a skittish glance.

He shook his head, to reassure her and to set Yorg Waskin straight. "Quite sure."

In his haste to refill his pack and take their leave, Rath shrugged his cloak back over his shoulder.

"Hold a moment!" cried Yorg, staring at Rath's belt. "Where did you come by those?"

Rath glanced down. The three flaxen plumes he'd cut from the Hanish soldiers back in Prum hung from his belt. What folly had made him hang on to them? They were dangerous little trophies to be carting around Westborne for some Han to glimpse.

At least he had not revealed the copper wand that hung from the other side of his belt. That he meant to keep, for it had proven its usefulness. From now on, it had better stay hidden.

"I reckon it would be better for you not to know that." Rath narrowed his eyes in a look he hoped would discourage any more questions.

He twitched his cloak back in place. "It might be better if you forget you saw anything."

"Fear you not." Yorg gave a broad wink. "No one will hear a word about it from me. But you had best think twice about toting those much farther. Somebody might catch a look and get the wrong idea."

Yorg would never believe what had really happened. Looking back, Rath could scarcely believe it himself. "Do not fret about us. We can take care of ourselves."

"Of that, I have no doubt." Yorg rubbed his hands together. "But if you would like to rid yourselves of those dangerous trinkets and make a nice coin or two, they are worth a good deal more than that rubbish you carry for gear."

"What would you want with such things?"

"Not me, friend. The *zikary*. They will pay for anything that makes them look more like the masters they fawn over."

The notion appealed to Rath. Make some coin, and a good bit by the sound of it, selling plumes he'd stolen from the Han to those *zikary* scum.

But he feigned an appearance of barely roused interest. "I might want to get them off my hands for the right price."

"Five silvers each!" cried the trader, forgetting to curb his eagerness.

Rath thought for a moment, then shook his head. "If you will give me that for them, I can surely get a better price in the first town we come to."

"If the Han do not spot your *bounty* and carve you up first," warned Yorg. "Seven each."

"Twelve," Rath countered.

"Twelve?" The trader began to sputter all the reasons that would ruin him.

Rath caught Maura's eye and jerked his head toward the door. They shouldered their packs.

"Eight!" cried Yorg.

"Ten," said Rath as he and Maura walked toward the door.

"Done!"

Stifling a smile of satisfaction, Rath stopped.

"Oh, very well." He pulled the three long hanks of pale hair from this belt, each knotted at the end to hold them together. "I am sick of toting them, anyway."

He held out his hand. "Let me see that silver, first."

"You shall!" Yorg scurried off through a curtained doorway.

While the jingle of coins sounded from the room beyond, Maura fixed Rath with a look of mock-reproach. "There are more ways to steal than lifting purses, Rath Talward."

"You mean Yorg?" Rath pointed toward the curtained door. "He will charge the *zikary* twice what he gives us. If they are eager to pay it, that cannot be stealing, surely? Or are you feeling sorry for those poor Han, going around with their pretty hair lopped off?"

"Hardly." Maura plucked some bits of cobweb off the pile of pots and tucked it into her sash. "They were fortunate you did no worse to them."

Under his breath, Rath muttered, "Oh, I wanted to."

The curtain over the rear door fluttered as Yorg scurried back holding a little cloth pouch bulging with coins. He exchanged it for Rath's *merchandise* with an air of mistrust on both sides.

Once they had made their bargain, Yorg scrutinized the three hanks of hair while Rath counted out the silvers to make certain he had received the promised sum.

"A pleasure striking a bargain with you, Yorg." Rath tucked the coins into the pouch on his belt. Suddenly he felt far more hopeful about this last leg of their journey. "Any chance you might have a riding animal for sale?"

With a decent mount and coin left over to keep them in food and lodgings, they might make it to Everwood by Solsticetide with days to sparc. Rath reminded himself, once again, that it did not matter *when* they reached Everwood, since the Waiting King would not be there.

Somehow, the need for haste continued to goad him.

Yorg shook his head. "You would not want it if I had."

"Indeed? Why is that?"

"The Han keep a close watch on the roads, friend. They don't favor folks traveling as a rule. The ones as do, they keep a right close eye on."

"I did not like the sound of that," said Maura a while later, as they trudged down the gentle slope away from the trading post. "How are we to get from here all the way to Everwood, with the Han watching travelers?"

"There must still be some folk moving from place to place." Rath's gaze roved restlessly, alert for the slightest hint of danger. "Food has to move from the countryside into the cities at the very least. Besides, I am used to making my way around without drawing much notice."

When he was younger perhaps. Now Maura could not imagine him easily blending into a crowd. It was not only his size and his rugged good looks, which appealed to her more with each passing day. That air of danger she had first sensed about him was as potent as ever, though she no longer feared it…at least not in the same way.

Something else made him stand out, too. A bearing of command she had first glimpsed back in Betchwood when he'd tried to rally his outlaw comrades.

"I still have some hundredflowers." Maura tried to muster her optimism. "And I will keep an eye out for more, though I do not know if they grow on this side of the mountains. One thing we must do is get rid of that copper wand while we have the chance."

She braced for another argument. "If the Han find that vile thing on you, the two of us are as good as dead."

Rath stopped in midstride. "By Bror, you are right!"

"I am?" Maura stopped, too. She did not doubt she was right, but it surprised her to hear Rath admit it.

"Indeed." He reached around and hauled the copper wand from his belt.

Just looking at it cast a shadow over Maura's spirit. She remembered the suffocating darkness that had enveloped her when she had wielded it. Thank the Giver, Rath was finally getting rid of the vile thing. If she'd had her way, they would have tossed it into Raynor's Rift.

Rath shrugged off his pack.

Perhaps he was trying to unhamper himself so he could hurl the wand a greater distance. Maura did not like the thought of someone stumbling upon it. She opened her mouth to suggest they dig a hole and bury the thing, instead.

But other words burst out when Rath unbuckled his pack and thrust the wand into it. "What are you doing?"

He glanced up. "Just what you suggested. Making sure the Han do not catch me with it. At least, not without a search."

"Are you daft?" If she could have brought herself to touch the copper wand again, Maura would have wrested it from him. "Have you not seen how dangerous that thing is?"

"I have *felt* how dangerous it is!" Rath's jaw tightened and his hands worked with ferocious strength far beyond that required for closing up his pack. "I have felt what one can do in the hands of my enemies and I have seen how this one countered that attack. I would no more toss it away than I would throw down my blade before a fight."

"Beware, Rath Talward. That blade has two sharp edges. Do not be surprised if the Echtroi turn it back against you."

"I would rather chance that than go into combat unarmed." He shouldered his pack. The stern, resolute look on his face declared the matter closed.

A tense, angry silence crackled between them for the next few hours as they picked their way down the wooded foothills to the plain. The prospect of making their way through hundreds of miles of that wide, flat expanse gave Maura a feeling of perilous exposure. It galled her to be so dependent upon a stubborn man who scorned everything she believed in.

And yet…she could not deny they had managed to strike a balance between their many differences to forge a formidable partnership.

Daylight had begun to wane when they happened upon a small farm tucked in a shallow scrap of valley between two low ridges. A thin plume of smoke rose from the chimney of the small house. A few fowl scratched near the doorstep. From inside the house came the shrill wail of a crying infant. In a field nearby, a wiry man and a slender boy turned slats of mown hay with long wooden forks.

Though this place looked far poorer than the snug, modest prosperity of Hoghill Farm, the sight of it provoked a soft ache of longing in Maura. In another few weeks, Newlyn and Sorsha would be making hay. Where would she be by then?

The more she had seen on her journey, the stronger had become her desire to summon the Waiting King, and the greater her realization of the vast challenge that lay before them. Would he even recognize the kingdom he had left so long ago?

"Hail, friends!" Rath called in Comtung. He stopped and held his empty hands out in front of him to demonstrate that he was unarmed.

Maura followed his lead.

The man in the field raised his hayfork in a threatening stance. He spoke to the boy, who scurried to the edge of the field and returned a moment later with a hand sickle. The man called out a wary challenge.

Rath replied with calming reassurance—something about their goodwill and meaning no harm.

As the two men continued to talk back and forth in Comtung, the farmer appeared to be growing less guarded with every exchange. Rath had a way of winning people's trust, when he wanted to. After all they had been through together, Maura had to admit, such trust was far better deserved than she had once thought.

While Rath and the farmer spoke, the boy stared at the strangers with undisguised curiosity. Maura met his gaze and smiled at him. After a moment's hesitation, he smiled back—a wan, pinched smile that looked as though it did not get much use.

A moment later, a woman emerged from the house with a fretful baby in her arms, while a young girl clung to her skirts. When Maura smiled at them, the woman's worried frown only deepened, and the little girl hid behind her mother.

"Rath?" Maura interrupted him. "Can you ask the woman what ails the child? Perhaps I can help."

The woman started at her words. "You speak Umbrian, still?"

Maura nodded. "It is almost the only thing I *can* speak."

She edged slowly toward the woman and her children, ready to stop if bidden. Behind her, she heard Rath and the farmer lapse into Umbrian as well. Something about this hay crop and a journey north.

"We come from the far side of the mountains," she told the woman. "We are only passing through on our journey. We mean you no harm. If the little one is ill, I know some healing."

"You do?" The woman brushed back a few lank strands of hair that had fallen over her brow. "There have been no healers in these parts since Auntie Roon passed over. The Han say the strong will thrive and—"

Maura could not listen to the rest for fear she would say something dangerous. "We are not Han."

Surely that could not be taken for openly rebellious talk. Yet, in a way, that simple statement was revolutionary.

They were not Han. They could never be Han, and they should not try to be. They were different. With a different language and beliefs they must not abandon. Or they would be nothing.

The woman seemed to understand. The tension in her pale, haggard face eased. She held the baby out to Maura, a gesture of trust that touched Maura's heart. "He's a-wasting, poor mite. Food goes through him, but does him no good. I have lost three other babes to the wasting."

As Maura cradled the frail, starveling child, pity for its mother subdued a bubble of eagerness. "I have a tonic that will help, if you can boil me some water."

"That I can!" The woman headed for the house, almost tripping over her skirts in her haste. "Come and welcome. Pardon our rude greeting. Some travelers that come from out of the hills are not the kind we want to linger. While you are tending the little one, Velsa has the worms and Young Blen has a sore swelling on his neck."

"I will do what I can." Maura followed the woman into the house. Before they departed, she vowed she would leave this family in better health than she had found them. And she would teach the mother as many of the most common remedies as she could, with a promise to pass them on to her neighbors.

Perhaps the infant sensed Maura's intention to help, for it quieted in her arms. With a gentle touch of her finger, she caressed its tiny cheek.

Behind her, Rath called, "Do you mind if we stay here a few days? Blen says if we help him bring in his hay crop, we can ride with him all the way to Venard when he takes it to market. He says he would be glad of my help to guard it."

"I would not mind at all." Maura turned back toward him, the sick baby cradled in her arms. "It sounds as though we can all do each other a good turn."

Even from a distance, she could not mistake the softening of his features as he gazed at the child. "A lucky chance we happened on this place."

A breeze stirred the cooling embers of her faith and purpose. A ride for them both in the kind of vehicle that would never rouse Hanish suspicions?

"This is not chance, Rath. Nor is it luck."

Once again, it seemed the Giver had smiled on them.

22

Rath bit back a grin as Blen Maynold's well-laden hay wagon trundled along the high road to Venard. They had passed several toll posts already. At each one, Hanish officers had waved them through with scarcely a glance.

He knew Maura considered this a boon from the Giver. Much as he wanted to scoff, the solution was so elegantly tailored to their need, Rath was tempted to credit something other than chance.

Glancing around to make certain there was no one within earshot, he leaned back toward the towering load of hay. "How are you faring, Maura? Can you breathe in there?"

He did not envy her, having to sit on the wagon pallet, covered with hay. But there had been no help for it. The driver's bench had only room for two, and Blen claimed it would look odd for a woman to be seen traveling with them. Apart from the discomfort of her hiding place, Rath was not sorry to have Maura out of sight for their journey.

Since their brush with the Han at Raynor's Rift and the past several days helping out on Blen and Tesha's small farm, her well-being had come to occupy more and more of his thoughts. Even in sleep, he could not escape. She ran through his nightmares pursued by lecherous Han and murderous Echtroi, and he was always powerless to protect her.

Three nights ago, he had stirred from one such vile dream to find her lying nearby, safely caressed by moonlight, wrapped in the relaxed, innocent beauty of sleep. Overpowered by relief, he had lain awake keeping watch over her. His arms had tingled with a phantom pain he had heard men suffered after losing a limb.

Now the hay rustled behind him, and Maura's voice seemed to drift from out of nowhere. "It is hot, and the straw makes my neck itch, but I can breathe well enough."

"We shall have to stop soon." Blen looked around as if reckoning how far they'd come and how much farther they must go.

"Old Patchel needs to graze and drink." He nodded toward the big, raw-boned gelding that pulled the wagon. "I'll keep an eye for a quiet spot where you can safely slip out and cool yourself, mistress."

Rath thanked the farmer. "How many more days before we reach Venard?"

He and Maura meant to part company with Blen before he entered the city to peddle his hay crop. Would they be lucky or blessed enough to find another ride to bear them farther north?

"No more than three, I should say." Blen directed a grim

stare at a bank of clouds gathering on the western horizon. "If the weather holds."

The two men fell to talking about the weather and about Blen's struggle to make his small farm support his family and the high taxes levied by the Han.

"If it wasn't for the hay crop, I do not know how we'd manage." Blen's shoulders seemed to sag under a huge, invisible weight. "Ours and our neighbors' ripens sooner than any in Westborne and it fetches a good price in Venard since there is so little grazing land around the city. I do not suppose you would come back south with me, afterward? Last year, my supplies from the market in Venard got pilfered on my way home. It has been a hungry winter. No wonder the wee ones are all ailing."

"I wish we could." Rath meant it.

He had worked hard during their short stay on Blen's farm. Though he had told himself it was only a fair exchange for the favor of a ride north, the sense that he was helping Blen, Tesha and their children brought him a glow of pride and satisfaction.

It had warmed him further to watch Maura work her healing magic on the children. There had been more to it than herb teas and pungent balms. Her smile, her laughter and her stories had kindled the beginnings of a sunny cheer in the children that seemed fitting somehow. Whenever Rath had caught a glimpse of her gently tending Blen and Tesha's baby, a spasm of renegade tenderness had taken him by the throat.

With all his heart, he wished the two of them could return south with Blen and forget all about the Waiting King.

"We are…expected," he added by way of explanation, "up north in a fortnight."

That reminder of how swiftly his time was running out

gouged a deep pit inside Rath. Strange, that he found it so hard to believe in the Waiting King who would free Umbria from Hanish tyranny. But the Waiting King who would claim Maura and take her away from him loomed all too real.

Suddenly a small crowd of ragged children burst from the bushes beside the road. Rath recognized their kind. After Ganny's death, he had run with a similar gang of young beggars and petty thieves.

A pair of Hanish soldiers came chasing after the children.

Blen's old gelding gave a shrill, frightened whinny and reared. One of the soldiers, who just missed being struck by a great flailing hoof, bellowed a foul curse in his own tongue. Rath was glad Maura would not understand it.

"What was all that commotion?" she demanded in an urgent whisper.

"Just a couple of Han after some young scoundrels," muttered Rath. "We will be past them soon."

The hay rustled. "What can we do to help them?"

"Nothing." Much as he admired her for wanting to help, Rath could not help bristling with impatience. "Young whelps like those are cunning enough to take care of themselves. The ones unwitting enough to get caught…"

"'None should mourn the weak who perish'?" Maura quoted from that hated Hanish maxim.

"That was not what I meant." Perhaps it had been…a little. "We cannot afford to attract notice from the Han. And we owe it to Blen's family not to draw notice to him, either."

"I suppose…" Maura did not sound convinced.

"That sort spend half their lives getting chased by the Han. They are plenty clever at dodging and hiding. Do not fret yourself about them." The whole thing stirred up memories Rath thought he had successfully purged.

He wanted to swat Blen's old horse on the rump to make it move faster. He wanted to flee the harsh memories those children provoked as fast as they fled from the Han.

The hay rustled again.

"Maura, what are you doing? Don't be daft now!"

"It was not me," she insisted.

A moment later, a squeak of dismayed surprise sounded from the back of the wagon.

Before Rath or Blen could ask what was going on, Maura spoke again. "It seems we have an extra passenger."

Her words were followed by a boy's voice, pleading softly, but desperately, in Comtung.

"Let me stay here, just a little while, worthy one! I hurt my foot on a sharp stone and cannot run fast. If I do not hide here, the Han will take me." That was what Rath thought he heard in the desperate gabble.

When Maura did not answer right away, the boy added, "If you make me leave and the Han catch me, I will tell them you are hiding here."

"Why, you young…" Rath growled under his breath, quelling the traitorous notion that, under these circumstances, he might have made the same threat when he was the boy's age.

He twisted around in his seat, ready to thrust his hand into the pile of hay in search of a scrawny neck to throttle.

Maura's voice stopped him. Though they had mostly spoken Umbrian with Blen and Tesha, she must have picked up more Comtung, perhaps from the children.

"I will heed a plea faster than a threat, boy." A little garbled with a heavy Norest accent, but understandable. Then her voice softened. "When we stop, I will tend to your foot."

"Blen?" Rath nodded toward the pile of hay behind them. "Will it be all right? Just until we stop to water the horse?"

The farmer's sharp features clenched in a worried frown as he pondered Rath's request. Clearly the young scoundrel's *threat* carried more weight with him than any plea.

"I...reckon he can stay," Blen said at last in a grudging tone. "Only, keep him quiet. And if you are found out, I will swear I do not know either of you...not that it will help me much."

"You heed that, you little musk-pig," Rath growled in Comtung at the unseen beggar boy. "If any harm comes to the lady on your account, I will make you sorry the Han did not get you!"

Even though no one could see her, Maura rolled her eyes and shook her head. Rath's excessive protectiveness could be almost as vexing as it was...touching.

How she wished she *could* touch him. Just lean her head against his shoulder for a moment, or slip her hand into his. She did not mind the minor discomforts of hiding in the hay for this part of their journey, but she did miss the chance to keep company with Rath—now that their time together was running out.

She wanted to know even more about him than she had already learned. Since that was impossible at the moment, perhaps she could do the next best thing, by learning about the boy who reminded her so much of Rath as he had been when they first met.

"Are you hungry?" she whispered in Comtung.

"I guess." Hay rustled as the boy crawled toward the back of the wagon. "Why? You got food?"

"A little." Maura groped in the hay beside her for her pack. "A roll and a bit of cheese. Would you like some?"

"How much?"

"Not a lot." Maura's hand closed over the food. "But you are welcome to it."

"Not how much food." The boy spoke in a scornful murmur. "How much do you want for it?"

"Your pardon." Maura chuckled. "My Comtung is poor."

"What did you speak before?" asked the boy, his tone suddenly wary. "Hanish?"

Maura smothered a hoot of laughter. How long had it been since she'd laughed? "Not Hanish. Umbrian. The true language of our people."

At least it had been before the Han had stolen it from so many.

"Never heard of it."

"I ask no payment for the food," she told him. Then remembering how Rath had once been suspicious of aid freely given, she added, "But to help me practice my Comtung."

After a moment's hesitation, the boy asked, "Are you *twarith?*"

"Twarith?" Maura knew what it meant, but hearing that word on the lips of a child who knew no Umbrian took her aback.

"That is what they call themselves," said the boy. "They speak a queer tongue. They tell queer stories. They give folks things and help folks."

He sounded as though he found their generosity as unfathomable as their language and their stories.

"I reckon I am *twarith.*" The word meant "believer" and

she had believed enough to journey clear across the kingdom. "But I belong to no group. I would like to meet these other *twarith*. Where can I find them?"

"Give me the food and I will tell you."

"Here." Maura thrust the roll and the cheese into the hay and felt them snatched from her hands. "I give it whether you tell me or not."

"Good." The boy spoke while he chewed. "Because I don't know."

"Mind your mouth, whelp!" snapped Rath, whom Maura had forgotten must be listening. "The lady is treating you better than you deserve."

Twarith. Maura savored the name and the idea while she listened to the boy eat with muted gusto. So there were Umbrians here in the most oppressed province of the kingdom, keeping alive the old language and following the precepts of the Giver?

She wished she had time to find them and talk with them. Give them hope that the Waiting King would soon come to their aid and reward them for their faithfulness during these dark days.

"Have you a name, boy?" she asked when he had finished eating.

"Snake," he declared in a defiant tone, as if daring her to question or ridicule it.

In her mind, Maura heard an echo of Rath's words from many weeks ago. *No one gave it to me. Like everything else I have ever wanted in life, I took it.*

"Snakes are quick and cunning," said Maura. "Sometimes dangerous."

The boy made vague noises of agreement.

"I know a story about a very cunning snake. The Three-headed Serpent of White Rock. Would you like to hear it?"

"I guess." The boy made an effort to sound indifferent, but Maura heard an edge of hunger in his voice. Hunger of the spirit that could only be sated with the stories, songs and beliefs of which he had been starved.

"Once," Maura began, "in the shadow of White Rock, there hatched a tiny snake with three heads."

"Keep the story for later," Rath called back. "We are coming to a village. I do not want anyone to hear you and get suspicious."

"Is this village your home?" Maura asked the boy. "Would you like us to let you off here?"

"Got no home. We move about."

With that young Snake fell silent, robbing Maura of any distraction from the sounds that had become distressingly familiar to her on their journey north. Ailing infants crying. Women scolding older children in shrill voices of hostile desperation. Hanish soldiers bellowing orders and harassing folks. The sounds of blows and cries of pain. Now and then the flat, listless voice of a slaggie seeking a temporary escape from it all at a perilous cost.

Part of her wanted to cover her ears and block it out, too. But another part insisted she must hear the sounds and see the sights of Hanish oppression, to fuel her resolve. That did not make it easier to sit and listen, unable to help.

Gradually a quieter sound joined the others. It took Maura a moment to realize the boy had fallen asleep, lapsing into a soft snore.

She had done something to help, after all. Befriending a single boy might not seem like much, but it was a place to start.

The noises of the village began to fade until Maura could only hear the subtle, soothing music of the countryside—birds twittering, the drone of bees, the whisper of wind through the leaves. It comforted and encouraged her to be reminded there were some things even the mighty empire of Dun Derhan could not subdue.

After a short while, the hay wagon slowed and veered off the road. Maura heard the nearby gurgle of flowing water as the rhythmic clop of the horse's hooves slowed and the wagon rolled to a stop. Next came the familiar sounds of Blen and Rath climbing down from their seat.

"There is no one about," said Rath. "You can come out… both of you."

Maura wriggled out of the piled hay, careful not to knock too much of Blen's precious cargo onto the ground.

"There is only me." She pulled back the hood that protected her hair from chaff, relishing the cool tickle of the breeze on her flushed face. "The boy fell asleep."

She looked from Rath to Blen. "Can we not leave him be and fetch him along with us a little farther? The more distance he puts between himself and the Han who were chasing him, the better for us all, don't you think?"

Rath scowled. "I would sooner you slipped the young rascal a little dreamweed and we leave him here. That way if he takes it into his ungrateful young head to tell someone about us, we will be long gone."

"Do you believe he truly meant that threat?" Maura strode toward the narrow brook that beckoned her with its promise of refreshment. "The child was using the only weapon he could command to sway us. Would you have done any different at his age?"

Rath ignored her question.

"Snake," he grunted as he stooped to refill his water pouch. "An apt name for a young viper. Mark me, you let him too close and he will sting us all."

"Please, Blen?" Maura turned to the farmer. "This boy can be no older than yours. I doubt he is running from the Han for amusement's sake."

"Aye, well…" Blen knelt by the edge of the brook and splashed water in his face. "I reckon it will not hurt for us to fetch him a bit farther. He cannot cause a commotion if he is asleep, can he?"

"Thank you." Maura rewarded the farmer with her warmest smile. "You honor the Giver with your kindness."

Rath and the farmer exchanged a look.

"The lad had better mind his tongue and his thieving fingers, though," Blen insisted in a gruff tone. "Or I will bounce his backbehind out in the dirt and let the Han have him."

"I will vouch for the boy," Maura promised. "And keep a sharp eye on him. I know the two of you think I must be daft to give him a chance, but I am not blind to what he is."

She fixed her gaze on Rath. "Perhaps he is not to be trusted, but how will anyone know unless someone dares to try?"

How reluctant she had been to give Rath Talward a chance. But circumstances had forced her to rely on him, and he had never let her down.

If only she could convince him to give others the same chance Langbard had given him.

Give to others as you have been given. Maura could not count how often Langbard repeated the Third Precept to her over the years. At the time, she had thought he meant the giving of material things.

Now, when she had almost nothing but the clothes on her body and the herbs in her sash, she glimpsed the need in her poor, broken land. She had plenty to give…from her heart, if she could find the courage to do it.

Did she think him too dense to understand what she meant? Rath wondered as he helped Blen unharness old Patchel for the night.

Langbard had trusted him at a time when even he had doubted his trustworthiness. Maura had overcome her well-warranted suspicion to have faith in him. Perhaps he owed it to them both to place a little of that trust in others. One day, he might overcome his natural wariness enough to do it.

But not if it threatened to put Maura in more danger than she was in already. Each night he lay down to sleep caring more for her than he had just that morning. Looking back, he saw it had been going on almost from the first.

Every day he glimpsed some new petal of her beauty opening for him. The way she looked when she glanced up to find him watching her. The practical grace of her hands as she performed some task for his comfort. The stubborn set of her lips that made him long to kiss them into cooperation.

Though he had to admit such a kiss might win her his surrender, instead.

Most of his life he had thought of nothing beyond his next meal, his next theft, his next fight. Until he'd met Maura, survival and freedom had been enough for him. He had never allowed himself to slow down long enough for the emptiness of such a life to catch up with him.

Now that he had let someone else matter to him, he could see what a hollow, brittle shell his old life had been. Would it become that way again if some harm befell Maura? Rath feared so with a jagged-bottomed depth of dread he had never felt before.

For a man with certain skills, it was a good deal easier to keep himself from harm than to protect someone else. Especially someone who did not look out for her own safety as much as she ought to.

An expectant silence wrenched him out of his brooding. "Your pardon, Blen. Did you say something?"

"Just that I would fetch you and Maura back some supper from the inn once I have eaten."

"I hope for all our sakes the food is better here than the place we stayed last night." Rath fished a silver from his money pouch and tossed it to the farmer.

Blen tried to give it back. "Put that away. You will need it soon enough. Besides, who ever heard of a man's hireling paying him?"

"Keep it," Rath insisted. "We would have spent more to come this far on our own. And drawn all kinds of unwanted notice from the Han, I daresay."

It gave him a sense of sly satisfaction every time they rode under the noses of a Hanish patrol or got waved through a toll gate. Neither surprised him, though. A number of well-laden wagons like Blen's were making their way to Venard on this road. Most had a hired guard along to help the farmer protect his load.

Blen and Rath fit in well, and the Hanish garrisons along their route had enough to keep them busy without delaying the routine spring shipment of hay to Venard. Rath could not have ordered a swifter, more secret means of smuggling Maura north.

"Since you put it that way…" Blen gave him a parting salute that looked almost jaunty. "I will not be long, I promise."

Rath led Patchel to the trough in the inn's courtyard for a good long drink, then brought him back to hitch beside the hay wagon. While Blen spent the night in the inn, his "hired guard" would keep watch over the horse and hay. Maura would probably insist on taking a turn during the darkest hours so he could catch some sleep.

Glancing around the courtyard to make sure there was no one within earshot, Rath whispered, "It looks safe for you to come out, now."

When he got no reply he tried again. "Maura? Are you awake?"

He thought he heard a faint rustle in the hay.

"Maura?" He jammed his arm into the pile all the way up to his shoulder. "Are you all right?"

His hammering heart slowed a little when his hand closed over her arm. "Your pardon! I did not mean to wake you. I only worried that…"

Wait! That sleeve did not feel like Maura's wool tunic, nor her linen undergown.

Rath hauled on the limb he was holding, dragging out a squirming boy by what turned out to be the left leg.

He was a rangy, underfed youth, like too many Rath had seen during their long ride through the heart of Westborne.

The lad was missing the little finger off his left hand and under a coating of chaff, his face was streaked with black.

That puzzled Rath for a moment until he realized the lad had tried to darken his hair with something, soot perhaps, which had run when he sweat.

"Oh, it's only you," muttered Rath in Comtung. He had all but forgotten about the boy.

"Let me go!" Snake writhed like his namesake. "I wasn't doing nothing! Just staying out of sight like the lady bid me."

Rath let go of the boy's leg, then before he could run off, grabbed him again by the breast of his coat, a bulky men's garment with the sleeves crudely hacked to half their original length.

"Where is the lady?" Rath gave the boy a shake for good measure. He knew from his own youth that Snake had been up to no good. "If you have harmed her…"

The boy abruptly stopped squirming.

"Do I look daft?" He fixed Rath with an indignant glare that appeared ridiculous coming from such a tattered scarecrow. "Why would I harm the only one who's done me a good turn in as long as I can reckon?"

Those words struck Rath a stinging blow such as the boy could never have landed with his hands. That still did not mean he trusted young Snake. Rath had known too many like him—been too much like him, once.

"Where is she, then?" he growled.

The boy shrugged his bony shoulders and almost got a cuff on the head for it. "Right after we stopped, she heard somebody crying. She went off to look. Told me to stay here. That's all I know."

Rath cursed. Then he took a risk he might not have taken if he'd had longer to think about it.

"I am going to find her," he told the boy. "Stay here and keep watch on the horse and wagon. Yell at the top of your lungs if there is any trouble and I will come in a hurry."

The boy nodded.

At least Rath thought so. He was too busy worrying about Maura and wondering where she had gone. Someone crying usually meant trouble. The kind a body should stay away from—not go in search of.

Slag! If he had to surrender his heart to a woman, why could he not have picked one with a healthy sense of self-preservation?

Because, he decided as he made a circuit of the courtyard, checking for hidden nooks, listening for the sound of Maura's voice, that was one of the things he…loved about her. Might as well use the word, at least in the privacy of his own thoughts. Calling it something else did not lessen its hold on him.

That was one of the things he *loved* about Maura. Her vast desire to help people, especially people no one else would see any benefit in helping. Because there was no benefit to helping outcasts…like him.

Or maybe there was, to her. A benefit as intangible as her Giver. And perhaps as powerful, if it existed and had done everything she claimed.

Where was she?

He wanted to bellow her name as loud as his voice could ring. But he dared not draw that kind of attention to himself, or to her.

When he finally caught the soft murmur of her voice, the

intensity of his relief made him light-headed. He followed that sound toward a narrow opening between the main part of the inn and a side wing. Suddenly a door opened in front of him and a pair of Hanish soldiers strode out.

By good fortune, they were headed in the other direction.

Rath scrambled for cover behind a two-wheeled dairy cart abandoned in a corner of the courtyard. When his foot landed on something yielding and a bit slippery, he glanced down to find several nuggets of horse dung around his right foot, and one under it. He swallowed a curse.

The soldiers walked past the narrow alcove from whence Rath had heard Maura's voice. Then, a few steps beyond it, one stopped and doubled back.

After a quick glance, he called the other fellow back and the two of them slipped into the alley. The swagger of their steps and the rough heartiness of their voices alarmed Rath.

Do not move! he ordered himself. *Keep your wits, for you will need them and so will she.*

Perhaps he had misheard and Maura was not there at all. If she was there, she might be able to get herself out without any interference from him. She had done it before, after all. No sense doing something rash that might draw too much unwelcome attention to their presence unless he had to.

The next few moments stretched on and on with every part of Rath clenched so tight he feared something would snap.

Then he heard sounds of a struggle and a cry he knew was Maura's. Before he could stir, she appeared, her arms pinned behind her by one of the Han. A slender trickle of blood seeped from the corner of her mouth.

Her gaze searched desperately around the courtyard. For

him, no doubt. But whether to beg his help or warn him away, Rath could not tell.

Not that it mattered. For there was only one thing he could do now.

23

Maura cursed her own foolishness and lack of caution. She had not even noticed the Han until they were upon her.

The sound of brokenhearted weeping had lured her from Blen's hay wagon into a tight little alley beside the inn's kitchen. There she had found a girl a year or two younger than herself, eating scraps begged from the innkeeper's wife. With her improved command of Comtung, Maura soon learned that Angareth had run away from a pleasure house in Venard that served Hanish soldiers and government officials.

"They're only supposed to mate with their own kind, so they do not foul their superior race with half-casts." The girl passed a hand over her slightly swollen middle in a protective caress. "If one of the bed girls has a baby, the bawdwife does away with it soon as it is born. Sometimes sooner."

The thought made Maura's gorge rise and her heart clench.

"I do not care so much what happens to me now." Angareth scrubbed at her eyes with the wide sleeve of her tunic. "If only my baby can have a chance."

She glanced up at Maura. "Do you think I am foolish to care for it when it is not even born yet?"

When Maura began to shake her head, the girl added with anguished defiance, "Or wicked to love it even if it has Hanish blood?"

"No!" Maura reached out to stroke the girl's cheek, but Angareth flinched back. "Loving is never wicked."

Something about the girl stirred a memory within her, but Maura had no time just then to dwell on it. "Where are you bound, Angareth? How can I help you?"

The girl named a place that meant nothing to Maura. "It is a town west of here. I have family there. I only hope they will not turn me out for shame when they find out about the baby."

"Surely they will not." Maura wished she could sprout wings and fly to the Secret Glade. For the sake of girls like Angareth and boys like Snake. For Blen and Tesha and their children. And thousands more in need of deliverance. "I would let you come with me and my friends, but we are bound by a different road. Would a coin or two help speed your journey?"

Hearing the firm tread of a man, she knew Rath must have come looking for her. She wondered how she would persuade him to part with a silver or two to help this girl. He would put up an argument, no doubt, but she could not resent it. She recalled his words from the previous night when he had caught her making a poultice for a beggarman suffering a mild case of flesh rot.

"You can protect yourself from the Han if need be, lass.

You are quick and clever and strong." His praise had surprised and touched her all the more because she had expected a scolding.

"If I can protect myself from the Han so well," she had teased, "why did you come with me?"

He'd shaken his head and caressed her face with a gaze as fond as it was exasperated. "I came to protect you from yourself. I know you want to help folks and I admire you for it. But if you keep this up we will soon not have a coin between us and I will be on my way to the mines while they drag you off to a...someplace just as bad. You do not have the power to help everyone who needs it, but this Waiting King of yours will. The best thing you can do for all these folks is to reach him as quick as you can. That means staying hidden and not giving away all your herbs and all our coins."

"What if there is no king waiting for me in the Secret Glade, as you believe?" She had challenged him, hoping he might recant his doubts.

Her question had made him think, at least.

As he turned away, shaking his head, she'd heard him sigh. "If there is no Waiting King, then none of this matters."

Now she turned to cast him a pleading gaze. She would ask five silvers for the girl, then let him bargain her down to two. In exchange for which, she would agree not to go away from the wagon again without his leave.

Angareth drew back with a high, frightened whimper.

"Do not be afraid," Maura reached for the girl's hand. "This is a friend of mine, he means you no harm."

Instead of Rath's resonant, mellow voice that made even

Comtung sound tolerable, another voice rang out, loud and harsh. "What friend, wench? No friend of mine."

Before Maura could reach into her sash, the Han grabbed her and pinned her arms. Another one squeezed past them to seize Angareth.

"So which is the runaway the innkeeper reported?" the Han holding Angareth asked.

"I care not." The Han against whom Maura was struggling fetched her a clout on the side of the face that made the outlaw Turgen's blow seem like a love tap.

Maura cried out.

"They both look serviceable enough for a pleasure house." The Han shoved Maura back out of the alley. "Let's go."

What now? Maura forced herself to breathe more slowly—to watch what was going on around her and to wait for an opportunity. True, she had fallen into the clutches of the Han. But she had fought them before and won. She knew they were not invincible.

As they emerged back into the courtyard, Maura's gaze flew to Blen's hay wagon. Though she saw no sign of Rath, she did catch a glimpse of two dirty bare feet disappearing into the hay pile. Hopefully Snake would have the sense to stay there until the danger had passed…if it passed.

What took place next happened so fast that it startled Maura quite as much as it did the Han.

Something hurtled through the air. Then the Han who held her cried out and pulled her arms so hard she feared he would wrench them from her shoulders. The other Han bellowed a curse, too, as the reek of horse dung assaulted Maura's nose.

Rath. She knew it must be him even before she heard him

shout some Hanish words. They must have been a taunt or a vile insult, judging from the reactions of the two soldiers.

The next thing she knew, she was flung to the hard-packed dirt of the courtyard. Angareth fell on top of her, for which Maura was glad…once she recaptured the breath Angareth knocked out of her.

While she lay there gasping for air, she heard the rapid thunder of hard-shod boots against the ground and the furious cries of the Han moving away from her.

"Angareth," she gasped when she had breath enough, "are you…all right? The baby?"

"You have come to worse hurt than me." The girl rolled off Maura and tried to help her sit up. "What happened?"

Maura shook her head as she pulled herself up. It would take her too long to explain.

She needed to go to Rath's aid—the fool. It had been one thing to create such a diversion out in open country, from a good safe distance, with a horse hidden nearby to make a quick escape. In the close confines of the inn courtyard, in the middle of Westborne, it was dangerous folly.

Something tugged at her elbow.

"Come, lady." The boy, Snake, hovered over her. "You must get away…now. Follow me!"

"No!" Maura staggered to her feet. "We must help Rath."

People were emerging from various doorways that opened onto the courtyard where Rath was leading the two soldiers in chase.

Snake clamped his bony fingers around her wrist with surprising strength. "Come with me! I know this town. There is a place you can hide until night falls."

"Take Angareth." Maura tried to pull her arm away. "Rath needs me!"

The boy clung to her with stubborn insistence. "He does not need you caught by the Han, too. That is what will happen if you do not come with me now!"

A grudging part of her acknowledged the boy was probably right. His warning sounded like something Rath might tell her if he were able.

Perhaps Snake sensed he was winning her over. "Wait and see what happens. He may escape the Han on his own. Or if he is caught, you will have a better chance of rescuing him once all the fuss dies down."

"Please," begged Angareth, "let us get away from here before more Han come!"

The girl sounded ready to shatter from fright and the strain of her ordeal. Rath, on the other hand, had proven well capable of looking after himself. He had staged this diversion to give her a chance to get away. He would not be pleased if she refused to take it.

"Very well, then. Lead us to this hiding place of yours, Snake."

When the boy let go of her arm, Maura fished in the pockets of her sash for a pinch of madfern and a few strands of spidersilk. She meant to be prepared in case anyone tried to get in their way.

If only she'd been prepared when the Han had come down that alley, rather than taken unawares, Rath would not be fleeing for his life now.

* * *

Good! The Han were chasing him—both of them. Rath had hoped to draw off one, at least, so Maura could take care of the other. Two in pursuit of him alone was better still.

Well…perhaps not.

The Han appeared to know what was what and where was where in this village. He did not.

He heard them bellowing for reinforcements to join the chase. He had no one to help him—unless he counted Maura and Blen, whom he did not want to get involved.

His years as an outlaw had taught him to be fast on his feet and to think fast in a tight spot. This was one of the tightest he'd ever landed in.

He leapt over a fence, ducked under a line of drying clothes, climbed a rough stone wall, then twisted his ankle when he jumped down the other side.

If only he could find a spot to hide until nightfall.

Spotting a fowl coop set a little off the ground to discourage predators, he dove underneath it.

The stench of droppings made him gag, but he would have stayed there had he not heard a woman shriek, "There he is, under the coop! Get him!"

Rath rolled out, scrambled to his feet again and headed off in a direction from which he heard no Hanish voices.

He ducked into an alley, shinnied up a drain pipe and ran across the ridge pole of a roof.

An arrow whizzed in front of him. A step faster and he'd have been done for.

As it was, the shot startled him—checking his pace for an instant too long, making him lose his footing. He tumbled down the steep slope of the roof, arms flailing, hands groping for anything to check his fall. But they found no hold.

He had only time for one thought as he plunged toward the ground. It was more of an appeal, really, in case there was a Giver and it could hear his thoughts.

"Let me land hard enough to kill me."

Any other outcome could only be worse.

When the racket from the streets finally quieted, Maura feared the worst.

She and Angareth cowered in a hollow gouged into the embankment beneath a bridge. She had sent Snake to see what he could find out, and to fetch the packs from Blen's wagon. While she waited for him to return and for darkness to fall, she fought to keep her fears at bay.

"Is it dark enough to come out now?" asked Angareth.

"You may go if you like. I had better stay until the boy gets back." *If* the boy got back. "I wonder what can be taking him so long?"

Maura leaned out of the hollow to listen, but a sinister hush seemed to have fallen over the town. All she could hear was the gurgle of the river, the patter of rain and the distant regular tramp of feet that sounded like a night patrol.

Where was Snake? Why had he not returned? Had she been wrong to trust him?

Perhaps he had run off with their packs to sell what he could in a neighboring town.

No. She would not let herself think that. "I hope no harm has come to him."

Angareth began to weep again. Sorry as Maura felt for the girl, she could not stem a rising surge of impatience. As Rath had once told her, in times of crisis folks could not afford to indulge their feelings too much if they meant to survive.

"I am so sorry I brought this trouble on you and your friend," Angareth sobbed. "You are one of the few folk who have shown me any kindness. Then your friend risked his safety so we could escape. I fear it may have all been for naught."

"Take heart, now." Maura wrapped her arm around the girl's shoulder. "We both made a choice, my friend and I. You are not to blame for our decisions. But you can make certain we did not act in vain."

"How is that?"

"Do not give up. Do whatever you must to make your way home. Raise your child well and be ready to give a hand to someone else who might need it. 'Give to others as—'"

"Shh!" Angareth pressed her fingers to Maura's lips. "I think I hear something."

Once Angareth fell silent, Maura heard it, too. The soft furtive sounds of someone approaching. Thinking it might be Snake returned at last, Maura brushed Angareth's hand from her mouth to call out to him.

Then it occurred to her the muted scramble of footsteps might belong to a Hanish soldier trying to sneak up on them. She pulled a wisp of spidersilk from her sash and waited, her heart beating a rapid tattoo against her ribs.

"Psst!" Snake called in a whisper. "Are you still here?"

Maura's pent up breath gusted out of her in a sigh of relief. She leaned out of the hollow. "We're here. Are you all right? What news?"

As the boy moved closer, Maura heard the soft scrape of

a bulky object along the loose-packed earth of the embankment. He had the packs, bless him! One of them, at least.

"There!" The boy sank down on the lip of the hollow. "We are even now for your hiding and feeding me." His gruff tone rang with a contrary note of satisfaction.

"I told you," Maura reminded him. "Our help was freely—"

Before she could finish, Snake interrupted her. "Do you not want to hear about your man?"

Her man? Those words sent a sweet ripple through Maura that was far too beguiling. Rath Talward was not hers. Nor could he ever be. But until that moment, she had never admitted to herself how much she wished he could.

"You saw him? He is alive? Why did you not bring him?"

"Hush!" snapped the boy. "Do you want every Han in this miserable village to hear you?"

Maura clenched her lips tight. She had not realized how loud she'd spoken. "Please," she whispered. "Tell me."

"He is not dead," said Snake, "and that is a bit of luck, for he fell off a roof."

"Can I go to him?" Maura's mind churned with balms and tonics she would need to prepare.

"Are you daft?" asked the boy. "The Han have him, of course, and you want to stay clear of them. I overheard two of the soldiers talking. They plan on sending him to the mines tomorrow, with their regular batch of prisoners."

A horrible sensation seized hold of Maura, like the one that had gripped her when she'd first looked over the edge of Raynor's Rift. She'd been horrified when Rath had told her of the mines—the brutality, the danger, the slag poisoning a man's senses and his spirit. She had heard the dread and despair in his voice. He had been there once, or come near to it. Or perhaps someone dear to him had.

"The poor man," Angareth whispered in a tone she might have used if the boy had reported Rath dead.

Snake gave an indifferent grunt of agreement. "He was not the pleasantest fellow, but he led the Han on a fine chase, I hear. The whole town is buzzing about it."

"I told that farmer fellow to get out of town before the Han started asking questions," he added. "And I fetched your packs. They were heavy to carry. Got any more food in 'em?"

A bewildered numbness eased the first sharp wrench of fear and grief that had torn Maura's heart. "I gave you all I had, but there might still be something in Rath's pack."

She groped in the darkness at the two packs, recognizing Rath's by its shape and the faint scent of him that clung to it. She reached in and hauled out a hard sausage and some bread. A shiver ran through her when the backs of her knuckles brushed against the copper wand.

An idea began to take root in her mind.

Breaking the bread and sausage in two, she gave half to each of the others. "I am sorry I have no more to offer you."

"Where will you go?" asked Snake, while chewing a large bite of food. "Now that *he*'s gone?"

"He is not *gone!*" Maura clung to that feeble crumb of comfort.

"He might as well be. And it will not be safe for you or the other lady to linger in this town after sunrise. Once I eat, I am off."

"Where will *you* go?" Maura turned the question back on him.

"Away from here."

"I will not need both of these packs." Maura pushed hers toward him. "I can give you one to use or to sell as you wish."

"For what?"

"For helping Angareth, here, get back to her village. She needs the aid of someone like you, who knows his way about and how to survive."

When the boy did not reply right away, Maura fumbled in the darkness for his hand. "Will you...please?"

He only let her hold it a moment before he pulled away. "I reckon so."

"Good." Maura wondered how she could feel such a weight of responsibility for two people she had barely met. "Now, I need one last favor from you before we part. Not because you owe me anything. You have already more than paid any debt between us. And not because I can barter for it, because I have nothing left that I dare give away."

"What?" Snake sounded altogether suspicious of such a one-sided exchange.

"Earlier you said you do not know where to find the *twa-rith*." Though torn about what she must do next, Maura knew she would need help. "Please think. Is there anywhere I might go to look for them?"

"Sorry," said Snake. "You get to hear about them from folk. Or one of them turns up out of nowhere, then disappears just as quick."

Maura swallowed her disappointment. Once she made her choice, she would have to operate alone. The prospect daunted her but she would not let it stop her. She had come too far and learned too much for that.

Angareth tugged at her sleeve.

"Your pardon," said Maura. "I know you must want to get on your way while the darkness lasts."

"I do," said the girl, "but it is not that. I know where you might find the people you seek. At least, I think I do."

"Truly?" Maura caught the girl's hand in a tight squeeze. "Where? How?"

"In the next village north. I was looking for something to eat and an old woman told me I might get help at a tavern called The Hawk and Hound. When I found the place, I saw some Hanish soldiers coming and going, so I kept away."

That did sound suspicious, even to Maura.

But Snake piped up, "I hear the *twarith* like to work right under the noses of the Han, but I never knew what that meant."

"It makes a kind of sense, I suppose." Maura pulled Rath's pack toward her. "I reckon I must go and see for myself."

If nothing else it would put her some distance closer to Everwood. And the walk would give her time to decide what she must do.

Follow the dictates of duty and destiny? Or do as her heart bid her?

The pain brought him back to consciousness. Rath cursed his ill luck for being alive now that he had lost his freedom.

And yet, a small but stubborn part of him clung to life. For he now cared for something more than his life or even his freedom. Not just Maura as a woman, but also as a token of something greater.

The pain struck him again. On the other cheek this time,

accompanied by a jingling sound. At least it was ordinary pain, not mortcraft. Rath wondered how long his luck would hold.

"What is a dung-throwing hired guard doing with so much silver in his pouch?" someone asked.

Rath coaxed his eyes open a slit to find himself tied to a chair in a bare room, facing a dark-masked Echtroi who swung his well-laden coin pouch with lazy menace. Staring at it, Rath regretted every silver he had kept Maura from giving away. If he'd shared her generosity instead of guarding against it, those coins would have done some good, rather than making the pouch heavier to strike him.

Though he knew it would invite another blow, at the very least, Rath could not resist shrugging his shoulders and giving an impudent answer to the death-mage's question. "Perhaps I am very good at what I do."

To his surprise, the Echtroi let out a raspy laugh at his show of audacity. "An Umbrian with some spirit—what a novelty. I am also very good at what I do."

The coin pouch flew upward, catching Rath under the chin in a blow that jerked his head back and made him bite his tongue.

"Enough jesting," his inquisitor snapped. "Where did you get the silver?"

Rath spat a mouthful of blood onto the floor. "Stole it."

"That is better." The Echtroi tossed the bag of coins into the corner as if it had served his purpose and no longer interested him. "Who did you steal it from?"

"A trader." That was almost true.

"Where did you come from?"

"The Hitherland."

The death-mage's parched lips curved in chilling mockery of a smile. "What a pity you did not stay there."

A man in his right wits should be terrified at this moment. Paralyzed, soiling-his-breeches terrified. Rath was not.

Perhaps unmasking that death-mage back in Prum and seeing the frailty that lay beneath the menacing image had robbed the Echtroi of their power over his fears. Or perhaps that fall from the roof had knocked all sense out of him.

"I will make you a bargain." Rath coaxed the words around his swollen, throbbing tongue. "I will go back where I came from if you go back where you came from and take your whole slagging race with you."

The Echtroi whipped out his wand. It was wrought of a rare green metal known as *strup*. In its tip glittered a venomous green poison-gem.

Now fear snaked through Rath's marrow. He had heard what poison-gems did to a body—the excruciating corruption that swelled and twisted limbs, making the victim retch blood while his flesh broke out in festering sores.

"Nefarion!" A voice rang out from behind Rath.

Though it was scratchy and strident, Rath thought it as sweet as birdsong, for it delayed his coming torment.

The death-mage glanced away from Rath. He switched from Comtung to Hanish. "What are you doing here, Varoque?"

"I have come to fetch more workers for the mines," announced the other man—another death-mage, Rath assumed. Ordinary Han did not speak to the Echtroi in that contemptuous tone. "They are dying off faster than we can replace them up there. Our production is falling and the Governor is not pleased."

Though Rath grieved the dead miners, he was glad they were finally free of the mines and the slag. He even admired them for dying at a rate to cause trouble for the Han. Closing his eyes, he struggled to keep his features slack, so the Echtroi would not guess he understood them.

"Climbed a little too high, have you, Varoque?" asked Nefarion, his tone as venomous as his wand. "It is a steep fall from where you perch, and there is always someone looking to give you a little nudge over the edge."

"Are you too comfortable here, fool? Torturing petty miscreants to keep your powers from failing?" Even in a foreign language, Rath understood that threat. "Perhaps you would like to be sent on a mission over the mountains? The Governor thinks we have not kept a careful enough eye on those barbarians."

"You would not dare give me such an opportunity to prove my worth."

"A chance to be broken or stripped, you mean. Mordake shattered his power on some old fool of a sorcerer. Vulmar has disappeared along with two of his men. And Nithard did what honor required after he was stripped of his mask and wand."

That piece of information intrigued Rath and made him struggle to conceal a flicker a pride. Did he understand right? If someone took a death-mage's wand and mask, then the mage was obliged by some twisted code of Echtroi honor to do away with himself?

He must find a way to live long enough that he could relay this news to someone capable of using it to advantage.

The first name that leapt to mind was the Waiting King.

24

By the time she reached The Hawk and Hound, Maura was reeling from fatigue.

She had hoped to reach the tavern before too many customers arrived, especially Hanish ones. Unfortunately she had lost her way for a time in the dark after parting with Snake and Angareth. It had not helped that she'd been too preoccupied with the struggle inside herself to keep her wits about her.

Part of her insisted she must leave Rath Talward to look after himself while she made haste to Everwood. The ivory maps sewn into the hem of her tunic seemed to grow heavier with every step, reminding her of the responsibility with which she had been entrusted. She must not put the quest at risk to gratify her own selfish desires. Even if he did not believe in the Waiting King, Rath would not want her putting herself in danger on his account.

She did not *need* him to reach the Secret Grove. Every challenge overcome since leaving Windleford had helped convince her she was more capable than she had ever believed. Once she woke the Waiting King, she could beg him to deliver Rath from the mines—the first and only favor she would ever ask of her lord.

Despite all those excellent arguments, she could not bring herself to abandon Rath without at least trying.

That was what had brought her here, to a village whose name she did not know and a tavern rumored to host some people who might help her.

Under her breath, she murmured a plea to the Giver, an old one Langbard had taught her many years ago. "Light my path. Guide my steps. Throw the mantle of your protection around me."

With that, she hurried across the street and pushed open the tavern door. For a moment she stood just over the threshold, letting her eyes grow accustomed to the dimness inside. The smells of hearty food and strong ale washed over her along with the sound of music from a flute and drum all but drowned out by a few loud voices.

When her vision brightened she saw the place boasted a dozen tables, less than half of which were presently occupied. Some Umbrian villagers sat at those nearest her, while most of the noise came from a far corner table where three Hanish soldiers sat, quaffing the contents of oversized ale mugs.

Even though she was mostly screened from their view by the other patrons, and two of the soldiers had their backs to her, she still felt horribly exposed and vulnerable. Flitting from shadow to shadow, she made her way to the bar where a short woman was filling mugs from an ale keg.

"Pardon me," said Maura in Comtung.

The woman moved closer and turned an ear toward Maura. "Speak up, lass, or I'll never hear you over all the tunes and talk!"

Maura sucked in a deep breath then blurted out the words she'd been practicing. *"Ban henwa chan Anreg, reg fi dimroth."*

In Old Umbrian, it meant, "In the name of the Giver, let me have water." An innocent enough request to make in a tavern. Except that *dimroth,* the *twara* word for "water" sounded a great deal like *limroth,* the word for "help." To anyone who did not speak Old Umbrian, it would mean nothing.

The last words were just leaving her lips when the music suddenly stopped, and most of the talk lulled at the same moment. Her strange speech seemed to hover in the silence, calling everyone's attention.

All that kept Maura from fleeing was her certainty that the Hanish soldiers would be after her in no time. So she waited, scarcely breathing, groping for the small amount of madfern she had left, hoping it would be enough if they approached her.

Behind the bar, the woman dispensing ale seemed unaware that the mug in her hand was full and overflowing. When she finally noticed, she set the mug down and bustled out from behind the bar, laughing. "This way, lass. The kitchen is this way."

Over her shoulder she called in Comtung to no one in particular, "Up-North girl looking for work. How queer they talk! I could hardly understand a word."

The music started up again, louder than before. When

Maura heard no obvious sounds of pursuit, she started to breathe again.

The woman propelled her down a narrow galley way, talking loudly in Comtung about food preparation and waiting on tables. Abruptly, she pushed Maura into a shallow alcove that held shelves of crockery.

Switching to Umbrian, she demanded in a vexed whisper, "Were you not told to come around back?"

Maura shook her head, chiding her dangerous lapse in not thinking of that herself.

The woman reached past her and gave the left-hand wall of the alcove a solid shove. The whole wall swung out like a door leading to an even narrower passageway.

"What happened to your face?" whispered the woman. "Is your man a slaggie? We see a lot of that."

"No!" Maura's hand flew to her bruised cheek. She remembered how anxious Rath had been that folks not believe he would harm her. "A soldier did this."

"Well, mind your step," the woman warned once the door had closed behind them, plunging the passage into darkness. "Or you will have more bruises to match that one. There's stairs coming. Just feel your way down."

Fearing she might tumble and break her neck, Maura groped her way down the tight, winding stairwell. Until about halfway, when some feeble light from below made it possible to see where she was going.

A few steps later, she emerged into a large, low-ceilinged room lit by a few candles. A woman and two small children were sleeping on a pile of straw in one corner. In another corner stood a small workbench around which hung bunches of dried herbs. An old man working at the bench turned toward Maura and the barwife, beckoning.

"You go talk to Clavance," whispered the woman. "I'd best get back up to keep the ale flowing."

She glanced at the old man. "Can you give me a bit of muddlewort to make our customers forget they saw this lass come in?"

Clavance plucked a linen pouch from the bench and tossed it to her. "That is our last until the new crop blossoms. Make it go as far as you can."

He turned back to Maura. "Now, my dear, how can I help you?"

The words had barely left his mouth before he flinched at the sight of her face. "Foolish of me to ask. I could try to apply a poultice but…"

"…they are hard to bind on to the face. I know." Maura shrugged off her pack and sank onto a stool near the workbench. "It is not for healing that I have come. Are you the ones folk call the *twarith?*"

Not that she had any doubt.

"Folks call us many things." Clavance passed a hand over the bald crown of his head in a gesture that reminded Maura of Langbard. "Fools, busybodies, dreamers…even sorcerers. We prefer to call ourselves *twarith.*"

He regarded her with a cautious, probing stare. "Do you know what that means?"

Maura nodded and smiled. She had never realized how comforting it could be to have contact with someone who believed as she did.

"Sholia ban Anreg marboeth." She chanted the familiar words of the First Precept. *Trust in the Giver's Providence.*

The man's gray brows shot up. He peered closer at Maura's sash. "Who *are* you, daughter?"

His hushed tone betokened fear…or awe.

"A traveler," she replied, "with far still to go and much to do. One who needs your help."

Clavance nodded. "Rest here and eat, then. You look weary. I will call a gathering for tonight."

Where was Maura, now? Rath wondered as the cart carrying a new shipment of miners lurched up a winding trail into the Blood Moon Mountains.

The Great Plain of Westborne spread out below. With his gaze, Rath traced a route northward, willing Maura to follow it.

The man to his left stirred and yawned. "Didn't we get lucky," he muttered quietly so the Hanish guards would not overhear. "A ride all the way to the top. Before, they always marched prisoners up. Lots died on the way, I hear."

Was it luck? Rath wondered. Or an opportunity from the Giver? Would it hurt him to pretend so, at least?

He leaned toward the man who had spoken and whispered just loud enough for a few others nearby to hear. "They are losing men faster than they can replace. They need to look after us better if they want to get their stinking ore out."

A low buzz rippled through the cart as that news passed from man to man. Vacant eyes flickered with life, or the possibility of it. Limbs slack with despair, moved and straightened.

Those subtle signs gave Rath enough encouragement to

add, "No group of prisoners coming to these mines ever had a better chance of getting out of them alive than we do."

"Alive?" An older man gave a hollow, barky laugh, then covered it with a cough. "What kind of *life* is that? Slaves to the slag?"

"Where would we go if we did escape?" muttered another. "The Echtroi would only find us and fetch us back."

"Or worse," grunted a third fellow.

Rath could feel the slow suffocation of despair settling over them again. "What if I told you the days of the death-mages in this kingdom are numbered and fast running out?"

"I would bid you spin a story that's easier to swallow," the older man grumbled.

But the younger fellow sitting beside Rath asked, "What makes you say so? You seem to know a good deal."

"I know the Waiting King is coming."

Several of the other prisoners broke into hoarse laughter.

A whip cracked above their heads and one of the Hanish guards bellowed, "Quiet, lowlings! See how much you laugh in the bowels of the mountain!"

For a time they fell silent, as ordered. Then the young fellow beside Rath whispered, "The Echtroi must have made your brain rot with that cursed wand of his. The Waiting King is a tale for children and daft folk."

"So I thought," said Rath. "But I have seen the Destined Queen with my own eyes."

A vivid image of Maura rose in his mind. Of that first day in the Betchwood when she had turned him invisible. Of the way she had subdued that houseful of Han in Prum and how she had found the map. Of their battle with the lank wolves and how she had braved her fear to cross Raynor's Rift in defense of her beliefs. He remembered the stories she had told him, the spells she had taught him and the healing she had worked on him.

"I tell you—" his voice pulsed with conviction "—the lady is on her way to the Secret Glade at this very moment."

He braced himself for the other men to laugh again, but they did not. They stared at him, their eyes and their features betraying the inner battle waged within each man—between doubt and faith, between despair and hope.

Perhaps he had no right to speak with such fervor when he still had not vanquished all his own doubts. But this was the only means he had left to serve Maura. He would not let some quibble about belief hold him back.

He watched as the others mulled over his claims. Their scowls and furrowed brows bespoke their disbelief. Yet hope quickened in the depths of their eyes in spite of their efforts to quench it. No matter what they might try to tell themselves to the contrary, they *wanted* something to believe in.

As he had, without ever realizing it…until now.

"Destined Queen!" the older man muttered in a tone of scorn. "Waiting King! What if that hogswill is all true? By the time they could do us any good, none of us will care about anything beyond our next sniff of slag."

Rath wished he could deny it, but he could not. They would soon arrive at the mines to have their necks branded and their first sniff of slag forced upon them. After that, no force would be necessary. Unless Maura found some magical means to fly, she would have at least a week's hard traveling ahead of her to reach the Secret Glade. Then…

Then, nothing, perhaps.

His gaze strayed back toward the plain, then fell to a straggly cluster of weeds that had taken stubborn root in the thin, rocky mountain soil at the edge of the road. The sight of that plant kindled a memory.

"Maur—er…the Destined Queen told me of a mountain plant that helps a body resist the slag."

In furtive whispers, he shared the description of freewort that Maura had given him. On the slim chance it might help, he lifted a silent plea to the Giver to let them find some.

"If we can find this plant, and if it does what I claim, will that be proof enough for you? Will you follow me and rise up like men instead of cowering like slaves?"

Though he'd delivered it in a whisper, Rath still thought it a stirring speech. From the time he'd reached manhood, he had rued his dubious gift for attracting followers. Now he hoped he had not lost the knack just when he needed it most.

But he had, it seemed. For none of the other men spoke, or would look him in the eye.

Well, he would rebel against the Han, even if he had to act alone, with no hope of success. After all…

"What have we got to lose?" muttered the older man with a shrug. "If it all comes to naught, at least we are out of our torment that much sooner."

That should have been a discouraging thought. But Rath found it strangely liberating. The other prisoners appeared to share that feeling. A faint murmur circulated among them. Not zealous or exultant in tone, but grimly defiant and resolved.

He held out his hand, palm up to the older man. Unless

he was sorely mistaken, this fellow had the makings of a fine second in command. "Rath Talward of Nonce. Some call me Wolf."

"Hail, Wolf." The man placed his hand on top of Rath's. "They call me Anulf. If we can find this weed of yours and it does all you claim, then count me with you."

Before Rath's grin could spread too broad, Anulf warned him, "Mind, though—*if* can sometimes be a big word."

"You mean to go where and do what?" The tallest of the men gathered around Maura in the cellar of The Hawk and Hound shook his head as if to correct his faulty hearing. "Lady, you must know that is madness! No Umbrian goes up into the Blood Moon Mountains of his own accord."

Maura had hoped the support of the *twarith* would shore up her resolve and perhaps show her the Giver's will. Strangely, their opposition had tempered her determination and made her believe that small, stubborn whisper in her heart might speak for the Giver.

"This Umbrian will go of *her* own accord," she declared. "With or without your aid, though I would welcome it."

A pretty young woman with large, soulful eyes spoke up. "I admire your courage, mistress, but what you ask has never been the way of the *twarith*. We offer help—food, shelter, healing, hiding to those in need. Thus we live our belief in the Giver's precepts and strive to pass them on to others along with the material gifts we provide in the Giver's name."

Maura made the gesture of respect. "I honor your faithfulness to the Giver in these dark times. Others might have been tempted to doubt in the existence of a generous creating spirit.

Or been moved to hoard what little they received for the benefit of themselves and their own."

Though the woman acknowledged Maura's praise, her fine mouth was set in unmistakable opposition. "Already the Han persecute us for what we do, though not as hard as they might. We have heard of Hanish women in Venard secretly appealing to the *twarith* for healing of their children. Our quiet, steadfast example may win them over one day."

"True, Delith. Very true." Several folk standing near the young woman murmured their support.

Delith lifted her hand to signify that she was not finished speaking. "The Han tolerate us because we engage in no open rebellion against them. If we take part in what you propose, they will make it their business to crush us. Then what will happen to the innocent victims of their tyranny?"

Not long ago, Maura would have been swayed by Delith's eloquent sincerity. After all she had experienced and with Rath's life at stake, she must not lose faith in her destiny, now.

"If the Han are driven from our borders, there will be no more tyranny. The *twarith* will be at liberty to continue your work. Though, with the Giver's blessing, there may be less need…or perhaps different ones."

"Who said anything about driving out the Han?" the tall man asked.

"I say it," replied Maura. "The Waiting King will wait no longer. The day of his return is at hand, and when he rises, Umbria must rise with him. To do otherwise would be to spurn a most generous gift."

"The Waiting King?" cried the tall man. "And who are you? His herald?"

"In a way, perhaps." Maura quailed before the disbelief she saw in all their eyes. Was this some sort of punishment for her own early doubts?

"You must follow the voice of the Giver as you hear it." She turned away from them with a sigh. "And so must I."

"Wait, mistress." For the first time since the other *twarith* had gathered to hear her plea, the Wizard Clavance spoke. "I am old, and perhaps of more bother than help to you in such an enterprise. But I knew the Blood Moon Mountains before the Han ever began their cursed delving. If a guide will be of use to you, I will come."

For a moment, Maura did not trust herself to speak, or to turn and face him. One of the heaviest burdens of this destiny was the knowledge of how grave a price good folks had paid to aid her, and how many more might before she was done.

Rath Talward had never thought the day would come when he'd be grateful for slag.

But as he lay on the hard floor of the Beastmount Mine's third level, his voice all but drowned out by the heavy snoring of true slag-slaves, he savored the way the black dust blunted his fear and tempered any rash impulses that might have doomed him and his comrades.

It had been a welcome surprise to discover how heavily the Han relied on slag to maintain control over their prisoners. The number of miners each guard had to watch was absurd, and those working below the first level were not well armed.

Rath had passed five of the longest days of his life in the Beastmount Mine. Five days of grinding toil, vile food, stale air, suffocating darkness and fights between irritable prisoners hungry for their next sniff.

They had also been busy days of gathering information, laying plans and a growing bond with his fellow rebels. Privately Rath wondered how much of their resistance to the slag came from chewing on freewort leaves and flowers. And how much from having a little hope and purpose.

The time had now come when any more knowledge they could gather about the operation of the mine would not be worth the delay it cost them. The longer they stayed, the deeper into the mine they would be transferred and the more likely something might go wrong to trap them here forever. Besides all that, their precious supply of freewort was dwindling fast.

As the footsteps of the guard faded into the distance, Rath flexed his aching muscles. "It looks like our time is at hand, lads. Does everyone remember his part?"

One by one, the men around him stirred from their feigned sleep and muttered their instructions. By the time they all finished, his whole body was itching for action. So were theirs, it seemed, for they sprang to their feet, some quivering in their eagerness, others taut as drawn bowstrings ready to fire.

"Hold a moment." Rath motioned them toward him in the close dimness. A bewildering impulse had seized him and he could not deny it.

"Come." He thrust out his hand. "Everybody in. Before we start, let us ask the Giver's favor on what we are about to do."

He expected at least one of them to scoff...maybe more. Instead, they rallied to him readily, with an air of reverence that defied this unholiest of places.

He managed to string together a few words of Old Umbrian, though he probably mangled them beyond the understanding of anyone *but* the Giver. Still, he fancied he could hear Maura whispering those words in his ear. They lit a blaze of confidence deep inside him. Rath sensed it in the others as well. It was as if the act of praying alone went some way toward answering their prayer.

Off in the distance, the guard's footsteps began to draw closer again.

"To your places, everyone!" Rath whispered. "And wait for the right moment."

He settled down on the floor near Anulf and commenced a pretended snore, all the while listening for the guard.

At just the right moment, Anulf began to twitch and gasp and make the queerest noises Rath had ever heard. If he had not known better, Rath would have been convinced the man was truly in the grip of a palsy fit.

Anulf did not have to keep up his performance long. The guard's footsteps quickened.

"What is all this?" he demanded.

The rest of the men continued their feigned slumber. Anulf continued his feigned fit.

"You!" The Han bent down to give Anulf a shake.

At that instant, Rath and four others leapt to their feet and grabbed him. Odger, a former blacksmith with massive hands, clapped one over the guard's mouth. Theto, a nimble-fingered young pickpocket from Ulwin, deftly removed the pouch of slag from the guard's belt, opened it and held it to the Han's nose.

In a very short time, his struggling ceased and they were able to gag him and strip off his armor.

"Goar!" a voice called in Hanish. "Any trouble down there?"

Now came the moment Rath had been preparing for. He had been listening to the night guard, Goar, particularly when the fellow spoke in his native tongue to the other guards.

He called back in Hanish, using his best imitation of Goar's voice, "Just one of these cursed lowlings having a fit."

"Kick him hard in the head," the other guard advised. "That will quiet him quick enough."

Rath dredged up a rumble of malicious laughter, knowing how soon the other guard would join his comrade.

As the one closest in size to Goar, Rath donned the Han's armor as quickly as the others stripped it off. Once he was ready, he called for help. Soon both guards lay bound, gagged and slagged, while two of the rebels were armed.

Before long, they were in full control of level three. Now came the next big challenge. Each level of the mine was connected to the ones above and below by long rope ladders that were only lowered when someone needed to descend a level, then were immediately raised again. If necessary, the Han could cut access to the upper levels, starving out any rebellion brewing below.

Was that what had happened recently to create the current shortage of miners? Rath wondered as he and his men approached the passage between levels two and three. Well, the Han had not reckoned on a group of prisoners resistant to the slag, with a leader who could speak passable Hanish.

One of his team had spied out the procedure for getting the ladder lowered.

Now Rath called up, "Some trouble on level six. They're sending a messenger up to report to the Leader."

"Always level six, isn't it?" grumbled the man above as he lowered the ladder. "What do they expect, the guards get almost as big a dose of slag as the prisoners. Hope I never get booted down that deep."

By the time the ladder guard had finished his litany of complaints, Rath had subdued him, and the team of Umbrian imposters in Hanish armor had clambered up to the next level.

With their disguises, they secured level two even more quickly than they had level three.

"Now..." Rath struggled to curb a sense of elation that no amount of slag could subduc. "It is time for us to split up. Anulf, you take your men and go after the lower levels. Rouse as many of the prisoners as you can and send them up. I want them boiling up to the surface just about the time their night dose wears off."

"I will see you up above, Wolf." Anulf clasped his hand. "And if I do not make it, I will go to the Giver happy to have been part of this."

"Do not talk so daft, man!" Rath growled. "Of course I will see you up above. I am counting on you."

An unfamiliar sensation twisted deep in his gut as he watched Anulf's men depart and turned back to the ones he would lead. Never again would he be able to lose followers without it cutting him to the bone.

He forced his mind back to their mission. "Keep your wits about you, everyone, and nobody get cocky. The Han did not overrun our kingdom because they are cowardly or stupid."

Perhaps not. But they had become as dependent on the slag, in their own way, as the miners had. Tonight they would pay the price for it.

Rath knew the conquest of level one would come at greater risk than those on two and three. Since the upper level housed newer prisoners, not yet fully subdued by the slag, the guards were more numerous and vigilant.

All went according to plan, until one guard they approached noticed the lack of plumes on their helmets. He called out an alarm before the blacksmith snapped his neck. Other guards came running and Rath's men were forced to fight with unfamiliar weapons in a dim confined space.

When the pickpocket, Theto, took a bad wound to his arm, Rath feared the tide of their small battle might turn against them. But he had not reckoned on the level one prisoners.

Roused from sleep by the noise, not yet fuddled by slag, a few of them recognized what was happening. Unarmed, they threw themselves upon the Hanish guards.

"Wolf!" One of Anulf's men staggered up to Rath panting. "Have you secured the last ladder yet? The prisoners from the lower levels are pouring up. There will be no holding them if they get this far."

Rath cursed. "Pull up the ladder between here and level two until I send word." He turned to his own men. "Hunwald, find something to bind Theto's arm. Strang, stop any prisoners from the lower levels who reach here until you hear me call. Then relay my signal and let them come."

He motioned to the blacksmith and two others who had given good account of themselves with their weapons. "Odger, Tobryn, Wake, you are with me."

They rushed to the ladder passage where Rath called up the lie that had gotten them two levels so far.

"Level six?" called down the young Han in charge of the

surface ladder. "What kind of trouble? I was told to let no one up until the change of guard at daybreak."

"Daybreak?" Rath bellowed. If they did not get up that ladder soon, all could be lost. "I will break your head when I get up there, you unlicked whelp! And put you on report to the Leader for letting the situation down here get out of hand!"

"Very well, then," replied the young Han in a sullen tone as the ladder unfurled. "But you will take responsibility if there is trouble. What did you say your name was again?"

"I did not say." Rath pushed the young guard through the hole to the first level.

Below he heard Tobryn calling to the others that the way to the surface was clear.

"Best take off these Hanish helmets, lads," he advised his men as they climbed to the surface. "So our own folk do not turn on us."

He knew once the prisoners came pouring up, it would only be a matter of time before an alarm was raised and they found themselves under fierce attack. "Remember, we hold the head of this ladder until the last Umbrian climbs out of that cursed pit. After that, where each of you go and what you do is up to you. But you will go with my thanks and blessing."

He pulled the Hanish helmet off his head and threw it as far as it would fly. Seldom had he felt a more welcome sensation than the cool breeze of a mountain daybreak blowing through his hair. He did not have long to savor it.

The first wave of miners came scrambling out of the mountain, like ants from a colony under attack. Most of them were black as ants and some were armed with stingers in the shape of Hanish blades taken from the guards below.

Their escape did not go unnoticed for long. A small party of day guards ran toward the mine head with blades drawn. Between Rath, his crew and the emerging prisoners, the Han did not last long. But two managed to escape the rout and dash back to the barracks.

An alarm bell rang from the barracks tower, loud and wild. Soon after, Hanish soldiers poured from the barracks faster than miners were climbing from the pit head.

As the first wave broke upon them, Rath threw himself into the fray with all his strength, speed and cunning. It felt as if his whole life, he had been a weapon in the hands of some greater power, being perfectly crafted and honed for this fight.

"Wolf!"

Rath was able to turn in the direction of the voice, for one of the prisoners had dealt a mortal blow from behind to the Han who had attacked him.

"Anulf!" he cried. "You made it! Well done!"

"You have not done so badly, yourself." Anulf hefted his stolen blade and glanced around the pit head, as if looking for a Han to use it on, but finding none readily available. "I would say Beastmount Mine will be ours before the sun is fully risen."

Then, above the cries of battle, a shrill, eerie wail rose.

"Slag!" Anulf spat on the ground. "It is one of those cursed death-mages."

Rath knew what he must do, though his courage faltered at the thought. "He has a fearful weapon in that wand, but he is only one man for all that. While I draw his spell, you must take some of our lads and go for his back."

"Are you sure, Wolf? I have taken a lick from one of those cursed things, and I would not willingly put myself in the path of one again."

"I am not *willing,* but it must be done and I cannot ask another man to do it." The screaming stopped as abruptly as it had begun. Perhaps the Echtroi was looking for a worthier victim. "Once he goes for me, strike hard and fast. I may not be able to stand it long."

With that, both men set off—Anulf readily, Rath forcing himself each step. Was he mad—to put himself in front of a wand-wielding death-mage, knowing what awaited him? He had better not think about it too much, or he might turn and run.

The Echtroi was all that stood in their way now, Rath told

himself. Once Anulf and his men brought the death-mage down, any other resistance was sure to collapse.

So he strode through the fray, determined to appear braver and more confident than he felt. The fighting seemed to part before him until he caught the Echtroi's attention.

"Death-mage!" he bellowed, followed by a Hanish insult.

This was getting to be a habit with him—making himself a target for the Han. Only, this time he would not run away and lead them on a chase, with at least a hope of escape.

The Echtroi raised his wand.

Rath tried to brace himself for what would come. But that was impossible.

Still, he locked his lips together, a mute challenge to the Echtroi to make him cry out. Then the pain hit him.

It was a different kind of pain than he had suffered before— a lethal brew of fear and all a man's worst nightmares. He saw Maura violated and murdered before his eyes, one hand reached out to him, her gaze imploring. But he could not go to her aid.

One tiny, detached part of his mind tried to reassure him it was only a wicked illusion, but his heart could not believe that. With each beat, it ached to bursting.

He was vaguely aware of Anulf and the others fighting the Han who guarded the death-mage's back. This would soon be over—it must, before it shattered his mind and heart, making him crave the slag as his only remedy.

Then a cry went up from the Han and the death-mage eased his grip on Rath for an instant. But it brought Rath no ease.

He saw a second Echtroi surging up the mountain to join

the first. At his back marched a troop of Hanish reinforcements to crush the revolt.

The sight robbed Rath of all hope. For he could not deny *it* was real.

The frantic ringing of a bell and the distant tumult of battle roused Maura from a restless doze.

Was she too late?

After laying their plans, gathering supplies and recruiting helpers, she and some of the *twarith* had started up the mountain the previous day. Maura could hardly wait to tear off the black robe she had been wearing since then.

Though it had never belonged to a real death-mage, there was still something oppressive about the hastily sewn disguise. As though it might transform her from the outside in. Or perhaps that was the insidious effect of the copper wand. Either way, she longed to rid herself of both, once and for all.

As soon as she had liberated Rath from the mine.

Her small troop was ready. On the way up the mountain, they had ambushed enough Hanish checkpoint guards to provide everyone with armor, however ill-fitting. More than once she had jolted out of a moment's abstraction to feel a fleeting twist of terror at the sight of herself surrounded by Han.

Some of the *twarith* were willing to fight the Han with their own weapons. Others, Maura had taught the binding spell. Their meeting cellar beneath The Hawk and Hound had provided a well-stocked arsenal of spidersilk. Clavance and two others skilled in the healing arts had come prepared with herbs and linen to tend any wounded.

Within a short distance of the mine, they had stopped to eat and rest before the attack they had planned to make once all the day guards went down to relieve the night guards. Then there would be the fewest Han above ground for her party to subdue.

That information had come secondhand from an escaped miner the *twarith* had given aid to a few months before. It made a kind of sense, and it was all they had. Maura hoped it was still correct.

The noise from up the mountain did not sound promising. But the Giver had brought them this far. They could not turn back now.

In case any of her followers was even considering it, Maura urged them on. "Come! The miners may have risen up. They will need our help. Fly to their aid!"

She could not have spoken any words better calculated to rouse and inspire the *twarith*. For years they had labored in secret opposition to the Han. Now was their opportunity for a bold act of defiance in aid of their most oppressed countrymen.

Maura barely had time to pull the despised black hood over her head and grab the copper wand before the rush of *twarith* carried her the final short distance up the mountain.

All was chaos around the mine head.

Miners fought Hanish guards with no weapons but their fists and feet. The sight brought Maura a surge of hope.

But what was this? Some Han fighting their own comrades with blades? The situation puzzled her for a moment, until she realized many of the men in Hanish armor wore no helms. Nor did they have the long flowing plumes of flaxen hair.

She turned to her comrades, half laughing in a frenzy of

relief. "Take off your helmets and keep a sharp eye who you attack! Some of those men in Hanish armor are Umbrians!"

A cry went up from the *twarith,* as they came to understand what was happening. Casting their helmets aside, they threw themselves into the fray.

"You had best take off your disguise, too, Mistress," Clavance called to Maura. "Else someone may strike you down for a death-mage!"

"With pleasure!" She all but ripped the hood from her head and tore the robe in her haste to remove it.

She was about to hurl the copper wand away, too, when her gaze flew to the other black robed figure among the combatants, and his wand of *eisendark.*

Clearly he had it pointed at someone. But where were the screams?

Then she saw him. A tall figure in Hanish armor, a few day's growth of beard stubbling his lean cheeks. Tawny hair streaked with dark mine dust, desperately needed another good washing. No sound escaped him, but the taut twist of his limbs and features betrayed mute torment.

Maura ran toward him. Blades clashed above her head. A hand snaked out to grab her ankle, but she kicked free of it.

The last time she had thrust this wand between a death-mage and his prey, she had not known what she was doing nor had she guessed what might happen. This time, she knew.

She would have given almost anything to avoid doing it, but there was one thing...or rather one person, she could not abandon to the cruelest of mortcraft. No matter what it cost her.

She stepped between Rath and his tormentor.

For a delirious instant, a rush of power and mastery swept

through her. Some seductive intuition whispered that she could be mistress of this potent dark force if only she had the courage and the will to dare it. It reminded her of all the evil the Han had committed against her people, urging her to take vengeance.

With such power at her disposal, what would she need with the Waiting King? She could be a warrior queen in her own right, second to no man, free to take a consort of her own choosing.

How that notion tempted her!

She glanced back at Rath to discover he had fallen, spent from his ordeal. His gaze sought hers, surely to urge that she claim the power offered her.

Instead he stared at her with aversion, as though she had suddenly grown repulsive to behold. Her grip on the power wavered, as did its grip upon her. Then it reasserted itself.

Never mind about the man, it urged her. *If she wanted him, she would have the power to make him love her.*

"No!" She wrenched her gaze away from Rath to face the death-mage once more.

Is it you who put such thoughts in my head to beguile me?

Better than that. I slither through your mind, collecting your deepest desires, then I offer them to you. You can have that same skill and more if you will only take it. Be warned, though. Either you master this power and make it your own or it will master you.

Suffocating darkness loomed over her, a warning of what she risked by defying him.

Then, as her desires lured her and her fears pushed her, she heard her own voice asking Langbard, "Why me? I am nobody special. I have no wish to be queen."

She'd had no such wish then, nor did she now. Perhaps that was what made her special and fitted her for this destiny.

Only if I try to master this dark force will it truly master me…as it has mastered you.

Though she held on to the wand with all her strength, it felt as though she had let go the leash of a huge, ravenous beast.

Which now turned to consume her.

Maura had rescued him from the death-mage's torment only to thrust him into worse. Where the Echtroi had taunted him with visions of Maura despoiled in body, Rath now saw the danger that she would be violated in spirit.

Never had she looked more beautiful or more regal, poised upon the field of battle, in a duel of wills with the death-mage. But she looked nothing like the woman he had come to love. There was something vain and cruel in her eyes that mocked him and his presumptuous feelings for her. If that was to be the price for saving him, he would rather perish.

Sensing her struggle to resist, he tried to call out to her, but he could not make his voice heard above the tumult of the fighting. He tried to rise and go to her, but his limbs were still half-numb.

This was one battle she would have to fight *for* herself and *by* herself. The only thing he could do was believe in her as he had never been able to believe in anyone or anything else. He must trust that her strength and goodness would prevail.

As he watched, Maura's body tensed and she twitched a little from side to side, as if pulled in two different directions by powerful forces. Then the wand in her hand burst apart with a violent crash, like a tall tree struck by lightning. Maura swayed and crumpled to the ground.

At the same instant, the death-mage's wand shattered, too. Rath scarcely noticed.

From somewhere, he dredged up the strength to drag himself toward Maura. Picking up the blade that had fallen from his hand when the death-mage attacked, he prepared to defend her with what was left of his life.

When someone rushed toward him, he swung the blade with more strength than he'd thought he possessed. Fortunately Anulf had quick reflexes.

"Steady on, Wolf." He dodged Rath's blow. "It's only me."

"Sorry." Rath let his arm fall.

Anulf knelt beside them. "We got him—the Echtroi." He made an oddly gentle gesture toward Maura. "Thanks to the lady."

He gazed at Maura's face. "That's her, isn't it? The Destined Queen."

Rath nodded. "She should not have come here."

"Aye, that's true enough. Nor should you have, the shape you're in." Anulf spared a swift glance at the battle raging around them. "I reckon we'll win the day now that the Echtroi is down. But there's bound to be some fierce fighting for a bit. We need to get the two of you away from here."

"We need to get farther than you think." Rath pulled a morsel of dried quickfoil from Maura's sash and cradled it on his tongue until his strength started to return.

He staggered to his feet. "Help me bear her."

Together, they carried Maura behind a clutch of small sheds. As they laid her down, a bearded old man in Hanish armor came puffing after them. "Who are you and what are you doing with the lady?"

Rath cast a withering glance at the Hanish blade in the old fellow's hand. "Put that down, before you do yourself harm. I am the reason the lady came to this benighted place. We only moved her away from the fighting so I might tend her."

"Have you skill in healing?" The old man handed his blade to Anulf with a grimace that showed he was glad to be rid of it.

"Only what I learned from her," Rath admitted. "If you can serve her better, then do, I beg you."

"I will do what I can." The old man knelt beside Maura and bent his ear to her lips. "Could one of you fetch me water?"

Rath caught Anulf's eye and nodded. Anulf hurried away toward the barracks.

"Hot if you can get it!" The old man called after him.

Then he glanced up at Rath, hovering over him. "Clavance of Vaust at your service...and hers."

"Rath Talward." Rath picked up one of Maura's hands and chafed the limp flesh. "This happened to her once before, though not so bad. I was able to bring her around with a quickfoil tonic."

Clavance nodded.

"She has a lot of herbs and things in her sash." Rath pointed toward the pocket that now contained only a tiny amount of quickfoil. The grave, worried set of the old man's features made him add, "You will be able to help her, won't you?"

"So I hope." Clavance blew out a sigh. "Her strength is ebbing fast."

Rath seized the old man's arm. "She cannot die! She has something important she must do." Far more important than coming here to fetch him.

"I know." Clavance began drawing pinches of herbs from Maura's sash. "Long ago, I was a pupil of her guardian, Langbard. Did you know him?"

Rath nodded. "Only a short while."

"Solsticetide will soon be upon us. Do you have far to go?"

"Everwood, up in the Hitherland."

"I know the place." Clavance's wrinkled features settled into even deeper furrows of worry. "If I could heal her completely at this very moment I fear you would still be hard-pressed to reach there in time."

"Reach where?" asked Anulf, who had returned with a steaming kettle and a mug.

Rath hesitated for a moment. But what was the good of secrecy now, among friends of proven loyalty? "Everwood. We must get there by Solsticetide."

They must get there by Solsticetide. The intense urgency that pulsed within him convinced Rath that he believed the whole preposterous story, whether he wanted to or not.

Clavance sprinkled the herbs in the mug, then poured hot water over them. "Even if you had fast horses, none of the roads in this part of the mountains lead north."

Anulf nodded toward the sound of the fighting. "After this, the Han will even be turning their court boys out of Venard to watch the roads."

Rath lifted Maura's shoulders so Clavance could dribble the hot tonic into her mouth.

"Perhaps…" Anulf mused. "No. It would be folly!"

"What?" demanded Rath. "Tell me."

Even if Anulf's suggestion was daft, it might distract him from his fear for Maura.

"None of the roads go north," said Anulf, "but the river does."

"The river?"

"Aye. It is how the Han get their cursed ore down to the plain—in barges. If you rode one of those down, and could get ashore before it reached the off-loading ports near the mouth of the river…"

"If you can make it that far," said Clavance, "I can give you names of some *twarith* in downriver towns who would help you on your way from there."

"How can we?" Rath passed his hand over Maura's hair. "With her still like this?"

For all the tonic Clavance had given her, she showed no sign of reviving.

"There is nothing more I can do for her here," he said, "than you could do on your ride down the river. Perhaps getting away from here and closer to the Secret Glade might help her. Her wounds are not of the body, but of the spirit."

Rath knew that well enough. And he knew what Clavance said might well be true. Yet something held him back.

When he had been captured and brought to the mines, he'd made a kind of peace with losing Maura. Now that he truly believed she would find the Waiting King in Everwood, could he bear to lose her again of his own free will?

Suddenly, a tumult of barking and baying rang out above the noises of battle.

"Slag!" Anulf spat. "They have loosed the hounds!"

Rath lurched to his feet. "Show me the way to the barges."

She had lost. She had failed.

The sense of that loss haunted Maura in the dark, desolate

void into which she had fallen. The weight of her failure threatened to crush her spirit.

Was she dead? If she was, then neither Rath nor any of the *twarith* had survived to launch her into the afterworld with the ritual of passing. She would be forever lost.

Some intuition told her if she surrendered to the darkness she would find a kind peace in oblivion. It was bound to come sooner or later. To struggle would only prolong her suffering.

No one could help her now.

Perhaps that was the very reason she *needed* to fight.

From the beginning she had felt unequal to her fate. Always in need of help—from Langbard, from the *twarith* and always from Rath. But she had helped him and others, too.

She had stood alone against the grim power and temptation of the Echtroi, and she had prevailed. She would not give up now. She would keep fighting—until she found her way back to herself once again, or until her strength failed at last.

She marshaled her weapons for the battle. The wisdom Langbard had bequeathed to her. The sacrifice of Exilda. Memories of all the people who were relying on her. Tender thoughts of Rath and all he meant to her. If she gave up now, he might lose his budding faith.

She thought of the Waiting King, too. Not as some mythical, heroic figure of legend, but as a real person, like herself. Perhaps he had been caught in a dark void like this for a thousand years. Perhaps if she could find her own way out, she would be able to help him find his way, when the time came.

As Maura armed her spirit with all of these, the weight that pressed down on her began to lighten. And the darkness around her began to shimmer. From an enormous distance, she heard the rush of flowing water and the beguiling whisper of a voice.

Though she could not make out the words, she followed it.

The roar of the river assaulted Rath's ears from every direction—ahead, behind, from both sides and beneath. Even above, when the bow of the ore barge plunged into a wave, sending a great spray of cold water splashing over him and Maura. He tried to shield her from it as best he could, though part of him hoped a good dousing might jolt her awake.

He gasped and sputtered and shivered in his sodden garments, half wishing he'd kept the Hanish armor on. But Maura did not flinch, nor did her eyelids so much as flicker.

Empty of its usual heavy cargo, the barge rode high in the river's swift feral current.

"You should open your eyes a moment, Maura," he urged her. "The trees on the shore are rushing by so fast, they fair set me dizzy."

When not sputtering from a wave of spray, Rath had been talking to her like that ever since Anulf had slain the barge guard and set them adrift. He doubted she could hear him, but on the slender chance that she could, he kept talking. Besides, it distracted him a little from his heaving stomach and his stark terror.

"There is another stream flowing into this one, Maura. I suppose there must be another mine up near its headwaters. When you find the Waiting King, I hope that will be one of his first tasks—to liberate all the miners. Then I expect you will find a way to wean those poor creatures from the slag. A proper team the two of you will make. Him to battle the Han and you to heal all the harm they have done to folks."

The barge lurched again, sending another wave of spray over them. With the cuff of his sleeve, Rath wiped the drops of water that clung to Maura's face like tears.

He shook his head and forced a laugh that sounded more like a sob. "There. You will be happy now. My hair is getting washed again. I am glad to have that cursed mine dust out of it. A pity I did not have some of those sweet-smelling herbs you forced upon me when you barbered me back in Windleford. Remember?"

Perhaps she did not. No matter. He recollected it well enough for both of them. And afterward, that bantering walk into the village when he had threatened to kiss her.

He kissed her now, upon the forehead, with all the tenderness he had come to feel for her since then. "Come back, Maura. Please. Umbria needs you. *I* need you…even if you can never be mine."

The barge hurtled on down the mountain, the way events had driven him and Maura these past weeks, at breathtaking speed over abrupt, stunning drops and through treacherous rapids. But Maura lay cradled in his arms—cold, silent and still. If she *could* come back to him, he believed with all his heart that she would.

He had only one hope of getting her back, though he shrank from asking.

"Giver…"

Rath phrased his appeal in Umbrian, for he feared he could not find the right words in his limited *twara.* Surely a spirit wise and powerful enough to create the whole universe would understand his ordinary speech just as well.

"…likely I have no right to ask such a boon, since I have only come to you so late. I have done plenty of deeds in my life that go against those Precepts of yours. I wish I could change them, but I cannot."

All at once, in the roar of the water, he sensed the power of the Giver. In the cool caress of the breeze, he felt its mercy. He had the attention of the force that quickened all living things. It made him feel small, trifling, yet in some strange way, he felt important, too. As if he and what he wanted *mattered*.

"Anyway…it is not for myself I am asking…at least…only in part. I mean…Maura *is* the Destined Queen, and a fine choice if you ask me. How can she fulfill this quest of yours if she cannot walk or speak? You have gotten us out of some tight spots in the past. Surely you would not let us falter, now, when we are so close?"

The river continued to roar and the breeze to blow, but Rath could not hear the Giver's answer in either. Perhaps he had not made himself plain enough?

"I know I have not believed in you before, but I do now. I am grateful for what you have given me. I swear, from now on, I will try to give as I have been given. And I will trust in your Providence. Only, please, please rescue her spirit from wherever it is trapped."

After one final jarring lurch, the barge settled into deeper, slower-moving water.

Rath held his breath, waiting for Maura to open her eyes or even for her heartbeat to rally. But nothing changed. She lay there in his embrace, her beauty taunting him with its empty perfection.

26

The depth of his disappointment surprised Rath. He had been so ready to trust in a power greater than himself. Then the strangest thought blossomed within him and he had the baffling sensation of entertaining an idea that had come from outside his own mind.

Look for my power within yourself, Elzaban.

Rath made a wry face at the thought of his preposterous birth name. How much ridicule and how many beatings had he taken as a boy before he'd had the sense to call himself something less high-flown?

He did not have much time to ponder those bitter memories. Ahead on the river, one of the small Hanish vessels that towed ore barges hove in view.

Slag! He had not realized the barge-tows plied their work this far from the mouth of the river.

Rath had no time to plan, barely any to think. If he did not act quickly, the current would carry the barge to the waiting ship where he and Maura would be captured.

He had no intention of letting himself fall into Hanish hands again. Nor Maura, either, even if she was beyond their power to harm.

The temporary strength he had gained from that tiny scrap of quickfoil was rapidly wearing off. With as great an effort of will as he had ever mustered, he lifted Maura up to the rim of the barge. Then, twining his arm through her sash to lash them together, he dove into the river with her in his arms.

The water closed over them in a cold, primal embrace that entreated Rath to yield. If he had been alone, he might have. But for Maura's sake, he struggled up, until his head breached the surface of the water. He had only strength to lift her head free, too, and to let the current bear them where it would.

Suddenly, ahead of them loomed the remains of a tall tree that had fallen into the river. Some of its roots still anchored the trunk to the shore.

Catching hold of an outthrust branch, Rath slowly inched toward shore, towing Maura into the shallows. There he collapsed into the warm mud until he revived enough to haul Maura ashore into the cover of a small thicket near the river's edge.

He pressed his fingers to her throat, searching for a pulse, however faint. He lowered his ear to her lips, scarcely daring to breathe, himself, as he listened for hers.

Maura showed no signs to life.

Magic had not worked. Prayer had not worked. There was only one thing left to do.

Wringing a few drops of water from his sodden garments, he moistened her brow with them.

"*Guldir quiri shin...hon bith shin...*" He spoke in a hoarse, hesitant murmur. "*Vethilu bithin anthi gridig aquis...a bwitha muir ifnisive.*"

Wash the cares of this world from your thoughts and let them be made pure for a better life in the next.

It tore at his heart to do this, but he had made Maura a promise. And she had promised he would hear her voice and share her memories.

He needed that.

Their last parting had been too abrupt, and their reunion had been no more than an exchange of gazes in the midst of a battle. If she was on her way to the afterworld, there would be no harm in revealing how much he cared for her.

He trickled a few drops of water on her lips, then on the palms of her hands, reciting the ritual words in a broken voice. Then he bent his head over her and opened his spirit.

Maura, where are you? You told me I would hear you.

No reply came. Not even within his thoughts.

Had he been right, after all? Was there no Giver? No afterworld? Nothing but this one, too-brief life in which folk had to look out for themselves first and last?

Once, he had been afraid to believe otherwise. Now...?

A stubborn little seed of faith had taken root within him, and it refused to die no matter how many disappointments might wither it.

Rath?

It was no more than a distant whisper. But it filled him with a sense of wonder, hope and grace.

Their bodies did not move—hers there on the ground, his hovering over her. But in a baffling way Rath could not describe, their spirits sought each other and came together in a haunting embrace of selves. Closer and closer, until suddenly... they were one.

He saw her past, through her eyes, and he felt her do the same through his. He saw himself through her eyes and tasted her love for him—with all his senses as well as some sweet, mysterious knowing that went beyond the limited scope of sense.

It did not feel like she was dying, but rather like he was being reborn.

Take me with you! his spirit pleaded. *I cannot bear for this to end.*

Nor I.

All at once, they knew they had a choice. He could go with her, to be one in the afterworld together. Or she could return with him to a life where destiny would part them.

There was no need for words. No way to hide their true feelings from one another. Together they felt the pull of two much-desired futures that would be forever contrary.

When at last the decision blossomed, it bore no blight of discord. And their shared wistfulness for what might have been only shaded its color to a softer, more delicate hue.

Rath opened his eyes. Maura opened hers.

The ache and loneliness of separation from her trembled on his lips in a mute cry. But when their gazes met, he knew that in some baffling way a part of each of them would always remain with the other.

* * *

"There it is," said Rath, the barest trace of a sigh shadowing his words. "Everwood."

He and Maura stood on a low bluff looking down toward the mysterious northern forest. Each of them held the reins of a horse that cropped the new summer's sweet green grass as if this were any ordinary day and this ride any ordinary ride.

After rising from the dark innards of the Beast, the colors of the world looked sharper and brighter to Maura. The varied greens of the grass and trees, the vibrant yellows and purples of wildflowers, the deep abiding blue of the Hitherland sky.

Now she stared at the sky where a silvery-white phantom of the rising full moon shimmered in waning daylight. "I suppose we had better get moving so we will have light to see the symbols on that tiny map of Exilda's."

Reluctance tugged at the hem of her gown.

She and Rath had risked their freedom and their lives for this quest. Now they risked their hearts and their future happiness, as well. Part of her wanted to fly toward her destiny on swift hooves, so it would be over and done with no risk of her recanting at the last moment. Another part wanted to delay it for as long as possible—eking out every second between now and then in Rath's company, with the love they had acknowledged for one another wrapping around them.

"I have studied that map enough, I could find my way blindfolded." Rath reached for her hand. "Still, in case there are any Han coming after us, perhaps we had better be on our way."

Maura knew how doubtful *that* was.

When they had sought aid from some *twarith* in northern Westborne, word had already begun to spread of the successful revolt in the Beastmount mine. Once or twice, during their ride into the Hitherland, they had glimpsed other riders in the distance, all rushing south at great speed, with no heed to spare for a pair of wary travelers.

Maura made no move to remount, no move to release Rath's hand. There was something she needed to know and this might be her last quiet moment to ask.

"What will you do…after…? Where will you go?"

He lifted her hand and laid it to rest over his heart. "I will go…where you bid me. I will do *anything* in your service. The King may be your husband, and I swear I will never do anything to sully that. I only beg leave to be your champion."

His words brought tears to her eyes, hard as she fought to hold them back. After what she and Rath had shared, he would not need to see those tears fall to know they were locked inside her and to understand their source as well as she did.

"Will that not be unbearable for you? For both of us? To be always near but never near enough?"

Rath shook his head. "We have been as near as a man and woman can be. I trust that somehow, someday we will be again. Until then, let me at least serve you and protect you. Let us work together with the King to free and heal this land of ours."

He made it sound easier than Maura knew it would be. Likely he knew it, too. Which of them would it be harder for?

Her? To wed another man, share his throne, bear his heirs? Wanting to be a faithful and dutiful wife, but forever torn?

Or Rath, to watch all that and ache?

He was right about one thing, though. They must not dwell on what might have been, but concentrate on what *could be.*

This quest that had brought them together was only the beginning. They owed it to themselves, to each other and to a great many other people to see it through to its end.

"You have proven yourself a worthy champion, Rath Talward." She lifted the hand he had placed over his heart to rest against his cheek. "Even a queen could ask for no better."

"Then you accept my pledge of service?"

"With all my heart."

As if pulled by some invisible force, half against their will, he bent toward her and she raised her face to meet him. They sealed their pledge with a chaste, wistful kiss that neither dared to hold longer or take deeper, for fear they would never be able to stop.

Then they mounted their horses and rode toward Everwood as the full moon of Solsticetide grew brighter and brighter in the darkening sky.

"What shall we do with the horses?" asked Maura, when they reached the edge of the forest.

Rath lifted her down, then handed her the reins of her mount. "Bring them this way. Unless Everwood has changed a good deal, there should be a small glade not far in where we can leave them until we return."

Their return—of course, Maura mused as she followed Rath through a narrow gap between the trees. Though she knew better, what they were about to do still felt like an end of something. It was hard to imagine what would happen after she had wakened the Waiting King.

No doubt Rath was right. They would need the horses, later.

"Not changed a whit," said Rath as they entered the glade. He sounded pleased and a little surprised. "Good grazing, a bit of a brook over there, out of sight of any chance passerby. A body would think it had been put here on purpose, just for us and this day."

"Perhaps it was," Maura whispered to herself as the flesh on the back of her neck bunched.

There was something silent and watchful about this forest, as if every tree stood guard. No wonder the folk in neighboring villages had been frightened of the place and warned their children to avoid it.

While Rath turned the horses loose to graze, Maura picked a few interesting leaves and flowerlets that caught her eye.

"Old habits die hard," she explained when he shot her a puzzled look. "This would be a fascinating spot for gathering. I wonder if anyone knows what some of these plants are called, or what they can do?"

Rath shrugged. "Some of the old folk in the villages around here might. Ganny's friends, if they are still around."

Maura looked around. "Which way do we head, then?"

"We follow the brook for a while." Rath pointed toward it as he pulled Exilda's ivory map from his pouch. "Until we come to a large rock. There we should find a path."

"Lead on." An anxious eagerness had begun to brew deep in Maura's belly. Now that she and Rath had made their choice and sealed their pledge, her feeling of reluctance was waning.

They had done it. Trekked through almost every province of Umbria to find the map, then followed it to the Secret Glade. When she thought of all the perils they had faced and challenges they had overcome along the way, the difficult, dangerous task of reclaiming their kingdom from the Han no longer seemed quite so daunting.

And what would he be like—the king who had slumbered so long, who would now be her husband and her lord? Though her heart belonged to Rath, she hoped and believed the Waiting King would be someone she could honor and admire.

Just as Rath had said, the brook eventually wound its way to a large moss-covered boulder, behind which they found a path that looked well trodden, though Maura doubted many folk had ever ventured this deep into Everwood.

The path led Rath and Maura deeper still, to a giant hitherpine.

"My word!" Maura stared in amazement. "That trunk is so thick a body could take a chunk and carve a cottage the size of Langbard's out of it. Which way, now?"

"A moment." Rath handed her the little map, then pulled a small torch from his belt and set it alight with his flint. "There. I wanted to get that done while I still have light enough to see what I'm doing."

He pointed to another tall tree in the distance. "According to the map, there are six of these. We should be able to see the next one clearly from the last."

And so it proved.

As they rested a moment at the base of the fifth tree and took their bearings, Maura stared up at the night sky, where thousands of glittering stars paid homage to their monarch, the full moon. "After all we came through to reach Everwood, this seems almost too easy."

"I have been thinking the same thing," murmured Rath. "I never did trust anything that came without a struggle."

The torchlight flickered over his face, giving it the impudent look Maura remembered so well from their early days together. "Perhaps the Giver decided we deserve a little ease at last."

"Perhaps so." Maura rose. "We had better not take too much ease, though, if we want to reach the Secret Glade while the moon is still high."

They picked their way through the forest to the last of the large trees.

"Next…" Rath peered at the map by the light of his torch. "We must find…a waterfall, I think."

"Hush," whispered Maura, "I hear one over that way."

They followed the sound until they came to a narrow cascade, tumbling from a high ridge, its waters sparkling in the moonlight. Rath found a set of stairs carved into the rocks on one side, which he and Maura climbed.

"The Secret Glade is very near here." Again Rath consulted the map, then held his torch aloft. "Do you see anything that might point us the way?"

Maura saw *something,* though when she tried to warn Rath, the words stuck in her throat. Finally, she got his attention by plucking his sleeve.

"What is…?" Rath turned to look. "Uh, slag!"

There, one good leap away stood the largest tawny wolf Maura had ever seen. If it had not been so deadly, she might have admired its wild majesty.

"Hold this." Rath thrust the torch into her hands. Dropping the ivory map into his belt pouch, he slowly drew the Hanish blade he had stolen in the mines.

The fierce weapon looked feeble against such a beast, especially if it was not alone. Maura knew tawny wolves always traveled in packs.

"Back away, slowly," said Rath. "Keep the torch in front of you. If he goes for me, run."

But the creature showed no sign of going for either of them. It did not growl nor bare its teeth. It stood watching them, then turned and walked a few steps, before stopping to glance back.

"Rath, I think it wants us to follow it."

"Inviting us back to its den for dinner, you mean."

"It does not look very hungry to me." Maura took a few tentative steps in the direction of the great beast.

Once again, the wolf began to walk ahead, then turned to see if they were following.

"Just so you know," said Rath as he hurried to catch up with Maura, "I do not like this. Unless it leads us to the Secret Glade soon, I…"

Maura never did find out what Rath meant to do, for as he spoke, they stepped through a gap between two slender whitebark trees and found themselves in a place of moonlit enchantment.

It was not large, but ringed with whitebarks at regular intervals, like so many elegant columns. Rich grass covered the ground, groomed to the ideal height for a luxurious carpet. Not a single fallen leaf marred its perfection.

Before Maura could notice more, the tawny wolf raised its muzzle to the night sky and let out a loud, resonant howl that sounded almost like a trumpet. Then it slipped away so quickly and so silently, it seemed to disappear before their eyes.

"So here we are at last," Rath whispered, sheathing his blade. "But where is the Waiting King?"

"Why, he must be…"

Maura held the torch aloft. She had been so absorbed by the mystical beauty of the place, she had not realized what was missing. *Who* was missing.

She had expected some finely carved resting place, with the Waiting King sleeping upon it, still wrapped in the thousand-year-old spell of his beloved.

But there was no sign of him.

As he stared around the deserted glade, Rath felt like someone had chopped his legs off at the knees. He could only begin to imagine how Maura must feel.

Putting his arm around her shoulders to steady her, he took the torch from her hand.

She shook her head, as if in a daze. "I do not understand. Were you right all along? Is the Waiting King nothing more than a story? After all we went through. All the trouble we stirred up. All the false hope we gave folk. How can it be?"

"Do not lose heart now." Rath could scarcely believe those words were coming out of his mouth. Could his fledgling faith continue to soar when reason and hard evidence would cut off its wings? "This is the Secret Glade. If ever there was a place full to the brim with magic, this is. The map led us here. You *are* the Destined Queen. I know it surer than I have ever known anything…except perhaps that…I love you."

This was what he had envisioned, back when they set out into the Waste. That Maura would face bitter disappointment at the end of her quest, and that he would be here to console her and make her his own.

Now, in spite of what it meant for him, he *wanted* the Waiting King to be here. He wanted Maura's destiny fulfilled.

"But, look." She made an empty, hopeless gesture. "There is no King here for me to wake."

"Perhaps he will not appear until the moon hits just the right spot in the sky," Rath suggested. "Or perhaps there is a magical trumpet or a gong you must sound to summon him."

Maura nodded slowly. "Perhaps."

"What is that, over there?" Rath lifted the torch and nudged Maura toward the center of the glade. "Perhaps it will give us a clue. And do not forget what you told me."

"I have told you a good many things." A ring of confidence returned to Maura's voice. "Some of them pure foolishness. Which one do you mean?"

"This was not foolishness." Rath assured her. "You told me tales may be fancies of things that never happened but they may still hold great truths. Perhaps the tale of the Waiting King is one such."

"I suppose it might be." Maura strode toward something sticking out of the ground, like a tall tree stump. "But how are we to puzzle out the riddle?"

Rath stared at what looked like a giant's goblet. It appeared to have been carved from a good-sized tree, the roots of which still held it in place. From the base, a slender stem rose, with a wide bowl perched on top of it.

"What can it be, do you suppose?"

Maura inspected it closely. "I cannot guess. None of Langbard's stories of the Waiting King ever mentioned anything like this."

She knelt before it, peering at the base. Then she beckoned Rath to lower the torch. "There is an inscription carved here."

She groaned.

"What?" asked Rath, anxious for her.

"It is in *twara,* which I can speak a good deal better than I can read."

She murmured to herself for a bit in a questioning tone.

"Well?" Rath prompted her when he could stand the waiting no longer.

"I believe it says, 'Gaze ye here by the summer moon's light, behold the King who has been woken, and meet your doom.'"

"Slag!"

"Aye." Maura gave a soft chuckle that held no merriment. "Slag."

She rose. "I suppose there must be some enchanted potion in the font. Langbard told me the Oracle of Margyle sometimes looks into the future that way.

"Put out the torch, if you please." She bent to gaze into the font. "The instructions say to look by the moon's light."

"No!" Rath pulled her back. "I do not like that 'meet your doom' business. Let me look first. Then, if no harm comes to me, you may look to your heart's content."

"Rath, this is my quest…my destiny. There may be something here to be seen that only I can see."

"So there may." As Rath looked around for a way to douse the torch, it went out on its own. "Or there may be danger. When the Waiting King is woken, he will need you. I offered myself as your champion and you accepted. Let me do my duty."

"Very well." Maura did not sound pleased with the idea.

She reached for his hand and clung to it with all her strength. "Look, then."

Rath bent over the bowl. For a moment he saw nothing but darkness. Then his eyes became accustomed to the absence of the torchlight. Or perhaps the solstice moon waxed brighter.

And he beheld something that puzzled and amazed him.

"Rath." Maura tugged on his hand. "Are you all right? Do you see anything?"

"I see…something," he murmured, "but I do not know what it means."

"Let me look."

Maura's face appeared in the font's shimmering water beside his. The light of the solstice moon sparkled on their brows like a pair of luminous crowns.

A faint gasp escaped Maura as she understood what the Giver was telling them. Then one tiny circular ripple disturbed the still water in the font, followed by another and another as her tears fell.

"Do you see what this means?" she whispered.

Rath shook his head.

"The water shows us the King, who has been woken." She turned and slipped her arms around his neck. "You, Rath Talward."

"Elzaban."

"What?"

"Elzaban," he repeated in a daze. "That was my name once. I took so much grief for it from the other boys in the village, that after Ganny died, I took a new one, less apt to get me picked on."

"You never told me."

"I never thought to." He sank to the grass, taking her with him. "It has been years since I thought of myself by that name. Until the Giver called me by it when I begged for your deliverance, in the barge."

"When I saw your reflection in the water crowned with stars, I knew what it must mean. It was as if Langbard and my mother, and all my forebearers back to Abrielle, herself, were telling me. I need no more proof from the Giver. But if I did, that would convince me beyond any doubt."

She hesitated for a moment, trying to take it all in. "There is one thing that puzzles me, though. I was told I must waken the Waiting King. I did not wake you."

"You did." He pulled her closer into his embrace, and she feared her heart would burst to contain the joy that swelled within it. "You woke me in a hundred ways. I was sleepwalking through life, caring for nothing beyond my own survival, believing in nothing beyond my next meal. Blind and deaf to everything it means to be Umbrian.

"You woke my heart." He planted a tender kiss upon her palm, then rested it against his chest. "You woke my spirit and my honor."

Hearing him speak of it, Maura knew it was true.

"I find it hard to believe I might be King." Rath stroked her hair. "But if I can be, it is because of you."

"What will we do now?" Gazing around the moonlit glade, Maura wished they had the luxury to make it their palace and shut out the troubles of the world. But to do that would be to betray their quest and their shared destiny.

"I do not know." Rath shook his head. "For the sake of our

people, I wish the Waiting King had been a great, magical hero, reborn. I cannot think where we will begin."

He lifted her thick braid and untied the ribbon that bound it, while he dropped a soft but provocative kiss on her nape. "But let those worries wait for morning. Perhaps it will bring us some of the answers we seek. For the rest of this night, let us think of only one thing."

"And what might that be, Your Majesty?" asked Maura, as if she could not guess.

Rath fanned her unbound hair over her shoulders like a regal veil. Then, with the crook of his finger, he turned her face toward his. "Only that I am King of your heart."

His lips whispered over hers, no threat to her destiny, but a fulfillment of it. "And you are Queen of mine."

His touch and his kiss were sparks to the tinder of her once-forbidden desire. She recalled the very first time he had held her—standing in that cold brook in Betchwood while danger passed within a stone's throw. Hard as she tried to deny it, the first fragile sprout of a bond had taken root between them, that day. Over time it had grown lush and strong, over-growing every bound she'd tried to place around it.

"I love my Lord Elzaban with all my heart." Her hands ranged over his face and through his hair, reveling in this sweet wanton freedom. "But the outlaw, Rath…"

With strong arms that had fought in her defense and held her when she wept, he now lowered her to the velvety grass of the Secret Glade. "Aye, what of the scoundrel?"

She tugged free his shirt and slid her hands beneath it to caress his chest. "I burn for him!"

"And he for you." With delicious, deliberate movements

that belied his impatient tone, Rath began to peel off her clothes and make the most intimate acquaintance of her body.

After so many weeks of haste, danger and stealth, Maura could dimly foresee many more ahead of them. For this one, precious night, she savored the luxuries of leisure, safety and…exposure. "Do you recall that first night we spent in the Waste?"

Rath gave a chuckle from deep in his throat. "When we had to rub that stinking liniment into each other's backs?"

Maura nodded, stroking her cheek against his. "It was the strangest thing. I felt the most pleasant sensations in places you never even touched.

"Here." She guided his hand to her bosom, then gave a quivering purr when he fondled her.

"And here." She could barely gasp the words as she drew his hand down to the sensitive flesh of her thighs—and between. "Though I knew it was wrong…I could not help wondering how it might feel if you did…touch me there."

If she had guessed the delight he could bring her, would she have been able to resist the temptation? "Mmm, now I know."

Rath silenced her with a deep, lush kiss. His fingers remained where she had led them, stroking and petting her to a hot, sweet pitch of desire. Then he lowered his lips to her breast. "Now you are only beginning to find out."

Maura knew better than to presume he would make an idle boast. As the night unfolded, he proved the truth of his promise, coaxing her body from one peak of pleasure to another, higher and sharper. When he eased her down to begin a fresh conquest, she indulged her intense curiosity about his body. By diligent exploration, she came to discover some of the means to make herself mistress of his delight, as he was master of hers.

At last, in a hoarse whisper, Rath asked if she was ready to join with him. "I have never lain with a maid, but I've heard it can be painful the first time. If you would rather wait…"

"Is that why you have tarried so when I am ripe to bursting for you?" With the same fleet agility she had once used to escape his hold on her, she rolled Rath onto his back and thrust herself upon him, holding him captive beneath her. "Have you ever known me to let a fear of pain come between me and what I wanted?"

Indeed, compared with the hurts she had taken on their quest, it had scarcely felt like pain at all. Once it passed, sensations of pleasure soon returned.

Her hostage lover writhed and gasped beneath her. "By all that's holy, lass, I surrender!"

"I accept your surrender." A twitch of her hips sent ripples of ecstasy trembling through her, with a promise of even more potent raptures. "And yield you my own."

Together they moved, racing in a fevered quest for release, until it seemed that the stars burst and showered around them and within them.

When at last they lay still, borne on warm, lazy waves of satisfaction, the Solstice moon shimmered over them like a fond benediction from the Giver—a blessing on their union and their mission. It cleansed any tiny lingering uncertainty in Maura's heart, filling her with the precious gifts of peace, joy, hope and love.

With a sigh of magical fulfillment, she murmured, "Our time has come."

SPOTLIGHT

HAPPILY NEVER AFTER

A modern Gothic tale set in a small New England town.

National bestselling author

Kathleen O'Brien

Ten years after the society wedding that wasn't, members of the wedding party are starting to die. At the scene of every "accident," a piece of a wedding dress is found. It's not long before Kelly Ralston realizes that she's the sole remaining bridesmaid left…and the next target!

Available in August.

Exclusive Bonus Features:
Author Interview
Map
and MORE!

SPHNA

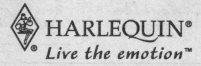

MINISERIES

Coming in August...

USA TODAY bestselling author

Dixie Browning

LAWLESS LOVERS

Two complete novels from
The Lawless Heirs saga.

Daniel Lyon Lawless and Harrison Lawless are two
successful, sexy and very sought after bachelors.
But their worlds are about to be rocked by the
love of two headstrong, beautiful women!

Where love comes alive™